THE GEMINI FACTOR

10TH ANNIVERSARY EDITION

PAUL KANE

Copyright 2022 © Paul Kane
All Rights Reserved.

The characters and events in this book are fictitious.
Any similarity to real persons, living, dead or undead is
coincidental and not intended by the author.

No part of this book may be reproduced in any form or by
any electronic or mechanical means, including information
storage and retrieval systems, without permission in writing
from the publisher, except by a reviewer who may quote
brief passages in a review.

Encyclopocalypse Publications
www.encyclopocalypse.com

PRAISE FOR
THE GEMINI FACTOR

'*The Gemini Factor* draws on the twins mythology to create a modern-day thriller of supernatural proportions. The plot is both involving and rewarding while the actual storytelling is quite excellent. Paul Kane manages to create a realistic portrayal of victim/killer/hunter without going over the top as many other writers do… a very well-crafted and rewarding novel which I have no hesitation in recommending.'

SCIENCE FICTION & FANTASY

'What you get within this book are characters who jump off the page, some great dialogue, and a plot that's as twisted as this author's mind can conceive which only adds to this reading experience. Dressed up as a traditional crime novel, it's the way in which the author has managed to blend Urban Fantasy, a touch of Sci-Fi and mixed it all up with a wicked sense of humour. It's a cracking title and one that I really had a blast reading.'

FALCATA TIMES

'Paul Kane's *The Gemini Factor* breathes some fresh air into the serial killer subgenre… There's no doubt in my mind that readers will think they know where Kane is leading them, only to have the rug yanked out from beneath them time and again. Kane's style is such that you can't help but turn the page to see what he's going to do next, and it's that unpredictability that has earned my readership in the last couple years. Simply put, the man can tell one hell of an entertaining yarn! If you're looking for a fun summer read, go grab a copy of *The Gemini Factor*, and while you're at it, pick up a couple more of Kane's books. He hasn't disappointed me yet, and I'm guessing you'll enjoy his writing too.'

HORROR DRIVE-IN

'Paul Kane has created a brilliantly detailed and utterly

believable setting – hopefully one that is revisited in later books. The Gemini Factor is a tightly plotted, well-planned thriller. A disturbing villain stalks a compelling, British noir setting, while heroes combine modern forensics and ageless intuition to stop him. Not just something for everyone, but something very good...'

PORNOKITSCH

'Kane's no nonsense writing style makes this book read like a modern crime novel, but anyone aware of Kane's previous work may suspect that there is something more going on than a standard crime thriller, and so there is, although I'll leave what that is for you to discover. The fatal final twists will leave your head spinning... This is such a fun book to read, so easy, it feels like the story just wraps you up. It's like reading those other classic genre storytellers King and Koontz. Kane certainly has the pedigree and this crime/genre novel is marvellously well crafted.'

MORPHEUS TALES

'The reader stays interested from page to page, from beginning to end, as they explore Kane's well-crafted Norchester, and get to know his heroes as they strive to end the spate of brutal killings. Overall, Paul Kane's *The Gemini Factor* offers a very interesting twist on the usual serial killer fiction, with some very, very creepy bits mixed in to keep you thinking about the story for a while afterwards. So, go ahead and pick up this book; get to know a new kind of evil. If you are a twin – sorry; this novel may be particularly disturbing.'

HORRORBOUND

'I was struck first by the dark poetry of Kane's writing. Then I was grabbed by the story and the characters... It's a good story, with good characters and great writing and for all that there is a supernatural aspect, it's the human element in the book that provides the real horror.'

UN:BOUND

'Well-written and very atmospheric, especially towards the

end. The characterization was excellent, too. I particularly liked Deborah. I have to say that I have a deep prejudice against books featuring twins. I have written a lot about this but it probably just boils down to the fact that I am the mother of twins and dislike the way twins in books are ALWAYS sinister. It's a tribute to Kane's book that I could overcome this prejudice and enjoy the story.'

ELLY GRIFFITHS
BESTSELLING AUTHOR OF THE RUTH GALLOWAY
THRILLERS, INCLUDING *THE CROSSING PLACES, DYING
FALL, THE STONE CIRCLE* AND *THE LANTERN MEN*

TABLE OF CONTENTS

PREVIOUS PUBLICATION HISTORY

'The Gemini Reloaded' (original to this book)

The Gemini Factor (first published by Screaming Dreams, 2010)

'Introduction by Peter Atkins' (first published in *The Gemini Factor*, Screaming Dreams 2010)

'Gemini Rising' (first published in *Nailbiters*, Black Shuck Books, 2017)

'The Gemini Factor: Pilot TV Episode' (original to this book)

THE GEMINI RELOADED
BY PAUL KANE

So, *The Gemini Factor* anniversary edition. Wow!

It doesn't seem like five minutes since I was sitting down to write the first few words, the first few chapters of this one. Or even when the idea came to me and I jotted it down, expanding it into a synopsis and chapter breakdown – the first time I'd ever done that (it's the way I always work now, which doesn't mean it's set in stone, just that it gives me a rough idea of the novel as a whole).

I mention the process of idea, expansion and writing because this was the first piece I ever did which followed that route. Before *Gemini*, and we're talking late '80s/early '90s, I'd done bits and bobs of writing while I was at school, tried my hand at a few shorts that never went anywhere, and had a crack at a couple of novels. The first was called *Night Beast* and was actually more of a novella. I always talk about this one in interviews because it was a bizarre Garth Marenghi-esque horror which ripped off authors like Jim Herbert, Shaun Hutson, Graham Masterton and such, and had people in choppers roaming the moors with Magnums attempting to kill the Night Beast in question. Which, incidentally, crash-landed from space into a swamp (those of you who've read my short story 'Star Pool' will spot the connection).

The second crack at a novel – which I still might put out at some point if I'm brave enough, simply as a curiosity and after I've totally re-edited it – was a meandering, sprawling book I just wrote without any real idea of where it was going. But, in writing, nothing's ever wasted and it was in the pages of both of these that I learned how to create characters, pen dialogue, do action scenes... Everything I'd ever need for later in my career.

Fast forward a few years, during which I'd been to art college, then to uni where I did some professional writing courses and ended up going into freelance journalism for newspapers and magazines. It was around this time I discovered the small presses and started writing short stories again, firing them off anywhere and everywhere. You can read some of the better ones in my 'best of' collection *Shadow Casting* from SST Publications, but many are still being reprinted today. I figured it was easier to get shorter work published than say a novel, but it wasn't long before that urge was nagging at me again. Short stories and novels actually require very different skill sets, rather than one being a stepping stone to the other – which a lot of folk believe. But the main difference is that in a novel you have the time and space to get to know characters well, to engage with them – hopefully, if us writers have done our jobs properly – over a much longer period. That's what I really wanted to try.

All of this is by way of an explanation as to *why* I began writing *Gemini*. But not why I chose that particular tale. I love crime fiction just as much as I love horror, indeed a lot of the horror books I grew up with used the framing device of a cop investigating some kind of weird crime. And, when you think about it, if you take out the 'supernatural' elements of *Gemini* what you're left with really is a police procedural murder mystery. If I'd written it like that, my career would have been very different indeed – and in fact I'm circling back around to straight crime now with my P.L. Kane books for HQ/HarperCollins *Her Last Secret* and *Her Husband's Grave*… But anyway. *Gemini* ended up being a crossover, a horror/ crime novel, and now I can't see it as anything else. It ended up being what it was always meant to be.

The germ of the idea, however, came from a newspaper piece, or magazine article – I can't remember which – that talked about the loss of a twin. How the sibling left behind felt, what they experienced… I think in this case it was twin sisters. What fascinated me was that the twin left alive still 'talked' to the dead one, even thought they were around at times. Like the notion of a twin experiencing pain and the other one feeling it – writ large. There's no greater pain than grief. So, from there I did more research into the subject and started to plot a story based around a murdered twin, who's directing his brother towards his killer. And, as serial killers tend to have MOs – themes and patterns, like Hannibal Lecter's cannibalism – I figured the most logical slayer of this twin would be someone who's going around doing a lot of that. Who has that compulsion, for whatever reason.

And, so, The Gemini was born.

As I say, I plotted this one out, figured it was a good enough premise that it deserved a bit of thinking about. Some degree of planning, not just in terms of story elements but also characters. I think it was around about then that the twist popped into my mind – which I won't spoil for those of you coming to the book for the very first time. All that remained after this was parking myself down and writing the thing, which was easier said than done. My previous attempts at writing a longer piece had taught me that I *could* do it, so it was just a matter of sticking with it and working as hard as I could to get to the finish line.

I think I completed the book around the time my first collection *Alone (In the Dark)* sold, so about 2000. *Alone* came out through a small press as well, because collections are a notoriously hard sell to a mass market publisher. But I'd been told by the likes of Simon Clark (he of *The Night of the Triffids* fame) at conventions that you at least stood a chance with a novel. So, I spent ages sending my polished version of *Gemini* off to places… and got precisely nowhere.

Enter the late, great Steve Harris. Steve was one of those people whose work I'd read and admired, like *The Hoodoo Man* and *Black Rock*. I can't even remember how I came into contact with him, probably through a friend of a friend, but I only ever got to talk to him via email. In fact, I interviewed him for my fledgling *Shadow Writer* site, and it was after this that I mentioned my first 'proper' novel and what a hard time I was having placing it. He offered to take a look, and when he'd read it and told me it had promise, he offered to edit it for free. I couldn't believe my luck, nor Steve's kindness – I've never forgotten his generosity and it's the reason why the book is dedicated to him.

Steve didn't pull his punches, though, and his edits and comments were at times brutal. But every single change he suggested made the book better, and indeed made it the much-loved novel it is today. You'd think it would be easy to sell the damned thing after all that, right? Wrong. It still took a few more years, after I'd made a name for myself with other books like the mass market *Hooded Man* novels for Abaddon/ Rebellion and novellas like *The Lazarus Condition* – which included the short story 'Dead Time' that was turned into an episode of LionsGate/NBC's *Fear Itself*.

Regardless of all this, I still wasn't able to sell the novel mass market, probably because at that time larger publishers were shying away from horror as a genre. But Screaming Dreams – who were doing some amazing work in the field

– took it on and published the novel as a trade paperback, which launched at the World Horror Convention 2010, held in Brighton. Ten years after it was originally written, it saw the light of day at last! A reminder, if any were needed, never to give up. Through my association with Clive Barker and the *Hellraiser* world, I'd also met and become friends with that lovely chap Pete Atkins (who wrote *Hellraisers II-IV* and novels like *Morningstar* and *Big Thunder*). Pete very kindly offered to read the novel and write an introduction, which you can find in this publication. His weren't the only lovely words written about the book, mind. Reviewers universally loved it, and over time it gained something of a reputation, spawning a prequel short story (again, you can read that one here) and TV interest (the original pilot script is also included here).

Now, I also like to link my tales together somehow (my good friend Steve Volk, who wrote *Afterlife*, called it 'Kaneworld'), and the most observant amongst you will find nods to *Gemini* in the likes of 'To The Power Of…', *Blood RED*, even my recent short novel from PS Publishing *The Storm*. There are also plans for a follow-up novel at some point. But the original has been out of print for a while, since Screaming Dreams is sadly no more, so I'm grateful to Jason and Gestalt Media for championing this anniversary edition. Something for fans of the original to cherish and to bring the tale of The Gemini to a whole new audience.

When I suggested the book, Jason asked if I'd be willing to write this foreword and explain why *Gemini* is so important. To me, personally, it's the pivotal book of my entire career. The first novel I wrote with an aim to having it published and read – without it, there'd be no *Arrowhead*, no *Before* or *Arcana* or P.L. Kanes – it's been with me for so long I can't remember a time without it. *Gemini* came out ten years after I wrote the first draft, and now here we have a brand, spanking new gorgeous edition ten years after it first saw print. There's something just a little bit perfect about all that, isn't there?

Okay, I'll get out of your way now so you can get on with the most important thing of all: the reading. To remind yourself why it's so important to you, or maybe discover why it's so special for the first time. If that's the case, then I envy you – you're in for quite a ride!

I know I've definitely been on one, and loved every single moment of it.

Enjoy.

Paul Kane

Derbyshire, May 2020.

THE GEMINI FACTOR
BY PETER ATKINS

So here's how it goes.

Somebody asks you to scribble a few words of introduction for their new book and you say yes for all the usual reasons. They're nice. They're talented. They always stand their round. And, best of all, they must think you're terribly clever and important, or why else would they ask you?[1]

So you're happy to oblige. More than happy. Full of bonhomie and good intent. "Delighted," you find yourself saying. "Send it over, me old tosh," or words to that effect. And they do. And then you read it. And – at some point between the perfectly good first sentence and the perfectly good last – you find yourself slapping your idiot forehead and wondering why the hell this always happens to you. "Shit," you might well say, or some witty variation thereof. Because you realise it's one of those books. No, don't be stupid. Not a bad book. A *really* good one, in fact.

---

1   Well, actually, the usual answer to that is that the seventeen people they asked before you were too busy. But let's not go there.

But one of those that can't be talked about without giving away certain things that in a perfect world would remain as surprises within the book itself. So suddenly, despite your best intentions, you're the spiritual brother of the arsehole who tips off his mate that said mate's girlfriend isn't just cooking dinner that night but has arranged a surprise birthday party for him. With cakes and jugglers. Or cocaine and hookers. Depending on the nature of the mate and the girlfriend.

It's a drawback specific to our field, I suppose, that catch-all field of mystery and suspense and fantasy and horror where nearly all the stories (and certainly nearly all the good ones) rely to some extent on misleads and surprises and the judicious (but never unfair) withholding of certain information from the reader. I'm convinced it must be very much easier to write non-spoiler introductions for mainstream fiction. If I knew people who wrote books that were handy little slices-of-quotidian-life, I probably wouldn't have this problem. But then if I hung around with tossers who wrote crap like that, I'd have shot myself in the head long ago.

No, I hang around with people who think up really weird shit and then, no doubt giggling to themselves, hide it like land-mines in what at first glance appears to be a perfectly straightforward thriller. People like Paul Kane.

So anyway, long story short, I'm asking you to consider this a signpost. One which reads Caution: Spoilers Ahead. Please drive carefully.

The Gemini Factor begins with a nasty little killing in the nicely named Fagin's Row area of Norchester, a fictional town somewhere in the middle of England. The town may be fictional but there's very little doubt that the story takes place in our world, a world which Paul establishes smoothly and easily with the invisible skill of a canny writer who never pauses for omniscient description of the look at all the research I did variety but instead lets us see and feel things always through the eyes and the thoughts of his characters, characters whom we recognise as people very like ourselves, with very real lives and very real concerns.

The chief investigators of what soon proves to be a series of killings are Detective Inspector Roy Mason and Detective Sergeant Deborah Harrison. It's not long before Deborah, the novel's heroine, mother to Izzy and daughter to Wendy and survivor of an abusive marriage, meets Jack Foley, a former historian, potential romantic interest, and – more disturbingly – someone who seems to know just a little too much. Not only about the current murders but about the several that have preceded them over a course of many years. Because we eventually learn that Norchester is simply the latest – though perhaps for many reasons the final – killing ground of a terrifying serial murderer whom the media soon dub 'Twinkle' but who prefers to think of himself as The Gemini, partly because of his choice of victims – who are invariably one sibling of a pair of twins (whether they know it or not).

It's not only the main characters of the novel who are brought convincingly to life by its author. Paul peoples his story with a supporting cast of characters who seem just as real, just as full of virtues and vices, of dreams and desires. He has that enviable knack of encapsulating entire lives and personalities into a few brief paragraphs so that we learn to like them. You know, just before they're killed.

In some ways – and I mean this only as a compliment – *The Gemini Factor* is deceptively conventional: It moves along like a well-structured thriller – moves like a fucking rocket, in fact – but what's fascinating to me (and will be, I trust, to you) is how it's actually something else at the same time.

PAUL KANE

In an extremely well executed example of form imitating content, the novel itself is 'twinned'. The surface narrative has a secret brother walking constantly alongside, hiding its footprints in those of its sibling, keeping always to the shadows of subtext and carefully delineated implication.

Reading *The Gemini Factor*, you will feel you are reading a first-rate example of the realistic Police Procedural, one with an adorable and admirable heroine and many other characters about whom you could actually give a shit. All the time, though, you will have a sense that another story is taking place, one that you can't quite see, one that is being told only in whispers, one that is a supernatural echo of the main narrative, its shadow self, its dark brother. You might tell yourself you're imagining things. But you're not. You don't have to. Paul Kane got there first and has imagined it for you. And – once the stories converge in the tension-filled and well-staged climax in a series of subterranean cells hidden deep beneath the modern city and long lost to history – you'll be grateful that he did. Grateful and impressed. Grateful, impressed and, just a little bit, appalled.

Peter Atkins
January 2010

For Steve Harris

Twinkle, twinkle, little star,
How I wonder what you are.
Up above the world so bright,
Like a candle in the night.

PROLOGUE

It is a miracle, pure and simple.

And in these times of scientific wonder and technological achievement, it remains a natural marvel. Something that cannot be explained, that probably never will be. It simply is, and has been since humanity was young.

This event depends upon many factors, the odds against it. But still it happens, time and time again. If two eggs are released during ovulation, and then fertilised, the resultant embryos will be linked but in a different way. One may be female; the other male. These are known as the dizygotics (literal meaning: two eggs), or more commonly as the fraternals. They will be close. Closer than any normal siblings can possibly be.

Though not as close as some.

If only one egg is released that month, the usual amount for a healthy adult woman, and this is seeded, the consequence is life. A single living organism, either male or female. A person.

But if this egg should divide, then that's when the miracle really occurs.

If the split comes at the end of the first week after

conception, or into the second, the embryos become a mirror image of each other. A reflection. If one should turn out to be right-handed, the other will be left. If one happens to have a hair parting on the left-hand side, the other will be granted a parting on the right. If they should look at each other face-to-face, it will be like looking into a three-dimensional mirror.

If the separation is somehow delayed and comes during or after the second week, it will never be complete. The embryos will be linked, not only mentally, but also physically. Attached to one another at the chest, the side, the head… Depending on the circumstances this may be operable. Or it may be permanent. Two bodies two people destined to live forever as one. In the more extreme cases, one may even have to be sacrificed so that the other can live, resulting in a great many moral and religious ramifications. They are known as the conjoined or the Siamese, the latter after the famous nineteenth century performers Chang and Eng Bunker, and account for around five percent of babies born this way.

But if the division appears during the first week, exact duplicates will emerge just under nine months later, genetically identical. The same in appearance, in looks if not in personality…even as infants they will display very different characteristics. However, the fact remains that no matter how 'individual' they grow up to be, they started off as a single entity. And, whether they like it or not, they will be alike in just as many ways as they are distinct.

Inside the womb, the developing foetuses interact.

They kick and nudge each other, perhaps trying to get back that which they've so recently lost. To meld together again. To share existence. Or are they possibly just communicating with the being they will come to call their 'other half'? A secret code only they can decipher, only they can understand. Some might say these are merely reflex spasms, the same ones most babies have from time to time. The jolt a mother feels as her child lets its presence be known.

One thing is for certain: there *will* be a dominant baby. One that takes more sustenance from the parent, and is accordingly that little bit heavier on delivery   seven pounds as opposed to six pounds eleven ounces, for example. Of the two sharing part of their blood supply, this will get the most, in some senses feeding itself on the less assertive child. This explains why most births of this kind are premature, delivered early, sometimes by caesarean section.

And occasionally the first to be delivered might seem inert, a stillborn. Only to wake up screaming as soon as its double eventually surfaces. As if waiting to take that vital breath together, to start *their lives* together. They share a bond that can never truly be broken; not by time or by distance.

Not by anything.

PART I

28

CHAPTER ONE

The city has two faces.

This thought had often occurred to him and seemed especially relevant tonight. Two faces. One: respectable, happy, smiling. Carefree. At times even beautiful on the right day, in a particular light, usually during the summer when the parks and streets were filled with families, children. Or even at this time of year as its residents geared up for Christmas and the shop fronts were plastered with decorations.

Then there was the other face. Ugly, contorted, vicious. Half-hidden by the shadows it had teeth, crooked and sharp. And it could bite. This was the face it hardly dared show to the world, made up of drug pushers and vagrants, prostitutes, muggers and rapists.

If you were lucky you never got to see this face. But then Roy Mason had never really believed in luck.

He cast his eyes over Norchester's streets tonight. This Sunday night. The endless sea of tiny lights, the people out and about…the traffic, of which he made up only the tiniest of proportions in his dirty, silver Granada. Mason slid the steering wheel through his hands, breaking off from the main procession. He turned left down a narrowing road.

I'm staring into the eyes of that ugly face right now, he thought.

Fagin's Row, so called because thieves were everywhere, picking more than just a pocket or two, was a collection of old flats and office buildings that should have been torn down long ago. As it was, people still lived in over half of the flats and a handful of small businesses continued to run from the office buildings, mostly ones involving pornography or buying and selling stolen goods.

Fagin's Row also contained its fair share of derelict buildings, boarded up places that were simply not fit for human habitation. It was to one of these that Mason was speeding now, a building just off Arndle Street that used to be a fudge-making factory way back when quite a famous one, too, if Mason remembered his history. He wondered what had happened to its owners after the company went bust. Perhaps they were still living here somewhere, hiding *their* faces behind locked doors and listening out for any noises on the landing-ways.

Even if he hadn't known this city as well as he did, Mason would still have been able to find the place quite easily just by following all the flashing blue lights. The next corner yielded a picture he'd seen so many times in his career; there weren't many who hadn't. Squad cars, men and women in uniform flitting to and fro. A crowd contained behind the cordon, peering past the people dressed in black and white. A TV camera crew with a reporter doing a piece into the lens, standing off to one side. Newspaper reporters were jotting down notes on pads. Photographers were clicking away, one flash following another. Mason tucked his car in by the side of the road and sighed.

Climbing out, he locked up the vehicle and readied

himself.

The television people were the first to see him. The male reporter intercepted Mason on his way to the building. "Excuse me… Excuse me, Detective Inspector Mason. It is D.I. Mason, isn't it? I wonder if we could have a word."

Mason grimaced. A word: there were quite a number of words he'd like to give him. "I have nothing to say at this time."

The other reporters could sense blood in the water. *Feeding frenzy*, thought Mason. They joined the TV crew and pointed Dictaphones and cameras at him.

"Is it true there's a dead body in there, sir?" asked the persistent TV man.

"If you'll let me get by, I'll have a look and tell you."

"Do you think this might be a gang-related killing?" This question came from one of the print reporters.

"No comment."

Mason pushed past them, a little too forcefully. A young constable could see he was having difficulties and called over some of his colleagues to deal with the situation. They let Mason through, and he immediately strode towards the building, grumbling under his breath.

Mason was handed a pair of disposable, elasticated slippers and he quickly put them over his own shoes. The side-door was already open and he could hear voices coming from inside. With another loud sigh, he entered the crime scene.

It was dark inside the old factory, in spite of the temporary lights that had been set up for their benefit. Mason saw a smattering of people in white suits Scene of Crime Officers gathered a bit further in, and the police photographer's flash blitzing the zone. Then he spotted the person he was really looking for. She was a little over five feet tall and wore a dark-grey overcoat. Her chestnut hair was cut quite short, coming to a stop just shy of her shoulders. When she turned, he saw she had on a trouser suit beneath the coat. What little of her blouse was exposed shone a brilliant white in the glare from the lights.

"Sir," Deborah Harrison said by way of a hello.

"So much for the day of rest, Sergeant," said Mason. "What've we got?"

"It's probably best if you see for yourself."

She led him to the reason why they were all out here on this chilly late November evening. There, in the corner of the room, next to a wall with broken bricks spilling out of it from several different wounds, was a body. It looked like it was asleep, propped up, with its head lolling on its chest and legs taking on the shape of an inverted 'V'. At first glance it could have been mistaken for a wino who'd had too much turps, or a drug addict who'd overdosed on heroin. But the man, for as Mason came closer he discerned it was a man, was missing his right hand. And there was a massive patch of red staining the wall behind him. Blood, dried now and glued to the brickwork.

"Shit, what a mess."

"That's one way of putting it." Mason spun around at the sound of another familiar voice. Standing behind and to the right of him, crossed hands holding a leather case, was pathologist Rosy Lim. She smiled a smile that seemed most inappropriate given the circumstances, twin dimples forming in her cheeks. Mason remembered her telling him once that she was one-third Chinese, but it was a very telling third. Rosy's oriental looks gave her aspect a beautiful, and extremely powerful, grace. Mason noticed her hair was tied back in a ponytail which meant that she'd probably already given the body a cursory examination; Rosy always made sure her long black hair was out of the way before getting down to business. "Although I doubt if I'll be putting that down in any of my reports."

Mason nodded. "Miss Lim."

"I won't keep you in suspense, Inspector. I've given our man here the once-over, and cause of death is probably a puncture wound to the lower back...or I should say the consequent loss of blood. However, only a fraction of that blood is actually on the wall and floor, which means he was almost certainly killed elsewhere and dumped here afterwards. At a guess I'd hazard he's been dead for several days. The hand was most likely removed after his death. A clean cut; nothing sloppy."

"Any sign of the hand?" Mason asked his sergeant.

Deborah shook her head. "Not yet, sir. But the Scene of Crime boys are far from finished. It's quite a large area to cover."

"What can you tell me about the wound itself, Miss Lim? Are we talking gunshot here? Knife?"

Rosy looked from Mason to the corpse. "I'll know more once I've conducted the autopsy, but if you pushed me I'd have to say it was some kind of spiked instrument."

"What do you mean, like a needle?"

"No, larger. There are holes in the back of his shirt, quite large holes. But no slits. I don't believe it was a knife."

"Right. Well, thank you, Miss Lim." Mason turned to Deborah. "Who found the body?"

"A group of homeless people, sir. Broke in looking for shelter against the cold I expect. Found more than they bargained for."

"I'm surprised they called it in. Where are they now?"

"Back at the station, giving their statements. I thought it was best not to let them wander about out there," said

Deborah.

"And, of course, they get to spend the evening in a nice warm nick being fed tea and biscuits. You're too soft for your own good, you know that, Blondie?"

"Sir."

"But you're right about one thing, we don't want them gabbing to the press about all this. Not yet, anyway. Which reminds me, someone had better speak to those arseholes out there."

"And tell them what?"

"*You'll* think of something."

Deborah cocked her head and gave him a scornful look. "And what are you going to do in the meantime, *Sir*?"

"Talk to a higher authority, Sergeant."

"I don't think praying's going to do much good," commented Rosy, who'd been listening to their conversation.

"I was thinking of a much higher authority than that, Doctor." Mason took out his mobile phone and thumbed it on. "Hello," he said, "could you put me through to Chief Superintendent Bingham, please…"

Deborah was pretty pleased with how she'd handled the collective media outside.

Professional, yet understanding. Detached, yet candid. She'd given them a few crumbs to broadcast on the news that evening and put in their rags tomorrow morning, withholding pretty much all of the valuable information, as Mason would expect her to do. She fended off the precarious questions to the best of her ability, and sent 'the arseholes' away with what they thought they wanted. *And everyone's a winner*, she thought. *Apart from that poor devil back there.*

It was still the worst part of the job for her. Murder investigation. Anyone would've thought she'd be used to it, especially after everything she'd seen. But they'd be wrong. You never got used to seeing death up close and personal like that, staring it in the face. Never. What was even more disturbing, though, was the notion that somebody had done that to another human being. Out there, somewhere, was a murderer. Perhaps even *murderers*. The capacity for violence was almost limitless when it came to some people. Nothing was taboo. Not setting a person on fire, not placing a gun up to their head and pulling the trigger, not rape and strangulation. Nothing.

Deborah rubbed her eyes. It had been a long day; trust her to be on duty when something like this happened. She'd started off that Sunday morning questioning two teenage youths about a spate of burglaries in the Partington Lane area of the city, a quiet, well-to-do spot crammed with big, expensive-looking houses each one boasting a lengthy driveway and enormous garden. Deborah couldn't help feeling envious when she'd visited them, first to go over the crime scenes, then to make enquiries door-to-door. What a place to live! She could just imagine herself in one of those houses, sitting on the patio sipping cocktails in summer, watching as some stripped to the waist Diet Coke man mowed her garden. When she won the lottery, perhaps. In the meantime she'd managed to crack the case in hand by tracing some of the stolen items to a well-known fence called Bernie Hastings, who'd willingly given over the names of his suppliers in exchange for a leniency she promised but knew she couldn't deliver.

No sooner had she caught up on the paperwork for that investigation, than the call had come in about the discovery of a body on Fagin's Row. Not a particularly surprising occurrence in itself, but apparently this one was missing its right hand and had blood all over it. She'd driven down there as fast as she could, leaving a string of messages on Mason's home answerphone. Deborah had spent the rest of her day what was left of it coordinating the operation. It was now almost eight-fifteen. She'd been up since six and was shattered. There was no such thing as shift work in the Criminal Investigation Division: when they needed you, you had to be there.

Deborah looked up. She suddenly had the strangest feeling. Like someone was watching her. Someone *was* watching her, of course. Lots of people were staring at her from behind the cordon, including most of the press who'd decided to hang around a bit longer in case anything else developed. But no, this was something else. One set of eyes. Deborah felt an iciness that had nothing to do with the freezing winter climate. She twisted her head, looking this way and that.

There.

She saw him, at the back of the crowd. Eyes fixed on her and her alone. A man with wavy hair and a beard. His stare was boring into her; she felt… Deborah made a move in his direction, slow at first, then more urgent. She didn't know why but she needed to speak with that man.

"Debbie?"

Deborah willed herself not to turn, not to lose sight of the bearded man; *not to break contact.* But instinctively she responded to her own name, and felt the connection fracture, then sever completely like the dead man's hand back in the dilapidated building behind.

"Debs? Is everything okay?" Once she'd found out who was speaking to her, Rosy Lim's face blotting out her view, Deborah swung her head back round to search for the stranger in the crowd. As she'd suspected he would be, the man was now gone.

"You all right? You don't look so good."

"What? No, I just thought I saw…" Deborah realised what she was about to say would sound incredibly stupid and stopped herself at the last moment.

"Thought you saw what?"

"Nothing. It was nothing." Deborah gave Rosy a shrug. "Anyway, what's up?"

"Message for you from Mason. I quote: 'Tell Blondie she can get going once she's sorted the media out. Tell her to go spend some time with that kid of hers.'"

"Gee, *thanks* Roy. I do all the hard work and he steams in at the last minute." Deborah laughed quietly to herself.

"Isn't that what inspectors are supposed to do?"

"Maybe it's just his way of telling me I look like warmed-over dog crap."

Rosy smiled her dimpled smile. "You do look tired."

"Yeah, well I'm not complaining if his lordship wants to take command of the troops."

"Hey, by the way, there's something I've been meaning to ask you for a while now. Well, ever since you came to work in our pleasant little city, really," Rosy said as they moved away from the cordon. "Why does he keep on calling you Blondie? Is he colour blind or something? Your hair's brown."

"It's just a stupid nickname that's followed me around. Mind you, he's the only one with the balls to use it."

"You used to bleach, right?"

Deborah let out a snort.

"Really. Come on, give."

"All right, but don't say I didn't warn you. What's my name?"

Rosy thought for a second or two, then a look of enlightenment dawned on her face. "Ah, *I* get it. Deborah Harrison. Debbie Harry. Now that *is* lame."

"Told you it was stupid."

"Oh, I don't know. It could have been worse." Rosy smiled again. "I can think of a few—"

Deborah held up a finger. "Don't even go there, Miss *Lim* the pathologist. I mean, who ever heard of a doctor with a name like that? It's like becoming a banker when your name's Mr Cash or something."

Both of them laughed softly. It seemed a strange thing to do, almost disrespectful considering what they'd witnessed that night. But in a way it made sense; humour was a good way to relieve the tension and helped them forget about it all…for a couple of blessed minutes.

As Rosy waved her on her way, she called out to Deborah, "See you tomorrow, '*Blondie*'."

"You will?"

"The autopsy's at ten-thirty. Mason's booked you both ringside seats."

"Great."

Deborah waited as one of the female constables let her through the cordon so she could get to her car. And while she waited, she found herself looking over again at the place where the mystery man had been standing. Wondering just who he was and what significance his arrival held. But then she shook her head, said thanks to the policewoman, and made her way to the car she'd parked just down the road.

39

CHAPTER TWO

D.S. Deborah Harrison guided her dark blue Peugeot through the maze of streets off Fagin's Row and joined the heaving throng of traffic back out on the main road.

Glimpses of the dead body invaded her mind as she mirrored, signalled and manoeuvred, changing gear to blend in with the flow. The blood down the back of that wall and on the floor, the missing hand God alone knew where *that* was. It was a good job she had a fairly strong stomach, unlike some of the people she'd known on the force. What about that guy she'd served with down south, Jenson? Couldn't even stand to see the photographs…made him bolt for the toilet every time. No wonder he'd ended up handling all the petty crimes. That's why he'd never got a crack at any of the big cases.

Big cases like the Coulthard Murders, the investigation that had seen her make sergeant that much sooner than she'd expected. Three generations of the same family slaughtered in their own home a grandmother aged seventy-five, a mother and father in their mid-forties and a daughter only fifteen years of age all beaten to death with what they eventually discovered was the metal bar from the inside of a set of dumbbells. With no possible suspects or motives, the investigation had remained at a standstill for months. Before Deborah, then only a 'humble' Detective Constable, discovered that the father had sired another child with a mistress Sara Flynn some twenty years ago. The affair had been called off not long after Mr Coulthard found out his lover was pregnant. He wanted nothing to do with the woman or her bastard child. And so she'd moved away, only telling her son Karl the truth about his origins when she was diagnosed as being terminally ill with leukaemia.

Just over a week after her death he'd come looking for Coulthard, revenge in mind, and had decided at the last minute to wipe out his entire family: a family the lost son had never been a part of. And, surprise, surprise, Karl was also a fitness fanatic. When the police raided his flat they discovered a pair of dumbbells the bar from one, though cleaned, still had minute traces of blood on its cylindrical shaft. That and the DNA match was enough to put Karl Flynn away for a very long time.

Deborah noticed the car in front was speeding ever so slightly. *What the hell*, she thought. Murder kind of put that particular crime into perspective. Anyway, she was in a hurry to get home herself. Now if it was a built-up area, or near a school, that would be different...might even be worth the paperwork. Deborah increased her speed to match his.

If she was quick about it, she might even get back before Isabel had to go to bed. It was a school night, after all. Isabel. The images inside her head of the dead man were replaced by a snapshot of her seven-year-old daughter, just like the picture she always carried around in her wallet. Normally she only had to close her eyes to see it...right now it was hovering just ahead of her on the windscreen. In the holiday photo, taken a couple of years ago, it was a bright summer's day, Isabel was laughing—

Now imagine her brains beaten in like that Coulthard kid.

Deborah told herself that was never going to happen. That she'd always be there to protect her. To love and care for her.

But you just never know. In your line of work… Imagine her a bit older, folded up in some alleyway on Fagin's Row, surrounded by trash and needles. And imagine the blood all over her—

Stop it!

Isabel was the only thing that made any sense to Deborah. The only thing in her life that… Deborah did this job to protect her, to make sure she didn't have to grow up in a world where you were frightened to go out, frightened to stay in. There was no way she'd ever let anyone hurt her, ever! The poor kid had been through enough already, having to grow up without a father who was worth a shit.

Deborah didn't know where Phil was right now, the scumbag. Didn't care either. She'd made no effort to get maintenance or child support from him. The fact that he was out of both of their lives was recompense enough.

There had been a time when she'd thought she was truly happy back there. A loving husband, a house, a career that gave her job satisfaction. It seemed like a lifetime ago now, a distant memory.

She'd met Philip Croft just after joining the police force, when she was in her very early twenties, at a housewarming do a couple of her friends were throwing. He was such a charmer in those days, and he appeared to have it all. A good vocation in the advertising industry, a flashy sports car. All that was missing was the perfect wife on his arm. Little did Deborah know that she was to become that other accessory he was lacking. He wined her, he dined her. Sent flowers and gave her jewellery. Told her he liked the fact that she was a copper, made him feel secure when he was with her. It was only when they were married, eight months or so after first meeting, that she realised *she* was the one who needed the protection.

He changed once that ring was on her finger. She'd heard the stories, seen the documentaries about it. She'd even come across it at work, and tried to get women to bring charges against their husbands. Deborah just couldn't see how they could let those men get away with such things, go back to them as if nothing had ever happened. Until she was in a similar situation herself, that was. It's the drinking that's doing it, she convinced herself. If she could stop Phil hitting the bottle… But that was impossible. He was out most nights of the week with the movers and shakers, and invariably he'd come back looking for an argument. Any excuse to start a slanging match. As time went by and his position at the ad-agency looked more and more tenuous, he drank more and more booze mixed with a little of the white stuff every now and again, Deborah suspected. And then the arguments would end up as fights. Once he even kneed her in the stomach, leaving her winded on the living room floor. He was careful never to hit her in the face, where her colleagues might see it, and she was very good at hiding the bruises about her person. She had her excuses ready, though, just in case; embarrassed more than anything, that this should happen to her of all people. Deborah would claim they were done in the line of duty if someone happened to notice them in the locker room…not that anyone ever did.

The only thing he'd ever done right the whole bloody time they were together was to help make Isabel: a one-night stand while he was experimenting with getting his act together. But he'd gone berserk when she told him she was expecting, reaching for the whiskey, ranting on about how they were fine by themselves talk about deluding yourself! that they didn't need a bawling kid around. It was simply another excuse for all the problems they were having, another way of deflecting the blame from himself.

(Was that how Mr Coulthard had reacted when Sara Flynn informed him about Karl? Was that why he'd been punished, and his family alongside him?)

But Phil went too far that night, smacking her in the face and almost breaking her nose. He knew she would go to her workmates this time, he could see it in her eyes. The hatred, the loathing. And so, with his marriage in tatters and his career heading the same way, not to mention possible jail time facing him, Phil skipped out on Deborah and the baby. She'd never seen him since. Seven and a half years and she didn't even know if he was alive or dead. Dead she hoped, deep down inside.

She'd changed her name back to Harrison soon after the 'split', and went through labour with the aid and assistance of her mother who was happy to help following the recent death of Deborah's own father. It gave her something to do, kept her mind occupied and stopped her from dwelling too much on the past. The three of them had coped like that ever since. A weird sort of family, some might say, but it worked.

The only problem Deborah could foresee was if Phil should suddenly come back. But she doubted that would happen. How was he to know she'd never pressed charges against him for assault? That she'd called in sick until the swelling went down. He wouldn't run the risk of returning and being arrested. That didn't stop Isabel asking about her daddy, though, which she'd started to do constantly these days. Who was he? What did he do? Isabel hoped he was a pilot she was obsessed with all things aeronautical and wanted to fly a plane herself when she grew up. Did she perhaps inherit this interest from her father?

Deborah had always changed the subject, diverted Isabel's attention away from thoughts of him. But how much longer she could continue doing that, she didn't know. Deborah imagined a scene played out some time in the future, where Isabel was pushing her and pushing her until finally she had to come clean:

"Your father was a worthless piece of gutter slime who liked nothing better than to get drunk and beat up on his wife. Is that what you wanted to hear? He abandoned the both of us because he didn't want you, Isabel. Can't you understand that? He. Didn't. Want. You! And if I never see him again as long as I live it'll be too soon."

The incident always ended with Isabel in tears, screaming that she hated Deborah. That her mother was a lying bitch and that she'd find her father, no matter how long it took. She'd find him and he *was* a pilot, and he'd fly the two of them to some foreign land, away from her… Deborah felt herself becoming lost in the daydream, close to tears for real. She had to fight hard to keep her emotions in check.

Signalling to turn left, she waited for a break in the traffic.

It wasn't long before she was home, a small house on a small estate, located on the outskirts of the city, that had served them well for the past ten months since her last transfer. She eased into the driveway, through the open gates. Deborah composed herself. She couldn't let Isabel see her like this, or her mother for that matter. Not that she could ever fool *her*. A curtain twitched in the living room. Opening the door, the detective climbed out and gave a brief wave. Before she'd even had time to lock the car, the front door was open, the light from the hallway opening up a second golden door on the concrete drive.

Wendy Harrison's smile was one of relief and concern, crow's-feet visible at the corner of each eye. She looked older than her fifty-one years today, the hair-colour she'd used to cover the grey fading somewhat, allowing traitorous streaks of silver to burst through. Wendy kissed her grown-up daughter and shut the door after her, always pleased to have her back safe and sound. "I don't patrol the streets anymore, Mum," Deborah had told her many times. "No, you just go chasing after dangerous drug dealers and killers," was her mother's standard reply. Deborah mirrored the greeting when she saw her own offspring inside, passing the kiss on down the line.

"I've missed you today, Izzy," said Deborah, taking the girl into her arms. Isabel hugged her back, then pulled her head away slightly.

"You said you'd be back early."

Deborah looked into those gorgeously wide eyes and brushed a strand of reddish-brown hair away from her daughter's face. "I know, but something came up. I couldn't get away."

"I hate it when you have to work Sundays."

"So do I, Izzy. So do I." Deborah looked at her daughter more closely now, matching her up to the photo in her wallet and in her mind's eye. Already it was so out of date. Isabel was changing, growing so fast; and there was nothing she could do about it. These were the days she should be spending at home with her, while Isabel still wanted her to. Before it became *uncool* to be seen hanging around with your mum at weekends.

"Did you have a good time at Claudia's this afternoon?"

"Yep."

"What did you two get up to? I hope you behaved yourself, young lady."

"*Mu-um!*" Isabel said, perplexed. "I'm not a kid, you

know."

Oh yes you are! You always will be if I've anything to say about it.

"Okay, but you do realise if you're lying I'm going to have to run you downtown for interrogation." Deborah started to tickle Isabel under her arms. She squirmed around, giggling, pleading with her mother to stop. "All right, on one condition. You tell me what happened on the soaps tonight after I've grabbed something to eat."

Isabel agreed and broke away from Deborah, pulling a face at her before running off back towards the living room. When she opened the door, the sound of an advert jingle on the TV wafted through the hall. Deborah grinned and shrugged off her topcoat.

"Here, let me take that," said Wendy.

Deborah refused to hand the coat over and hung it up herself on a peg by the door. "I can manage, Mum. 'I'm not a kid, you know,'" she said, parodying Isabel. "Why don't you go and put your feet up."

"Why don't *you* tell me what happened today?"

Deborah headed into the kitchen without replying. Her mother followed her through. "Leave it for now, Mum, okay? I just want to make myself something to eat and sit and watch TV with Izzy before she has to go to bed."

"I can't help it, Debbie. I worry about you."

"I know, Mum. But really, it's okay." Deborah flicked on the kettle, slid a couple of slices of bread into the toaster and unzipped a tin of baked beans using the electric tin-opener.

"She's been asking about Philip again," Wendy told her as she lit the hob.

Deborah turned, anxiously. "And what did you say?"

"It's not my place to say *anything*, sweetheart. But she's curious. It's only natural."

Deborah unloaded the beans into a pan, then spooned herself some coffee into a mug. "I don't want her knowing anything about him. In fact, I've been thinking about telling her he died before she was born."

Wendy stepped forward and touched her arm. "You're not, are you?"

"It's better than telling her what he was really like."

"I'm not sure that's such a good idea. She's bound to find out the truth eventually, and when she does she'll hate you for it, love."

Deborah bowed her head. "I-I just don't know what to do, Mum. She's built up some kind of idealised image of him in her mind. I'm frightened that if I tell her, she'll blame me."

"For what? You have nothing to feel guilty about."

The toast chose that moment to pop up, effectively ending the conversation. "I just want to leave it a bit longer, Mum. Just a bit longer."

Deborah buttered the toast, layered the beans on top, and added boiling water to the coffee. She loaded everything onto a tray and followed her mother into the living room.

"Mum," she heard Isabel say as she walked through the door. "Mum, look. You're on the telly!"

Deborah was shocked to see her face on the screen, talking to journalists outside the dilapidated factory on Fagin's Row. The local news reporter was giving a voiceover: "Police were refusing to either confirm or deny the body—"

Quick as a flash, Deborah abandoned the tray on a nearby chair and pressed the off switch on the television. The picture disappeared, leaving the screen blank. Two baffled faces stared at her.

"Mum, what did you do that for? I wanted to—"

"It's time for bed, Izzy," said Deborah, flustered.

"But it's still early."

"I said it's time for bed. You've got school tomorrow."

"But you said—"

"Bed," snapped Deborah. "Right now."

Sulking, Isabel jumped off the couch and pushed past her mother. Deborah closed her eyes and pinched the skin at the top of her nose. When she looked at her mother, she saw fear in the woman's eyes. But it wasn't fear of her daughter that she detected.

Instead, Wendy Harrison was afraid for her only child.

CHAPTER THREE

The structure had majesty.

Hardly surprising with a name like *The Imperial Hotel*. However, just like the Empire itself   and the Royal family come to that   it had seen better days. He tilted his head back to take in its size. Squares of light were dotted about on its surface, indicating the occupied rooms. They gave the towering rectangular edifice the appearance of a giant handheld puzzle, the object of which was to move the tiny plastic pieces around in order to make a coherent picture. Either that or a gigantic crossword puzzle, the figures at certain windows resembling letters of the alphabet.

The architectural style wasn't a mystery to him, the pillars at the entranceway giving this away. An exaggerated classical approach favoured during the Victorian era, seemingly at odds with the industrial style also popular during that famous revolution in the nineteenth century. Feeling like a Greek or a Roman stepping into a temple of the ancient deities, he took the steps two at a time and passed between the pillars, then carried on through the doors proper   revolving doors no less.

Into a foyer that was trying its best to look plush:

complete with red carpets and pot plants. The receptionist, one of the part-time staff he assumed, probably studying at the nearby college or university and working here to pay the bills, beamed at him from behind the counter. His eyes were drawn to the name-tag attached to her maroon waistcoat, resting on top of a cream-coloured blouse. 'Felicity' it read in joined up text that was meant to look handwritten, but was quite obviously spat out of a bubble-jet printer.

"Hello, sir. How can we help you?" she said in a sickly-sweet voice. It was obviously the royal 'we', or as royal as this place got these days.

He smiled awkwardly. "Er…I'd like a room."

"Certainly, sir. Can I ask if you've made a reservation?"

"No…I'm afraid not." His voice cracked; he'd never been very good at talking to women, even in situations as commonplace as this. "Will that be a problem?"

"You're in luck, sir. We're not fully booked at the moment. Will you be wanting a single, a double…"

"Ah… A double please, I think." He needed some space right now, and a bed slightly larger than himself.

"All our rooms come with en suite bathroom and satellite television," Felicity informed him as if it was something remarkable these days. "Now if you could just fill this in, Mr…"

"Foley…Jack."

She handed him a simple registration form and he passed it back a few moments later, completed.

"Thank you, Mr Foley. Do you know how long you might be staying with us?" Was there a hint of desperation in her voice?

"It's…hard to say."

"Only…"

"Yes?"

Felicity was having trouble maintaining eye contact with him. "Do you have a credit or debit card…?"

"Oh, right, I see." He took out his wallet and handed over a card so she could swipe it. Security against him doing a runner.

The transaction completed, she gave him a room key not a card key, he noted, but a *real* key with the number '307' stamped on its label. "Yours is room three-oh-seven. That's on the third floor."

"My cases are outside in the car, er…do you think…"

"I'll have someone park your car and bring your luggage straight up to your room, Mr Foley," Felicity said.

"Thanks. It's the red Mondeo," he clarified, giving her a set of his own keys. "You can't miss it."

"Thank you, Mr Foley. I hope you have a pleasant stay with us here at *The Imperial*."

"I hope so too." There wasn't much conviction in his voice.

He made his way to the lift, one of the old-fashioned kinds with a gate across the front. As usual, it was open and on the ground floor at this time of night. Inside waited a man who looked about eighty years of age, wearing a more elaborate version of Felicity's uniform and sitting on a tall wooden stool. His name was appropriately enough – 'Albert' according to his laminated badge. He asked which floor the man required and then punched the button to take him there.

On the way up the old operator almost fell asleep, only waking when the lift ground to a halt at the requested level. He opened the gate for the guest, who thanked him for his trouble.

"You're most welcome," replied the geriatric, who sat back down on his stool and appeared to nod off again as the lift descended.

The room took a bit of finding. Indeed, he'd only just walked in when a burly man with two small cases came up behind him. His name-tag was missing for some reason.

"Foley?"

"Yes."

The fellow, who looked like he'd worked as a bouncer at some stage in his life if he hadn't, then it was certainly an option for the future dropped the cases on top of the double bed.

The bouncer waited a moment at the door, and then coughed.

"Right, sorry."

"Thanks," he said after receiving his tip. "Much appreciated."

The door clicked.

At last he was alone.

He sat on the end of the bed. Diagonally opposite was a dresser with a mirror against its back. He caught sight of his reflection and barely recognised himself. The coarse roughness of the beard, the lines marring his brow.

Jack Foley looked like a distorted version of himself, much older than his thirty years. His clothes were rumpled and creased, (no wonder Felicity thought he might run off without paying…). His body ached from sleeping in the car, when he allowed himself to sleep, that was. When he had to face the fact that he was so tired he might doze off at the wheel, just like Albert back there in the lift. That he might roll the car into a ditch or cause an accident and end up killing innocent motorists. That was the last thing he wanted.

But he'd had to get here as soon as he could. As soon as he knew *where* to go. Even so, he'd arrived too late. Again. It was already over. Again. If only he'd driven faster, if only he'd been able to figure out where…

Jack flopped backwards on the bed, next to his cases. He'd almost forgotten what it was like to sleep in a proper bed. He'd promised himself he wouldn't rough it again tonight. Now that it was over…for the time being. He couldn't do much anyway but wait.

After a little while, he got up and put his cases on the floor. Jack wandered into the bathroom, pondering whether or not to have a shower. He needed one, that was for sure. But it had waited this long so it could probably hang fire till the morning.

He got out of his grubby clothes, though, fishing through his luggage for a clean pair of boxers. While he was changing, he noticed the remote control for the TV on a table next to the bed. Grabbing it, he pointed the instrument at the black box suspended on an armature in the top left-hand corner of his room.

The box sprang to life, showing him a miniature representation of Arnold Schwarzenegger. Even that size, the Austrian Oak was an impressive figure. Jack watched as Arnie dispatched the men who were chasing him in various grisly ways, blood flying in all directions as guns let loose with their deadly volley. Watching the big man reminded him of something…

Pounding against muscle, feeling the strength there.

A big black shape: huge.

A hand around his neck.

Tight, ever so tight.

Then being lifted up off the floor   struggling was no use.

Something out of the corner of his eye, a flash of metal. Then pain, incredible pain. Christ it was agony!

Then…

Jack shook his head. He turned off the lights, pulled back the crisp, clean sheets and slipped inside the bed.

Channel hopping to clear his mind, he came across a music station: some guy in a hotel room a bit bigger than his own, singing a lament for 'the lovers' apparently. Jack pressed the button again, and was rewarded with a trite comedy about a city couple making a new life for themselves in the country. Next he stumbled upon the end of a local news programme. To his amazement there was the woman. The woman he'd seen tonight.

"...further when we know more," she finished, then it cut to another story. She was on the screen for all of thirty seconds and he'd only managed to catch a fleeting glimpse of her name underneath: D.S. something or other. He continued watching for a bit, waiting to see if anything else came on about the murder it didn't then flipped backwards and forwards to see if he could catch another news broadcast. But it looked like he'd missed the last one, and the satellite news channel didn't even mention the story; they were too busy reporting a foreign hijacking. One more quick sweep for some reason Arnie was now wearing a wet towel on his head; Jack had seen this film once, but couldn't for the life of him recall what it was about and he shut the TV off again, vaguely disappointed that he couldn't find any history channels.

Eyelids heavy, Jack settled down in the bed.

He stared at the stars through his window and remembered a time when his father had taught him the names of the constellations, sparking his imagination. Jack used to dream about ancient mariners using them to navigate their way around the globe. But that was long, long ago. His father was dead now. His whole family was gone.

Jack closed his eyes, fatigue taking hold of him. He dreamed that night, but not of ancient mariners. And he went to sleep thinking about the woman he'd seen standing outside that building tonight.

The woman who'd looked at him so strangely.
The woman with short chestnut hair.

CHAPTER FOUR

"Come on, come on."

Mason parped his horn at the car in front. The congestion was due to roadworks, or at least that was the general idea. A temporary traffic light system had been set up, orange and white cones had appeared from nowhere as if it were suddenly their mating season, but for the life of him Mason couldn't see any actual *work* being done on the *road*.

"I said we should have set off sooner."

"Yes, thank you, Blondie. We'd be all right if those pricks in front would just… Ah, here we go."

The lights had changed to green on their side some time ago, allowing a handful of cars to sneak past. But they changed abruptly back to red again as soon as the Granada pulled up.

"Oh, I don't believe this!"

If he doesn't calm down he'll have a stroke, thought Deborah.

Mason was a heavy man: not exactly fat, but certainly on the verge. And he looked even bigger crammed behind the wheel of a car. His thick neck strained against the sides of his shirt collar, the tie he wore looking for all the world like it was strangling him. His chin was angular, as was his nose though not to the point of being overlarge and he had eyebrows that arched neatly over each eye, their salt and pepper texture akin to that of his ruffled hair. The material of his raincoat bulged at the shoulders as his hands gripped the wheel. Fat turquoise veins stood proud on the backs of those paws, his grasp tightening in frustration.

Mason's angry expression reminded her of Isabel's face that morning as Deborah had given her a lift into school. She'd tried to apologise to the seven-year-old over breakfast, but she wasn't having any of it. They hardly spoke after that, sitting like strangers in the Peugeot as it ferried them to the school gates. *Give it some time*, thought Deborah. *I just need more time…*

When she'd arrived at work, Deborah had spent an hour or so looking over the statements of the homeless people who'd found the body, finding nothing of real significance in their words. Then Mason had eventually rolled in, and she'd had to wait while he went to get a sandwich from the vending machine, making them late in the process.

Mason tutted loudly now.

"We'll get there," Deborah said.

Unconvinced, he beeped the horn again registering his disapproval with the quartet of workmen who'd actually bothered to show up. The last of the cars came through the gap and finally the lights showed green again. Mason pressed the accelerator hard, zipping through and out into two-lane traffic again.

They pulled into the morgue's car park a little after ten-thirty. A single-storey concrete building padded out with lots of glass, anyone who didn't know what happened inside might mistake it for a leisure centre or even God forbid a nursery.

Mason checked in at the front desk and was told where they could find Dr Lim: just down the corridor, first on the right. Mason bounded down the wing, Deborah bringing up the rear; in no hurry to get there if the truth be known. Luckily, or unluckily depending on how you looked at it, Rosy Lim had only just started the autopsy.

"Ah, Inspector Mason. Nice to see you again so soon," said Rosy when he burst in. "Don't worry, you haven't missed a thing. I believe you know Eugene…" Eugene was one of Rosy's technicians, a squat man with bags under his eyes.

"Hi there, Blondie," said Rosy, waving.

Deborah groaned and nodded a greeting to the pathologist, dressed in surgical scrubs and what looked like a shower cap. Rosy's hands were encased in latex, making them look deathly white. As white as the naked cadaver laid out on the table before her. Mason joined Rosy at that table, Deborah keeping just a fraction behind him. The smell was only now beginning to reach her, antiseptic and butcher's offal. She was nearest to the victim's head and could see his face quite clearly. No longer was he just a lolling figure in the dark recesses of some broken-down factory. He was a person, a human being. Or he had been, once upon a time.

"I was just about to examine the puncture wounds on his back, the ones I told you about last night. Eugene, would you mind?" Eugene rolled the body onto its side, then onto its front, and Rosy bent over the two marks halfway down the dead man's back. To Deborah they looked exactly like big craters in the flesh. The doctor spent a good few minutes just gazing at them.

"Mmmm," said Rosy.

Mason came closer. "What're you thinking?"

"Well, at first glance I did wonder if they might have been made by something like a barbecue skewer, or an ice pick."

The inspector's nose twitched. "Like in *Basic Instinct*?"

"Never seen it," admitted Rosy. "But if you like."

"Good film, that," said Eugene.

Everyone stared at the technician, then turned back to Rosy. "Right... Anyway, I scrapped that theory. See how close together these holes are?" Mason looked on with interest.

Deborah stepped round her boss. "Yep. What do you think made them, Rosy?"

Rosy faced her. "In my opinion the murder weapon was some sort of pronged instrument."

"We're back to the barbecue motif again," said Mason. "What can you tell us about the hand?"

Rosy moved down the body on the same side. "I can confirm it was removed after death."

"After he'd been stabbed with the fork?" asked Mason.

"That's correct. He'd already lost a great deal of blood before his hand was separated from his arm. As I said before, it was removed very cleanly, possibly using an extremely sharp cleaver or hatchet. One fluid motion." Rosy chopped a hand into her palm for effect.

Mason pulled a face. "All right, Miss Lim, we get the picture."

Rosy lifted up the appendage in question slightly so they could see it better. "It wasn't sawn off because there'd be ragged edges here." The pathologist ran her fingers down the cut. Thankfully from this angle Deborah couldn't see the bone and meat packed inside the arm. Rosy lay the extremity down again. "But I'll tell you this much, Inspector: whoever did it was strong."

"What makes you say that?"

Rosy laughed. "What, apart from the fact they can chop off a hand in one go? Have you ever tried to detach a hand from an arm, Inspector?"

"Not lately, no."

"No, of course not," said Rosy, shaking her head. "All I'm saying is it would take considerable effort."

Deborah came around the far side of Mason. "So what's the other reason?"

"I'll show you. Eugene?" Rosy skirted round the table until she was positioned across from them, then waited for the technician to roll the corpse back over again. She took hold of the dead man's chin and pulled it gently towards her. Mason and Deborah saw the marks on his neck, great indentations stretching back behind his ears. "The killer reached around and held him by the neck while he went to work with the fork. I'm not certain yet, but I believe the victim might even have a broken or at least fractured neck."

"That's why his head was hanging down back at the crime scene," said Deborah, thinking aloud.

"Exactly. And I can't be one-hundred-percent certain until I open him up, but I'd say he rammed the murder weapon home, probably almost to the bridge of the fork. I'll be able to tell you the length of it too, once I see what kind of damage it's inflicted on the inside."

Mason folded his arms. "Thank you, Miss Lim. That would be most useful, seeing as we haven't managed to locate the murder weapon itself yet."

Rosy acknowledged his gratitude with a bat of her eyes.

"Could the attack have been carried out by more than one person, Rosy?" Deborah was still looking at the marks on his neck.

"Possibly… But I would say unlikely in my opinion. Whoever was holding him would just have gotten in the way of the person with the fork."

Rosy Lim waited for any more questions they might have, then began getting ready for the autopsy proper, describing all of her findings again into the recorder hanging down over the table as more photographs were taken of the corpse. The detectives stayed and watched as much as they could, but when she started slicing open the deceased and removing internal organs, they told Rosy they'd wait outside till she was done. As Deborah walked towards the door of the autopsy room, she heard Rosy's saw crank up; then struggled to curb her nausea as its edge connected with cranial bone.

Outside the building, Mason lit up a cigarette and leaned against the concrete wall of the morgue. Deborah walked up and down, questions filling her head. Who was the dead man on that table? Why was he killed? Was it gang related as the reporters were suggesting? Certainly Fagin's Row was a hotbed of such activity...but then why was his hand removed? Deborah had heard of some hit men taking souvenirs of their kills, or removing both hands and heads so people couldn't be identified, but...

And where did the fork come into it? Surely a conventional weapon would have been more appropriate. A gun or a knife?

There was no point driving herself crazy with them, not when they only had a vague outline of the story. But she couldn't help it. Once the puzzle was presented, she had to solve it: and the sooner the better. As Mason often told her, it was one of the characteristics that would see her make inspector herself before too long.

"Missing your days back on the beat, Blondie?" her superior enquired, blowing out a mouthful of smoke.

Deborah stopped her pacing. "Just thinking, sir."

"Yeah, I know what you mean."

"None of this makes any sense."

Mason grinned. "Who said it had to make any sense? Life doesn't make sense, Sergeant, in case you hadn't noticed. If it did, then..." Mason shook his head and took another drag on the cigarette, narrowing his eyes as he appreciated its flavour.

Deborah decided not to ask what he was going to say, probably only another one of his bad jokes anyway. But Mason was right about one thing. Life didn't make sense, not even at the best of times. If it did, she never would have ended up with a bastard like Phil. She'd be married now to an understanding, caring partner. And they'd be a proper family, her, Isabel, and him...with her mum in a granny flat or the house next door. In a perfect world it might have come true.

But this was the real world.

And in the real world bad things happened all the time.

CHAPTER FIVE

This wasn't real, any of it!

Yet it was. A perfect world.

He was running through a cornfield; exploring, charting the farmland around where he lived. A little boy again, pretending to be on a famous expedition. He ran and ran and ran. Basking in the glow of the fat summer sun, relishing life to the full. He was laughing, enjoying himself so much. Except something was missing. Something was so wrong. He heard a rustling in the ears of corn, the swishing as someone approached. His dad had always told him that if the farmer ever found out there'd be hell to pay.

Hell to pay.

So he ran again. Ran away from the person in the corn, the person chasing him now. He became lost in the sea of gold. But he could hear footsteps, heavy footfalls.

Clump-clump, clump-clump.

Solid, the sound of shoes on asphalt, and speeding up. How could he hear footsteps when the ground was so soft? The corn seemed to whip him much harder. He touched his face and saw blood come away on his fingers. Looking up, he noted the sun setting in the sky. Where before it had been round, a rich yellow ball warming him, now it was boiling red and orange; drowning in a darkened sea of clouds.

Night was fast approaching.

Clump-clump, clump-clump, clump-clump... The big farmer was coming for him, with his pitch-fork.

And then a sound. Heavy breathing. He was running through the corn...through the streets. The stars were out above and there were streetlamps all around, but neither seemed to offer much light.

Clump-clump, clump-clump, clump-clump, clump-clump, clump-clump...

He sprinted, gaining pace; heart hammering in his chest. For some reason it felt like his life depended on it. Had to get away from the farmer, had to escape from—

The streetlamps were flickering. One by one they fizzled out and died with a crackle of electricity.

The footsteps suddenly stopped.

He risked a look over his shoulder but saw nothing. The farmer was gone. He was safe.

As he faced front again, panting and sweating, the shadows came alive around him, stretching out to devour him. He bumped into the solid mass, bounced off and landed badly.

A hand shot out and grabbed him, seizing him by the throat. The boy struggled, trying to free himself from the farmer's grip. Except he knew now that this wasn't the farmer. It never had been. He was being hoisted up into the air with hardly any effort at all. Eyes wide, he quaked with fear. As he was brought closer, as the stars revealed his attacker's face. His faces...

Jack's eyes snapped open. He could see only whiteness, blinding whiteness. For a second he thought he was dead;

he felt so cold. Then he realised he was curled up on the bathroom floor, staring directly at the white porcelain of the toilet's base.

Grunting, he lifted his head. He remembered coming in here, having a shower, and then… It had happened again, just like the first night. Only different. The same but different. It was like that every time.

Jack reached up a hand and grabbed the sink basin, using it to pull himself to his feet. He looked himself over to make sure he wasn't bleeding. Touched his neck to see if it was sore, if there were any indentations. But how could there be? It was just a dream…just a vision. An aftershock, a reliving of past events. Quite appropriate considering his former career.

Jack glared at himself in the bathroom mirror. That wasn't him, not the Jack Foley of old. He opened the bathroom door and was startled to see a middle-aged woman in an overall making his bed. She turned, almost as surprised as he was. Jack jumped back behind the door, covering his naked body with the wood.

"W-Who are you?" he shouted, poking his head round the corner.

"Housekeeping, love. Come round at eleven every morning," she said, grinning. "I knocked, but no one answered. Thought you were out and about. No 'do not disturb sign' on the handle."

"Oh…I'm sorry. I didn't realise."

"No need." The woman smirked. "You ain't got nothing I haven't seen before. It's been a while, granted…"

"I overlaid, you see," said Jack, his cheeks turning red. "Then I took a shower."

"You don't have to explain to me. I'm only the hired help."

"Er… Look, you couldn't pass me my overnight bag, could you? The black one on the chair."

The woman, 'Miriam' according to her badge, held up the bag. "This one?"

"Ah…yes, that's it."

She brought the bag across and handed it to him. "Here you go, love. I'll leave the bathroom today, shall I then? Or do you want me to come back?"

"No, that's okay. Thanks."

Jack shut the door and locked it. Placing the bag on the toilet seat, he fished around inside until he found his razor and shaving foam. He ran a bowl of steaming hot water and squirted a generous amount of foam into his cupped hand. Jack dampened his beard, then massaged the white froth into it. His razor became clogged a few times as he stripped away the top layer, but tapping it sharply on the sink basin soon fixed the problem. When he'd finished, Jack ran a fresh bowl of water and washed his face again, the liquid bringing him back to life. He dried his skin on the hand towel provided, rubbing it gently. By the time he brought the towel away from his face, the steamed up mirror had cleared. Jack paused, recognising himself in the reflective glass.

It was his face, the one he wore. The one that reminded him every time he looked in the mirror.

The face of Jack Foley.

CHAPTER SIX

What a difference a day makes.

Isn't that how the old song goes? Deborah was beginning to see the wisdom of those lyrics now as she waited for Mason in one of the many corridors of Yardley Street Station, a corridor which just happened to contain the gents toilets.

Yesterday they had been stumbling around in the dark with virtually nothing to go on. Rosy Lim had come up with very little else during the course of her extremely thorough autopsy the results of which were now on Deborah's desk in black and white except for the fact that the fork prongs were approximately six and a half inches long, and that they'd been driven right through the victim's ribs, the lower portion of his right lung, and his kidney. The forensic examination of the crime scene and the man's clothes had yielded nothing yet either: no fibres, no fingerprints, no blood other than the victim's own. There were some scuffed bootprints, but these could well have come from the homeless people who broke into the building, and would tell the police nothing in isolation. The search had continued for both the murder weapon, now officially a dual-pronged fork, and the severed right hand. Indeed, it was continuing even today, but no one was expecting anything to be found; most people, Deborah included, now concurred with Rosy's theory that the victim had been murdered elsewhere and simply dumped there. Flat to flat enquiries turned up the usual blanks, but what could you really expect in Fagin's Row? And Mason had put the word out in case any of his sources knew anything, which had also proved a waste of time up to now.

Then early this morning they'd hit the jackpot. Their trawl through the missing persons reports had come up trumps, a recent photograph marking out the victim. The man was one Stuart Redbrook, thirty-four years of age, who lived at 17 Hedgemere Avenue, on the east side of the city. Apparently he had been reported missing on the Thursday of last week. The late Mr Redbrook was a programmer in a computer data company and kept informal hours. But when he hadn't shown up for work two days on the trot without checking in, alarm bells had begun to ring. In fact no one had seen him since the previous Tuesday, when he left the offices at around seven o'clock, just before the boss himself. His girlfriend was abroad so there was nobody to confirm or deny whether he'd returned to his home that night. Redbrook's family, understandably concerned, had rung around all the hospitals first to see if he'd been in an accident, then registered him as missing. They'd been told to wait a while before jumping to conclusions in case he showed up.

Well, he showed up all right, thought Deborah. *The news could have been better, though. Those poor people.*

Now Deborah was the one waiting to see what Mason wanted her to do next. When she'd told him about Redbrook, he'd immediately dashed off to see the super, who'd specifically asked to be kept informed. That meeting had come to a close some ten minutes ago now and Deborah had finally tracked Mason down, thanks to an observant P.C. called Clark who had spotted the inspector heading in the direction of the loos.

The varnished door of the gents opened and Mason appeared, shaking his wet hands. He didn't seem the least bit shocked to find his sergeant outside. There was a pungent odour of cigarette smoke hanging around his person that intensified the closer he came.

"The drier in there's packed up again. Remind me to give maintenance a call, will you?"

Deborah held out her own hands. "So what happens now, sir?"

"Well, they'll come and fix it, I hope. Can't stand wet hands, personally." Mason smiled. "In the meantime, I'm going to Redbrook's place of work. Have a chat with a few of his colleagues, see if I can dig anything up."

"And..."

"Ah, now Blondie, I want you to—"

"Don't say it, sir."

"I want you to go and have a talk to the family. There, I've said it."

Deborah frowned. "You know I hate giving news like that, sir."

"Someone's got to do it. Take one of the uniforms if you like, get them to break the ice. But I want *you* to find out if he had any enemies, anyone—"

"Anyone who might want to crush his windpipe, stab him with a barbecue fork, then cut off his right hand?"

"That about covers it, yeah. And they'll need to make a formal identification as well. What about the girlfriend, any idea when she'll be back in this country?"

"Not yet, but I'll find out."

Mason began walking down the corridor. "Thanks.

Look, I'm sorry about this but I really think it's better if you handle…that side of it."

Deborah kept up with his strides. "Why, because I'm a woman? Tea and sympathy, is that it?"

Mason glanced across at her. "Is that what you really think?"

"No," said Deborah. "I think you just don't want to do it yourself, so you're palming it off on me."

"You know me too well. It's called delegation, Sergeant. When you're the inspector, *you* can send people off to do all the dirty jobs. Until then…" Mason stopped and waved his hand in front of the double doors ahead of him. "Ladies first."

Mason jabbed repeatedly at the button, but the 'WAIT' symbol on the crossing steadfastly refused to light up.

"Shit," he muttered, then dashed across the road. An approaching vehicle only just missed him, its beeps hounding his progress as he made it to the other side. Without a doubt he would have done the same if he'd been driving. But his Granada was parked back at Redbrook's offices, out front on the double yellows. He was a pedestrian now, however temporary the situation might be, and he reacted with a pedestrian's mentality, sticking a middle finger up at the speeding car as it disappeared into the distance.

It made more sense to walk over here rather than go all the way around the one-way system, he'd told himself. It would also be quicker, and Mason was all for things being quicker. He'd never had much patience at the best of times, as those under him had found out over the years. Slip up when Mason's around and you're for the high jump.

Which was probably why he'd gotten nowhere with Redbrook's workmates. He'd seen it all before, the shiftiness, the guilt; everyone has something to hide and when the police come knocking it makes people nervous   no matter how innocent they may be. Obviously that made life a thousand times more difficult if you were trying to track down a murder suspect.

Mason talked to everyone there, starting with the man in charge of the outfit, an uptight suit called Harvey Wheeler. They sat in Wheeler's rather small office while the inspector told him of Redbrook's death. He seemed shocked and concerned, though more for himself than for Redbrook, Mason suspected.

"Dead? God, how could this happen?"

"I'm afraid I can't tell you that at this time, but we are treating the matter as suspicious. You might have been the last person to see him alive, we believe," Mason informed him quite early on in the conversation.

"But… But the first to notice he was missing."

"True."

Both men eyed each other up distrustfully. *Guilty,* thought Mason. *But of what? Of falsifying his taxes, of adultery, of stealing a chocolate bar from a shop when he was a kid? Or maybe just littering?*

"I-I really haven't known Stuart long," Wheeler kept insisting. The company, egocentrically named 'Wheeler's', had only been formed a year ago, but was made up of 'Good people', Stuart Redbrook numbering amongst its finest, if modest number of employees. The fact that Wheeler had poached the man from another firm seemed like something akin to standard business practice in his book.

"Happens all the time, Inspector," Wheeler promised him, attempting to hide his discomfort behind a façade of cool credulity. "It was all very amicable."

"Really? I don't think I'd be very 'amicable' if someone had just lured away a member of *my* staff, especially if he was good at his job."

"No, I don't suppose so." Wheeler opened a desk drawer and took out a bottle of scotch. He poured himself a drink without bothering to offer Mason one.

"Forgive me for saying so, Mr Wheeler," said Mason, looking around him, "but this operation doesn't exactly strike me as top flight."

Wheeler laughed dryly and took a sip from his glass. "You think maybe I blackmailed Redbrook into coming to work for me, because I couldn't afford to pay him?"

Mason shrugged.

"Redbrook's salary was quite a substantial one, Inspector. Feel free to check the company records if you don't believe me. We may not appear 'top flight' at a glance, but it's because we don't splash out on superficial luxuries that we're able to make more money behind the scenes. Haven't you heard, it's the way of the future." Wheeler drank again. "We don't even have our own car park here because the space in this building is rented."

"So I noticed."

The discussion had gone downhill from there. Mason asked question after question, confirming the time when Wheeler last saw Redbrook a week ago, what mood he seemed to be in and so on. All routine things he had to ask. But he soon got fed up with the short, uninformative replies Wheeler was giving.

Taking his leave of the man, Mason turned his attention to the rest of the team: going through the motions. There were seven Wheeler workers present and he got just as much out of them. Three barely knew Redbrook. A couple knew him fairly well as he liaised with them on a regular basis. The sixth was the closest thing Redbrook had to a friend in the office and regularly played squash with the man. While the last, an attractive woman who did the company's accounts, claimed not to have had much to do with Redbrook, though the tears she'd choked back told Mason she was almost certainly *liaising* with the fellow more than she cared to admit. None were able to offer insight into what might have happened, though. Indeed, none of them had even been around at seven o'clock last Tuesday evening. Mason wondered whether the accounts woman had arranged to meet Redbrook somewhere that evening and been stood up. Redbrook's girlfriend was away, so they had room to manoeuvre. Perhaps she was so used to being jilted when something more important came up, she'd thought nothing of it, nor the fact that he'd not turned up for work the next day. Or maybe she'd been embarrassed to call attention to the fact in case anyone suspected her true feelings. But Mason couldn't just come right out with it and ask her directly. Quite apart from anything else, he didn't really see the point.

He did have a couple of leads to follow up, though. The company Redbrook had worked for before he switched over to Wheeler's: a grudge angle. And then there was Wheeler himself. He was worth investigating further... But Wheeler had inadvertently given him his closest lead to check out. Because there wasn't a private car park attached to 'his' premises, the staff tended to use the multi-storey just across the road. Wheeler had some kind of deal going with the owner, an old school buddy he supplied cheap technical advice and they got discount parking.

The configuration itself was like one of those miniature garages Mason had spent so many hours playing with as a lad. With different levels, spiralling tracks and supporting beams. Ring the bell and go through the wash... *Ding, ding!* The very top was open to the elements; Mason looked up and saw one or two people peering over the side. They simply couldn't resist it in spite of the risk. They had to look down. It was like going on a roller coaster; the thrill of facing the danger. Of knowing that one little slip would cost them their lives. The figures pulled back out of view.

Mason found the side-entrance door and opened it. He was confronted with a ticket machine, a flight of concrete steps, and a metal lift. For a moment he stood in the entranceway, looking around. Then he heard a disembodied voice speaking to him.

"Hello. Yes, you. Do you require any assistance?"

Mason located the source of the question. Above him and to the right was a C.C.T.V. camera, and next to it was a speaker. The inspector imagined some small computer geek locked away in a broom cupboard upstairs, surrounded by monochrome screens, watching everyone who went in and out of the entranceway. George Orwell would have been gratified to learn just how uncannily accurate his future predictions had proved to be.

Mason reached into his coat pocket and pulled out his I.D. wallet. The leather flipped open as he held it up to the camera. "Police," stated Mason. "Could I have a word?"

There was a pause before Big Brother answered. "I'll be there in a minute."

"Cheers." For some reason Mason found himself repeating the same phrase over and over to himself as he waited for the man to arrive. *Ignorance is strength. Ignorance is strength. Ignorance is strength...*

Deborah coaxed more power from the Peugeot as it scaled the hill towards a junction. Beside her was P.C. Kevin Peel, at least ten years her junior. It was true what they said, policemen   and women, she wasn't falling into that trap *were* getting younger every day. She half-expected to turn and see him sat there licking a lollipop and reading the latest issue of *The Beano*, or whatever passed for comic books nowadays.

You'll fit right in working with this division, sonny.

To her amazement, Peel stuck his hand in his pocket and produced a bag of Liquorice Allsorts. He popped a pink one into his mouth and shook the bag in her direction.

"Sergeant Harrison?"

Deborah had to bite her lip to keep from sniggering. Composing herself, she said: "No thank you, Peel. Not while I'm on duty."

The worried constable's hand shook and all the colour left his face. "I'm sorry, I didn't mean to… You won't report me, will you?"

"*Report* you?" Deborah did laugh now. "If I reported every copper who scoffed sweets on duty, Peel, I'd be doing the paperwork from now till doomsday."

"Sorry." He edged back into the seat and silently chewed his Allsort. Peel was scared of her, that much was obvious by the way he nearly wet his pants when she spoke. Part of her wanted to tell him it was okay; she'd been a P.C. once upon a time and just because she'd risen in the ranks it didn't make her the Bride of Frankenstein and Margaret Thatcher all rolled into one. But another side of her personality, a distinctly sadistic side that reared its ugly head every now and again, actually quite liked it. With fear came respect, and when you had respect you had it made in this game.

Turning left at the junction, the car went over a bump in the road. Peel dropped his bag of liquorice on the floor, spilling them over the car mat in the front. He lunged forward in a desperate bid to gather them up, some rolling under the seat where he couldn't get at them.

"Leave them till we get there, Peel,' said an exasperated Deborah.

"It's okay, I've nearly got them all—"

"Leave them, Peel! Christ, I don't have this much trouble with my daughter in the car."

Peel sat back, sufficiently chastised. "I'm sorry," he repeated.

"It's all right. Just relax." Out of the corner of her eye Deborah could see his face turning a bright shade of scarlet making up for the previous lack of blood in his cheeks the black and white colour of his uniform exacerbating the contrast.

If nothing else, the sweet incident convinced her that she couldn't let this virtual rookie deliver such bad news to the Redbrooks. He'd probably start blubbing the moment they did. Either that or not be able to get the words out in the first place. No, she owed it to them – exactly why she couldn't explain – to deliver the news personally. *Properly.*

Deborah put the subject out of her mind. She'd have to deal with it soon enough when they arrived at Redbrook's parents' place. But for now she concentrated on her driving and nothing else, ignoring the odd twitch as Peel shuffled about in his seat, his hand reaching down the side groping around for those last few Allsorts underneath.

Finally they arrived at the address given when Redbrook had been reported missing. It was a nice house, white with bay windows and a lawn just big enough for a retired couple to maintain. Deborah felt her stomach doing somersaults as she set the handbrake. Peel waited for her to get out of the car before rescuing the remaining sweets he'd dropped.

Got them all?'

Peel nodded, still red with shame, and put on his

peaked cap.

"Good. Glad we got that settled." Deborah leaned back against the Peugeot and stared up the driveway to the house. She saw movement behind the nets inside. Right now they were probably wondering who the visitors were, sharp intakes of breath all round as they spotted Peel's uniform. Perhaps Stuart had been found, their lost son alive and well? Deborah gave it a minute, left them with their false hopes a few moments longer. Then she opened the gate and began walking up the drive.

"Stay behind me," she whispered to Peel, who was bringing up the rear. "Let me do the talking, and for goodness sake don't offer them any of your sweets."

Peel shook his head, taking the commandments on board like they were handed down from Mount Sinai itself.

The walk up the drive seemed to take forever. Deborah's feet moved in slow motion, one before the other. Then, abruptly, she was at the door: a lovingly varnished door with glass squares embedded in its body and a polished brass knocker which hung below a polished brass letterbox. Deborah was about to use the knocker but the very thought of that *rat-ta-tat* sound, of brass against brass, made her shiver. Instead, she rapped on the wood lightly with her knuckles.

She heard a lock turning on the inside; her hand reached in her bag for I.D. The door opened inwards as she brought up the wallet, her photo frozen in the blue of the identity card, badge shining golden in the weak sunlight from above.

The I.D. slipped from her fingers, dropping to the floor like a heavy autumn leaf. Her mouth gaped wide and her face froze like the image in that passport photograph.

She stared at the man in disbelief. He stared back. There was no doubt in her mind. *You're looking…* Deborah told herself. *You're looking right at him.*

PAUL KANE

You're gazing into the face...
Into the face of a dead man.

PART II

CHAPTER SEVEN

True to form, he spent much of that day in the library.

Bored with staring at the same walls for days, of watching the same dross on TV, Jack had finally decided to venture outside of the hotel. To explore, as he had done so often as a child. To see just what kind of city he'd found himself in. The city of Norchester

He hadn't had an attack since that first morning and felt confident enough to rejoin the rest of the human race, for a few hours at any rate. The shops in the city centre were impressive, he had to admit. He counted at least five big clothes stores on the same street, and even bobbed into one to get a couple of fresh shirts and a jumper Jack didn't bother looking at the style or colours, he just made sure they were his size. There seemed to be more music, Blu-ray and computer games shops than anything else, reflecting the technological age he was living in. An age that would have seemed like make-believe when he was young.

Jack had a wander around these, to pass the time more than anything, then grabbed himself some lunch in a nice, but busy, café near the plaza. He ordered a warm quiche and a coffee over the counter. He even thought he spotted Felicity from *The Imperial* moonlighting there as a waitress, dressed in a yellow blouse and black skirt today, with her hair taken up. She was dashing about from table to table, smiling that same generic smile, and didn't even notice him. *No reason why she should*, thought Jack, must have a lot on her mind holding down two jobs while she attended uni or college or whatever that is if she *was* a further or higher education student. *But then haven't we all got a lot on our minds?* When he'd finished, he left a tip on the table for her to collect.

His next port of call was the massive library located near enough in the centre of the city, or so the pamphlet that he'd picked up in *The Imperial*'s lobby claimed. You could feel the warmth as soon as you stepped through the automatic glass doors, and Jack was grateful to be out of the winter winds. No wonder so many homeless people chose to congregate inside such places, if only to keep out the bitter chill.

Jack moved deeper into the library, glancing up at the signs above. He located the reference section no problem, and it was only a short step from there to the rows of shelves containing books on history. He scanned them, searching for something of interest.

There was a book on Christopher Columbus, one of his own personal heroes, written to coincide with the 500th anniversary of the Genoese explorer's discovery of the New World. Jack thumbed through the pages, then read a bit:

But Columbus was still convinced that he could sail to the Far East by heading West across the Atlantic, thus pioneering a new route to his destination. Having failed in his efforts to gain funding from King John II of Portugal, Columbus presented his ideas to King Ferdinand and Queen Isabella of Spain. The main problem would almost certainly be the length of the voyage, which had hitherto been calculated as four months considered impossible by most right-

thinking individuals of the time.

Four months. If only all journeys could be over so quickly. The author Hubert Konrad, probably a pseudonym had obviously taken the pop-biographical route here to cash in on the occasion, but Jack found comfort in these pages, regardless of how well he knew the tale himself. He skimmed through most of the book before moving on to another, all about the Russian Revolution.

When he'd done with that, Jack went from book to book, reading up again on events as diverse as the Gunpowder Plot, the American Civil War, another one of his favourites, the Treaty of Rome… And people like Oliver Cromwell, Ghandi and Patton. Then his eyes caught a glimpse of one particular spine. He pulled it from the very bottom shelf and held it up. On the front, in big letters, it read: *The Real Robin of Sherwood: A Study by John Foley.* He opened it up and read the printing date, then the dedication. It was one of his first publications; he was surprised they even stocked it. Flipping back to the front he saw that it hadn't been taken out in months. Jack laughed painfully to himself and put it back where he'd found it.

That was another life, all in the past.

Maybe one day he'd return to what he did best, perhaps when he'd figured all this out. When he'd got to the bottom of whatever was happening. But it was impossible at present. How could he even contemplate starting another project when—

For one thing he couldn't concentrate for more than five minutes at a time, and when the blackouts, the dreams… when *they* came… For another he was always on the move always forced to leave a place not long after he'd arrived. It hardly made for a stable working environment. He knew he'd have to pack up and leave this city soon. It was always the way.

God, how he wished he could just turn back time, like that character in his favourite novel by Wells. Prevent what had happened; stop it happening time and time again. Get his life back, his real life, not this…this whatever it was.

Jack knew he would never be complete, never be *whole* again until this was over. One way or the other.

He was so caught up in his own thoughts, he hadn't noticed the library assistant crouching on the floor: a brittle-looking man with glasses on a chain around his neck. He was busy putting back books that had been discarded by people who couldn't be bothered to return them to the shelves. Jack all but tripped over him.

"I'm sorry," he called down to the man.

The library assistant tutted, then raised a finger to his lips. Jack saw what he was getting at. "I'm sorry," he whispered, almost inaudibly this time. That seemed to satisfy the man and he nodded contentedly to himself, getting back to the task in hand.

Jack looked at his watch and realised he'd blown all of the afternoon in the library. He started looking for the way out again, but inadvertently stumbled upon the reading room where all the day's newspapers were kept – reporting more recent history. The tables were littered with crumpled paper, the wire racks alongside containing only specialist journals and periodicals no one here would ever be interested in, but which the library had to stock because of its mandate to provide for all; publications such as *Wicker World* what a terrible pun and *Taxidermy Today*. The librarian with the finger fetish would have a field day tidying up in here at the end of his shift, thought Jack. The papers had been picked over, then abandoned, like carcasses on the Serengeti Plain. A headline or two caught his eye, though none on the front page:

       'POLICE NO FURTHER WITH MURDER CASE'
       'FAGIN ROW DEATH, POLICE BAFFLED'

The press was still running with the story even after they'd broken its back. He'd read a number of the write-ups when they first appeared, just to get a sense of the background to the murder   and to discover *her* name, if he was honest… D.S. Deborah Harrison. The victim was a man named Stuart Redbrook. His injuries had been described as 'extremely severe' in the rags he'd looked at, which probably meant they had no idea as yet.

There was hardly any mention of Stuart's nearest and dearest, especially the most important part. The reporters seemed content to keep on regurgitating what little they already knew about Redbrook's death. 'A close friend of the family,' it said in one particular tabloid, 'told us they are in a deep state of shock. They can't understand why anyone would want to do this.' A close friend of the family: that usually meant they'd made it up because nobody would speak to them or give them a juicy quote.

Jack walked by without looking more closely at any of them. It only served to remind him how he'd failed. Failed to get to Norchester in time, failed to save Redbrook, failed to—

Clutching the plastic bag with his shopping inside, Jack made his way through the maze of bookcases and out into the wide reception area. The glass frontispiece told him it was already dark outside, broken up only by the pretty Christmas lights hanging here and there. All over the city people would be getting ready to come back home from a hard day's work. Jack was glad he hadn't brought the car into the city centre, but didn't relish the prospect of a walk back to his hotel in the cold. Then again, maybe it was just what he needed to clear away the cobwebs.

Gritting his teeth in preparation against the inevitable blast of frigid wind, Jack stepped through the automatic doors and began his hike back to *The Imperial*.

It was a quarter past six when he finally arrived.

He'd lost his way more than once and had been forced to stop and ask people for directions on the busy city streets. Some just stared at him as though he were from another planet, others lied and said they were strangers 'in town' themselves. Fortunately, there were a couple of decent citizens who helped him out, and he was very relieved when he turned that last corner to see *The Imperial* towering in front of him. Over the last few days it had come to seem like a kind of home to him. Jack realised it was dangerous to think like that he might be called away at any time but he couldn't help it. He'd gotten to know some of the staff, in particular Miriam, with whom he always had a chat now in the mornings, and of course Albert.

From them he'd gained some sense of the history of *this* place. *The Imperial* had seen it all in its time. Royalty had favoured this establishment many moons ago, that went without saying, but stars from the world of film, sports and television had also graced its halls.

It had quietened down somewhat in recent years though, due mainly to the new management from what Jack could gather. "A foreign entrepreneur with a bit of a reputation," was how Miriam described her current employer. He'd maintained a front of respectability whilst simultaneously cutting the money spent on the place and on their wages, relying more and more on a staff of part-timers and pensioners who were paid peanuts. "You wouldn't catch royalty within fifty miles of the place now," she said, "but some of us still take a pride in our jobs."

Jack squeezed between the pillars and pushed on the revolving doors. Inside, he nodded a greeting to the receptionist on duty. "Hello, Ralph."

Ralph smiled a smile he appeared to have borrowed from Felicity for the evening. "Mr Foley. Been shopping, I see."

"Just a few bits and pieces."

"And will you be dining here in the hotel tonight, sir?"

"Haven't really thought about it. Are you booked up yet?"

Ralph pulled a face that said: 'Of course we're not booked up, and we're not likely to be either. In fact I can't remember the last time we *were* booked up.' But his actual words were, "No, I'm sure we can find room if you decide to eat in. Dinner is at—"

"Eight, yes I know. Thanks Ralph, I'll maybe see you later." Jack was about to head for the lift when he stopped and turned back to ask something. "Er, Ralph?"

"Yes, sir."

"You wouldn't happen to know if Felicity has a day job in the city, would you?"

"A day job?" The concept was apparently alien to Ralph.

"It's just that I thought I saw her today. I might have been mistaken."

"I really couldn't tell you, Mr Foley; I don't know much about her. You see, she's usually not around when I'm here."

"Right. I just wondered if you knew."

"You could always ask her yourself on Saturday night. That is if you're planning on staying until then."

It was hard for Jack to think that far in advance. The time between now and then was an eternity in his world.

"Okay, thanks again."

Jack made for the lift and waited while the cage descended to his level. It popped open and he said hello to Albert. "Don't they ever let you go home?" he asked as the lift set off.

The old man laughed. "Seems that way, doesn't it?"

"They work you far too hard, you know, Albert."

"Oh, I don't mind. This keeps me young," replied the lift operator with a sparkle in his eye. "So what do you think of this fair city of ours, Mr Foley?"

"I've told you before, call me Jack. Well, I can't say as I've seen a great deal of it, but what I did see was…interesting."

"Interesting," agreed Albert.

"You've certainly got one hell of a library here."

"That we have. That we have. Finest records section you'll ever hope to find."

"I only looked at the books," Jack admitted, feeling somewhat guilty about it.

"Next time you ask to see Marv. He'll show you around downstairs."

"I'll do that, Albert," said Jack.

The lift came to a sudden halt at Jack's floor and he thanked Albert for the ride.

"Anytime," Albert told him.

He had no trouble finding his room today, and reached into his coat pocket for the key to the door. The tag rattled against the key as he brought it up, shoving it in the lock and turning.

The door fell open and Jack fell inside with it.

His vision clouded as he dropped to his knees, his shopping on the floor beside him.

Jack crawled inside the hotel room, though he no longer knew *where* he was. He saw a small footbridge, water…a river, a canal? And a path off to one side, separated from the main road by an embankment and a set of railings.

There were lights down there, and people. They were safe.

Jack watched them walking along. Not right…not right… They were all on foot.

Jack's eyes watered, the tears streaming down his face.

Then he heard the noise. *Tring-tring, tring-tring!* A bicycle bell. This was the one… A figure riding a bike over the bridge, then down onto the path, ringing the bell to get people to move. *Tring-tring, tring-tring…*

And closer now, he saw the rider was wearing a sweatshirt and a cap. Somehow Jack knew instinctively it was a woman… She always comes this way, she's on a health kick goes for a long ride before and after work every day always the same time, always the same circular route.

And *He* can see her face. *He* knows the face, *He* recognises it: *He* knows her routine, *He* has studied it. *He* knows everything about her.

He has followed her often enough.

Jack reached out, his hands clutching at empty nothingness.

He is waiting for her to come down the path, to leave those people behind and turn right, up towards the shortcut she always takes to get back onto the road…through the narrow ginnel, flanked on either side by tall, thick hedges. It's fairly dark in there, but it's such a short short-cut. She usually makes it through in no time on the bike, through to the next population centre…

So why is she slowing her approach now, thinking twice today about entering?

Get out of there, turn around and get out of there! Jack tries to warn her, to stop her. But he knows she isn't really here with him, any more than he is there with her.

She shrugs off the jitters and goes in. Building up speed, so fast, so fast, keeping to the path, watching out for anyone who might be coming towards her.

Tring-tring, tring-tring!

So close now. So close…

He can smell her scent.

So close…

And she's so focused on the path ahead, she doesn't notice those arms reaching out of the bushes, timed to perfection, big hands snatching her and the bike up and dragging them sideways through the hedge; through into another dimension almost.

She's flying. She hears the sound of the bike smashing to the floor, the sound of the bell (*tring-tring, tring, tring…*) but it's so far away and now she's landing, landing awkwardly on her back, the air plucked out of her mouth.

The cyclist's baseball cap has come off, and her long, blonde hair has spilled out from underneath. She's confused, dazed even, but manages to lift herself up on one elbow. She blinks, trying to see through the darkness, a darkness that appears to be moving, coming towards her.

Get-out-of-there, get-out-of-there, get-out-of-there…

Closer. Treading on the bike and crushing it

Get-out-of-there, get-out-of-there, get-out-of-there…

Crushing the bell.

Tring-get-tring-out-tring-of-tring-there…

Then a voice, so deep and gravelly it seems to shake through every bone in her body, says: "Ride's over."

He's quick. Oh so quick. Sweeping forwards like a force of nature.

She flips over onto her front and starts to crawl away.

Get out of there! Get the fuck—

She wants to scream but can't, and then there's a pain in her left leg. *He's* brought down something pointed and sharp and it's staked her to the ground, through her thigh. Now she screams, or starts to: but she only has time to let out one frightened cry before *His* hand grips the back of her neck, reaching right around, cutting off the sounds emerging. *His* fingers press against her throat; yet she continues to try to scream, grinding throat muscle against *His* hand. *He* pulls her head back and to the left, twisting the thing in her thigh at the same time. Out of the corner of her eye she glimpses the face the faces? of her attacker. And, oh God, oh Jesus, *He* has two faces. Two faces when there should only be one.

There's a fraction of a second between the snapping of her neck and the pain kicking in. A moment of pure terror and pure tranquillity. Or somewhere between the two.

Then she realises that she is, in fact, dead.

He would have done it sooner, but wanted to see the expression on her face.

Voices… Close? Getting closer?

No time to savour this one. It's possible that someone might have heard her cry, heard the scuffle. Not very likely, but possible. *He* can't take that chance. Pulling free the bloodied fork, *He* tucks it out of sight, replaces it with another implement. A knife.

He clears away the fine strands of hair, then jabs this into the side of her head. She spasms involuntarily. More blood seeps out as *He* cuts. The edges will be ragged *He* hates that but at least it will be done.

The knife, so sharp it could cut through aluminium, traces the shape of her ear. Drawing an outline around it in red. When *He's* finished, it comes away in his hand with a satisfying squelch, leaving behind a raw hole on the side of her head. She doesn't care anymore. She's past caring. Past living.

Work completed, *He* leaves her prone form on the grass, next to her broken bicycle. *He* takes one last look at the scene…and is gone.

But Jack cannot look away. He still sees the body of that woman. Still sees the blood flowing out of her, darkening her sweatshirt. A freeze-frame—

Only when he topples forward onto the carpet does he snap out of his daze.

Jack saw through his own eyes again, was in control of his own sight, his own actions again.

Scrambling to his feet, he only just made it into the bathroom in time. He spent the next few minutes throwing up in the toilet pan, retching after there was nothing left inside. When he felt the heaving subside, he splashed water on his face from the sink, towelled himself off and dashed back into the hotel room.

He'd seen another death, but where? That was the question. The next city, the next town? A hundred miles away? A thousand or more? The killer had had a whole week to get to his next location.

And the vision had come too late again.

CHAPTER EIGHT

The rain bounced off the plastic covering of the tent.

It sounded like fingers tapping on the membrane's surface. *Pitter-patter, pitter-patter.* The effect was oddly relaxing, almost therapeutic. D.S. Deborah Harrison closed her eyes and listened to the beat. Shutting out the sight below her. For a moment she almost forgot where she was, carried away by the sound of the rain. But the moment didn't last long. Such moments never did.

"I'd say this happened last night." Rosy Lim's voice was clear and precise, dragging Deborah back to reality. She opened her eyes again and saw Mason standing next to the pathologist.

"Time, Doctor?"

"Best guess, somewhere between six-thirty and eight, maybe eight-thirty."

Deborah looked down again at the figure on the ground, her damp body bent into an unnatural position, one leg underneath her, head to the side, spine twisting round. She kept expecting the woman to pull her leg out and straighten up, like a restless sleeper suffering from cramp. Deborah had to keep reminding herself that this was another sleeper who would never awaken again. Never rise to the sound of the alarm again, to the sound of the paperboy or postman.

If she was ever in any doubt, all Deborah had to do was focus on the blood, most of which had soaked into the woman's tracksuit bottoms and sweatshirt. Or maybe the gaping hole on the side of her head where her ear had been removed. She must have been so pretty before... No, she didn't want to look at that anymore. Instead, she cast her gaze over the mangled shape of the bicycle, but found no comfort there, either.

"The murder definitely occurred here this time," continued Rosy. "The blood's confined to this one area. And her neck's broken, just like Stuart Redbrook's."

Stuart Redbrook. That name still made Deborah flinch. She recalled the scene almost three days ago when she'd visited his parents' house. Her shock when the door had opened. Seeing the dead man standing there. Stuart Redbrook in the flesh. The last time she'd seen him was on Rosy Lim's table, his skin a lighter shade of grey, being sliced open from sternum to crotch. Yet there he was, inches away, a worried frown on his face because nobody had told him he was meant to be dead.

At first she thought she must be imagining things, pasting Redbrook's face onto another body, her mind playing tricks. He was too young to be Redbrook's father, that was for sure. And anyway, who'd ever heard of a father looking exactly the same as his son? Except perhaps in Hollywood films where the same actor took on two roles? Similar perhaps, but not the same. At one stage Deborah even considered the possibility that this was Redbrook's ghost. She had a fairly open mind about such things, but even so...

To her surprise the callow Peel had stepped in to save the day. Realising that his sergeant had seized up, he quickly made the introductions, giving her time to come to her senses. As soon as she saw the man at the door nodding, reacting to what Peel had to say, she came to terms with the fact that he *was* real not a figment of her imagination, nor a spectre come back from the grave.

"I'm Theo Redbrook," he said. "Stuart's brother."

Stuart's *twin* brother.

Embarrassed, Deborah had retrieved her I.D. from the doorstep and asked to see his parents. Then she'd broken the news to them as gently as she could. Mr Redbrook comforted his wife, rocking her backwards and forwards in his arms, his own eyes glistening with moisture. But it was Theo's reaction that she found the most curious. He cried, of course he cried: he'd just been told his brother was dead. However, it was almost as if he'd known before she said the words. Known since his sibling went missing. There was a kind of resolved look on his face; all he'd needed was confirmation really. Somewhere deep inside he was already aware of Stuart's departure from this world. But now he could grieve properly.

He joined his parents on the sofa and the three of them melded together, a ball of arms and sobbing faces. Finally, when she felt it was appropriate, Deborah broached the subject of identification. The body was now in a fit state to be seen by next of kin, thanks to Rosy's professionalism and understanding. It had to be done, a formality, a necessary evil… They were all insistent on going together, in spite of the fact that only one person was needed. It reinforced the notion that they'd bonded together; become one being sharing this inconceivable anguish, but at the same time tripling the support.

Deborah would never forget their faces as the sheet was drawn back. Mrs Redbrook's hand reaching out to stroke her son's cheek, then breaking down and finding her way back into Mr Redbrook's embrace. Theo leaning over his brother, gaining a glimpse of what the future had in store for him, seeing a reflection of his own dead face staring back at him. Did he understand now why Deborah had reacted the way she did at the door? Then he asked of his brother: "Who did this to you, Stuart? Tell me, please tell me." And he lingered, ear cocked above Stuart's mouth, willing his brother to come back just long enough to impart the identity of his killer. Deborah waited with him, listening for the whispered name as stupid as it sounded now, she waited for Stuart to talk.

But he never did, at least not out loud.

"Seems reasonable, doesn't it, Blondie?"

Deborah travelled back to the present where Mason was eager for her reply. "Sorry, what?"

"Are you all right?" Mason asked her, stepping up and placing a hand on her arm. "I know this is rough, but—"

Deborah nodded. "I'm fine. What was Rosy saying?"

"She thinks whoever killed this woman also murdered Stuart Redbrook, and I'm inclined to agree with her."

Rosy pointed to the woman. "Same M.O., the neck, the wound. I can't be sure without removing the sweatpants, but I'd bet you anything the weapon driven through the thigh there was a dual-pronged fork. The only difference is the ear."

"With Redbrook the hand was missing," said Deborah.

"Right."

Mason grimaced. "So what, you think this guy—"

"Or girl," interrupted Rosy. "We haven't established yet that it's a man we're looking for. Okay, they're strong, but I've met quite a few women who were that in my time."

"So have I," concurred Mason. "All right, you think this *person* is collecting body parts?"

"Don't you?"

"Buggered if I know what's going on inside their

mind," said Mason. "And I'm not sure I want to, either."

If only they'd been able to come up with something from the multi-storey car park, thought Deborah, then at least they might have a description to go on. Unfortunately there was nothing on the C.C.T.V. tapes but interference and static for that particular night. Then again, there was nothing to say that the attacker was waiting for him when he went to fetch his car. Maybe Redbrook ran into him or her on the way home. It was obvious he never made it to his house, no signs of a break-in or a fight inside.

Which left them where? With another murder on their hands. The press had already been on their backs because they hadn't made any progress with the first one yet. What did they want after less than a week? Some cases took years to solve. This would send them into high gear. And she wouldn't be able to hide what was going on from Isabel then…

It was a twist on the classic cliché: a man out searching for his missing cat had discovered the body at around nine o'clock this morning. It made a change from the usual dog walker. Unlike Redbrook, this woman had been attacked on the spot then left there. Had the killer panicked? Perhaps the woman screamed, not loud enough to attract any attention, obviously, but it was enough to scare whoever did this. The cuts were less exact around the ear, not a perfect severance like Redbrook's hand. Done in a rush. As much as it pained her to admit it, Deborah knew they would have to ask the media for help in tracking down witnesses. The same media that had been systematically pulling them to pieces for days.

At least they knew who the woman was; her purse, containing driver's license and credit cards, was in the bag on the back of the bike. Her name was Haley Archer. Address, 14 Cavendish Road. Not too far away.

"This fucking rain," said Mason. "We might've been

able to lift an impression or something if it wasn't for all that."

Without offering any sort of explanation, Deborah opened a flap in the tent and walked outside. The rain *was* still pouring down, had been since the early hours of the morning. She put up her umbrella, stepping past men in white suits. Deborah decided to trace the woman's final movements for herself. She made her way up through the ginnel, and out onto the towpath that ran parallel to the old canal, up towards the small footbridge. Only then did she discard the slippers, uncovering the boots beneath.

From here she could see the iron bars of the fence separating the embankment from the main road, the green paint peeling away, rusty scars here and there that would spread after today's sudden downpour. The rain had put off most of the assembled media, but some were still waiting impatiently above. As were the usual band of ghouls, people who'd noticed all the police cars there and had stopped to get a better look. Someone pointed a camera at her, but she couldn't tell if they'd taken a photograph or not. Deborah took in the faces of the crowd, reporters and public, eyes hopping from one person to the next.

If there had been more people present she might have missed him. As it was, her hawk-like vision picked him out straight away, standing beneath his own brolly. There, on the fringes, not really a part of the flock. The beard had gone, but she would have recognised him anywhere. It took her a second or two to remember quite where she'd seen him before, though it *had* been one hell of a week, after all. That night on Fagin's Row after she'd talked to the press. He'd been in the crowd then as well…watching. A coincidence? Hardly likely. Deborah had heard of killers returning to the scene of their crimes, to revel in what they'd done without anyone else knowing who they were. Supposedly it turned them on. Some even liked to get on TV so they could watch themselves later on the news.

Was that this man's game? Was he killing people and then getting off on all the attention? Something told her no, but she had to find out.

Deborah caught his eye, just as she'd done the other night. And just as she'd done before, she started to walk in his direction. He held her gaze for a minute, maybe more, then broke away. Agitated, he pushed back from the bars and turned around.

Not this time you don't.

Deborah scrambled up towards the fence. Two uniforms protecting a gap in the railings noticed her approach and got out of the way just in time, puzzled looks on their faces. The reporters moved down as one, chasing Deborah as she chased her 'suspect'.

She lost him briefly, then picked him out again crossing the road and climbing into a car, a red Mondeo. Her Peugeot wasn't far away and she sprinted after it, collapsing her umbrella as she went. Beeping it open, she got in and slid behind the wheel, gunning the engine. The mob of reporters were hot on her trail, swarming at the window as she pulled out, only just missing a car coming up behind her. Angrily, Deborah waved them off the road, searching for the man's car and spotting it just up ahead.

Rubber wipers smeared the rain across her windscreen as Deborah yanked the seatbelt across. The Mondeo was six, no, five cars away now. She changed gear, looking for a chance to overtake. The streets were narrow in this part of the city, made even more so by the number of cars parked on either side of the road.

The green estate in front was taking its time, commendably sticking to the speed limit. On any other day she would have applauded the driver, there were far too many lunatics on the highways as it was. But right now Deborah wished he would just clear out of the bloody way.

By craning her head she could still see the Mondeo. Whoever was driving seemed hesitant, as if he didn't know his way around Norchester. Good, that might work to her advantage.

The estate slowed down even more, its right-hand indicators flashing. It crawled to a full stop to wait for a break in the traffic. Deborah didn't have time for this. She wrestled with her steering wheel, overtaking him on the left-hand side. The Peugeot sneaked past and earned a blare from the green estate's horn.

"And you," muttered Deborah under her breath. Mason would have been proud of her. Now there were only four cars between her and the Mondeo. It was still too many. There was a space between the Renault ahead of her and the Ford ahead of it. Hardly big enough for her to slot into, but it would have to do.

There was a van approaching on the other side of the road.

You can make it, she told herself, not believing it for an instant. *Now!*

She started to overtake the Renault, pressing down on the accelerator. The van was coming up fast. Deborah glanced sideways and saw a red-faced man shouting abuse at her. Two panes of glass prevented her from hearing it, but she could pretty much guess what he was saying. With an extra spurt, she turned the wheel hard and nipped into the space at the back of the Ford. The Renault was forced to brake in order to accommodate her and she saw the driver through her rear-view mirror, still spitting nails.

She was in luck. The Ford hung a left and vanished

from sight probably trying to put as much distance between him and the Peugeot as possible.

The Mondeo turned right at the next available opening.

As soon as she drew level, Deborah did the same. She smiled as the Peugeot drove between two sets of tall buildings. He *really* didn't know where he was going.

The driver had turned down a dead-end road.

"Got you," said Deborah.

CHAPTER NINE

He knew it had been a mistake to stop.

It was too late; he couldn't help that poor girl now why even bother? But once he realised the murder had taken place in the same city, and after hours of driving around and around in the dark… It had never happened before. Not two in the same place. Not in all this time, and Heaven knows how many years before that. *He* had never struck in the same place twice.

Curiosity had got the better of Jack, he supposed. He had to see where she'd been slaughtered. What was so special about it, about *her*? The police were there, he knew that. It was dangerous; he knew that too. But it hadn't stopped him. He might have known that the woman would be there, D.S. Harrison, the policewoman from the news, the one who'd looked across at him that night. She recognised him instantly, as he did her.

So why run? He had nothing to feel guilty about. He'd done nothing. If anything that was the problem he'd done *nothing*, and the woman was now dead. He'd done nothing *wrong*, then.

Tell that to the copper now pursuing him.

How could he explain all this to the police, when it didn't make sense even to him? If at all possible Jack wanted to avoid a run-in with the law, no matter how trivial. This was his business and no one else's.

That was why he'd taken off, and why he'd turned up this side-street. But the Peugeot was still behind him, doggedly pursuing him. He simply couldn't shake her off. And now he'd chosen to drive up a dead-end road.

The blocky shapes of garages were racing to meet him, cutting off his exit route. Reluctantly, Jack was obliged to bring his Mondeo to a halt just shy of them. He looked in the mirror. The Peugeot was slowing too, its driver angling the car sideways so he couldn't get past.

It stopped just twenty metres away. The door opened and the policewoman climbed out.

Deborah marched round the front of the Peugeot, rain splattering her face

The thought occurred to her again: what if this was the murderer? She'd run him to ground down what was virtually a deserted back alley. Now what? Call for assistance? If he *was* the killer she'd be dead before backup ever arrived, on the receiving end of a very large two-pronged fork.

And yet she continued to walk towards the other car, as if her body was no longer under her command. She found herself standing on the passenger side of the car, bending down and peering inside.

Stupid. Stupid.

Deborah looked at the man inside. He looked back, but he wasn't staring so intently at her anymore. Right now he resembled a woodland animal caught in the headlamps of an oncoming truck. Harmless, and scared stupid.

Of course, appearances could be deceptive. He might

be reaching down the side of his seat just like Peel had done in her car. But instead of sweets, his fingers would be closing around the butt of a sawn-off shotgun, ready to hoist it up in her direction, the explosion shattering the passenger window and taking half her face off in the process.

Nevertheless, she tapped on the glass, mouthing the words: "Get out of the car."

He hesitated, no doubt wondering if there was some way to escape this situation. There wasn't, and he knew it. The man opened his door and got to his feet.

"Let's have your hands where I can see them," Deborah told him, still keeping the bulk of the Mondeo between them.

He shut the door, then held his hands out at the sides.

The man was in his late-twenties, early-thirties she guessed, five-foot ten give or take, with light brown hair verging on blonde. He wore a sage-coloured jacket, dark patches spotting the material where the rain had left its signature, and beneath that a jumper   the collar of a shirt jutting out at the neck. As she moved cautiously around to his side, she noticed his trousers were dark, possibly black denim, and he had forest boots on his feet that appeared to have a good thick tread.

"Am I under arrest?" he asked, squinting as rain droplets ran down his face.

Deborah considered this, then said, "That all depends."

"On what?"

"On why I've seen you at the site of two murder scenes in the last week. And why you ran when you saw me coming over to talk to you."

He said nothing.

"Look, you can either tell me here or back at the station. It's up to you."

Again nothing.

"Right, hold out your hands."

The man looked sideways at her, then complied. Deborah snapped on a pair of handcuffs, the hasps making a clicking noise as they locked tight. "There's no need for these," he said.

"I'll be the judge of that." Feeling reasonably secure, the D.S. speedily patted him down to make sure he wasn't carrying any concealed weapons. Jack twitched once or twice as her hands passed over him. She found no knives or guns, not even a mobile phone (which she found weird), just a leather wallet, which she put in her pocket. "Right, now get in the car." Deborah made sure he walked in front of her, but kept close enough to grab him should he decide to make a run for it again.

"What about my car?"

"Just get in." Deborah watched him clamber into the passenger seat of the Peugeot. She walked back to the Mondeo, keeping one eye on her own car all the time. His keys were still in the ignition, so she leaned in to take them out. There was a crook lock under the seat, but she didn't bother with that. Deborah figured using the auto-lock on the key-ring would be sufficient. It'd be safe enough here for the time being, and the people who kept their cars in these garages could just about get through.

Dripping wet, Deborah returned to the Peugeot and got in.

"Okay?" she asked him.

"Thanks."

Deborah glanced at the man again. He didn't look like a murderer. But then, what did a murderer look like? Killers came in all shapes and sizes, from frail old octogenarian poisoners, to little kids barely old enough to comprehend what they were doing. Neither of those two examples fit the bill on this occasion, but the man sitting next to her right now was in theory at least physically capable of ending the lives of both Stuart Redbrook and Haley Archer. She lowered her gaze to his cuffed wrists. Had those same manacled hands broken the necks of both victims? Had they gripped the fork and shoved it into back or thigh, hacked off parts of the body to keep for Christ knows what purpose?

"Now then, let's see who you are…" Deborah took out his wallet and read the name on his driver's licence. She said it aloud, reasoning that it might somehow tell her whether he was guilty or not. "Jack Foley."

"Yes," he said softly.

Was this the name of a homicidal maniac? Could she picture headlines containing the moniker 'Jack Foley'? No, that hadn't helped in the slightest. She put the wallet away again and started up the car.

The D.S. felt his eyes turning upon her. "I haven't killed anyone, if that's what you're thinking."

"We'll see." Deborah did a two-and-a-half point turn and drove back up the way she'd just come.

"It's true."

"Well, right now you're all we've got, Mr Foley."

He was about to say something else when Deborah's mobile phone came to life. It played an irritating tune, begging her to answer. She pulled it out of her pocket and answered the call with one hand. It was Mason, wondering where on earth she was.

"I might have something, sir." She turned her head towards Jack. "I'm bringing in a bloke called Foley for questioning."

Jack couldn't make out what was being said on the other end, but the voice was loud.

"Yes, I know that, sir. But…Yes, I'll explain when I see

you… Ahuh, yep. I'll meet you there in ten minutes." Deborah pushed the phone back into her pocket.

"My boss is quite keen to talk to you, whoever you are. Why don't you do us all a favour and tell me what you know."

Jack sighed and tipped back his head. "You wouldn't believe me if I did."

"Try me."

But Jack merely smiled and wiped away a droplet of rain on his face.

From her angle, it looked very much like the man was crying.

CHAPTER TEN

Yardley Street nick gave the impression of being the kind of building that was really suited to its vocation in life.

Sandwiched between two other office blocks, which were all glass and concrete in the main, its hard red-brown façade, with windows that looked like they had bars across them — but were actually more concrete struts — oozed authority: mid to late '40s, Jack guessed. Moreover, a black set of railings — bar symbolism again — separated the main road from the small front entrance, a concrete rectangle with two box-lights hanging on either side of the doorway and a golden crest badly in need of repair situated just below them. And in case anyone didn't quite get the message, over the entrance was a sign that read 'POLICE' in big white letters against a blue background. Access to the rear entrance was down a tight cut-off side-road leading round to the back of the station, and this was where they headed now.

The clouds above had finished relieving themselves by the time Deborah turned left into the side-street. After parking the Peugeot, she took Jack in through the back way — the part that actually contained all the cells. Jack felt sick with nerves as Deborah keyed in her code and took him into the station proper. She walked him past grey walls and offices, up stairs and along corridors, until they arrived at a small room with a wooden door.

Inside, there was a table on his right with four chairs placed symmetrically around it, two on one side, two on the other. There was also a recorder on the table and a small camera in the top corner of the room. On the left was one widow no larger than half a metre square, and so high up you would need to stand on a chair *on top* of the table to reach it, except for the fact that the table was bolted to the floor. Deborah ordered him to sit down on the farthest chair, next to the recorder.

She left the door open while she grabbed a uniformed constable and said something to him. Before she let the bobby go, Deborah called back and asked her 'prisoner' if he'd like anything to drink. He told her no. The P.C. carried on up the corridor and Deborah came back into the room, shutting the door behind her.

"Is there anything else you want?" she asked Jack.

He held up his hands and nodded meekly at the cuffs. "These are a bit tight."

"Sorry, I forgot about those." Deborah undid the handcuffs and returned them to the holder on her belt.

"Am I going to be charged, Sergeant Harrison?"

Deborah sat down opposite him. "How do you know my name?'

"You were on the news the night they found Stuart Redbrook. Plus it's been in the papers."

Deborah conceded his point. "What about that night, what were you doing on Fagin's Row?"

"Shouldn't there be another officer present or something? There always is on the TV."

"This isn't a formal interview. Not *yet* anyway. I'm

giving you one last chance to talk to me before Inspector Mason arrives."

Jack examined her closely, trying to make up his mind whether to trust her or not.

"I'm not stupid, you obviously have *something* to do with all this."

"How do you know I'm not a reporter?"

"Where's your press pass, your notepad? Your Dictaphone?"

"I might've left them in the car."

"You weren't carrying them when you ran off. A good reporter sleeps with his notepad, ever heard that saying, Mr Foley? And unless you've got a Pentax or video camera tucked up your sleeve, I'll assume you're not a photographer or a cameraman for ITN, either." Deborah folded her arms. "You'll have to do better than that when Inspector Mason arrives. He won't stand for people messing him about."

Again he seemed to be weighing her up.

"You say you had nothing to do with those killings. Fine. But you know something, I can tell. Are you covering for someone, Mr Foley? Do you have a guilty conscience, is that why you were there?"

"No, I—"

The door opened suddenly and Inspector Roy Mason filled the gap. Jack and Mason regarded each other coldly.

"So, what have you brought me, Sergeant?" the latter said at long last.

"This is Mr Jack Foley, sir. I saw him that night back on Fagin's Row and then again this morning. The first time I didn't really think much of it, but when I went over to talk to him at the canal… Well, let's just say he led me a merry dance."

"I see," said Mason, pulling up a chair beside her. "Like

hanging around crime scenes, do we, Foley?"

Jack clammed up.

Mason reached into his inside pocket and pulled out his cigarettes. "Do the honours would you, Blon…Sergeant?"

Deborah started the recorder and told the machine the time, who was present and which case the interview was connected with.

"Now this is for your benefit as much as ours," said Mason, pointing to the recorder. "You haven't been charged with anything, you're just helping us with our enquiries." Jack remained still as Mason continued: "What were you doing on Fagin's Row last Sunday, Mr Foley? Do you live in that area of the city?"

"No," said Jack. "I saw the crowds and—"

"You just happened to be passing and you were curious. That's understandable. There was a lot of commotion that night. But it's funny how the abandoned factory where Stuart Redbrook was found is so far away from the main road. I say again, what were you doing down Fagin's Row?"

"Nothing."

"And this morning? You were just passing again, right?"

"Right," answered Jack.

"You get around, Mr Foley, I'll say that much for you." Mason eased back in the chair and it creaked under his mass. "Perhaps you could tell us where you were a week ago last Tuesday."

Jack said nothing.

"Did you, for instance, happen to be in the vicinity of Ingle Street, of a firm called Wheelers'?"

"Never heard of the place." It was the truth, he hadn't.

"No? Doesn't ring any bells?"

Jack's face creased at the mention of bells. He heard the

bicycle bell so far away, the woman riding down that ginnel… the blood, the snap of her neck, the noise the slicing made as her ear was—

"What's the matter, Mr Foley? Does it bring back bad memories?"

Jack clenched his fists under the table.

"Were you waiting for Stuart Redbrook when he left his offices that Tuesday night, waiting in the multi-storey car park across the way perhaps? Did you force him to drive to some isolated spot and then kill him?" Mason's voice was becoming louder with each word he spoke.

"I-I've never even met Stuart Redbrook."

"You're lying. You know him, don't you? You've seen him. Answer me!"

"No," Jack lied. He'd seen Redbrook all right. He'd witnessed it all…just as he'd seen the woman with the bike murdered in cold blood. But he wasn't about to tell Mason that.

"You know what I think? I think you killed Stuart Redbrook that night and got a taste for it. Then you went out last night and you killed again, is that it? Is that what you did, you piece of shit?" Mason was shouting now, barking out each word. "Tell me!"

"No."

"You're lying. Tell me what you did."

"I-I didn't—"

"You sorry sack of—" Mason paused when he felt Deborah's hand on his arm. He followed her eyes to the recorder and then as they rolled towards the camera.

Mason nodded and took a deep breath.

Jack glowered at his interrogator opposite. "I didn't do it, Mason. You can sit here shouting at me all day long, but your murderer's still out there somewhere. Look, I can prove it. Check my cards, you'll see I wasn't even in the city last Tuesday. I arrived the night Stuart Redbrook was found."

It was now Mason's turn to say nothing.

"I'll get someone on to it," said Deborah, remembering that she still had Jack's wallet.

She took it out and opened it up, searching the compartments for his cards. But as she did so, Deborah caught sight of a photograph tucked away inside reminiscent of her own outdated picture of Isabel. It was a picture of Jack. Jack with his arm around someone. No, she couldn't believe it…

"You got them yet?" asked Mason.

"Er…yes, sir. Here they are." Deborah produced the items and folded up his wallet, leaving the photograph still inside.

Deborah looked at Jack open-mouthed. It was impossible, there was no way. But she'd seen the evidence for herself.

She just didn't know what it all meant yet.

CHAPTER ELEVEN

Jack Foley was released just after one.

Deborah insisted on driving him back to his car and Mason didn't stand in her way. The cards had checked out. They'd been used in Marlborough the week Stuart Redbrook died, then in various petrol stations and holes-in-the-walls between there and Norchester before Sunday night. Unless Jack Foley had arranged for someone to use them, and they were checking the C.C.T.V. footage on that, there was no way he could have been to blame for that man's death. However, as Mason reminded her, he was still in the frame for Haley Archer's murder. Foley admitted he'd checked into *The Imperial* hotel on the night Redbrook had been found, and his card had been used to buy sundry items in the city yesterday. So he had been local when she met her end.

But somehow Deborah knew he wasn't responsible. Connected, but not responsible. Especially when news reached them at the station about Haley Archer. About Haley Archer and her sister.

Mason had extracted nothing further from Jack; sometimes his heavy-handed approach just didn't work. She could understand his frustration, his feelings of helplessness as both the media and his superiors cried out for results. This just wasn't the way to go about getting them.

Jack sat quietly as Deborah rolled the Peugeot out of the car park. His elbow rested on the door and he rubbed his head. No matter how hard she tried she couldn't figure him out. Usually she was pretty good at reading people, it was what made her so proficient at her job. With Jack it was different. She'd felt it the first moment she set eyes on him. He was an enigma.

Deborah changed gears and broke the silence. "I'm sorry for the way Mason acted back there. He was out of order."

Jack gave a sarcastic laugh. "He just doesn't like being messed about. Your words, Sergeant."

"My name's Deborah. People call me Debbie. Well, most people do." She could feel the conversation drying up again, so she added, "Though not usually when I'm at work."

"I'd like to be able to say I'm pleased to meet you, Debbie…"

"I know – and I'm sorry for that, too. If it means anything. But you know, when you ran off like that…" Deborah shrugged.

"I suppose I *was* asking for trouble."

Jack seemed to be loosening up a bit, and she was glad of that. The direct approach hadn't got them anywhere. Maybe it was time for a change of tactics. "Look, it's my lunch hour, more or less. Are you hungry?"

Jack's hand dropped and he turned in his seat. "You're joking?"

"What? Just because I chased you all over the city, handcuffed you, and then ran you down the station for questioning, you don't want to eat with me?"

"Was this Mason's idea?"

Deborah smiled. "No, all mine. What do you say? I know a nice quiet pub not far from here that does great baked potatoes."

"I take it you don't think I'm your killer anymore."

"I never said I did in the first place." *I just said you know more than you're letting on.*

Jack's stomach chose that moment to let out a loud growl, the mention of 'baked potatoes' clearly triggering automatic hunger pangs.

"That's *one* vote for," said Deborah.

He hesitated, then shrugged himself and said, "Okay, sure. Why not."

"Right." Deborah grinned and changed gear, pointing the Peugeot in the direction of some food and drink.

Quiet or not, the place was still pretty full.

Deborah ordered them two potato lunches while Jack went off to find a decent table at the rear of the pub, away from the business types who'd also chosen today to eat somewhere different. Deborah found him again five minutes later with the orange juice he'd asked for, half a bitter for herself, and two pairs of knives and forks wrapped up in serviettes.

"Thanks," said Jack, accepting the juice. "How much do I owe you?"

Deborah waved her hand. "Forget it. Working lunch. So what do you think? Not bad, eh?" she said, sitting down on a velvet-topped stool.

"It's nice. Reminds me of some place."

"The Rover's Return?"

"The what?"

Deborah gaped in disbelief. "The Rover's Return. *Coronation Street?*"

"Oh right, the soap opera." Jack sipped his orange. "I

never watch soaps."

"Sacrilege. I never miss them. When I'm not in Isabel always tapes—" Deborah stopped, realising all too late what she'd said. The object was to get Foley to talk, not her.

"Isabel?"

That's it, you've done it now. You have to tell him. "Isabel is my daughter. She's seven."

"You're married?" said Jack. "You don't wear a ring."

"It's not the 1950s. You don't have to be married to have kids." *Too defensive,* she told herself. "But I am, yes."

"And what does your husband do?"

Don't say it. Don't you tell him… "He's a… He used to be in advertising. Look, we're separated." *You had to say it, didn't you?*

Deborah noticed a faint glint in his eye. "I'm sorry."

"No need. It happened a long time ago."

"It must be…difficult for you being—"

"What, a single parent? I get by." Deborah drank almost a third of her bitter.

"Forget I said that, it's really none of my business."

No, it isn't. So why am I telling you?

The meal arrived, brought over by a man in a white shirt and black tie. "Hope you enjoy it," he said as he laid the plates in front of them, the potatoes open and steaming.

Jack waited for her to start eating before he picked up his own knife and fork, spearing a piece of his side salad and dipping it in some pickle. Deborah used this break to steer the conversation away from herself. Now that he was eating, he was hardly likely to walk out on her. Was he?

She finished swallowing a mouthful of hot potato and said: "So, you know all about me—"

"I wouldn't go that far."

"More than I know about you. What do *you* do for a

living, Mr Foley? That is when you're not hanging around crime scenes?"

Jack picked up a crust of buttered bread and chewed it a while before speaking. "If you're Debbie, then I'm Jack."

"You haven't answered my question, *Jack*."

"No, I haven't, have I?"

Deborah chased a pickled onion around the plate with her fork. "Come on, at least tell me that."

"All right, all right. If you must know, I'm an historian. Satisfied?"

"Historian?" Deborah felt a smile about to surface.

"I…I write books about history. What's wrong with that?"

"Oh, nothing. It's just that you're not… I mean you don't look like—"

"I'm not an old fart in a tweed suit, is that what you mean?"

"I guess. An historian, then? Can't imagine that pays very well."

"I get by."

Deborah jabbed her fork into the onion with a smirk. "Have you written anything I'd know?"

"I doubt it. Although I did once publish a title about British law and order in the nineteenth century."

"Sounds right up my street." She couldn't help the sarcastic edge, but if Jack noticed he didn't show it. "And you're from Dealy, right?"

Now Jack stiffened. "How do you know that?"

"I'm a detective, remember?" She smiled. "*And* it was on your driving license."

"Of course," said Jack, drinking his orange.

"You're a long way from home, Jack Foley. What are you doing all the way up here? Researching your next book?"

"Something like that.'

Deborah studied his expression, searching for clues to his motivation. "And what were you doing in Marlborough before you came here?"

"Buying cigarettes."

Deborah laughed. "Well, Mason was spot on about one thing. You do get around a bit. Those cards of yours have been used all over the shop in the past few months. Not always in this country, either."

"Is that a crime?"

"No, I suppose not." Deborah finished her bitter, the last suds of froth sliding down to the bottom of the glass. "But you haven't exactly spent very long in any of those places."

"Maybe I decided to take some time off, travel around."

"Bit of a punishing schedule you've set yourself." Deborah sliced a tomato in two. She saw Jack wince as the pulp and juice spilled out, like he was fighting to keep more unappetising pictures out of his mind. "Level with me," she said.

"I don't know what you're talking about."

The time was right to play her trump card. "Who's the man in the photo?"

"What photo?"

"The one you carry around with you in your wallet. I noticed it when I took out your card."

Jack retreated into silence once more.

"Now, I carry a photo around with me of Isabel. She's my daughter, she's family." Deborah leaned in closer. "The man you're with in that picture looks exactly like you, Jack."

Jack slammed down his knife and fork.

"He's your brother, isn't he? Your identical twin brother?"

Jack's face was like granite, totally unreadable.

"And you want to know something else? Both Stuart Redbrook and Haley Archer that's the woman who was killed last night they were both twins as well. Now isn't that a coincidence, Jack?"

He said nothing.

"Has he got something to do with all this? Is he the person you're looking for? The one you've been roaming all over chasing?"

Again, silence.

"Is he the one doing this? Are you trying to... Jack? Jack...?"

Jack wasn't listening to her. He was somewhere else... He'd remembered why this place was so familiar; he'd seen one like it that night. *Although it was heaving back then, bodies wall to wall. Typical Friday.*

And there he is, laughing and joking with a gang of workmates. Attractive long-haired blonde sitting next to him, and he's chatting to her...chatting her up the same as always. It all comes so easily to him. What's her name... Hayley...?

No, Jesus! Not Hayley, not Hayley!

His best friend Larry has just returned from the bar, carrying a tray of drinks placing a lager down in front of him. Music is being pumped in from the speakers above: Madonna telling anyone who'd listen that she was going to keep her baby, no matter what. And someone complaining that they always have the same stuff on every week, like it's stuck in a timewarp or something. Someone else says Groundhog Day. *Reliving the same thing over and over, the same music, the same place...the same experiences...*

He's celebrating a big contract, selling a complete computer system to some big insurance firm who don't really need to upgrade, but are going to anyway because he's such a great salesman. Stands to reason: he can sell himself, he can sell anything. Christmas has come early and he might just be able to talk this very nice young lady into accompanying him back to his place if he plays his cards right. But at the back of his mind he's replaying the answerphone message left by Gloria, the woman he dumped the other week:

"Someone must've really screwed you up once. I hope you sort yourself out one day, I honestly do."

Boy, that really got to him. Leaving a string of broken hearts behind him when all he really wants is what Larry has with his wife and kids. No, it's better this way. No ties, no responsibilities. Love 'em and leave 'em. Except tonight it's going to cost him, isn't it?

Because he's going to turn down a lift home with Larry; he thinks he's in with the blonde, when he isn't really, and then he's going to have to walk it home because—

And now he's running…running so fast. Someone's following him, trailing him. He has a twin. No, not a twin, more a shadow dogging him. The footsteps…

Clump-clump, clump-clump.

Hard, heavy.

Speeding up, faster now, faster. Matching his own pace. Never letting up, never—

He pulls his mobile phone out to show…to show that he can call for help; that his one link to civilisation hasn't been cut. And if he can just make it to the road, flag someone down and…

He has to get away, has to…before… And then he sees that it's only a young lad on his way to catch the bus. And he thinks he's safe now, thinks he's so safe.

But he's not.

Fucking hell, fuck-ing-hell…

Hands around his throat, gripping him. Lifting him up. He drops the phone and it clatters to the floor. And there's a flash of metal, something sharp being rammed into his chest so hard. He's bleeding like a punctured juice carton. It feels strange, he's going cold.

But fucking hell, look at his face! There's something wrong with that face. There's something very *wrong with it.*

Jack tried to stand, knocking the table over as he did so. Deborah jumped back, then moved forward instinctively to steady him. Jack began convulsing in her arms, couldn't help it: shaking as if an electrical current was passing through him.

"Jesus, Jack? Jack…" He pulled Deborah to the floor with him, as a crowd of drinkers gathered around. The barhand in the white shirt and black tie rushed over.

"Is he… Is he all right?"

Deborah didn't respond; she had her hands full holding Jack down, his face a collage of terror and pain.

Then, as suddenly as it had started, the 'fit' ceased. Jack came to and looked deep into Deborah's eyes. She was concerned, that much was obvious, but he pushed her away from him and scrambled to his feet. Jack staggered past the onlookers, who muttered comments as he went.

He heard Deborah apologising for the mess, glanced back and saw her flashing her ID to the waiter, before racing after Jack. He was halfway down the street by the time she actually made it outside. Jack swayed like a drunken man, bumping into passing pedestrians. She caught up with him easily enough and grabbed him by the arms.

"Hey, what the hell's going on?" she demanded, disregarding the funny looks she was getting from people on the street.

Then, without any kind of warning, he broke down.

And he left her no choice but to take him into her arms, holding him until the mighty sobs wracking his body subsided.

CHAPTER TWELVE

For a long time neither of them spoke a word. They just sat in the car, speechless and motionless.

Jack looked like one of those soldiers they always showed in footage of the Vietnam War. *Shell-shocked.* Yes, that word described him exactly, thought Deborah. He point-blank refused to be taken to Casualty, though. And Deborah didn't want to push it. She was still coming to terms with what had happened herself, the last thing she needed was to bring on another 'episode'.

Then, eventually, Jack began to talk.

"My brother's dead," he told her.

"What?"

"He was killed. Murdered. By the person you're looking for." He let the information sink in, then hit her with the next revelation. "I saw it happen."

A hand went to her mouth. "Jack… Oh my God, I'm so sorry. When was this?"

"Two years ago."

"What?" she repeated. "So you were a witness to the murder. Why on earth didn't you just come forward and tell us?"

Jack shook his head. "Tried that once before. It didn't get me very far. The body was never found, you see. James, that was my brother's name, he was simply logged as a missing person."

Just like Stuart Redbrook, thought Deborah, *until* he *was found.*

"But you if you were there, if you saw what happened—"

Jack held up his hand. "I didn't say I was…there, exactly."

"I don't understand," said Deborah, frowning.

Jack sighed. "It's difficult to explain."

"Like I said before, try me."

Jack looked into her eyes again, then nodded. "Okay… I saw my brother get killed I saw it all, experienced it I guess you'd say. But I was a hundred miles away at the time."

Deborah gaped at him, her mouth open.

"You're looking at me the same way they did, back then. Like I'm crazy. I knew this was a mistake…" Jack made to open the door, but Deborah put a hand on his arm.

"No, Jack, wait." She could feel him trembling. "I didn't say you were crazy. It's just a little…"

"Hard to take in?" Jack turned back around and she removed her hand. "You should try it from my perspective."

"Right. So what're you telling me, that this is a twin thing? I mean I know that twins are close but—"

"James and I weren't particularly… We were once, but, well, we had a falling out. Towards the end we were barely speaking to each other. We were as different as we were alike. James was in Information Technology…"

One with a foot in the past, one with a foot in the future.

"But this wasn't… This was something else, something I can't explain." Jack rubbed his sore eyes. The release of pure emotion had obviously left him drained and vulnerable. Deborah might have felt bad about taking advantage of it if she didn't believe these outpourings were in some way beneficial. Not just to her, but to Jack.

"How did…" Deborah paused. "I'm sorry, but I have to ask. How—"

"Did it happen?" Jack finished for her again. "He was stabbed. The killer was waiting for him, grabbed him by the neck and… I saw it all, even felt the pain. I've been reliving it since that night, over and over. Like I did just then."

He was right. It was difficult for her to believe what he was saying, but *Jack* certainly did. The conviction was written all over his face. That he might have known his brother was dead, yes, Deborah could just about swallow that. She'd seen the way Theo Redbrook reacted when she broke the news to him – as if he'd already known Stuart was gone. And she'd also seen mothers who'd known their missing children were still alive, or that they were dead when the police refused to give up searching. It was a bond that couldn't be explained, but that didn't mean it didn't exist.

But to accept Jack Foley had actually witnessed his own brother's demise…that was another thing entirely.

"I don't expect you to understand," said Jack. "The authorities didn't back then. Thought it was grief, said it can affect people in certain ways."

This explained his reluctance to talk with her, with Mason. "That still doesn't explain what you're doing here now, Jack."

"But it does. Don't you get it?" Jack was becoming distraught again. "*James.* I don't know how, but ever since that night he… Oh, forget it."

"No, please. I want to know. I *want* to understand, Jack."

He wet his lips with his tongue. "Somehow James created a link between the killer and me. I've seen every murder since that night, every killing."

"You mean Redbrook and Haley Archer."

Jack shook his head and took her hand in both of his own; what's more, she let him. It seemed ridiculous that just a few short hours ago she'd been chasing him through the streets of Norchester, that she'd cuffed him and dragged him back to be interrogated by Mason. But then, life was seldom anything *but* ridiculous when you thought about it. "They're only the most recent victims."

Realisation slowly dawned on Deborah. "God Almighty, you've been following this maniac around, haven't you? How many has…has he—"

"Too many. But no one has ever connected them. He's way too smart for that. He does his homework. Some don't even know they're twins: but *he* knows. And he covers his tracks, spreads himself around. There are families out there right now, they still don't know… But this is the first time he's killed twice in the same place. The first time he's allowed his…allowed the victims to be found, like he doesn't care anymore. Like his patience is running out."

"He? You think it's a man then?"

Jack's face was blank. "*He's* not like any man you've ever met."

Deborah let this last utterance go. "Jack, you have to come back with me and tell them—"

"Tell them what?" Jack sneered. "They didn't believe me before, what makes you think they will now? *You* don't even believe me, I can tell. And would your friend Mason believe it? Answer me that!"

Deborah had to admit she was having big problems with what he was telling her. Maybe the murder of his brother *had* affected him if his brother was even dead created these delusions inside his mind. But then, how could she explain the fact he knew where to find Redbrook and Haley Archer? The only other way was Mason's explanation.

"And besides, when I see the things I see I have absolutely no idea of the location. Not at first, anyway. One alleyway looks much the same as any other, as does a canal or an abandoned factory, unless you see a sign or some kind of landmark. Even then it doesn't help unless you're familiar with the terrain." Jack became aware he was squeezing her hand too tightly, and he let go. "It takes time to sort out. Although the…visions, I suppose you'd call them, are much clearer than they used to be." He paused and looked out through the windscreen. "So what are you going to do now that I've told you everything?"

Deborah slumped back in the driver's seat. "I honestly don't know. This is all too…"

"What can I say to convince you?" Jack turned back to her. "I know. Something was missing, wasn't it?"

Deborah was puzzled again. "I don't follow."

"He took something, didn't he? Something that belonged to Haley Archer? Just like the bastard took something from Stuart Redbrook his right hand."

"That information was never released."

"I know." Jack considered her sternly. "I saw the killer cut it off, just like I saw him slice round Haley Archer's ear he wasn't as precise this time. Thought someone might come and interrupt him."

"Oh my Lord."

"I know because I saw it! I saw it *through* him. Just like I saw him scoop out my own brother's eye."

CHAPTER THIRTEEN

It's dark where he is. Very dark.

He lights a lamp, an old-fashioned gas-lamp like the ones they used to use before electricity. There are more in here, and candles too, but he only needs the one to see by at present. He places it on the desk, a semicircular desk, rotten now with age, then takes off his belt. He lays this on the desk and it clatters noisily. Nobody can hear it, though. Nobody can hear anything where he is.

He straightens out the belt with his tools attached to it. They fit in little loops on the band, loops he added himself, designed specifically for the implements he carries   with padded supports so they don't rattle when he moves. Next he reaches into his pocket and takes out a handkerchief made from black silk. There is something inside the handkerchief, something small. He places it on the bench beside the tools and begins to unwrap it, like a pass the parcel player once the music has stopped. He's wrapped it up so nice and neat, but now it's time to uncover what's beneath the folds.

The ear lays in the centre, afloat on a sea of sable sleekness. The blood has dried and for that he is thankful. He reaches out and selects a small bag attached to the toolbelt.

Inside here he keeps the specialist instruments, the ones he uses afterwards. Opening it up, he finds a miniature version of his toolbelt, only this time the loops are made from plastic instead of leather. His fingers run along the individual implements until he comes across the ones he needs. He takes out three. A small pair of scissors, a craft knife what he jokingly calls his scalpel and a pair of small tweezer-tongs.

Delicately picking up the ear between thumb and forefinger, he starts to snip away the ragged edges of skin with his scissors scissors which were actually designed for manicures, but which he has adapted perfectly for his… unique purposes. He made sure at the time to leave plenty of excess flesh on so that he wouldn't have to cut right up to the ear itself. Then he uses the 'scalpel' and tweezers to make sure the job is a tidy one: you could hardly tell the difference between this and a waxwork ear from Madame Tussaud's, such is the care and attention he puts into the piece.

As for the leftover pieces of flesh which now resemble lumps of raw bacon fat well, he simply sweeps them from the desk into his cupped hand and tips them into the waste bin he always keeps by the side of him when he's working.

There, all done. A pity he couldn't have spent more time on the detachment when he killed its owner, but that couldn't be helped. At least he is satisfied now with the thing. All that remains is to organise its storage.

He leaves the desk for a few moments to go over to a row of shelves behind him. This is where he keeps the empty jars.

Once he's found one of a suitable size and shape, he fills it with fluid from bottles he prepared earlier. His own special recipe, a variation on the usual formaldehyde or alcohol concoction. This should preserve the ear indefinitely. For evermore. Carefully, he takes the ear, carrying it in the palm of his hand like some small obscenely-shaped pet, and brings it closer to the glass neck of the jar. Then he picks it up with his fingertips again and drops it into the solution with a *schlop!* The thick liquid, which has the consistency of half-set jelly or paper glue, moulds itself around the human ear, caressing each contour, each curve. Content, he screws on the lid, then seals the jar with tape so that it's airtight.

Now it is ready to join the others.

He takes the jar in his huge fist, holding it up against the lamplight one final time, and delivers it to its ultimate resting place. It fits quite nicely next to the hand he took only the other week. This is contained in a slightly larger vessel and he finds the juxtaposition aesthetically pleasing. The hand brings to mind a bare tree in the autumn, fingers and thumb outstretched, part of the wrist standing in for a trunk. With a chilling smile, he recalls taking the appendage, the weight of the cleaver in his own hand, the rush of air as it came down, the sound as it chopped effortlessly through flesh and bone as he put his great strength behind the blow. The cleanest cut he's ever made.

Hardly any need for preparation, not like the ear.

Hands on hips, he admires the new addition to his 'display'. It's nice to finally have somewhere close by to keep them. Nice not having to spend days, weeks, at a time away from them. Not that he is ever truly parted from them.

But he can't stand here all day; there's still much work to be done. He goes back to the tools on the desk. The ones he's used need sharpening, that is the first task. Then, of course, he'll need to sleep. Because as soon as darkness falls, he'll be out again. New subject; new habits. He always learnt their movements before he struck, judging when it was safe to take them. No, maybe not safe it was never safe, as his last excursion had proved. Waiting for a window of opportunity, then.

He unclasps his weapon from the belt. The metal glints in the lamplight, reflecting the flame. The fork's dual prongs sparkle at each point. Holding it by the handle, he takes out a stone. It makes a grinding noise as he works, lovingly massaging the metal. By the time he's finished, both prongs will be razor sharp from hilt to tip.

As he labours on the fork, he casts his eyes over the photographs on the desk, scattered around in haphazard piles. He begins memorising the top picture a picture of a man's face. He smiles, unable to help himself.

As he fixes in his mind the likeness of his next victim.

CHAPTER FOURTEEN

It had been a tough decision to make.

And it was a decision she hadn't made lightly. But in the end, all things considered, Deborah had chosen not to tell Mason what she knew about Jack.

"You don't even believe me, I can tell. And would your friend Mason believe it? Answer me that!"

Those words came back to haunt her every time she thought about telling him. Jack was right, Mason wouldn't believe a word of his story. She could just see him now, half-laughing, half-boiling with rage because she'd brought this load of rubbish to him.

"What're you saying, Blondie, that he's some kind of psychic?"

"Not exactly, sir."

"I've seen that fucking film, we all have. You'll be having us reading the tealeaves next to find out when the murderer will strike again."

God forbid that the papers should ever get wind of it. They'd already found out about Haley Archer being a twin and put two and two together, if you'd pardon the obscene pun. Now it was front page news. And what, in their infinite wisdom, had they dubbed this psychotic?

Mason had stormed in the day it broke, dumping a pile of early editions on her desk. He didn't speak a word; he didn't have to. His expression said it all. When Deborah began to read, she felt exactly the same way.

'TWIN KILLER AT LARGE' said one in bold type, while another had already abbreviated this to: 'TWINKLE STRIKES AGAIN: LINK BETWEEN MURDERS FOUND'. The next day they were all using it.

Twinkle. Of all the stupid names… She'd like to get hold of whoever thought that one up and show them some of the photographs of Stuart Redbrook and Haley Archer, see how appropriate they found it then. This was a serious criminal they were dealing with, not some hobgoblin from a children's nursery rhyme or fairy tale. And, as Rosy Lim pointed out to her over the phone, "Now they've chosen a nickname, you've got a bona fide serial killer on your hands."

There was no way to hide it from Isabel after that, especially as she'd been taunted in the schoolyard about her mother's inability to catch said serial killer. Deborah had been forced to contend with all her seven-year-old's questions and tears but just how do you console your kid when you don't have the answers yourself? Was it true that the bad man was after *them* now? Isabel had asked. No, Deborah promised her. But how could they be sure?

She'd even begged her mother not to go to work until 'Twinkle' had been captured. "But honey, we're the ones who've got to catch him," she tried to tell her.

"I don't want *you* to catch him. Let somebody else do it!"

The argument had gone round and round in circles until Isabel finally fell asleep in Deborah's bed, eyes red raw, her cheeks still wet; the compromise reached that she could stay off school for a while and her mother would ring in every half-hour or so to let her know she was all right.

"Listen," she'd told Isabel, "I won't be in any danger myself. If…*when* we find Twinkle…" – the name stuck in her throat, but it had already passed into common usage – "uniformed officers will arrest him. Inspector Mason, that's my boss…remember, I've talked about him before? Well, he and I just have to do all the detective work."

"Like that time the police were after that crook in *The Street*?" Isabel was like a walking encyclopaedia of knowledge about soaps, in particular '*The Street*' as the programme was known in their household…it was an obsession they could both share. Still, anything that helped her cope with what her mother did for a living…

"Yeah, just like that. And he went to jail in the end, didn't he?"

Isabel nodded but still looked worried.

And if all that wasn't enough to contend with, Deborah also had a cold coming on probably due to chasing about in the rain the other day. She'd dosed herself up with paracetamols and cough medicine, but it had done little good.

As November blundered into December the situation was like this: they still hadn't made any connections between Stuart Redbrook and Haley Archer, other than the obvious, which ruled out some of the leads Mason had already been working on; the 'powers that be' were raking her superior over the coals as were the media pressing for immediate results with this one; and now, as she waited for the coffee machine at Yardley street to serve her, it felt like her head was full of cotton wool.

Was there any wonder she hadn't told Mason? She'd hardly had time for one thing. If he ever found out she could say she didn't want to bother him with talk of insights and intuitions.

"You *don't even believe me, I can tell.*"

But again, that was the real problem, wasn't it? *Did* she believe Jack or not? Was she simply withholding this information because she felt embarrassed? Embarrassed because a tiny part of her wanted to trust what Jack was telling her; because she felt a very strong compulsion to listen to his warnings? It was true that as he'd held her hand in the car, just before she dropped him off again at his hotel assuring him that she'd have his vehicle delivered; Deborah didn't want him driving after what she'd seen in the pub she'd had the strangest feeling that they shared a common goal. And if what Jack had said was really what was happening, then he could very well be the key to finding Twinkle. To putting this evil son of a bitch away for life.

So why hadn't she been in touch with him since that day? She'd tried, once, to ring him at *The Imperial*, but the receptionist said he wasn't in his room. If she'd really wanted to, Deborah could have driven over there to see Jack. At the very least kept on ringing until she caught him in. Why hadn't she? Because she was scared? Frightened to put her faith in him in case he did turn out to be a stressed-out, strung-out loony with an overactive imagination? Although the story about his 'missing' brother had appeared to check out... Or was she afraid of something else, the way she'd started to feel about—

"Here's where you've been hiding out, Blondie!" Mason approached her just as the plastic cup dropped into the compartment below. She picked up the boiling hot coffee cup by the rim and took a sip.

"Sir." It sounded almost like 'Dir' as her nose began to fill up again.

"You sound dreadful. Have you taken anything for

that?"

She gestured in the affirmative, drinking her coffee and sighing as the liquid relieved her aching throat.

"Good, you're no use to me laid up at home."

"Not going to happen, sir. Has something come up?"

"In a manner of speaking." He started to walk slowly down the corridor and she followed at his elbow. "How do you feel about shrinks, Sergeant?"

"What, you mean psychiatrists?"

"More like psychologists."

"How am I *supposed* to feel about them, sir?"

The grinding of Mason's teeth in the absence of a cigarette to suck on informed her how *he* personally felt about them. "That's up to you, Blondie. But we've been assigned one to advise us on this case, to knock up a profile of the killer."

"And you don't approve?"

"Frankly, no. I don't need some bloody Cracker wannabe getting under my feet."

"They might be able to tell us something, sir."

Mason growled. "What, that whoever did this feels guilty about playing with themselves? Who gives a shit? They like to kill, that's all that really matters. And the only way we'll find them is by good, honest police work."

Deborah finished most of her coffee, then binned the cup. Her sore throat returned with a vengeance two seconds later. "Then why...?"

"Orders from Chief Superintendent Bingham. I don't know, I think he's in the Brotherhood with this guy or something." Mason looked around to make sure no one had overheard him. "Name's Grieves, he lectures at the local university. Comes highly recommended," said the inspector acrimoniously.

Deborah blew her nose again before she was forced to sneeze. "So when do we see him?"

"The mountain has come to Mohammed, Blondie. He's waiting to see *us* right now in the briefing room, to tell us what he's come up with so far."

"Well, it has to be worth a shot, doesn't it?"

"I suppose so."

Deborah couldn't help it: this time the urge to sneeze caught her by surprise. Mason held her shoulders as she bent forwards, blowing into a tissue. "Okay?" he asked.

"Terrific." Again: *Derriffic.*

"I'll send Peel out for some Lemsip," he said to her. "My treat."

Deborah gave a mocking smile as he opened the door for her. In a way she was glad this had happened. It would take her mind off Jack for a bit and might even shed some light on the murderer. In spite of Mason's grudge against the profession, the use of psychologists had resulted in many arrests, not just in this country, but around the world. Hell, the FBI even had their own division dedicated to profiling such criminals. And if they were, as Rosy had intimated, dealing with a serial killer, then there would be rituals, methods, and behavioural characteristics that might mark him out (she'd thought of the killer as a 'him' ever since Jack told her this was so, but they still didn't have a shred of evidence to support the theory). *Who knows, this Dr Grieves might even come up with a way to catch the killer*, she thought. They certainly weren't having much luck on their own, were they?

Mason stepped through the door behind her and caught her up. They were nearly at the briefing room when he stopped her, pulling her back by the arm. "Listen, before we go in, Blondie, I just wanted to say something." Mason lowered his gaze, looking down awkwardly at his shoes.

"Sir?"

"Well, all it really was… I just wanted you to know I'm glad you're with me on this case. I couldn't have asked for a better or more competent officer as my sergeant."

Wow, is he *feeling ill?* thought Deborah. She smiled and said, "Thank you, sir. And don't worry, we'll catch him."

Mason cocked back his head and put his hand on the door. "Will we, Sergeant?" she heard him whisper as he pushed it open. "I'm beginning to wonder."

CHAPTER FIFTEEN

The Briefing Room was about half-filled with police officers, some uniforms and a smattering of Detective Constables assigned to Mason's murder squad.

Right at the back was Chief Superintendent Alexander Bingham himself; a short man with grey, wiry hair. What he lacked in stature he certainly up for in presence. No one but an idiot would ever lock horns with Bingham. He'd sent more grown men out of his office in tears than Deborah had had cold dinners in the station canteen.

"Inspector Mason, Sergeant Harrison," he said as the two of them entered. Again, his loud but strategically aimed voice belied his size and let everyone know where they stood in the great scheme of things. Below him. "Take a seat."

Mason and Deborah sat on two of the drab plastic chairs provided, while Bingham went on to introduce the man in the foreground. "This is Dr Michael Grieves, people, from Norchester University." Dr Grieves was much taller than Bingham, but was altogether a less intimidating presence and certainly no Robbie Coltrane. He wore a suit that didn't match (the jacket didn't match the trousers and the tie didn't match the jacket *or* the trousers), his bald pate was slimy with sweat and his hands shook as he rummaged around inside his battered leather case, the top of which served as a handy shield when he wished to crouch out of sight of the 'audience'. It struck Deborah that if Dr Grieves was ever to analyse himself, he might find the subject extremely interesting.

"Now, Dr Grieves has had a chance to review some of the material we've gathered, working in conjunction with our friends at the path labs…"

I bet Rosy just loved that, thought Deborah.

"…And he's here today to offer some insight into the mind of the person we're…" Bingham was about to say hunting, but changed the word to: "seeking." The superintendent nodded across to Grieves, who missed the signal entirely. "Michael? When you're ready," prompted Bingham.

Jesus, I bet the students rip him to shreds down the road, Deborah mused.

"T-Thank you, Alex… Superintendent, er Chief Superintendent Bingham," blurted Grieves almost inaudibly.

"Give me a fucking break," whispered Mason.

"From the evidence I've seen—"

"Sorry to interrupt," said Bingham. "But could you speak up just a little bit, Mike?"

Grieves smiled apologetically and started again, his voice still shaky but louder at least: "From the evidence I've seen so far, and remember these…er…these are just my own suppositions, I have been able to conclude several things about our killer. The first is that the same person carried out both attacks."

"We sort of guessed that ourselves," said Mason.

"Yes, thank you, Inspector," castigated Bingham.

"R-Right, yes…" Flustered, Grieves nevertheless pressed on. "Secondly, this person has either an overwhelming hatred for, or overwhelming obsession with, twins. Specifically identical twins of either sex."

Mason was about to say something else, but Deborah gripped his arm. He smiled at her.

"I-If, er, we work on the assumption that whoever killed Stuart Redbrook and Haley Archer has a hatred of the twin phenomenon, then perhaps these actions can be seen as…er, can be seen as his or her attempt to destroy that which they find unacceptable." Grieves paused, pleased with how it was going so far. "The mirror image, that point in childhood when we first see ourselves reflected in the mirror, a perfect representation, is a pivotal time for each of us. W-When we first discover who we are, what we look like and, erm, what…what…" Grieves forgot his next line and went on to something else. "I-It seems plausible to me that if hatred *is* the motivation, then the killer might see a living reflection of a person as inherently wrong. It is entirely possible that they find the sight of a double unnerving in some respect, the mirror image given flesh so to speak. If that *is* the case, then they would almost certainly want to…ah, obliterate the copy, leaving only one true individual behind. And, erm…all is right with the world again…that is, in their eyes."

"So what about the…disfigurements?" This question came from one of the uniformed men who didn't have the good sense to keep quiet.

"Ah yes, I was just coming to that. If revulsion is the prime motivation, then the detachment of a hand or an ear is perfectly explainable. I'm sure I don't need to tell you why." Grieves looked out over the room and found that he did. "Er, yes. Well you see these are parts of the body that come in twos, are they not? Granted they are not identical pairs, but they might still represent duality in the killer's mind." There was a collective murmur of understanding from the officers gathered.

Eyes, thought Deborah. *Eyes come in pairs as well…*

"And by removing this symbol, the murderer also ensures that even in death the twin is no longer an exact copy of its…er…of the other twin. By missing a hand or an ear, it is a flawed duplicate. The threat is expunged, the…er, the revulsion is relieved."

Mason held up his hand. "So you're telling us this person kills twins because the very idea of them offends him or her? Because he or she thinks they're evil?"

"T-That's…yes…that's certainly one theory." Grieves bent behind his case and wiped his brow; the edges of the handkerchief flapped out at the side like a surrender flag. When he rose again, he was still sweating just as profusely. "M-My other hypothesis concerns jealousy. Imagine the child, staring at the mirror image, seeing the ultimate playmate another figure exactly like them. Then…er, then imagine the disappointment as they reach out…ah, only to find reflective glass. The figure in the mirror is not real. There is no 'other' them."

"No twin," said Deborah.

Grieves smiled. "Ah…yes. In essence, yes. No copy, only a useless reflection. Now what do they see when they grow up, but other people who *do* possess another them, an exact copy in terms of appearance, you understand? Why could this not have happened to them, they ask? How cruel fate is, et cetera, et cetera… So, what to do? They set out to eliminate these reproductions. If *they* can't have a twin, if the mirror image cannot…er…come alive for them, why should it do so for anyone else? J-Jealousy, it…erm, I'm sure you'll agree being in your er…your line of work, husbands killing in jealous rages and so forth… It can be a very powerful emotion. All right…" Grieves pointed to the uniformed man who'd asked about the 'deformities'. "T-To return to your, er, the question you asked earlier, again. In this scenario the decapitations occur not to deform per se, because the killer is an admirer of duality they even use a dual-pronged fork to murder their victims, and might arguably have a dual personality but they take the items in order, erm…in order possibly to create the 'other' that was denied them when they looked in the mirror."

"Are you seriously suggesting that this sick… That they might be attempting to make another version of themselves out of parts taken from their victims?" said Mason.

Grieves nodded sheepishly. "I-It's a possibility."

"Oh well, that's it then, case solved," chuckled Mason. "Sergeant Harrison, round up everyone with the last name Frankenstein."

Some of the officers laughed nervously, but the room soon quietened when Bingham spoke up. "That'll do, Inspector."

"I'm sorry, sir. I just don't understand how this will help us catch the murderer."

"Then perhaps you might be altogether the wrong person to be leading this investigation." Bingham's words cut through Mason like an axe-head. "Go on, Mike."

Dr Grieves smiled apologetically at both Bingham and Mason. "T-The person we're, erm…*you're* looking for is probably a loner. Now before you say they always are, let me explain why this point is significant. I believe they grew up on their own, if not physically, then mentally. An outsider who found it hard to make friends. That's why the fantasy of the mirror image is so appealing, ah, important to them in either scenario it's crucial. A sense of abandonment, of loneliness, of not being able to communicate these fears to anyone—"

Mason got up and walked out, slamming the door

behind him. Deborah turned round in her seat and saw that Chief Superintendent Bingham hadn't even batted an eyelid. His gaze remained fixed on the psychologist ahead. She stayed and listened to the rest of the lecture, delivered in broken English, punctuated by more 'ums', 'erms' and stutters, suggesting more about the speaker's childhood than the subject's. But before she could slip out, Bingham came up and stood between her and the door.

"Tell Mason: my office, quarter of an hour."

"Yes, sir," she said, grappling with the need to sneeze again.

Then she left, just as Bingham stepped forward to thank Grieves for his time. After scouring the building, Deborah eventually found her boss sitting on a wall outside, enjoying another cigarette.

"Sir?"

He looked up through a dirty cloud of smoke. "I know. Bingham wants to see me."

She sat down beside him. "Why did you wind him up like that?"

"What, Grieves or the Super?"

"Both."

"I just can't stand wasting my time like this. We should be out there doing some real police work, not sat inside listening to a ponce like him going on."

"I don't know, sir. He had some interesting ideas."

"But none about how to stop whoever it is from killing again." Mason threw the burning butt onto the ground and stamped it out. "I just feel so useless, you know what I mean?"

Deborah pushed a piece of untamed hair back behind her ear. "You could get yourself thrown off this investigation, is that what you want?"

"I..." Mason shook his head. "Of course not. But *you*

know it and *I* know it, Blondie. We're just sitting on our hands here. Waiting around until the next body shows up, hoping they'll screw up this time. Meanwhile, the media is crucifying us slowly and the public are rapidly losing confidence. Do you know how many calls are coming in from worried twins, asking for police protection because they don't think we'll ever…" Mason didn't finish his sentence. Instead, he got up off the wall and said, "Time to face the music."

He headed in the direction of the entrance. Deborah watched him disappear inside, waited a moment or two, then followed him, clapping her arms about her to keep out the cold.

CHAPTER SIXTEEN

George Lovesy lined up the shot.

He squinted, estimating the distance between the red and the pocket. An easy pot. George drew back his cue, running it over the bridge of his fingers a few times. Then he hit the white and hoped for the best.

There was an almighty clack as the white and red balls collided, the red spinning off and missing the pocket by centimetres. George stamped his foot. Dammit, maybe he was in need of some glasses after all. Ten, no, five years ago he would have made that pot no problem. Could it really be that he was getting old?

George chuckled to himself. Well, he *was* retired after all. The only difference between him and the senile old souls you saw hanging around the library or charity shops being that he'd built up a successful sporting goods empire and retired at the age of only forty-five. *You jammy sod, Georgey.* What would his father have said to that, a man who'd worked well into his sixties in a profession that was sadly no more in these parts? All that was left of the metalworking industry in Norchester was a museum with a few sepia-toned pictures hanging on its walls.

But did it really matter what his father would've said? Was George still angling for his approval so long after the patriarch's demise? Probably.

Yes, by God, definitely! If he could, George would have raised Samuel Lovesy from the grave and said to him: "Look, look at all this. Look what I've achieved." As it was he'd managed to outdo Sam's blue-eyed boy, Harry, who was right this very minute tending bar somewhere in an altogether seedier part of the city.

Never a good word for George, never any encouragement. Well, he'd showed the both of them, hadn't he?

To this day George still believed that his father blamed him for the death of their mother. Was it his fault he came out second, that Mum had started to bleed internally and died right there and then in the delivery room? That was forty-nine years ago, for goodness' sake. Medicine was primitive by today's standards. If it had happened today and if his father'd had George's money, enough for Evelyn Lovesy to go private then…

But what was the use in harking back? You couldn't change the past. He was happy now, *rich* and happy. George had a beautiful wife, twenty-five years his junior (it was the money that attracted her, he was labouring under no misapprehensions there, but it was still great to go to bed every night with a woman as gorgeous as his Veronica); he had three wonderful kids from his first marriage to that po-faced bitch who'd tried to take him for all he was worth, and failed miserably; plus he still had his health (his latest medical had pronounced him fitter than many men half his age, which was good considering he was trying to keep up with a woman in her twenties). He put the latter down to regular exercise in the heated pool out back, and a couple of hours a day in the gym he'd set up in his basement. What was the sense in owning a sporting goods chain if you couldn't get hold of a few exercise bikes and rowing machines every now and again?

Best of all, though, he had this house. He was one of the Partington Lane brigade now, one of the 'elite'. It was something he'd always dreamed about, ever since he set up that market stall when he was in his teens. But he never doubted that he'd make it one day, if only to show his father and his brother. And now here he was, playing snooker on a very expensive full-sized snooker table: the kind they used every year for the World Championships. Playing snooker all by himself…

Not that Veronica would be interested in participating even if she were here, and not out for the evening at a Partington Wives committee meeting; something to do with a ball they were organising to celebrate the area's centenary. Yes folks, it was one hundred years since the first nob decided to build a house in this portion of the city, away from all the riff-raff, but George couldn't be bothered with all the whys and wherefores.

Maybe that explained why he was all alone here tonight, playing snooker by himself. His old, genuine mates didn't want to know, and no matter how much he tried to convince himself, George Lovesy didn't really belong up here with this clique. He didn't fit in (not like Veronica: she fitted in perfectly). Oh, they *tolerated* him. Played nice, sucked up. But you could tell they were thinking to themselves, *He shouldn't be here. He's gatecrashed our private party.* They were right, of course. He hadn't been born to this, hadn't inherited it from 'Daddy' like most of them. But in his eyes that made him better than the whole bleeding lot of them put together!

George lined up another shot, remembering all the

fun he'd had in the snooker halls downtown. Knocking back pints with the lads, having a few small wagers and a bollocking good time in the process. Back then he was just an ordinary working bloke with a family to support. *The good old days.* Having said that, George also remembered the bills he couldn't pay, the times they'd gone without meals or electricity or gas just to make ends meet.

He struck the cue ball again. This time the red went down and he clutched his fist in triumph.

"Old? My foot!" he said to himself. "You've still got it, George. You've still got it."

Jack lay on the hotel bed, trying to read.

Bored out of his head, he'd picked up a few novels and an *A-Z* of Norchester from a bookshop in the city. He'd walked there, the same as before. Deborah had been right, it wasn't safe for him to drive at the moment, the attacks coming more and more frequently. Normally he could have expected to relive his brother's demise maybe once a month, but he'd already had two flashbacks in as many weeks. And then there were the murders…

The book he was reading at the moment, or trying to at least, was supposed to be a techno-thriller set ten years in the future. His brother's influence again? It was so complicated and full of jargon Jack had cast it aside three times already. But he just couldn't give in once he'd started something, so he toiled away again until the words ran into one another and gave him a headache.

His mind kept drifting back to the conversation with Deborah the other day. He still couldn't understand why he'd told her all those things, opened up to her like he'd never done with anybody before. Not even in the years before James' untimely death. Every time he closed his eyes he saw her face, but she was looking at him like he was insane. He felt the touch of her hands as he tried to explain what was happening to him.

She'd called only once, when he was out buying the books as a matter of fact. No message.

Jack put the novel on the bedside table, using a scrap of hotel writing paper as a bookmark, then flicked off the small light above his head. The stars were bright again that night, hanging over the city like a choir of silent angels. Somewhere not too far away there was the flashing pink of a neon sign. It was only nine o'clock but the bars and nightclubs were gearing up for yet another busy night.

He listened to the sounds around him. Jack could hear voices coming from one of the rooms behind, the muffled blare of a TV several rooms away. And above him, the soft moans of lovers having an early night, eschewing the bright lights of the city in preference to their own company.

Jack closed his eyes, doubting whether he would sleep. He pictured Deborah again, but this time she was smiling not frowning.

George had cleaned up the majority of the colours. Now all that remained was the pink and black.

He lined up the cue again, drawing it back and—

The lights came on outside. George was in the games room around the back but could easily see the overspill from the front porch lamps, activated whenever anybody approached the house. Veronica must be home, although he'd never known one of her meetings to finish so early. Usually the Partington Wives cackled on well after the clock struck ten.

There was no point trying to listen for the car's engine, because George had bought her one of those quiet models for her birthday last August. Ran like a dream, hardly any noise at all.

The only way to find out for sure was to go and have a look through the window in the living room.

George exited the games room, snooker cue still in hand, and marched up the lengthy hall towards the south end of the house, flipping on the indoor lights as he went; dimmed to a comfortable level. The living room was three times as big as the games room, and came complete with a giant wall-mounted television great for watching movies on, just like being at the cinema a well-stocked bar, a curving beige-coloured leather sofa that could seat about twelve people, the accompanying armchairs with recliner option basically it flipped you back and hoisted your legs in the air and various *objets d'art* including a rather hideous sculpture Veronica had picked up at a fair in London purporting to be some kind of animal.

Like everything else in the room, the windows were big. George could see the whole of the driveway, leading up to the adjoining three-car garage, and the gate down the far end, which didn't even appear to be open. Needless to say it wasn't Veronica, unless she'd already parked her car inside the garage and closed the door. More likely it was a cat or something. Those lights had always been way too sensitive, he'd told that to the firm after they installed them.

The lights went out again, just like they always did when it was a false alarm.

While I'm in here... thought George, turning towards the bar. He lifted the counter lid and stepped inside, looking around for the gin and vermouth. He was going to mix himself the driest martini he'd ever tasted in his life. George brought up a glass from under the bar, then tipped in the gin. He added just a dash of dry vermouth. There didn't appear to be any lemon or olives handy, so he went without, stirring up the mixture with a transparent plastic stick. He sipped a tiny mouthful and smacked his lips.

George carried the drink and cue back through to the games room.

"Now where was I?" he asked himself.

"On the pink," came a deep, guttural reply from behind.

Jack snaps awake in the bed, his body quaking.

He sees a house, a *big* house. White with massive windows. And there is light everywhere, so bright it almost blinds him. Jack is dragged along for the ride, stealthily dodging around the side of the building, locating the alarm system and easily disabling it, forcing open the kitchen window and climbing inside, opening the door through to the hall and sneaking into another room, waiting behind that door, waiting…waiting for…

He waits for the man to enter the room, the room with the big snooker table in the middle. Hardly breathing at all, behind the door. And as soon as the man comes in—

George Lovesy stands stock-still.

The martini slides from his grasp, the glass shattering on the floor, the alcohol ruining his expensive carpet, and all he can think is:

Veronica's gonna kill me.

No, no she's not. There's someone else in the house, someone who'd got past the finest security systems money could buy, someone behind him. And *he* is going to kill George before Veronica will even get the chance. The sporting goods mogul feels obliged to turn, to see who is here with him. But he knows already, doesn't he? It has been in the papers, on the news.

"Twinkle," he says hoarsely. *Jesus, why me? Why not Harry? Why not pick on Harry, the golden boy? He's got so much less to lose than me. Can't you see that, can't you see what I've achieved here? I don't want to die! Please God, don't let me die…*

George is a large man, always has been, always will be. But the thing behind him is *gigantic*, a giant clad in the deepest, darkest black he'd ever seen.

And it has two faces, which for some reason George finds totally acceptable.

He has the crazy idea of swinging his cue at the intruder. Then, suddenly, to his surprise, he's doing it. He uses the wooden stick as a club, bringing it sharply up and sideways.

The cue breaks in two when it strikes Twinkle's arm. George looks on in amazement as the wood splinters, then tries to ram what is left into Twinkle's chest, or where he judges his attacker's chest to be. A hand comes up, snatching the cue from him and tossing it across the other side of the room, where it bounces off an easy chair and table.

George backs away, blubbering: "I have money. I-In the safe. You can take it, take what you want. Just leave me—"

"—alone." Jack sees the man's face, his panicky, fear-stricken face.

The snooker cue has proved an ineffectual weapon, snapping like a twig across *His* biceps. The man is wasting his breath. *He* doesn't want money; has no need for money. But will take what *He* wants, needs…

It's time to end this now.

He leaps forward, speed and agility incredible, especially in light of his size. The man raises his fist, but there isn't enough power for a punch, let alone room.

His hand moves to the belt, removing the fork.

Jack hears the man say: "Oh my God, please… Please don't—" But a hand is around his neck in seconds, cutting short the commotion of words. The man's eyes bulge, he beats at the hand that grips him so tight, that's lifting him off his feet and onto the snooker table.

He raises his other hand, the one with the fork in it…

George can't breathe. His hands flail helplessly about as he feels himself being hoisted through the air. His back slams down hard against the green baize of his cherished table, one of the balls digging into the small of his back: the pink he'd been hoping to drop.

The fork, the dual-pronged fork, the one he's read about, seen reported on the news, hovers in front of his eyes.

Then—

Jack sees the fork plunge down, and closes his eyes.

But the image doesn't go away. How can it, when it's *inside* his own mind? The fork rams down hard into the man's forehead, prongs coasting through skull as if it was tissue paper, as if there had always been slots in the man's head, waiting for the fork to be inserted, and—

George is vaguely aware of a violation within his own cranium, of something being inside there that doesn't belong just as he's never belonged up here with the Partington Laners. His eyes roll upwards in their sockets, and his brain itches…but he can't scratch it.

Blood runs from the holes in his forehead like lava from an erupting volcano.

As he dies, George wonders what it has all been about.

All the struggling, trying to better himself, to get his own back on his father and Harry. Only to be killed one night in his own home (a quirk of fate...*pot luck*, even?). His life over in seconds. He wonders this, but the only answer he is given is oblivion.

Jack is looking down at the man's head, cracked open like a walnut.

He yanks out the fork, still so sharp. Dripping redness comes with it, splattering across the snooker table. *He* wipes it off and then holsters the weapon, wondering whether or not to take the body.

In the end *He* decides not to. What does it matter now, anyway? People know of *His* existence, and this quest is almost at an end. The table is as good a place as any; the man's wife won't be back just yet. *He* has privacy...or so he thinks, little realising that Jack is observing his every move.

Out come the scissors. Not the manicure scissors, but a larger pair   one might even call them shears. *He* cuts the man's polo shirt open down the front, splaying the two sides wide, revealing his hairy chest and stomach.

Now out comes a knife, a large knife with jagged teeth down one side. *He* cuts the man open from neck to belly, methodically pulling back skin and muscle, then cranks open the ribs.

He plunges his gloved hands into the gore and feels around.

Jack heaves, his stomach convulsing.

With a sickening *squish*, one of the lungs comes free. A flabby red sponge, slipping over *His* hands like a living creature. *He* takes out a black plastic bag and puts the lung inside; it will do until *He* arrives back and can prepare the organ properly.

Then, very carefully, *He* pulls the two halves of the man back together and takes out a needle and thread…

Jack's vision suddenly clouded, he was aware of not being in the room anymore, of being somewhere else. Waves of nausea washed over him, but he controlled them long enough to shake his head and look at the figure in front of him.

It was James.

He was a ghastly pale colour, almost white. Jack shouted or thought he shouted at him: "Why are you showing me these things? What do you want me to do?" But James simply repeated the questions without answering them.

Then he heard a voice that might have been his own say, "Help me."

He ran towards James, ran so fast that he—

Smacked straight into the dresser with the mirror on its back. Jack howled with pain as he banged his knee and head.

Gradually he came to his senses, realising he was back in the hotel room at *The Imperial*. The connection was lost, and that which he'd thought was James was actually just his own reflection in the mirror, painted silver by the starlight outside. He stumbled backwards, slipping on a wet patch soaking the carpet. So he *had* thrown up after all; it was hardly surprising. He'd have to clean that up before Miriam saw it and started asking questions.

His bed was a mess of tangled sheets and he had knocked the book he'd been reading onto the floor.

Jack collapsed next to the bed and for a good few minutes he just sat there.

It was too much of an effort to move, too hard to think. He just wanted to go to sleep, pretend this wasn't real.

But it was. It had happened again.

And there was nothing he could do about it.

CHAPTER SEVENTEEN

Deborah called in at the library on her way home that evening.

It was the first time she'd set foot in the place since Isabel needed help with a school project at the start of term. She didn't particularly care for libraries. They reminded her too much of her own time at school, trawling through old dusty reference books and copying out reams of information just to get a pass mark in subjects she wouldn't even need when she grew up. How Jack could do this sort of thing for a living was beyond her.

Although she had to admit if the libraries round her way had been like this, she might have enjoyed her studies a great deal more. No long queues here or fiddling around with tickets; you just went up, they scanned your card, and stamped your book. Simple. Thank goodness she'd signed both herself and Isabel up when they came before…

There were other ways to do this, she knew, but there was so much information out there – a lot of it contradictory – and sometimes you just couldn't beat the old methods; putting in the time and the legwork. She discovered a very helpful if weird man at one of the information counters. He looked like he'd fall right over if you so much as breathed on him and wore his glasses on a chain around his neck.

"You're looking for books on what, sorry?" he said, so softly she had to lean forward to hear him.

"Twins," she replied, a little too loudly for his liking, before blowing her nose on a shrivelled up tissue. But his look of disdain whether it was because of her volume or her germs, she couldn't tell was soon replaced by one of delighted recognition.

"Ah, *I* recognise *you*," he said excitedly, though still keeping his voice at a pitch that only dogs could properly appreciate. "You're the police officer investigating those two murders, aren't you?"

"I'm one of the detectives involved with the investigation, yes."

"I knew it, you've been in the papers. And the books are connected with the case! Well, Inspector—"

Deborah smiled weakly. "Sergeant. I'm not an inspector quite yet."

"Sergeant, consider me at your disposal. You know, I've never helped the police track down a killer before."

She got the impression this would be one of the highlights of his career, if not his entire life, and that he'd never spoken more than a few words to anyone in a row before she came along and asked for assistance.

Not that any of it mattered. He was a damned good

librarian and within ten minutes had found her more than a dozen books devoted solely to the topic of twins, and something like twenty pertinent magazine articles and references in books, which he kindly photocopied for her free of charge, shoving his master key proudly into the Xerox machine.

Deborah skimmed through the books and chose four to take with her, as well as the wealth of photocopied material.

"Thanks," she said to the librarian before heading off to check out her load. "Really appreciated."

"Anytime. I mean that," he answered, waving her on her way. "We're always happy to help."

Deborah passed swiftly through the stamping desk, drawing more curious looks from the librarians there. *So this is my fifteen minutes*, she thought. *Pity it had to be under these circumstances.*

At the car she placed the books and papers on the passenger seat and phoned home.

"I'll be there in five minutes, Izzy. No, I'm fine. *Honest.* Tell Gran to put the kettle on and have a couple of paracetamol waiting." Deborah started the Peugeot and pulled out of the car park, glancing down at the books on her left. She couldn't help thinking about Jack again as she did so, wondering what he was doing right now.

After dinner a bowl of hot chicken soup, a cup of mint tea and her tablets and after changing from her work clothes (today an olive drab suit) into scruffy faded jeans and a sweatshirt with a picture of Bart Simpson on the front and the legend 'Bite Me!' emblazoned across the back, Deborah settled down on the settee with the books.

Isabel was on the rug next to the gas fire, watching TV. Every now and again Deborah noticed her looking across to see if her mother was still there. Wendy Harrison was on the phone to one of her old friends from down South she'd waited until after six so it wasn't as expensive.

The first book Deborah looked at was more concerned with twins in general, how they developed from a single egg, what happened in the womb and after they were born. It came as a big shock to discover that at least one in eight of all natural pregnancies were twins, even though only a tenth of these actually made it through to the birth. There was a case study of a couple who were having twins and the authors followed them through each stage of the pregnancy, chronicling every little twitch or bump. There was even a fuzzy ultrasound picture of the twins on one page. It was hard to make out the two distinctive shapes, but in the end she did. They were almost embracing each other, wrapped around each other inseparable. Where else were they going to go?

Deborah found out, by skipping ahead a couple of chapters, that twin babies can easily be told apart, in spite of what most people think, particularly by the mother. One will usually be the dominant twin, more lively than the other, more of a handful to put it plainly. How alike or dissimilar their personalities were tended to be more to do with when the egg split after conception.

She read about research into twins, once thought to be no more than a cause for mild amusement but now widely held to be the key to understanding who we *all* are…and what we might one day become. Studies were being conducted all the time. One which ran at the Gregor Mendel Institute in Rome, Italy, between 1953 and 1978, and was conducted by Professor Luigi Gedda, led to the 'clock of life' theory: that we all have a genetic blueprint for our lives encoded within us. The most famous, and arguably the most influential, study of twins was Dr Tom Bouchard's ongoing survey of the phenomenon. Since 1979, Bouchard, of the University of Minnesota, had tested and interviewed hundreds of identical twins each test usually taking a week to complete, involving medical examinations and personality evaluations. Samples of blood were compared, as were fingerprints and background histories. There was even a study much closer to home, at St Thomas' Hospital in London.

Research tended to confirm that genetics had much to do with how the twins turned out, but environment also played its part. Deborah read about the classic occurrences of twins being separated at birth but leading uncannily similar lives, and was amazed to find so many people who'd had twins out there somewhere and didn't even realise it. The one that especially stuck in her memory was the 'Jim Twins' story, mainly because it featured in all four of the books and a number of the photocopied sheets. A textbook case, you might say. Both named Jim, Jim Lewis and Jim Springer, the American twins weren't reunited until they were thirty-nine years old in 1979. It was then that they noticed a series of remarkable coincidences in their lives. Both men had worked for the police force as deputy sheriffs, then in fast food restaurants; both smoked, and smoked the same brand of cigarette at that, bit their nails and liked the same kind of beer; both enjoyed stock car racing but hated baseball; both married women with the same name and gave their first sons virtually the same names (James Allan and James Alan); they spent their holidays in the same place Florida; both owned a dog called Toy; both had had heart attacks, suffered from haemorrhoids and insomnia, and had been plagued with migraines as teenagers only to stop getting them at exactly the same time.

In another book she found a piece about German twins called Jack another one and Oscar, who were born in

Trinidad in 1934. Their parents split up, so Oscar went with his Catholic mother to Germany and Jack stayed with his father in Trinidad. Oscar went on to fight for the Nazis in World War Two, while Jack was raised as a Jew. When they eventually met in the '50s they couldn't stand the sight of each other and hated the fact that they were identical, not only in appearance but with regard to certain characteristics. Deborah couldn't help but be moved by such a sad tale.

More chilling than sad were three other stories she noted. The first was about a pair of twins called Greta and Freda Chaplin, from York. They claimed to be one person living in two bodies, talking in unison and finishing each other's sentences. They both also had the same obsessive, and aggressive, tendencies and had made their neighbour's life a misery for fifteen years. Deborah looked at the photograph provided: the longhaired sisters were dressed alike, yellow shirts and blue cardigans, and both wore the same expression, somewhere between misery and utter contempt. These two were 'mirror image' twins; Deborah thought back to Grieves' lecture about the killer being jealous of the mirrored 'other'.

The second report was about a man who'd killed his own twin. The case had been big news back in the US in 1964 apparently, and concerned brothers Tim and Todd Nicholson. Police had been called out to Tim's house, by Tim himself, one evening in December, only to find that he'd shot Todd in the heart with a .22 Winchester rifle. He was arrested for murder and tried the following year, in the midst of a media circus (Deborah could certainly relate to that) where it emerged that the twins, born into one of Chicago's richest families, had been dressed alike and treated alike since infancy. They never had a chance to become individuals, to have their own space if they wanted it, and subsequently found the whole experience of being a twin stifling and claustrophobic. In the context of that relationship the worst kind of sibling rivalry had developed. Todd, the older of the two by seconds, was the more dominant twin: he was also the more aggressive and violent of the pair. Tim claimed that he acted in self-defence that night, but was still charged with manslaughter and served three years of a one to ten year prison term.

The third tale was that of Raymond and Robert Brant. Here were twins who did everything together, too, but through choice not circumstance this time. In the summer of 1949 they were both working as linemen for a power company, usually going out in the same squad. However, it just so happened one day that they were sent out in different teams. Robert was up the side of an electricity pole when he received the fatal jolt that would end his life, and yet four miles or so away brother Raymond also felt the same shock. In that instant he knew Robert had been electrocuted and killed, stating that he felt his spirit departing. There wasn't a day went by after the accident that Raymond didn't relive his twin's death. It was almost as though half of him was missing, as if part of himself had died that day.

Deborah could see Jack in the pub, knocking the table over, writhing on the floor, his back arching. And later, claiming he was reliving *his own* brother's murder: the very moment the fork was rammed into…

Reading such remarkable stories as these, it no longer seemed like mere exaggeration or fantasy.

The last book she looked at was more about the mystical and historical side of twins. She read:

Twins have always been a constant source of fascination for others, but they have also been a source of great fear. In many different cultures throughout the centuries, the innate peculiarity of this phenomenon, of two beings who look alike and often appear to share some sort of unexplainable psychic bond, has resulted in people being frightened of twins. Frightened of the strange powers they were said to possess.

Certain Native American tribes executed twins at birth, believing them to be bad omens or evil spirits in human guise. This practice was also common amongst the Inuits of Greenland and the aboriginals of Australia. In addition, it was not unheard of in some cultures for a mother to be sacrificed alongside her 'unnatural' infants, as giving birth to twins was deemed to be proof that she had consorted with two men instead of just the one.

Deborah could see Isabel watching her out of the corner of her eye again. Thank God human civilisation had progressed since those days. Well, in some respects anyway. She couldn't imagine what she'd have done if anyone had… Deborah didn't want to didn't *have* to think about it. Such things bore no relevance to her case. Or did they? It proved that down through the ages people have been wary of twins. Maybe someone still felt that way today, felt strongly enough about it to try and wipe them all out? But why would he come here?

There she went again, thinking of a male killer. If she could accept Jack's word about that, why not about everything else?

She flipped through again, coming to a section entitled simply 'Gemini'. The Latin word for twins, the Gemini myth was tied in to a story about two brothers, Castor and Pollux. They were the offspring of Leda and Jupiter (or Zeus, depending on which source you read), who disguised himself as a swan in order to ravish the poor woman, and they were delivered initially as an egg. Deborah found herself smirking at the thought of making love to a bird, then giving birth to a giant egg. She'd never been a fan of classical myths again, it reminded her too much of school but something made her read on.

It also mentioned that Helen, the cause of the Trojan war, was their sister, and that when two guys called Theseus and Pirithous kidnapped Helen from Sparta, the twins were the ones who valiantly went to her rescue eventually recovering her successfully. Castor was well-known for his horse taming abilities, while Pollux was famed for his boxing prowess: obviously the dominant, stronger twin, Deborah concluded. Like some of the other twins she'd read about, they were inseparable, and an unbreakable bond was shared between them. They'd also served as sailors on the Argonautic expedition (though she didn't remember seeing them in the movie version that creaked around every holiday time) and afterwards were considered patron deities of seamen and voyagers.

During an ensuing war with Idas and Lynceus, whoever they were, Castor was slain. Pollux, inconsolable at such a loss, begged Jupiter to let him give up his own life for his brother's. But, by all accounts, Jupiter allowed the two brothers to share their time, to spend alternate days as deceased mortals and as gods in the heavens, where they became the constellation known as Gemini today. It was also said that they appeared occasionally during later periods to fight in great battles, mounted on splendid white steeds, no doubt tamed by Castor.

Eyes roving down the page, Deborah found reference to the twins in a quote from Macaulay's *Lays of Ancient Rome*.

So like they were, no mortal
Might one from other know;
White as snow their armour was,

Their steeds were white as snow.

She skipped a bit, moving on to the last few lines:

Back comes the chief in triumph
Who in the hour of fight
Hath seen the great Twin Brethren
In harness on his right.
Safe comes the ship to haven,
Through billows and through gales,
If once the great Twin Brethren
Sit shining on the sails.

Deborah put down the books just as her mother walked in.

"Penny sends her love," said Wendy Harrison, joining her daughter on the couch. "She's off to Majorca for two weeks over Christmas."

"Nice," said Deborah, reaching up her sweatshirt sleeve for a tissue and blowing her nose again. "Are there any seats still available on the plane?"

For a fraction of a second Wendy thought she might be serious, and was about to say she'd find out. But it was only wishful thinking on her behalf. The policewoman couldn't fly off to kick up her heels with this case still hanging over her, no matter how much her family might want her to.

Deborah tried to relax the rest of the evening. She watched the soaps with Isabel, knowing all along her daughter would be glued to the repeats again the following day. They flicked from one channel to the other, and when the 'live' early evening shows were over, Isabel slipped in a tape and played her mum their daytime counterparts that she'd missed while she was at work. They covered the whole spectrum that night, much to the exasperation of Wendy, who would rather have watched the classic Hollywood musicals screening on Channel Four South Pacific, Seven Brides…and Oklahoma! back-to-back, she kept reminding them. Deborah and Isabel caught up on all the Australian, British and US storylines that evening; the DS losing herself in a world where unrequited teenage love and affairs between various husbands, wives and their in-laws or neighbours were the only things to worry about.

By a quarter to ten, Isabel was fast asleep in the comfortable armchair. Deborah carried her up to her room and put her to bed, deciding not to wake her up to get changed. She came down and said goodnight to her mother, who'd taken the opportunity to slip on the last hour of *Oklahoma!* An early night was just what Deborah needed, too.

Gordon MacRae's dulcet tones wafted up the stairs as she washed her face, cleaned her teeth, and changed into her cotton PJs.

Surprisingly, she fell asleep straight away.

And she'd only been in bed half an hour when she felt a hand on her shoulder.

"Wha…?" Her mother was bending over her, illuminated by the landing light.

"You're wanted on the phone, love," said Wendy quietly. "You left it downstairs again. I tried to tell them you were in bed, but… Well, they said it was urgent."

CHAPTER EIGHTEEN

This was becoming a habit.

A bad habit you wanted to quit but had absolutely no control over whatsoever. No, not a habit. Déjà vu. Wasn't that what they called it, when you seemed to be doing the same things over and over again, repetitively? Reliving things…

Deborah was looking at another mutilated body, another victim of 'Twinkle'. Another man, just like Stuart Redbrook. The same people were gathered around her, Mason, Rosy Lim, forensics experts, photographers. The same number of uniforms, the same scene waiting for her as she drove the Peugeot into the Partington Lane area of the city: lights flashing in a driveway, reporters and cameras ready tipped off by a 'concerned' neighbour, she later found out.

All the same, and yet not the same.

This time the attack had happened inside the victim's own home, a place that was supposed to be safe. A place where you could shut the door and leave all of the world's insanities outside. There he was, laid face up on his snooker table, his forehead covered in drying grue, his chest and stomach the same held together by almost invisible threads. Deborah recognised his face, but couldn't call to mind the name. He was one of the residents she'd spoken to only weeks ago about the burglaries in this neck of the woods. Langley? Longley? Lovesy! That was it. George Lovesy. *Connections… connections…*

If she remembered rightly he was a local businessman, owner of a chain of sporting goods shops. She could see him now on the doorstep, telling her all about how he'd only started out with a stall on Norchester market. And promising her he had one of the best security systems around. One of the best, but still not good enough.

Mason's face was alabaster. His clothes were all creased and crumpled, as if he'd been sleeping in them, and probably on the couch. Deborah had only visited Mason's flat the once, when he'd stopped off for something on the way to a crime scene. He had never been married she remembered someone telling her that, didn't she? or was she imagining things? and his place looked the very model of a bachelor pad. Untidy, unorganised and unloved. Hardly surprising, seeing as he spent so little time there. (But then, what state would her own home be in if she didn't have her mother staying with her?) On that one fleeting visit she'd noticed pillows on the couch rather than cushions, and she'd put money on it that Mason crashed out there most nights of the week rather than face a big, empty bed.

"So what've they taken this time?" asked Mason.

Rosy folded her arms over her chest. "Difficult to say until I've opened him up…again. At a guess one of the major internal organs."

"An organ that comes in a pair," Deborah chipped in. "That's if Dr Grieves' theory is correct."

"Well, it could be the kidneys, then. Or maybe the lungs."

"Jesus H. Christ," Mason whispered to himself.

"And his wife found him like this?" Deborah queried.

Mason said nothing, so Rosy confirmed that she had.

On her approach, Deborah had spotted a woman with shoulder-length frizzy hair sitting in one of the patrol cars, the door open and a coat around her shoulders. A female PC was on her haunches next to the woman, who looked to be in shock. That must have been Mrs Lovesy, though the wife was very young and could easily have passed for his daughter if she hadn't been wearing a rather conservative high-necked dress. The fact that she'd been crying made her look even more like a little girl playing at being a grown-up, raiding her mother's wardrobe for dressing up clothes.

It was a pretty awful thing to think, but it did cross Deborah's mind whether or not she was crying over the death of her husband after all, a good proportion of his fortune would now go to her or if it was just because she'd had to find him inside like this. An image she would probably take to her own grave. Deborah knew that *she* certainly would.

Watching all those soaps has made you so cynical. Isn't it possible that she might, just might, have loved him? That the age difference meant nothing to her? Or don't you believe in love anymore, Deborah?

"Can't tell if the neck's broken yet," commented Rosy.

Deborah took a step back from the snooker table. "I'd say that would've been the least of his concerns."

"But the fork was used again, I'd stake my reputation on that. Right here…" Rosy tapped the middle of her forehead. "And right in again. Like I said before, strong."

A mobile rang out and they each checked their pockets. "Mine," said Mason. "It'll be Bingham wanting a progress report." He took the call, walking carefully over to the corner of the room.

"I'll leave you to finish up here," Deborah told Rosy.

"I've already seen more than I would've liked to, and there's something I want to check out."

"Okay. See you outside."

Deborah made her way past the men in white outfits cluttering up the hall, and emerged into the frigid night air again. Her nose had stopped running now, but there was still a residual tickle at the back of her throat. A nagging irritation that she couldn't shake off   just like there was something nagging her about these killings. Something she was missing. Something that, when she uncovered it, would crack the homicides wide open.

Mrs Lovesy had already departed. She'd probably been taken to the hospital so a doctor could give her the once-over. Then, when she was ready, if there'd ever be such a time, she'd have to make a detailed statement, raking over every little detail again. Deborah didn't envy her.

She wandered down the driveway towards the entrance. Deborah looked at the gate, through the gate. And – sure enough – she saw him there, hiding in the crowd.

The same but not the same.

Because this time he didn't disappear when she approached. What was the use? She knew where she could find him. No, this time he waited. There was a certain inevitability about their meeting again.

She knew it and he knew it.

Deborah had to speak to Jack Foley.

CHAPTER NINETEEN

She knew she shouldn't be, not here and certainly not now, but Deborah was pleased to see him.

Even if she wouldn't admit it to herself, there was a slight flutter inside as she told the P.C.s to open the gate and admit him.

"How come he gets to go in?" whined one of the waiting paparazzi.

"Yeah, which paper are you with?" asked a reporter.

"I'm a freelance," Jack told them. It wasn't a lie, he *was* a freelance writer of sorts.

"Friends in high places," another member of the press wagered.

The rest gave a collective "Ah", and some even offered to cut him a deal when he came out.

Deborah gave him a scolding look as she dragged him inside. "I don't think that was wise, do you?"

"It'll stop them plastering my face all over the front of tomorrow's rags."

He walked with her down along the side of the wall, out of earshot of press and police alike. "Why did you come here?" she said.

"You know why."

"If Mason sees you—"

"Then why did you let me in?"

Deborah avoided eye contact. "I don't know."

"I have an alibi, if that's what's bothering you. The receptionist at *The Imperial* will vouch for my whereabouts all evening."

"Who's to say you're not working with an accomplice?"

Jack turned to face her. "Is that what you think?"

She hesitated before answering. "No... I don't know."

"But Mason might."

"He might. Did you... Did you see what happened in there?" Deborah could hardly believe what she was saying.

"Yes."

She raised her head. "Tell me."

The cold transformed Jack's breath into vapour as he let out a sigh. "He disabled the alarm system somehow, I've seen him do things like that before. He's got a knack with electrical equipment. Then he broke in through the kitchen window, waited for the owner of the house—"

"George Lovesy," she informed him.

"He waited for Mr Lovesy in the games room, behind the door. Lovesy tried to defend himself."

"We know. We found the broken snooker cue."

"He was just too strong. He got hold of the man by his neck, then slammed him down onto the table." Jack wore a glazed expression as he described the scene; it was like someone dredging up an incident from their own past. "Then he brought out the fork and plunged it into Lovesy's forehead, right about here." Jack pointed to the exact same spot Rosy Lim had indicated. "The man died more or less instantly as far as I could tell. Then he opened Lovesy up with a knife and removed one of his...organs before sewing him ever so neatly up again. There, how did I do?"

Not for the first time, Deborah was at a loss for words.

"Look," said Jack. "I don't know why I'm being shown these things any more than you do. But it's happening to *me*. It's been happening to me for two years. Back in the hotel room I thought…"

"What?"

"No, it's crazy."

"Show me something about this that isn't."

Jack pushed his back up against the wall. "I thought, just for a moment… Well, I thought I saw James."

"Your brother?"

"I think he was trying to speak to me. I think he's trying to…I don't know, tell me something."

Deborah stood in front of him. "Jack, why have you been following this killer's trail? You tell me he's done this before, lots of times."

"He has."

"But why are *you* chasing him? You can't do any good here. Lovesy's dead. You saw it happen yourself."

"Don't you think I know that?" he snapped. "But what would you do? Crawl away someplace and just quietly lose your mind? Believe me, at times it's quite a tempting thought."

Deborah saw his point. Putting herself in his shoes, she tried to imagine what it must be like to experience the murders that way. To witness every blow, every horrible detail, and know there's nothing you can do about it. Nothing but follow the killer to the next town, the next city. Hoping that one of these days you might be able to—

"You're here to try and stop him, aren't you?" she said suddenly. "You think that by shadowing him you might just get lucky, that you might be able to get to him before he can commit another murder?"

"No."

"Don't lie to me, Jack."

He rubbed his tired eyes. "Maybe. But it's never going to happen. I'll never get to him in time."

Deborah took him by the shoulders, forcing him to look at her. "And what if it does? What then? What do you think you're going to do, say, 'excuse me, would you mind putting that fork down?' then escort him to the nearest nick? Jack, for Heaven's sake he's dangerous! You more than anyone else should understand that." Why was she so concerned? Was it work or something more? The intensity of her feelings surprised her somewhat.

"As I said," Jack spoke slowly. "It's never going to happen."

"But something is. I can see it in your eyes. This thing's building to a head, isn't it? He's staked a claim, and one way or another it's going to end here."

Before Jack could answer, Deborah heard footsteps behind her. She let Jack go and turned to see Rosy Lim approaching. The pathologist cocked her head, as if waiting for an explanation. Or an introduction.

"Rosy," said Deborah, partly relieved it wasn't Mason.

"Who's your friend?"

Deborah stepped aside, allowing Rosy a clear view of Jack. She noticed her associate looking him up and down. "This is Jack Foley. Jack, this is Rosy Lim, our pathologist."

Recognition dawned on the doctor's face. "*The* Jack Foley? The guy you were telling me about."

Jack looked from Rosy to Deborah, seeking clarification. He didn't get it. The policewoman felt like a schoolgirl who'd just been sprung gossiping about the class heartthrob. She nodded bashfully.

"Well, well," said Rosy. "You're not quite what I

imagined, Mr Foley."

"No?"

"Wait a minute," Deborah cut in, changing the subject. "How did you get here? You drove, didn't you?"

Jack held up his hands in surrender.

"After I specifically told you not to."

"Sorry. I didn't think there was—"

"Rosy, would you mind doing me a favour?"

Rosy frowned. "Depends."

"You're just about finished here, aren't you?"

"It's all over bar the shouting."

"Which Mason will be doing if he catches Jack hanging around. Would you give him a lift back to *The Imperial*?"

Jack made to protest, but thought better of it.

To him she said: "I'll have someone bring your car back, *again*." Then she turned to the pathologist. "What do you say, Rosy? It's on your way."

"You don't even know where I'm going."

"I'll owe you one."

"You already owe me several..." Rosy shrugged. "Okay, okay. But let's get going. I don't want to be in the middle of something with you and Mason."

Deborah thanked Rosy and watched her haul Jack off by the arm towards her Vauxhall. They climbed inside the green car, which looked almost black tonight. As he got into the passenger seat, Jack's eyes found Deborah's once more. It was another one of those long, lingering looks they'd shared before. She was reluctant to break it, and so was grateful when he finally closed the door.

The officers at the gate opened it up to let Rosy through.

Deborah hugged herself, and coughed. Then she made her way back up to the house to see Mason.

CHAPTER TWENTY

Rosy couldn't help staring at the man sitting in her passenger seat.

Keep your eyes on the road, she said to herself. Night driving wasn't a speciality of hers and she really ought to focus on one thing at a time or they'd both end up in the place where she worked. But it was hard, especially after what Deborah had told her about Jack.

She doubted whether even Mason knew the whole story. If this was ever to hit the fan, would she be in trouble for withholding evidence? After all, Deborah was the police sergeant, not her. If she chose not to tell her inspector everything, what had it got to do with Rosy? And anyway, Mason probably wouldn't believe a word of it. Rosy wasn't at all sure Debbie did, or even herself for that matter.

Moreover, she'd been told in the strictest confidence. Deborah had needed someone to talk to; they were pretty good friends. It was the only reason Rosy knew the things she did about Jack Foley. And she wasn't about to betray that trust.

Jack was quite a handsome man, but acted as if he didn't really know it. He seemed shy, awkward. Nervous.

Rosy couldn't tell if it was because of her or the predicament he'd found himself in. His brother murdered, and him following the killer around. It was bound to take its toll. Yet she suspected Jack hadn't been overly confident before, probably hadn't been cocksure in his entire life. Some people were just naturally timid. Unlike her good self.

Then, as if to prove her completely wrong, Jack said, "What has she told you?"

Okay, not the best icebreaker in the world, but it would have to do. "You mean Debbie?" She wasn't quick enough to catch his nod, but she knew the answer to her own question anyway. "Not much."

"'Is this the guy you were telling me about?' That's what you said back there."

Rosy smiled and answered quietly, "Enough."

"Great."

"Look, she told me as a friend."

"And I suppose *you* think I'm crazy, as well."

"Define crazy." Rosy changed gears and glanced in the mirror. "I'll admit, your story sounds a little off the wall—"

"Just a little?"

"But for what it's worth, I don't believe Debbie thinks you're crazy. In fact, judging from what I saw tonight, I'd say she was more worried about you than anything."

Jack released a faint laugh into the wild. "I suppose she worries about all her murder suspects."

"You're not still a suspect… Are you?" Rosy suddenly looked worried herself. "No, Debbie wouldn't do that to me."

"Mason thinks I've got something to do with the murders."

"That's different. Mason suspects everyone. Guilty until proven innocent, that's his philosophy. It's what makes him a good inspector."

"And Sergeant Harrison's different?" He waited, but Rosy kept silent. "So what makes her such a good police officer?"

"Her instincts."

Jack sat back in the seat. "How long have you known her?"

Rosy shot him a look, then mentally did one of her shrugs. "Not that long, but we seemed to hit it off."

"So you're good friends?"

"I'd say so, yes. Why do you want to know?"

"No particular reason," said Jack casually.

"She doesn't mix business with pleasure, Mr Foley. None of us do. It's a recipe for disaster."

"Are you speaking from personal experience?"

And here was I thinking he was timid, thought Rosy. "That's none of your business."

"I'm sorry," he said. "That wasn't why I was asking about… Forget it."

Neither of them said anything the remainder of the way back, until Rosy pulled into *The Imperial*'s car park. "Here you go, Mr Foley. Home sweet home."

"Thanks, but it's Jack. My *friends* call me Jack."

"Jack, then," said Rosy, finally accepting his veiled apology.

He ditched his seatbelt and got out. Before closing the door, though, he bent down and leaned in through the gap. "What do her instincts tell her about me, Dr Lim?"

Rosy didn't quite understand what he meant. "Excuse me?"

"Sergeant Harrison. You said her instincts made her a good police officer. What are they telling her about me?"

Rosy smiled again. "Goodnight, Jack."

Jack nodded and shut the door. Rosy brought her foot

off the clutch, found the biting point, and took the handbrake off. As the green Vauxhall pulled out of the car park, she took one more look in the rear view.

Jack Foley was still there, still standing in the semidarkness like a man who'd lost his way.

CHAPTER TWENTY-ONE

You could cut the tension at Yardley Street with a pair of scissors.

It had been like that for the last few days, ever since the 'third' victim had been found. Nothing miraculous was uncovered at George Lovesy's place, and nothing came of his autopsy. Bingham's superiors were now pushing for results and, like the killer, the press were out for blood. Lovesy was the most well-connected fatality yet, his fingers in all kinds of pies. A rumour was buzzing around that outside help might muscle in, people who specialised in this kind of crime. It was even going about on the grapevine that an extended TV appeal would be launched for information. And perhaps it wasn't such a bad thing, in spite of what Mason might think.

There were still no clues as to the identity of Twinkle, nor anything to indicate where he might strike next. The only thing they knew for sure was that he would target another twin. This had encouraged Deborah to do some more detective work.

She'd used the internet this time to aid her in her quest for answers. The 'net and the police computer systems helped solve cases faster than ever before. Maybe if they'd had TV, search engines and forensic science in the olden days, Jack the Ripper would never have evaded capture. But right now they had their own version of the Ripper to contend with. His name was Twinkle and Deborah had no intentions of letting him get away.

To begin with, she checked the news archives from the places Jack had visited on his some of his travels. She'd still not filled Mason in about what Jack said that day in the car, let alone told him she was starting to believe it. After some of the things she'd read about twins, it wasn't *totally* inconceivable. Perhaps if she had some tangible evidence, she could go to her boss and show him, although that would probably just place Jack in more hot water.

Regardless of this, she looked. Deborah still had the list of locations where Jack had used his cards. And she had dates. So all she had to do was look for any reports of missing people…missing twins.

In most of the places Jack had been to, she found plenty of missing people logged: though usually only locally. Surprisingly, just a couple had been listed as twins. At first she'd almost gone past them, using the dates on bank and credit company faxes to look up information. Then she realised her error. Jack had arrived *after* the killings, in some cases a long time afterwards. So she backtracked and discovered these reports, just as Jack had said yes, all this technology was great, but you still had to know what you were looking for to see the pattern. She thought back about what he'd told her. About his 'flashes' for want of a better word. About not always knowing where or what he was seeing till well after the event. For so long he'd tagged behind Twinkle, never catching him up…and those times he'd travelled abroad: *following Twinkle abroad?*

No, he'd never caught him up. Until now.

Because for some reason the killer had broken with tradition. Had decided to remain in one city, to murder more than once in that city. And not to cover his tracks, not to hide the evidence of his deeds. He was like a predator stalking his prey, using Norchester as his own private hunting grounds. But why? that was the question. Why here? It was a puzzle she intended to solve.

Deborah sat at her desk, tapping away on her computer. Her cold had all but cleared up and her head no longer felt like it belonged to someone else. And with that newfound clarity came inspiration. Perhaps Twinkle was sick of roaming, of going underground. Did he want some kind of recognition for what he was doing, a chronicle of his work? Did he want his 'name' up there in the serial killer hall of fame? It was so hard to stand out from the crowd nowadays, but Twinkle had managed to come up with a fresh spin. And when the enormity of his crimes were finally realised, when each twin killing was eventually linked (how many before Jack's brother? spaced out, perhaps years apart?), when the world was finally told about what he'd done, the things he'd taken… He would live on forever, wouldn't he? Be worshipped as a god by some, just like Gein, like Bundy. Who knew what kind of depraved headcases were out there, ready to found the church of The Twinkle, to follow his doctrines to the letter? It didn't bear thinking about.

That was one possible answer. But there was another. Predators go where the prey is, where that prey is in abundance. Like a shark circling the same stretch of ocean until its food supply is exhausted. Quite why she was comparing Twinkle to such a beast she didn't know, it just seemed…appropriate somehow.

Deborah keyed into the hospital records for Norchester and the surrounding area. Specifically records connected with births. The information wasn't publicly available, but Deborah had picked up a few hacking tips from a reformed young offender she still spoke to on MSN from time to time – and who had once almost brought the entire Midlands to a standstill with an 'I love you' computer virus.

Using her skills, it was a simple matter to collate the data. But it was time-consuming combing through all the information to pick out the relevant bits. These weren't detailed ledgers, of course: the hospitals wouldn't allow any old Tom, Dick or Harry to view private case histories. But that wasn't important. All she needed were rough figures.

She'd been at it most of the morning and well into the afternoon when a voice behind her said, "I hope you're taking the appropriate screen breaks, Sergeant."

Deborah would've recognised that deep timbre anywhere, and turned to greet Chief Superintendent Bingham with a half-smile. He wasn't much taller than her standing up, so she didn't have to tilt her head back very far in order to meet him face-to-face.

"I was just about to take one now, sir," she informed him.

"Good." His gaze fell to the screen and he leaned in to see what she was doing. "Hospital records, Sergeant Harrison?"

"Er…yes, sir. I have a kind of theory."

Bingham pulled up a chair and sat opposite her. "I'm all ears," he said.

"There are so many, and I've yet to start checking through any records for anywhere else, but what I've found so far is pretty interesting."

"Go on."

Deborah referred to some of the notes she'd made. "Without doing a comparison, it's impossible to say for sure, but Norchester…"

"Yes?"

"Well, there does seem to have been a significant number of twin births in this area over the last few years."

"Which proves what?"

Deborah looked up. "Maybe the same was true ten, twenty, maybe even thirty or forty years ago."

Bingham frowned. "Supposing you're proved right, that would give us a reason for Mr Twinkle's presence here. If he's got entire generations to choose from, and *if* those babies are still in the area…"

"It's still just a theory, sir."

"Yes, well… Keep on it, Sergeant, and let me know what you find out." Bingham rose and made to walk away. Then he turned sharply back as if he'd just remembered something. "Oh, you haven't seen your inspector today by any chance, have you? That's the main reason I came down here."

Deborah shook her head. "He said yesterday that he'd be having a word with a few of his sources today, seeing if he could turn anything up on the streets."

Bingham nodded. "Keeping out of my way, you mean?"

"I wouldn't know, sir."

"No, no. Of course you wouldn't. Right then, carry on Sergeant." With that, Bingham left the office. It was obvious to anyone with more than two brain cells to rub together that Mason wouldn't be working on the Twinkle case by this time next week. Which probably meant that she wouldn't be working on it either. Unless something drastic came up and soon, she'd be back running down small-time thieves over the Christmas period. There was always a rush on over the festive season.

Deborah gazed out into space for a few moments, at the spot her superior had occupied. She'd invested so much time and effort into this case already. It would be hard just to hand it over to a bunch of strangers.

No, more than that. It would be devastating. This was becoming personal for her, a matter of pride.

And what's going to happen to Jack?

The thought troubled her, though she didn't know why. What did she care what happened to him? She barely knew the man. And yet—

Deborah blinked, breaking the Sleeping Beauty spell. Time began to move forward again. She had work to do. The D.S. took a drink from the coffee cup beside her, all that was left of her lunch, and winced at the cold, bitter taste.

Then she placed her fingers on the keyboard again.

And she began to search.

CHAPTER TWENTY-TWO

Patricia counted up her tip money for the day and grinned.

Not bad. Not bad at all. At this rate she'd be able to afford something really nice for Danny, maybe an expensive watch or one of those electric razors she'd seen advertised on the telly, the ones you could take into the shower with you.

The thought of Danny-boy in the shower made her feel all tingly inside. Patricia closed her eyes and imagined the soapsuds dripping off his well-muscled body, and her climbing in beside him.

"Trisha? You about ready to go?"

Patricia opened her eyes and saw the man himself at the door, waiting to walk her home. Why bother with daydreams when you could have the real thing? She took in his film star face, like one of those teen actors who'd started off in dreary unrealistic US teledramas, but had since moved on to bigger and better things in the glamorous world of cinema. His perfectly black hair, those gorgeous green eyes and luscious lips… Oh, but the stubble he wore would have to go. Yet another reason to plump for the razor; he'd have no excuse then not to shave. Well, no excuse other than the fact he was a student and he thought it made him look kind of cool. Rebel without a Gillette.

"Hold on a sec," she called back, rummaging around in her handbag for her purse. Tissues, mobile, keys…why was it that whatever she was looking for always found its way to the very bottom? Finally she located the purse and stuffed the tip money inside. "I'm heading off now, Mr Harvey… Mr Harvey?"

Mr Harvey, a grey-templed man with a kindly face, appeared out of the back room like a magician arriving on stage. "Okay, love. See you…what day is it? Tuesday? I'll see you on Thursday."

"Half-day," Patricia reminded him as she put on her parka. Mr Harvey was just about the best person in the world to work for, but his memory was atrocious. She sometimes wondered how he'd managed to keep his business going for so long after his wife had passed on.

"Right, but you'll be here for the lunch-time crowd?"

"Yep, wouldn't miss it for the world. See you on Thursday!"

He waved as she left the café, smiling and shaking his head as if wondering what he'd got to do next.

"I swear he'll forget where he works one day and we'll never see him again," said Patricia, slipping an arm around Danny's waist. She was so glad he was here. Walking back to the bedsit was bad enough in the winter evenings, when darkness fell at around two in the afternoon or so it seemed and hung around like a bad penny until the sun could be bothered to show its face the next morning. But what with the madness that had been going on in Norchester lately… She would've ordered a taxi, only they cost the earth, especially at this time of year.

They walked down instead of up, away from the

main street. The bedsit they shared with five other students was closer to the university than it was to the shops, which probably explained why the rent was so high even though the facilities sucked. Still, at least she and Danny could be together whenever they pleased, which wasn't always a good thing when you were trying to get your head around coursework. Tonight, though, she'd be glad of the distraction. It had been a pig of a day, full days always were. Patricia hated wearing that false smile the whole time, masking the way she really felt. Tired, bored, and generally pissed off at the world and most of its inhabitants. There had been a long succession of people wanting to be fed and watered today, and it was her job to oblige.

At least the tip money had been above average. It was the only way she'd be able to afford a gift for Danny, what with her paltry part-time wages going on living expenses.

She had no idea how she'd find the money to buy gifts for her family, but she'd cross that bridge when she came to it. Danny was the most important one...next to her sister, naturally. She wanted to show him what he meant to her. How she felt about him.

This had been the longest relationship she'd ever had; coming up on a year now. Moving away from home had been a wrench at first, even though home was only the other side of the city. But having her sister with her had made things easier, regardless of the fact she'd chosen a different subject and lived quite a way away from her in the halls of residence. Then she'd met Danny. He had been in her psych group for those seminars with Dr Grieves; a bit of a shy guy, but she'd always liked the strong, silent type. They were just friends to begin with, hanging out together after class, helping each other with the workload, giving seminar presentations together. However, gradually, inevitably, they became much closer than friends should be. The mutual attraction was there, it was just a matter of coaxing Danny out of his shell.

The first year Christmas break had done them both good. Time apart had made Danny realise how he felt about her, so that when they returned in January, after the exams were over, they started seeing each other properly. Valentine's Day was the biggest landmark, though. They attended the annual February 14th bash on campus, drank a little too much cheap booze, and ended up back at Danny's room in the halls. One thing led to another and they finally spent their first night together. A good thing they'd gone to the dance prepared: it still made Patricia laugh when she remembered them both producing condoms at the same time. "Great minds think alike," she'd joked.

That night had been just about the best of her entire life. Danny had been so gentle, nothing like the other boyfriends she'd had. She felt for the first time that she was actually *making love*, not just having sex a purely physical, animalistic thing. And as they were making love, she figured out why that was: she was actually *in love* with this boy. It was a strange feeling, one that she didn't think she'd ever had before. Maybe she'd *thought* she was in love with some of the others…but with Danny it was the real thing. Unmistakable.

Even now when he said her name, or looked at her in a certain way, goosebumps spread all over her body. They held hands in public, ignoring the jeers. They kissed openly and often, and the touch of his hand on her face, on her arm, was enough to make her quiver like a jelly. God, that sounded so pathetic; like something her great-grandmother would have said when she was 'courting' back in the year nought-dot. This was supposed to be a post-feminist age, or so the lecturers proclaimed at uni, where girls took what they wanted, when they wanted, demanding an equal footing. She wasn't supposed to need a man to make her feel complete. And yet Danny invariably did somehow. Perhaps it was because theirs was a partnership in every sense of the word. They respected each other, and she was far more than just a piece of meat to him. Patricia had a mind as well, which Danny also loved. They spent long hours just talking, about life, the universe, and everything. And if they disagreed on a subject, they weren't afraid to tell each other.

But, best of all, they had trust. If Danny went out while she was working, or vice versa, they knew nothing untoward would happen. Neither of them would even so much as look at a member of the opposite sex in *that* way. Of course she had friends that were male, and he had some that were female; it was just an unwritten law that they didn't need anyone else. Jealousy never entered into the equation. Well, it hadn't *yet* you couldn't promise that it never would in the future. But, for now, she was content. The second year meant they had to move out of the halls of residence, so it was the perfect opportunity to find a place together. Okay, so they weren't totally alone, but it was better than nothing.

Her sister knew all about it, obviously, and was happy for her, although possibly a bit jealous because she didn't have anyone of her own right now. But you could never break, nor replace, that special bond *they* shared. In fact Patricia had seen her sister on campus the day after the Valentine dance, and the cheeky look she gave her said that she knew Danny had had his 'wicked' way. She'd probably even sensed the exact moment it happened…and not for the first time. Likewise, Patricia had always been able to tell when her sister was sexually active, too. It was just one of those quirky things you had to live with when you were like them.

Now, ironically, Patricia dreaded going home for the holidays. Last summer had been bad enough, and she'd visited Danny as often as she could at that…when funds would allow. The thought of spending Xmas cooped up with her parents, who'd ask Patricia and her sister all kinds of awkward questions, prying into every aspect of their lives, was enough to send her loopy. If only there was some way she could get out of it, spend those weeks here in the bedsit with Danny. Have the place to themselves…

It was a nice fantasy, but a fantasy nonetheless. Dad would be round like a shot to drag her back to the old homestead.

As they walked down Linden Road, Danny put his arm around her shoulder and she let him bring her in closer. "So, how'd it go today?" he said.

"Don't ask."

"Want to hear some good news?"

"Always."

Danny reached into his jacket pocket and pulled out two cardboard oblongs. In the light from the streetlamps they looked orange, but Patricia guessed they were probably pink. "You got the tickets!" Now *she* pulled him in close and kissed him on the cheek.

"You shall go to the ball, Cinders."

Patricia couldn't believe it. Tickets to see her favourite band, The Harmonies, live. "How did you get them?"

"I have my ways," he told her solemnly, raising one eyebrow. She laughed. "No, you remember Gary?"

"Sure." Gary was Danny's best friend back home. She'd met him several times while she was visiting her boyfriend in the summer months.

"Well, he knows someone who knows someone else, who has a brother-in-law who works for their record label."

"They're like gold dust!" said Patricia. "They must have cost you."

"Call it an early Christmas present. *And* it's the Saturday we get back, so you don't have to worry," he said, putting them away in his pocket again for safekeeping.

"I wasn't worried. Come here you." Patricia yanked him off the road and into a side-alley. "I love you, Danny Sirk." She kissed him full on the mouth and he responded, as always, passionately but tenderly.

"I love you too," he whispered when they broke off, then started to kiss her neck. She closed her eyes and breathed deeply. "Oh God, Danny…"

His hands fell to her waist, pulling the parka apart and drawing her nearer. She reached round and squeezed his buttocks through his jeans. Danny's left hand moved up, cupping a breast through the thin material of her waitressing blouse. Their mouths met again.

Patricia felt something cold land on her forehead, then her nose. She opened her eyes and tore her lips away from his. "Hey, Danny, look. It's snowing."

Danny glanced up. Giant fluffy snowflakes were falling all around them, and *on* them. It looked like the stars were falling from the sky. "So it is. It *must* be nearly Christmas." He began to nuzzle her again, his stubble tickling her flesh.

"It's so…" Patricia forgot her next word as Danny began biting her neck. She pressed herself up against him. He undid a couple of buttons on her blouse and his hand snaked inside. The feel of his fingers on her bare skin, stroking, rubbing… She was losing herself in the moment.

Someone walked past on the street. A man hurrying along, trying to get to wherever he was going before the snow came thicker. He turned his head briefly in their direction, but didn't slow down.

"Stop, Danny."

"What? He couldn't see anything."

"We'd better continue this at home."

"I'm not sure I can wait that long."

"Easy tiger," she said.

"Doesn't it turn you on? Out in public, knowing you might get caught?"

"Does it you?"

"Maybe."

"My, aren't we the dark horse?"

He smiled. "No, you're right. Let's head back. With a bit of luck we might get snowed in and have to spend all day in bed tomorrow."

Patricia's hair was glistening white with a fine covering of snow. "Tomorrow, bed. Tonight, shower," she notified him, picturing Danny all soaped up again.

"If there's enough hot water," he said, bringing her back down to earth.

"We'll make do—" Patricia could hear someone else walking down the road. Quickly, she pulled away from Danny, doing up the buttons on her blouse. The footsteps stopped. She could hear breathing near to the entrance of their alley.

Danny mouthed the word, "What?" and she pointed towards the shadow on the pavement, long and black. Whoever was out there, they were waiting. Perhaps waiting for them to emerge. The dreamlike image of Danny's naked body in the shower was replaced by newspaper headlines and TV reports.

"Danny, let's get out of here," she whispered.

"You're shaking. There's nothing to worry about. I'm here."

The boyfriend always says that, thought Patricia. *In all those scary movies the boyfriend always says, "There's nothing to worry about" right before he gets his head chopped off with an axe or a chainsaw or—*

Danny took her hand and they inched forward. The shadow vanished. Patricia kept behind Danny as they poked their heads out into the street. There was nobody there.

"Probably just someone who lost their way. It's pretty confusing down these backstreets," said Danny. Patricia relaxed slightly. Danny was right. He was here with her. None of the other attacks had happened to couples. Only to people on their own. And it was a big city.

But you are more at risk than other people, said the persistent voice of doom inside her head.

That doesn't mean I'm going to shut myself away like a hermit until I've finished my course, she told it. *Although if Danny's with me, then I wouldn't mind all that muc—*

She was suddenly aware of something above them, something dropping down on top of them. A large something. It seemed to glide across them, knocking Danny over and pushed Patricia into the wall, her handbag flying out of reach.

Where…where did it come from?

It was a stupid question; the important thing was it was *here*. Now. Covering Danny completely. He struggled underneath the shape, trying to roll over onto his back. Patricia heard a muffled grunt as her boyfriend was punched in the side, then a coughing noise. The concert tickets spilled out of Danny's pocket and wound up in the gutter.

It had its back to her, but she knew what it was, *who* it was: The Twin Killer. Twinkle. The voice in her head began singing a nursery rhyme from her childhood:

Twinkle, twinkle, little star. How I wonder what you are…

The snow was falling more heavily now, raining down on the struggling forms of Twinkle and Danny, locked together. She had to do something, but all Patricia could do was watch.

Up above the world so bright…

Another punch, and then Danny stopped moving.

Patricia roused herself. She should get help, scream… *Do something!*

The mobile…the mobile phone in her bag. She had to get to it.

Patricia picked herself up, still winded, but before she could go anywhere the attacker was upon her, shoving her back into the alley.

It was hard to see his face, even now: was he wearing some kind of mask? Suddenly there was a gloved hand over her mouth. "Keep still," he growled it was a man, definitely.

Like a candle in the night.

He was reaching around for something, something in a hidden pocket perhaps? Then she saw it. He raised the fork, a big fork with sharp prongs.

Patricia bit down hard on his hand. Her teeth sank into material, flesh, and quite possibly bone as well. He gave a yell and took his hand away. Patricia brought up her right knee. It connected with something, she couldn't tell what, it might have been his stomach, it might have been the part she'd been aiming for, but Twinkle bent over, wheezing. She pulled away, then felt herself running but standing still.

He had hold of her parka hood.

Patricia wrenched her arms out of the coat and escaped; she looked left and right for her bag. There it was on the floor. She ran over to it and opened it up. The first object she came across inside was the purse. *No, I'm not looking for you anymore! I need the phone…where's the fucking phone?*

Patricia risked a glance back. The dark figure was coming out of the alley, with the fork in one hand and now a large knife in the other. He looked like an enraged diner from the café, waiting for his main course.

Us, we're *his main course.*

It was an absurd notion, but Patricia felt sure he was going to eat them both. Raw. Carve them up right there on the street, and nobody would—

Danny groaned, shaking his head: distracting her.

When Patricia turned back, Twinkle was lunging at her. And she could see his face. His faces. *Jesus, the bastard has two faces*, she thought.

Both his weapons were drawn back.

Without thinking, she ditched the bag and reached forward. Grabbing him by his clothes   some kind of cloth outfit   she pushed her knee up against his chest. His own momentum carried him over her head and he went flying into a lamppost.

For what seemed like an age, she couldn't move. She couldn't bear to look in case he was standing over her, ready to bring down the fork.

But when she did, she saw Twinkle was flat out at the base of the lamppost, his weapons out of reach. Patricia rose shakily to her feet.

He must have hit his head, she guessed.

He looked so helpless lying there, the snow falling on him. She found herself staring at the man, at his knife on the floor   the blade at least eight inches long – at the fork he'd tried to stab her with.

Run! Get the fuck out of there!

No, your bag! Get the bag and phone the police…

Patricia inched forward slowly, bending, reaching for the strap of her bag. Almost there, almost… Twinkle suddenly jerked awake and jumped at her in one sinuous movement. He slapped her hard across the face. Grabbing her hair, he dragged Patricia round and into the lamppost.

Her vision blurred for just a moment, but then she saw him crouch and scoop up the fork.

You shouldn't have hesitated, should've just run when you had the chance. This time you're going to die. This time—

Twinkle appeared to sink into the pavement, shrinking before her very eyes. Eventually, she realised what was happening. Danny had rugby tackled him, slamming the man into the concrete. And was it her imagination or could she hear…

More footsteps, someone running.

Patricia blinked. There was a figure speeding up the road. The man who'd walked past them earlier. He looked from Danny, now spread-eagled on top of Twinkle, across to Patricia. Quickly working out the most likely scenario, he helped Danny pin down the villain. The men pummelled him with their fists.

Now Patricia picked up her bag again, finding the phone first time and switching it on.

She immediately punched in the numbers 999.

CHAPTER TWENTY-THREE

Excited, but on edge, Deborah opened the door and stepped inside.

Yardley Street was buzzing with police officers. And she'd had a job to get her Peugeot through to the car park at the back, as the place was under siege by hordes of journalists and TV news teams.

"I don't know what you think you're going to see here tonight," she sniped as she ploughed through them, her windscreen wipers crushing snow against the glass. Cameras flashed at the side-windows when she passed by, almost blinding her. Deborah was tempted to get out and give them all a mouthful, but how would that have looked on the evening news? Bingham would not be impressed.

Finally, she made her way through entering the inner sanctum where no press could possibly pass. But it had been just as chaotic parking, and then wending her way to the station's back door. And now here inside, people in the entranceway, some she knew, some she didn't…

Deborah pushed past the desk and keyed in her code. It was almost as bad in here, but she did at least spot Mason in the corridor. He was having words with one of the detective constables in their murder squad. When he saw her, he beckoned her across with one hand.

"Sergeant," he called over the heads in the crowd. "You got the message, then."

"Sir."

Said message had been a garbled phone call she'd taken on her mobile at a drive-through fast food joint near her home, instructing her to return to the station at once. "Twinkle's been apprehended," said the faint voice at the other end. Deborah thought she was hearing things.

"Say again."

"Repeat: Twinkle's been apprehended, Sergeant Harrison."

Before turning the Peugeot around, ignoring the horns of the cars behind her, Deborah had called to let her mother and Isabel know she'd be late back probably *very* late back. So what else was new?

"*Sorry, no burgers tonight, Izzy. I'll make it up to you, I promise.*"

Then she'd cut through the traffic and sped off towards Yardley Street again.

"They didn't tell me very much," she complained, drawing alongside Mason at last.

"Wasn't much to tell at the time. But there's a hell of a lot more now."

"So I see," said Deborah, looking around. "How did it get this busy, this quickly?"

Mason grunted. "Come on, let's find somewhere a bit more private and I'll fill you in."

The private place Mason had in mind turned out to be the gents lavatory. Everyone was too busy to use the toilet, and so consequently and conveniently it was empty: a shrine to the neglected art of micturition and defecation. It was the first time Deborah had ever been inside one of these places since she was a kid and she'd been caught short at the cinema with her father.

"Sir, I don't think I should be—"

Mason held up his hand. "Don't worry about it. At least we can hear ourselves think in here."

"All right," she said. "What's happened?"

Mason told her about the events in the centre of the city three quarters of an hour beforehand. About how Twinkle had attacked a young couple down a side-street – "The fucker only jumped on them from a fire escape!" – and got more than he bargained for. Along with a brave passer-by, they'd managed to wrestle the killer to the ground and hold him there until the police could arrive: two squad cars and a van within minutes of the call being made.

"And they brought him back here?"

"*No*," said Mason. "First they took him out and bought him a drink."

"You know, sarcasm is the lowest form of humour, sir."

Mason huffed.

"And the witnesses?"

"Upstairs, giving statements. But the important thing is, we've got him, Blondie. We've finally got him!"

Deborah and Mason looked in on Twinkle's captors, still in the process of giving their statements. The girl with the oh-so-sweet looks was Patricia Bailey, Mason told her. If she was shaken up by her ordeal, she hid it well. The lad sat next to her, clutching her hand as if it were a life-support, was the boyfriend, Danny Sirk. He too looked fine, though Deborah knew he was nursing a couple of bruises about his torso where Twinkle had punched him.

"The kid was beaten up a bit, but point-blank refused

to go get treatment until we had his statement. I don't think he wanted to leave his girlfriend alone. Understandable really," uttered Mason.

Deborah exchanged glances with Patricia. The girl smiled at her, again it was a sweet smile, if a fraction jaded. Deborah nodded, making her aware of the respect she held for the girl. Then she nodded curtly to Danny for the same reason. They'd done what the entire police force of Norchester had failed to do. By chance, granted, but they'd done it all the same.

In the opposite room was Benjamin Tate, the other member of public involved. He was a sprightly individual, aged thirty-nine, who lived only three streets away from the place where Twinkle had struck.

"I'd run out of cigarettes, you see," he was telling the interviewing officer. "Keep meaning to quit, but well, you know how it is. The newsagents in the plaza is only a short walk from my flat. I was just coming back from there. Guess it's a good thing I hadn't given up after all."

A good thing indeed, thought Deborah. All three would be on the front pages of the newspapers, maybe not tomorrow, but definitely the next day. And they'd better get used to being interviewed, because the TV stations would be pestering them for their story, too. They *were* heroes, after all, and the world loved needed? heroes.

The duo paid a visit to the evidence room next, and Mason was handed several packages on request.

"Twinkle was wearing this when we picked him up," said Mason, thrusting a transparent plastic bag at her. Inside was a black skin-tight hood, and attached to it were two realistic rubber facemasks, the kind you might buy for a fancy-dress party or for Halloween. They were flesh-coloured, with eye-holes and mouths, and artificial hair. When the wearer donned the hood, it might appear as if he had two faces, one on either side of his head. Deborah shuddered. It was the last thing Redbrook, Haley Archer and George Lovesy had seen before their deaths. Not to mention Jack's brother.

"God," said Deborah.

"And he'd been brandishing these."

Deborah gaped at the weapons, a long kitchen knife and a razor-sharp barbecue fork, both in their own private bags. She imagined the man coming towards Patricia Bailey, something with two faces, holding up these murderous implements.

At last, Mason took her down to the cells   the sea of officers parting to allow him passage. The desk sergeant, Kilbourne, escorted them through the barred doors and into a corridor with more solid metal doors on either side.

"He's in the last one on the left," said Mason. "I put him in there myself."

Kilbourne snapped open a small rectangular hole in the middle of the cell door. The room seemed to shine white through it. Deborah swallowed hard. She wanted to see, *desperately*. But then again, she didn't. Putting a face to the crimes, the horrendous crimes she'd seen: the blood, the snapped necks.

"Take your time," Mason advised her. He wasn't being sarcastic now; far from it. He understood it could be difficult to look upon pure evil like this. But in a funny way, what he said made her more eager to see. Determined to show him she could handle it.

Deborah bent over and leaned forwards.

There, sat on the bed, hands on his knees, was a man. Just an ordinary man. Nothing demonic about him, no horns or fangs. He was simply a human being. Which made his actions even more sickening, and that much harder to comprehend. He had short, spiky hair, raised to a peak by a combination of sweat and gel. His dark eyebrows dipped down into the middle of his forehead, the eyes themselves in shadow. His mouth was pursed, lips thin but red. He was clean-shaven, with one or two sore patches where the razor had burnt him, and he had an Adam's apple that jutted out, bobbing up and down as she watched.

His shoulders were broad, and the white T-shirt revealed that he was fairly muscular. He wore black tracksuit bottoms and black shoes (the laces of which had been removed), his feet apart, resting on the cell floor.

All of a sudden he seemed to realise he was being observed. He raised his head, the shadows around his eyes dissipating. His frozen stare was the very antithesis of Jack's. There was no warmth here, no humanity. Nothing. Deborah focused on him for as long as she possibly could, but it was like holding a hot coal in your hand. Inevitably, she dropped the coal and stood back.

"Gruesome piece of work, isn't he?" snarled Mason.

Deborah moved her head up and down mechanically, not really hearing her inspector but agreeing with him at the same time.

"And he says his name's Craine. Anton Craine."

CHAPTER TWENTY-FOUR

The first thing he saw that morning was the snow.

Jack Foley opened his eyes and marvelled at the giant flakes floating past his window, the sky heavy with the stuff, like fallout from a nuclear explosion. He rolled over in the double bed. The clock told him it was eight-fifteen.

He'd slept soundly last night, more soundly than he had in a long, long while. Perhaps it was the reading that had done it. He'd been determined to finish that blasted near-future techno-thriller last night big waste of time and he'd done just that, reading solidly all evening. At last he came to the end:

As the device ticked down to oblivion, humanity sat back and prayed for the end to be swift.

Was that why he'd compared this snow-laden morning to a nuclear winter, because of the lousy book? No, surely not. It hadn't had that much of an impact on him although in some ways the ending had called to mind images of Hiroshima. It was simply a mountain he'd had to climb, and then Jack had closed his aching eyes, snuggled down under the covers, and dropped off to sleep. He hadn't noticed the exact hour, but it must have been nine or thereabouts. Good grief, that meant he'd had eleven hours! Eleven whole hours. He couldn't believe it.

However, far from feeling refreshed, he found that he was actually lethargic and dopey. He couldn't stop yawning. Jack let them out freely, one after the other: loud and proud. Scratching his head, he cast off the covers and swung over the side of the bed.

He fumbled for the remote control on the chair not far away from him, and pressed the standby switch. A picture appeared in the top corner of the room and he pumped up the volume. Some woman on a brightly-coloured sofa was explaining how she'd discovered God after having a panic attack in Sainsbury's. Apparently, God had instructed her to write this bestselling self-help book   more like *help-yourself* and make a personal 'wellbeing' video which would help others find their inner calm…and pocket her loads of money in the process. Jack left her blaring away to the presenters and wandered off into the bathroom, almost colliding with the doorjamb on the first attempt. He washed his face and began cleaning his teeth.

Jack was partway through his shave when he heard the name 'Twinkle' mentioned on the TV. He did a double take in the bathroom mirror, wondering if he was still asleep and dreaming all this. A pretty unimaginative dream if he was; going through the mundane motions of getting up. Jack walked back through into the hotel room proper, most of his face still covered in shaving foam.

"…last night," said the man on the screen, a well-groomed newsreader in shirt and tie, sitting behind a mahogany desk. "Police have confirmed that they have detained a man on suspicion of committing the so-called 'Twin Killer' murders. His name cannot be given for legal reasons. More details as and when we get them. Other news, and the Prime Minister today announced that—"

Jack was deaf to the rest of the broadcast. He stood in the middle of the room, open-mouthed. His mind was buzzing with questions. How did they catch him? Where and when? Who was he? What did he *really* look like? Had that been why he slept so well last night, why James hadn't troubled him?

Hurrying back to the bathroom, Jack wiped the foam from his face with a towel. He emerged seconds later and sat down on the bed. Jack reached across for the phone, pressed the button for an outside line, and dialled the operator.

"Hello, could you give me the number for Yardley Street police station, please? Norchester."

The number came back in an electronic voice and Jack wrote it down on a pad next to the phone. He hung up, then dialled again. It was engaged the first few times he tried, but Jack persisted. Finally, as he was about to give up, it started ringing. It rang several times before a woman answered.

"Yardley Street police station, how may I help you?"

"Yes, hello. I'm trying to get in touch with a Sergeant Harrison."

"Could I ask what this is in relation to?"

Jack hesitated. "Er…I just really need to speak with her."

"I'm sure you do," said the woman snottily. "Your name, please."

"Jack Foley."

"One moment please."

Jack was put on hold and subjected to a medley of tunes played on the panpipes. They ranged from the ever-reliable *Greensleeves* to a modern reworking of the theme from *Chariots of Fire.*

The woman returned with a *Click!* "I'm sorry, Sergeant Harrison can't come to the phone right now. Can I take a message?"

"Did you tell her who was calling?"

"Yes I did." He just knew she was lying. "Now do you want to leave a message or not?"

"No, that's okay." Jack hung up.

He started to dress, the clothes working against him. Socks slowing him down by not going on his feet properly, the holes in his fresh boxers eluding him, buttons not finding their correct slits on his shirt.

Once he was done, Jack pulled on his coat and grabbed his keys. He remembered what Deborah had said about driving and figured it wasn't a good idea to show up at the station in his Mondeo. What then? Walk? Too far. He needed to get there as soon as possible. A taxi? He couldn't wait for it to arrive.

Jack flipped off the TV and left the room, slamming the door behind him. He ran down the corridor towards the lift. It took only a few minutes for the carriage to reach his level. Inside, as always, was Albert.

"Morning, Mr Foley...Jack. You're off out early today."

"Morning, Albert. Listen," Jack said as the doors closed behind him, "you wouldn't happen to know anything about the bus routes around here, would you?"

CHAPTER TWENTY-FIVE

Deborah had pulled an all-nighter again.

Isabel and her mother would be livid. But it couldn't be helped. Deborah had to stick around; there was a lot to do now that Twinkle alias Anton Craine: no previous form according to a C.R.O. check on his fingerprints was in custody.

She'd managed to snatch only a couple of hours' sleep at her desk, sometime between two and five this morning she reckoned, and yet here she was, wide awake and fighting fit. Raring to go. Ready to interview Craine.

That's all he'd parted with last night when they brought him in, his name. He wanted them to know who he was it seemed, which went some way to confirming what she'd thought about him: that he was seeking recognition. It was feasible he'd even let himself be taken down. A picture of the shattered snooker cue in George Lovesy's games room entered her head. The broken or fractured necks of his other victims. Would someone who'd done all that really let a couple of students and a thirty-nine-year-old unemployed bank clerk stand in his way? Was it a cry for help? His subconscious saying 'stop me'?

Deborah looked at Craine across the table, shackled,

somewhat deflated, sitting alone after refusing representation. He still had that cold, hard stare, but it seemed more pitiable, more sad than evil this morning. As if whatever had possessed him had gone now. A cry for help? Anything was possible she supposed.

Mason was present, of course. As were two of the largest officers in the station, just in case things turned nasty.

The interview got off to a terrible start and went downhill from there. Craine had confirmed his name again his voice steady and calm but nothing more. Mason had asked him for an address, but the prisoner wouldn't play ball. Mason quizzed him about where he'd been on the night of Redbrook's disappearance, Haley Archer's death and more recently George Lovesy's murder. Craine said nothing about this either.

Mason brought out a plain brown envelope, opened it, and removed some photographs. He spread them over the desk. They were a mixture of close-ups of the murder victims' faces and the injuries that had been inflicted upon them. Deborah tried to look straight ahead, but caught a glimpse of Haley Archer's gaunt countenance mouth open, blood running down the side of her cheek from a shredded glob of flesh that used to be her ear. Eyes glassy and lifeless. Beneath it, she could just see the stump of what had once been Stuart Redbrook's hand; it looked like raw meat, cleanly cut by a master butcher. Next to it was a picture of George Lovesy's sewn up stomach. Deborah could actually imagine the knife going in, slicing though skin and fatty tissue, then finally the two halves being opened up and the lung removed.

She wished Mason had given her some kind of warning before he'd done that. On the other hand (poor choice of words given one of the injuries), if the laying out of these reminders of death had had such an effect on her, then they would probably have had the same impact on Craine. *Probably*.

"I am showing Mr Craine photographs of the murder victims," said Mason for the benefit of the recorder, not going into details about what the photos contained.

Craine wouldn't look down.

"*Mr* Craine, would you please look at the photographs and tell us if you recognise any or all of these people." He made it sound as if he was showing Craine holiday snaps of the three dead twins.

Craine's head moved slightly, but not enough to be able to see the photographs.

Quietly, Mason got up and walked around to Craine's side of the table. He looked across at one of the P.C.s on guard, before flashing his eyes up to the camera in the top corner of the room. The P.C. moved forward to block its line of vision. Satisfied, Mason bent down next to Craine's ear. "Mr Craine…" Mason grabbed him by the back of the neck and forced his head down. Craine wasn't fast enough to close his eyes, the full horror of those scenes accosting him. "Would you *please* look at the photographs and tell us if you recognise any or all of these people."

The P.C.s in the room said nothing; Deborah said nothing, although she was unsettled by the action. Craine said nothing, either, but his breathing came a bit faster, in and out through his nose.

"Think very carefully before answering, Mr Craine," said Mason, his face red, spittle flying out and landing on Craine's neck. Deborah could see Craine grimacing and flashed Mason a worried look. "Seen enough?" snapped her boss.

He let go of Craine's neck, but the man's head didn't spring back like she thought it would. Craine kept staring at the photographs, his eyes flitting from image to image. Mason's tactics might have been over-the-top, but they'd achieved their objective.

The inspector asked him again where he'd been on the night of the attacks, one by one. Craine continued to examine the stills. Every now and again, he'd incline his head as if remembering a specific moment.

It crossed Deborah's mind that perhaps to him they *were* like holiday pics.

And this one was taken just after I mangled Haley's bike down by the canal, and then did the same to her. Lovely scenery, though, don't you think?

Maybe he didn't equate these scenes with the things he'd done. Was it all like a fantasy for him, a movie inside his own head in which he was the anti-hero Twinkle? Did Craine possess the capacity for grief, for guilt or remorse? Well, it wasn't as if he'd known these folk personally; they were just pawns in his scheme to become famous. Weren't they? But they were still people, for God's sake! People with lives, with families…families like Stuart Redbrook's. His parents waiting patiently by the phone for any news of their missing son, a brother who almost seemed to know that his twin was dead before he'd been told.

Surely that had to count for something?

Not to someone who didn't place any meaning on human life. Not to Craine, apparently, with *his* perception of reality. Because now Deborah could see a smile playing on his lips. And she was stunned to hear him laughing as he stared at the photographs. The bastard was actually laughing.

She'd never had any experience of this sort of thing before. Oh, she'd seen criminals who weren't sorry for what they'd done, who didn't seem bothered by the jail term stretching out in front of them. But they were usually responsible for minor crimes compared to this: robbery; GBH; drug dealing. In a way it wasn't really their fault, it was their environment, their background, society. Could any of that excuse laughing at three murdered correction, slain people?

Even Karl Flynn, who'd killed the Coulthards, had shown…what? Resentment, fear, then finally guilt over what he'd done. But this, well this was something else.

"You think that's funny?" Mason said from behind him.

Deborah willed the inspector to back off. *Not here, sir. Not now.*

Mason tapped his finger on the table. "You think *that's* funny?" Craine laughed even louder. She could see Mason balling his hand into a fist.

"Sir…" she started.

Mason shut his eyes and walked away, facing the wall of the interview room.

Deborah waited for Craine's laughter to die down, then addressed him herself. "Why twins, Craine?"

He looked at her, tears streaming from his eyes.

"What is it about them?" she persisted. "Do you think they're…*unnatural*?" Deborah was drawing on Dr Grieves' theories in an effort to get him to speak.

Craine stuck out his bottom lip in contemplation.

"Do you want to *be* like them? Is that it? You think maybe this will help you become like them?" She realised she was out of her depth, but forged ahead anyway. "Or are you jealous of them?"

And why did you take the things you took? What did you do with them?

Craine smiled again. It was a chilling sight.

Mason came back round and sat down in his chair. "You're already going down for assault with a deadly weapon *weapons*, I should say. Attempted murder. You're looking at a lot of time behind bars, Craine. Why not tell us about the rest of them. We'll find the evidence we need sooner or later, anyway."

His face went blank.

"If you're looking for a nice cosy room at the local nut farm, forget about it. You're as sane as I am, Craine," barked Mason. Her boss didn't sound particularly sane at present. "I'll make sure you pay for this if it's the last thing I do."

Craine grinned like a nitrous oxide addict.

"I am…" he began. They were so surprised to hear his voice after all this time, they almost missed what he said next. It was: "The Gemini."

"What're you talking about, your star sign?" Mason sneered. "I'm an Aries, so bloody what?"

Craine shut up again.

"This is getting us nowhere," said Mason.

"No, wait." Deborah rested her hands on the table. "What does that mean, Craine? You want to tell us, don't you?"

He nodded. "I am The Gemini."

Craine would say nothing more. They asked him question after question, Mason becoming increasingly agitated, until Deborah decided it was time to take a break. She suspended the interview and flicked off the recorder, then invited Mason outside.

"I take it all back, he *is* fucking crackers," said Mason. "Maybe we ought to get Grieves back in here to give him the once-over."

Deborah thought about telling him to calm down, but knew it would do no good. "Hmm. Perhaps."

Mason looked at her sideways. "What is it, Blondie?

What're you thinking?"

"'I am The Gemini' he said."

"I know. I was there."

"Well, it's just something I was reading the other night. An old classical legend."

"What, about Gemini? I'm afraid classics weren't a part of the curriculum at my school, Blondie. Enlighten me."

Deborah folded her arms. "To cut a very long story short, sir, Gemini refers to a pair of twins called Castor and Pollux. Now this pair were inseparable, went everywhere together, did everything together. Until one of them was killed, Castor I think…"

"Right, I'm with you so far."

"Obviously Pollux was a bit upset by all this—"

"I can imagine," said Mason.

"So he begged Jupiter, that's the king of the Roman gods—"

"And there was me thinking it was a planet."

Deborah scowled and he took the hint, touching his finger to his lips. "Pollux asked Jupiter to bring his brother back to life. Now, in the original story Pollux offers his own life in exchange, but instead Jupiter gives them both immortality, so long as they spend alternate days as dead mortals and as gods in heaven or whatever passed for it back then."

Mason looked at his watch impatiently.

"I'm getting to the point, sir. What if our friend in there is a twin himself?"

"What, Craine?"

She nodded. "Or maybe he thinks he is. I don't know, I'm not an expert. Anyway, what if his brother died?"

"Or the imaginary brother he never really had died?" Mason pointed out.

"Okay. Perhaps he died at birth or just recently we'd

need to verify all this, of course but assuming for a second it's true, what if Craine thinks he can get this brother back by killing more twins?"

"You mean, he thinks *he's* Pollux?"

"No… I don't know. But it would explain the outfit, plus the sacrificial style killings of Redbrook, Haley Archer and George Lovesy."

"What, sacrifices to the gods? Instead of offering up himself?"

Deborah shrugged. "It seems a bit stupid now I've told you."

"No, no. It's not stupid at all. It's very interesting." Mason said, rubbing his chin. "Who knows what was going through Craine's mind when he committed those killings."

"Then again, he might just be using this cock and bull to make his story more colourful. 'I am The Gemini!' It's quite a catchphrase, don't you think?"

Mason put his arm around her shoulder. "Come on, Blondie. I'll buy you a coffee and you can tell me more."

CHAPTER TWENTY-SIX

By the time Jack arrived at Yardley Street, it was almost ten o'clock.

The busses were still running, and Albert's information had proved accurate about the routes and times   as if there had ever been any doubt. But they were far from running smoothly. Though the ploughs and gritters had been out in force early that morning, the sudden snow showers had taken most of the city by surprise: not to mention the national and regional meteorologists, who were busy apologising profusely on all their morning bulletins. Many roads were cut off and traffic jams gummed up the channels that were passable.

Which meant delays.

Jack travelled about halfway there by bus and then jumped ship at the next available stop. Using the *A-Z* he'd purchased just before George Lovesy's death, still in his coat pocket from that night, Jack chose a shortcut which would get him to the station this side of lunch-time. Wishing he'd brought his umbrella, he stomped up and down streets, the snow falling on him like confetti on a bridegroom.

The hidden sections of the city seemed deserted, apart from the occasional gang of kids throwing snowballs and enjoying the premature start to the Christmas holidays. One lad even threw a ball in his direction, but he didn't stop to retaliate. He heard the youth call something after him, but ignored it. He couldn't stop for anything, not now he knew where he was going.

For one thing he was playing the newscast over and over in his mind.

Police have confirmed they have detained a man on suspicion of committing the so-called 'Twin Killer' murders. His name cannot be given for legal reasons. More details as and when we get them...

And the telephone call to the station. *"I'm sorry, Sergeant Harrison can't come to the phone right now. Can I take a message?"*

Can't or *won't*. Maybe the snotty woman *had* told Deborah who was calling. What if the D.S. ordered her to make up an excuse because she really didn't want to talk to him? He'd been nothing but a pain in the arse since he got here. Was he wasting his time traipsing to the station? It didn't matter, he had to come, to finally...

See the face of his brother's killer.

Not just his brother's killer, but the man who'd taken so many lives, wrecked so many households. After all this time, he hardly dared think...

Jack rounded the next corner and saw the station house in front of him, just across the road. Snow had gathered on window ledges, and was clinging to the side of the building in patches. It looked almost festive, or as festive as such a place could possibly look.

His heart sank when he noticed all the media camped out on the steps, halfway round the side, and on the road. Of course they'd be here: *More details as and when we get them.* How stupid of him! This was breaking news. He didn't stand an earthly chance of getting past them.

Even if he did, what then? The police were hardly

likely to welcome him in with open arms, take him to see his tormentor in the cells.

"Mr Twinkle, we have a visitor for you. Meet Jack Foley, your shadow. Your...twin."

What had he been thinking, coming here this morning? Jack shook his head in desolation.

Then he saw her, pacing nervously on his side of the road. No, it couldn't be...could it? Jack started walking towards her. She was dressed in a puffed up parka coat and woolly tights covered her legs down to a pair of knee-high leather boots. Snow dusted her head and shoulders giving her the appearance of an extremely exotic species of bird, with white fluffy plumage. She was biting the skin on the side of a finger, her face flushed by the cold winds, and didn't see him until he was practically on top of her.

"Felicity?" The girl jumped when she heard her own name. "Felicity, is that you?"

She gawked at him, then pieced reality together bit by bit. "Mr Foley?" She took her finger away from her mouth and smiled sweetly, the instinctive smile she'd first given him when he checked in at *The Imperial*, and the same smile she'd flashed him not two nights ago when she'd finished her weekend shift there. "What are *you* doing here?"

"I could ask you the same question."

She seemed unsure at first, then said, "I'm wondering how I can get inside the police station."

"Really? So am I."

Puzzled, she pulled a face. "You? Why?"

"I have a...friend in there. It's important that I speak with her. Why're you here?"

With no finger to feast on, Felicity now bit her lip.

"It's okay, you can tell me."

"My sister's inside. Well, I *think* she's inside. You see I only got the message this morning I've been out most of the night and so I came down here—"

"Whoa, slow down. You're not making much sense."

Felicity took a deep breath, and started again. "I went out with a few friends from my course last night, and my phone battery died, then I ended up sleeping over at their place... Anyway, when I got back to mine, someone told me my sister had called."

I was right about her being a student, then, thought Jack.

"She left a message about coming to the police station, that there had been some trouble. You know, I knew something wasn't right last night. I could tell... I tried ringing them up but couldn't get through, so I came straight over. Well, not *straight* over...the snow and everything. But I came as quickly as I could. God, if she's been arrested Mum and Dad are going to go spare."

Jack mulled this over, then asked. Felicity, this sister of yours—"

"Trisha?"

Everything's connected, Jack... "Trisha. She wouldn't happen to be your identical twin sister, would she?"

"How do you know that?"

"Lucky guess." He stepped closer. "Have you seen the news this morning, Felicity?"

"No, I didn't get the chance. And anyway, I'm not really much of a *news* person. Why? Oh no, she's not been on the news, has she? What's she done?"

Jack held up his hands. "No, no, nothing like that. But I've a feeling she probably will be on the news later."

"What do you mean?"

"Felicity, you know about the...attacks that have been happening?"

Panic suddenly registered in her expression. "Oh my

God, I told her to quit that waitressing job! She hasn't been hurt, has she? Please, Mr Foley—"

"I can't tell you that for sure. But I do know that the police detained a suspect last night. And I think maybe your sister had something to do with it."

Once Felicity had gotten over her initial surge of alarm, Jack suggested they try to get inside somehow. There was no point trying the front entrance, as that was completely clogged up with reporters. Jack thought their best bet was to break through the throng and make their way up the side-street to the rear entrance the one Deborah had used on his last visit. He knew the girl beside him was his heaven-sent ticket inside there, and felt guilty about using her this way. But she needed to get into the station every bit as much as he did; more so probably. She needed information about her sister and he was only helping her get it.

They crossed the road together, then started to make their way through the forest of photographers, cameramen and reporters outside Yardley Street nick.

"Excuse us, sorry. 'Scuse…"

It wasn't easy. The assemblage was reluctant to let them into its ranks for fear they might scoop a story first and Jack was barged into more than once. But eventually they started to make some progress down the side-road.

Then the fight broke out.

"Oi, where do you think you're going?" someone shouted at Jack. He said nothing in reply, merely keeping his head down whilst trying to shield Felicity with his body. Then somebody from behind him threw a punch. It caught Jack a glancing blow on the base of his skull and he toppled forwards. Falling into the wall of bodies, he lost his grip on Felicity. Above him, someone else had punched his attacker.

Nerves were frayed; most of these people had been here all night in the freezing weather conditions, having to rely on thermal underwear and coats to keep them warm, to catch catnaps in vans and cars, with not so much as a sniff of an exclusive. They were cranky as hell and in the mood to lash out. It didn't take long for the fracas to escalate.

Jack felt boots trampling him as he sought to get up. He called out to Felicity but lost sight of her. The snow was still falling hard, which gave the scene a farcical appearance. Punch-up in a winter wonderland.

Suddenly Jack was hauled up by his collar and thrust against what must have been the side-wall of the station. Media now choked the small road leading to the car park and back entrance. A blow to his midsection doubled him over with a wheeze.

Before collapsing, he saw luminescent yellow shapes wading into the crowd: these characters seemed to have flat, chequered heads…at least that's what they looked like through his watery eyes. Of course, they might as easily have been peaked caps. Jack didn't care, all he was bothered about was the pain in his stomach and the feeling of weightlessness as he was plucked out of the battle by strong, firm hands.

"Come and have a look at this, Sarge."

Peel and a handful of his contemporaries were laughing as they looked down on the turmoil below. Deborah had stopped off at her desk after the coffee machine and was now walking through the corridor on the second floor. Curious, she went over to see what the constable found so amusing through the window.

"What is it, Peel? Has Santa Claus decided to visit Yardley Street early this year?"

"Better than that," he promised, making room for her

to get through. "The press are only having a scrap outside, aren't they?"

"What, right outside a police station?" Deborah rushed to the window and looked down. She shook her head when she saw the fighting. "Of all the stupid..." She stopped, leaning in closer to the pane. She could've sworn she saw... Was that Patricia Bailey down there, wedged between two police officers? It couldn't be.

But she soon forgot about that when she spotted another face in the crowd, being dragged out by two more P.C.s. It was Jack Foley; she'd recognise him anywhere.

And it looked as if he was hurt.

CHAPTER TWENTY-SEVEN

Deborah took the stairs two at a time, descending at a rate of knots.

She had to get down to the ground level as quickly as possible, and wouldn't wait while the lift found her floor. As she came round a bend in the stairs, she almost knocked over a female police officer heading upwards, but dodged sideways at the last minute to avoid the collision.

What did he think he was playing at, coming here? She would have contacted him eventually, let him know all about Craine when she had time (it was a wonder he hadn't come sooner; he probably saw the whole attack last night). The man had no patience, that was his trouble. It seemed a rather hypercritical thing to say when you were pelting down a flight of stairs at breakneck speed, but the thought never even entered Deborah's head.

She was angry, although that wasn't the real reason why she was rushing down these stairs, was it? Jack was injured, and something inside her had responded to his pain. As much as she hated to admit it, Deborah was concerned about him.

She hopped over the bottom step and ran up the

corridor to the back entranceway. Upon opening the door, Deborah saw several members of the press being escorted past the desk sergeant. *Well, they got their wish*, she thought. *They're inside.* Though she doubted any of them would've pictured it quite this way, heading for the cells to cool off.

Then came Jack. He was white: his hair, his coat, all covered in snow. It sparked a memory in her mind.

White as snow their armour was, Their steeds were white as snow...

He was arm-in-arm with P.C. Clark, another one of Peel's mates, more or less supported by the man. "By the look of things, this is the bloke who started it all," Clark told Sergeant Kilbourne. "Shoving through to the front of the 'queue'."

"Well, bring him on in. The more the merrier," said Kilbourne, chuckling.

"Wait." Deborah was just about to say the word herself, but somebody beat her to it. She whipped her head round to see the girl who looked so much like Patricia Bailey standing in the doorway. But it wasn't her, she could see that now (*the same but different*). Deborah finally twigged. This was Patricia's twin sister. "He was only trying to get me inside," Felicity protested. "He's not even a reporter...I don't think."

"Actually, he's an historian. Aren't you, Mr Foley?" Deborah strode forward as Jack met her gaze.

"He was only trying to get me inside," Felicity reiterated. "It was the others..."

"All right, Clark. I'll take it from here," Deborah said, grabbing hold of Jack's arm. He staggered as she led him to a seat by the back wall, but she kept him upright. Felicity came and stood beside them.

"Are you... Is he okay?" she asked Deborah.

"I don't know, are you?"

Jack moaned, then spluttered, "Never been better."

"What the hell are you doing here, Jack?"

"He was just trying to—"

"To get you inside, I know. You did mention it." Deborah smiled. "I'm sorry, it's been a long night. I take it you're Patricia Bailey's sister?"

"Felicity. She tried to contact me, but I only just got the message."

"Right, well she's upstairs. The doctor has had a look at her and Danny—"

"The doctor! Oh my God!" Felicity's hands went to her mouth.

"Don't worry, they're both fine. They just didn't want to go home last night; hardly surprising when you consider what they went through."

"What? What did they go through?"

Deborah let out a weary breath. That was right, the poor kid didn't even know yet. "I think the best thing I can do is take you to her and she can explain everything." She turned towards Jack. "As for you…"

"Don't worry," Jack said huskily. "I know the way."

It was heart-warming to witness the reunion between Patricia and Felicity Bailey.

The sisters barely exchanged a word for the first five minutes, they simply hugged each other tightly, the tremendous relief evident on Felicity's face. Close barely described their relationship and Deborah wondered what it must be like to have another person feel that way about you. To understand you inside out, like Patricia and Felicity obviously did.

It's a twin thing… The nearest she had to it was the unconditional love she gave to Isabel, and hopefully received in return. But even she would grow up, leave home, start a new life for herself without Deborah. Start her own family someday. With a twin you had a friend forever. In most cases. Deborah suddenly remembered the story of Tim and Todd Nicholson. *In most cases…*

It wasn't long before Danny was brought into the circle as well, and the three of them shared a moment together. But no matter how much Patricia loved him or he loved her, he would never be as close as those two girls were. Would never share what *they* shared.

As Deborah led Jack away from the visitor's room, she could feel him staring at her again. Oh no, how she wished he'd stop doing that.

"How're you feeling now?"

"Fine. It was only a punch in the stomach."

"You shouldn't have come, Jack. If you saw the attack, then you should've known—"

"But that's just it, I *didn't* see it. The first I knew about all this was when I put the news on in my hotel room this morning."

"No 'insights'? No 'hunches'? No voices from the other side?"

"Don't make fun of me."

"I'm sorry." Deborah pulled up sharply in the corridor, waiting for a couple of P.C.s to pass by. "You don't make things easy, do you?"

"Who for, you?"

"For yourself. For anyone."

"What's his name?"

Amazed he'd even ask, she said, "I can't tell you *that.*"

"Please. I need to know his name. The man killed my brother."

"And he killed Stuart Redbrook's brother, and Kimberly

Archer's sister and Harry Lovesy's brother and God knows how many more, if you're to be believed—"

"*If?*"

"But I don't see *them* here in this police station demanding to know the name of the man who did the deed. Just you, Jack Foley. Always you."

"I *have* to see him, Debbie." His doleful eyes drew her in. "You can understand that, can't you?"

"Absolutely out of the question."

"Is it Mason?"

"No. Well, yes…partly. But I'm a police detective, Jack. I can't go around giving members of the public access to the criminals. It just doesn't work like that, especially in such a high-profile inquiry as this."

Jack placed his hands on her arms.

"Take your hands off me, Jack."

"Please, Debbie. I'm begging you."

"I said…" Deborah tried to take a step back, but her body just wouldn't respond. She could feel herself trembling, and couldn't prevent it, couldn't control it.

"Don't ask me to do this," Now it was her turn to beg.

"Just for a second. *Please!*"

She sighed, finally shrugging off his hands.

Then, knowing she'd ultimately regret it, Deborah Harrison nodded her head.

CHAPTER TWENTY-EIGHT

There was evil here. He could sense it.

It was awake and alive.

He could smell it, feel it. Almost reach out and touch it. Jack had known since he entered Yardley Street police station that the killer was inside. Again it might have been James, the link they shared informing him that the murderer was near… (So what happened last night? Was it because nobody had been killed this time? Had James somehow known Twinkle would be captured?) Or maybe it was just your average gut instinct, like the ones Deborah followed all the time.

And as he waited to see his brother's executioner, Jack's palms became sweaty. The heat inside was in stark contrast to the snowy wasteland rapidly stacking up beyond these walls. His hair and clothes were now wet from melted snow, just as they were wet the first time he'd visited this place. After the rainstorm.

How surreal his life had become. If someone had told him two years ago that he'd be stalking a vicious predator, waiting for an…opportunity, and now waiting to see that beast for the very first time, he would have thought them insane. That was somebody else's destiny, not his. A mix-up in the Creator's plan; Jack's papers placed in the wrong file in the busy offices of biographical records upstairs.

But strangely enough it was all he knew now. It had been his existence for so long…it seemed he'd been on the road even longer than he'd been an historian. Although in reality it had taken up but a fragment of his adult life, comparatively speaking. This was his obligation and reason for carrying on. What would he do now the chase was over? Stick around for the trial, that went without saying. But what then? Go back to how it was before? What demented dreams could he think up that might come true twenty-four months down the line? Jack found he couldn't think of any, a life after this was void. Without meaning or substance.

No, he couldn't allow himself to wonder about that. The only thing of any consequence was seeing that face. And looking into its eyes.

Mason was waiting for her at the door of the interview room.

"Where have you been?" he asked Deborah.

"There was some trouble down below with the media. A fight."

"Couldn't the troops handle it on their own?"

"Probably. I just thought I'd lend a hand."

"You're a latter-day Good Samaritan, Blondie. Right then, shall we get on with this?"

Deborah fidgeted uncomfortably at the door. "Actually, sir… I was told on my way back that Chief Superintendent Bingham wants a word."

"A progress report, already? Well, didn't you tell him there's nothing *to* report, yet?"

"I think he wants to hear it from the horse's mouth, sir. There's a lot riding on this."

Mason swore under his breath. "All right. Give me five minutes and I'll be back."

Deborah said she would keep his seat warm for him, watching as he stormed off up the corridor and through the double doors at the far end.

Then she went to fetch Jack.

"Just a few seconds," she warned him. Deborah still didn't know why she was doing this; putting her job   her whole career   on the line. It was inexplicably and unforgivably stupid.

"That's all I'll need," replied Jack, attempting to keep up with her, his legs still a bit wobbly. His stomach ached as well, but he couldn't tell whether it was because of the punch he'd received in the scrum outside, or the anticipation he felt as he came ever nearer.

The door loomed closer. It looked like the same interview room he'd been questioned in himself not long ago. Probably wasn't, it was hard to tell in a station this size. And then they were there. Deborah looked both ways, checking that the coast was clear before knocking. She went inside, informing the P.C.s on duty that Mason had gone to see the Chief Superintendent and might be a little while longer. She kept the door ajar, but placed herself between them and the corridor, obstructing their line of sight.

Out in that corridor was Jack. He could see the spiky-haired man at the table, slouching in his seat. The killer looked ordinary enough. It was at this point that he expected it to come: confirmation, *revelation*. But there was nothing. Not even when the man raised his head and locked eyes with Jack. He saw nothing in those dead orbs, felt nothing when the man gave a smile that could chill champagne.

Then the man spoke. "I am The Gemini," he said. It

appeared to be his mantra, because he said it again: "I am The Gemini."

"Shut your mouth, Craine," shouted one of the P.C.s in a gruff voice.

Craine. So that was the man's name. Still nothing came to him. No *illumination*.

This wasn't how he'd pictured it at all.

James, tell me. I need to know!

"Foley?" The name was spat out with such hatred, it made Jack flinch. But he was reluctant to tear his eyes away from Craine. Only at the very last moment did he turn to see who was calling out to him, who was coming down the corridor towards him.

It was Inspector Roy Mason.

"What the fuck are *you* doing here?" he demanded. Deborah finished up inside and came back into the corridor, closing the interview room door behind her. She scrunched up her eyes, perhaps hoping she could make herself vanish into thin air or make everyone else in the corridor disappear, yes that would do just as well. Maybe if she wished hard enough she could—

"I *asked* what you *were fucking well doing here!*" roared Mason. He was covering the distance between himself and his pair of targets in long, measured strides.

Jack's mouth opened and closed like a fish.

It looked as if Mason was going to charge at the man, finish what he'd wanted to do in that same interview room or one just like it a couple of weeks ago. But he stopped short, standing in front of his sergeant with his hands on his hips. He waited for her to open her eyes, which she did one at a time, hoping her wish had come true.

It hadn't.

"Sergeant," said Mason, his voice lower but now

infinitely more menacing. "I'd say you have quite a bit of explaining to do."

CHAPTER TWENTY-NINE

Deborah knew now what it must feel like to be a criminal. To be on the other side of that table, facing a barrage of questions. Aware that by saying just one word out of place, you could incriminate yourself. Land yourself in more trouble than you knew what to do with.

It wasn't a particularly pleasant experience, but it was one she felt she deserved.

Mason was the person pacing up and down this time, just as she had done outside the morgue after coming away from Stuart Redbrook's autopsy. It seemed like years ago rather than weeks. Mason had cracked a joke, hadn't he? Something about her missing her days on the beat and yes, now she did yearn to have those days back again.

But he was in no joking mood today.

The first thing he'd done after catching them outside Craine's interview room, and after nobody would answer his question, was to have Jack Foley escorted from the premises. Frogmarched might have been a more accurate description. Jack had looked to her for assistance, for support. But she had simply glared at him, letting him know that *he* was to blame for this, for putting her in such a position. And telling him tacitly that she wanted him to go.

So he'd gone, without protest, without another word in fact. Head down as an act of contrition, possibly even despair. *He should be happy*, thought Deborah. *He's got what he wanted. Now I have to pay the price.*

The next thing Mason did was direct Deborah to the interview room just down the hall, the one Jack had waited in before laying eyes on his brother's killer. He told her to sit down, which she'd done, and then he shut the door, leaning up against it with his hands behind his back.

Time passed before he began to speak. "You know, I can bear most things life has to throw at me, although God knows recently I've…" He paused. There was a sad, melancholy edge to his address. "But lying. You lied to me, Sergeant." *No nicknames now. No Blondie this, Blondie that.* Deborah found she actually missed it. "I saw Chief Inspector Bingham's secretary on the stairs. According to her, he's not even *in* his office. He heard about the ruckus outside and decided to go and smooth things over. But then, you probably knew that all along. He didn't want to see me at all. You deliberately got rid of me, didn't you?" He refused to wait for an answer. "Just time enough. I get there, find out he's not in, then come back. But time enough for what? Come on, tell me. I need to get this straight in my head."

Deborah was too ashamed to speak.

"I thought we were a team, Sergeant. Thought we were in this together. And now I find you going about behind my back doing…doing what, exactly? You still haven't told me. What else aren't you telling me?"

"I…"

"Oh, she speaks."

"I'm sorry," she said softly

"I'm sorry too. Now are you going to fill me in on what

this is all about, or do we really have to go and find Bingham?"

So Deborah told him about Jack's brother. How she thought there might be a connection between the murders, that Craine had possibly struck elsewhere before he reached Norchester, and that she'd been searching for other twin disappearances for this reason. But she didn't mention anything about Jack's…curse, the link to his sibling the inspector still wasn't ready for that yet nor his quest to track Twinkle down, although Mason guessed about the last part.

"That's why he's done so much moving around, isn't it? He's been following him," said Mason. His expression was that of a child's after finishing a particularly difficult jigsaw. The pieces, or at least some of them, were finally slotting into place. "He's been searching for our man Craine, looking for revenge. So he's a vigilante on top of everything else. Brilliant! And *you* gave him access to his brother's murderer."

"I'm sorry."

"Yes, so you said." He was genuinely disappointed in her, and she didn't know how to put things right. Or, indeed, if she ever could.

"I mean, whatever possessed you? He could have done anything! Attacked Craine, killed him."

"I wouldn't have let that happen."

"And you were planning on stopping him how?"

What, I couldn't stop him because I'm a woman, is that it? Deborah let it drop. Now wasn't the time to get into another one of their arguments about gender, about women police officers doing the job as well as and in many cases better than their male counterparts. Not when she'd broken the rules so blatantly.

"He wanted to see Craine. I-I don't know—"

"What, so you felt sorry for Foley? Is that what you're telling me? You risked a suspension, possibly even dismissal, and all because you wanted to put his mind at rest? Or was there something more to it?"

Deborah felt her own anger welling at that remark. "No, certainly not."

"You've obviously spent time with the man—"

"Only as part of this investigation."

Mason's upper lip curled. "How can I believe a word you're saying, Sergeant? If you can lie to me about Bingham, why not about this?" He sounded like a jealous husband who suspected his wife of cheating on him. And why not? Their partnership was very much like a marriage, together day-in, day-out. If there was no trust anymore… Well, the next logical step would be divorce.

"I swear to you, I've never lied about anything before—"

"Before today? That's very reassuring. So how about tomorrow or the next day? What about the next time you decide it's in the best interests of the case for you to withhold vital information from your inspector?"

Deborah propped her elbows up on the table and held her head in her hands. "I *couldn't* tell you."

"Why not?"

"I just couldn't."

Noting her obvious distress, he let Deborah off the hook for the time being. "I'll have to think very carefully about this," he said. And that's when the pacing had begun.

Her whole life, her future career, was going to be decided in this very room. Nervously, she traced Mason's every step, his every deliberation. It would be just her luck to get thrown out as she was in the final stages of the biggest case of her career. Okay, so they hadn't caught Craine themselves, but the arrest would still look pretty damned impressive on their permanent records. And she'd had to go and ruin that for…for what? She still didn't understand why she'd done it, allowed Jack to get within ten miles of the interview room, let alone within metres of Craine. Had she felt sorry for him, as Mason suggested? It was true that she now believed his story, and she *had* seen him writhing about on the floor, reliving the night of his brother's death. No one was *that* good an actor; it was real, all right. Didn't he deserve the chance to see who'd done it? Was that why she'd agreed? If that was it, why not go through official channels? Arrange a supervised prison visit? Once Craine was tied in to the murders, it wouldn't have been difficult to sort out. But that could have taken weeks, months even. It might not have happened at all if Mason had gotten wind of it. Why was it so important Jack saw Craine today? Deborah couldn't think of a satisfactory answer to the question. *Or was there something more to it?* That's what Mason had said, and all it implied. No. Right now, she hated Jack Foley. Hated him for putting her in this predicament, for asking what he'd asked of her. For making her sit here sweating while her entire existence was decided on the toss of a coin.

Heads, Mason trusts her.

Tails, he doesn't. And never will again.

Common sense dictated it would be the latter. When you came right down to it, she had betrayed him for *whatever* reasons. Could she really blame him for not wanting to work with her again? How would she have reacted in his position, if say Peel was her sergeant, however unlikely that might be, and he'd done something as inexcusable as this? That was an easy one, but she didn't like the answer at all. Deborah convinced herself it was curtains. With each stride Mason took, she could imagine herself up before Bingham, his face red; more disappointment and recriminations.

She could hear his words over and over again in her

head: "We had high hopes for you, Sergeant. You've let us all down. Inspector Mason, your colleagues, everyone who's ever had any faith in your abilities. But most of all, you've let yourself down."

Then having to face her family, disgraced. Who was she kidding? Her mother and Isabel would no doubt secretly be pleased by the news. No more moving around, or late shifts. No more all-nighters like last night. She could play the role of a normal mother, perhaps with a nice safe part-time job somewhere. No more fears or worries about whether she was all right. But Deborah knew her mother too well. The idea of her daughter being sacked from any post would upset her, especially under these circumstances.

Mason prolonged the agony as much as he dared, teasing out the time. Penalising her this way first…and formally later? Then all of a sudden he came round and sat down beside her.

He fixed her with an intense stare, more intense even than Jack's. Than Craine's. It was like Mason's gaze was penetrating her very soul. She knew why; he had to make sure.

"We've known each other a good while, now," he said, breaking the deafening silence. "And without hesitation you're the best damned sergeant I've ever worked with. So, I'll ask you once, and once only. Is this ever going to happen again?"

Deborah wanted to blink, but was afraid to. Afraid it would affect the 'test'.

"No." It was an honest answer. She meant it from the bottom of her heart. And Deborah hoped prayed he could see that. But it was impossible to tell what he was thinking.

Something touched her, a hand on her arm. She didn't recoil, as much as it startled her. "Then I see no reason to take this matter any further. Bingham's got enough on his plate at the moment. We all make mistakes. But make sure this is your last."

Deborah gave a loud sigh as he withdrew his hand. "Now, I believe we were in the middle of an interview," he said, standing. Then he turned his back on her and went to the door. He opened it, and slowly walked out. Deborah sat welded to the chair, not altogether certain she *could* get up. Mason's face appeared again at the door. "Are you coming or not, Blondie?"

Deborah got up, made her way to the door, and followed Mason out into the corridor.

CHAPTER THIRTY

Mason trod the corridors like an animal on the prowl.

The world had turned around another day, and night-time was creeping up on them apace. He'd sent Deborah home an hour or so ago, told her to get some sleep in a proper bed and come back recharged first thing in the morning. She'd claimed she was all right but he could see through her act. She was exhausted, dead on her feet. And no help to him in that condition. She was probably also still worried about what had happened earlier on.

Good, that was the idea. Things were bound to be strained between them for a few days, but he was confident they'd get back on track again…eventually.

The rest of Craine's interview hadn't gone very well. They'd extracted nothing more from him, apart from the fact he was 'The Gemini', which they knew already.

The vast majority of the reporters still waited outside, but they'd calmed down somewhat after Bingham had spoken to them personally. As he did with the people under his command, the Chief Super, now at home himself, soon put them in their rightful place without them even realising it. He'd also been able to ease the passage out of the station of the Bailey twins, of Sirk and of Tate.

The station personnel had almost halved as well. Now that the initial fuss had died down it was business as usual for the Yardley Street plod. They went back to doing whatever they'd been doing before Twinkle Jesus, he still hated that nickname – a.k.a. Anton Craine had been taken into custody.

The thought had occurred to him, as he got on with some of his overdue paperwork, why not have a little private chat with Craine? Only this afternoon he'd had a pop at Deborah for stepping out of line. Now he was intending to do the same thing.

Mason passed through the inner doorway and approached Kilbourne, who stood virtually to attention on the other side of his desk.

"No need for all that, Doug. We've known each other far too long." Mason grinned. "How's our star attraction tonight?"

"Not heard a peep out of him, which is more than I could say about those reporters we had in here earlier."

Mason laughed now. "I bet you were glad to see the back of them."

"You're telling me! Threatening us with everything from a lawsuit to a front page story on police brutality."

"Speaking of which, is there any chance of bobbing in to see him?"

"Twinkle, you mean? Oh, I don't know, Roy."

"I was only joking about the brutality bit. You won't even know I've been in the same cell with him. Come on, you know me. I like to get results, but I know where to draw the line."

Douglas Kilbourne did know him; he'd known him for nigh-on twenty years. And if anyone could get that lowlife down there to talk, it was Roy Mason. But the only way to do it was without an audience.

"Not a finger on him, though, Roy."

"I won't harm a hair on his spiky little head. I just want to talk to him. That's all. Perhaps get him to think about what he's done overnight. He might even confess tomorrow, with a bit of luck."

"They do say it's good for the soul."

"Right. It wouldn't be bad for the image of this nick, either." Mason waited while Kilbourne went into his small private office for the keys, then he stood aside as the man opened up his desk. "If anybody comes in looking for me—"

"I've not seen you all night."

"Thanks, Doug. I appreciate this." Kilbourne let him through the bars, then followed him down to Craine's cell. Then he opened up the next door and let Mason inside. Craine was sitting on the bed, in exactly the same place he'd been hours ago. Mason walked in and the prisoner looked up.

"I'll come back in ten minutes," said Kilbourne.

Mason turned his head. "Make it twenty, Doug."

"A quarter of an hour, and that's the best I can do."

Nodding, Mason accepted his compromise.

"Although it beats me how you can stand to spend fifteen seconds alone with *him*. The guy sends my water cold," Kilbourne disclosed.

"Oh, he doesn't scare me. And I think we understand each other now, don't we Craine?" The convict managed a snort.

Kilbourne backed out of the cell. "Quarter of an hour," he repeated, then locked the cell door again.

Mason listened as Kilbourne's footsteps died away. Satisfied they were on their own, he walked even further into the cell. Craine watched him closely.

"I," said Craine, "Am…The…Gemini."

"All right, if you like," Mason replied. "Yes, you sick bastard. You are The Gemini."

CHAPTER THIRTY-ONE

Alone in his cell that night, Anton Craine looked out through the one small, perfectly square window above his cot.

The snow had stopped falling and now he could see the stars shining brightly in the sky. So beautiful; so, so beautiful. Unlike the pictures in his mind, in his head   pictures that would not go away. Faces trapped in the contortions of death. Body parts, blood. Too much blood. He'd laughed when he saw them, the photographs on the table in front of him. But now it wasn't so funny. It wasn't funny at all.

Now that he was on his own, he thought he heard the dead people talking to him. Questioning him: Why did you do this to us? Why? Why? Why?

And his answer, the one he'd been giving all day long, the one he'd given to the policeman who'd visited him earlier in his cell, was: *I am The Gemini.*

Not good enough. He couldn't fob them off as easily as the law. They knew why, they knew who he was. *You crave that which you are not*, they chorused.

That which you are not and never shall be.

Craine put his fist in his mouth, but the words escaped through his knuckles, muffled and incomprehensible. "But I am The Gemini."

No. You haven't finished your work yet. There is more to be done. You have failed.

"I am The Gemini! I am! *I am!*" he mumbled, but there was no conviction anymore.

The voices came louder now than ever before. So much guilt, so much bloodshed. All for nothing. All wasted. How could he ever put it right, stop the voices?

There is a way, they told him. *Prove to us you're sorry for what you've done. Make amends.*

Craine jerked his head up and down, his fist still blocking his mouth. "Anything. I'll do anything… I'm sorry."

Will you do this for us? Will you? Do you have the courage?

Again he nodded.

Then do it now. It's the only way. Bleed as we have bled.

Anton Craine took his hand out of his mouth, then opened the cavity wide. His tongue lolled out like a slimy-wet slug. He thrust it forwards as far as the muscle would allow. His eyes were wide, mad and staring.

Do not make a sound, they told him. *Can you do that? Quiet, ever so quiet.*

Craine nodded, placing one of his hands below his chin and the other on top of his head.

Then, as the P.C. back there in the interview room had ordered, he finally shut his mouth.

His teeth came down hard on the tongue, and though the pain was great, he applied even more pressure with his hands. Blood exploded into his mouth, into the back of his throat, and splattered out through his teeth. In a matter of seconds, the tongue had been sawn in two, one end dropping to the cell floor with a soggy slapping noise, the other flicking about inside his mouth.

Craine kept up the pressure until he could do so no

longer. He let go of his head and chin, opened his mouth, and let a stream of thick, red liquid flood out. Some he tried to swallow back, but didn't quite succeed.

Well done, they said. *Now you can rest.*

Craine fell backwards onto the cot. Blood continued to flow from his mouth, painted black by the night. He sprawled on the warm pillow of his own juices, letting another part of his mind worry about the fire raging inside his mouth, the swelling root of tongue that was left.

He would either die from blood loss or asphyxiation. It made no difference which. So long as they all knew.

Anton Craine could still see the stars from where he lay. So bright and so beautiful. For him it was over and he could slip effortlessly away.

He'd done what had been asked of him.

Now it was time to go to sleep.

PART III

CHAPTER THIRTY-TWO

Isabel had been awake since half-past three.

Deborah had sent her back to bed something like ten times since then. On one occasion, she'd even awoken to find the seven-year-old bouncing up and down on her bed.

"Out young lady!" she'd cried. "Or Father Christmas won't be bringing you any presents at all this year."

Isabel had departed, muttering something about Father Christmas not existing, but not daring to risk saying it out loud on the off-chance that he did. Deborah tried to get back to sleep again, but now found that sleep was playing hide-and-seek with her: she was the one seeking, though not finding. She was fully awake by quarter to six and decided to get up and get on with the ritual after she heard Isabel banging about again in the next room. Maybe it hadn't been such a good idea after all, taking a few days off over Christmas.

Still, she wouldn't miss these moments for anything. Enjoy them, her mother had once said to her, because before you know it she'll be gone, making her own way in the big, wide world. Of course, Deborah had pointed out that *she* was still living with her mother and she was in her thirties, to which Wendy had replied: "Yes, but you don't play with

Barbie anymore or blow bubbles in your milk through a straw." Deborah didn't see what that had to do with anything

Isabel did neither of those things anyway but understood the sentiment all too well. Kids grow up fast. Blink and you'll miss it.

Deborah pulled on her bedside light and went to the wardrobe, then veered sharply away in order to prop a chair up against the bedroom door. She didn't want Isabel bursting in and discovering her secret hiding place.

Deborah tested the door. The chair wobbled slightly, but it would keep out a nosy whippersnapper no problem. Returning to the closet, she pulled the clothes on hangers aside, then turfed out some of the junk that lived in the bottom. Tittering to herself at the deviousness of it all, Deborah felt down the back of the wardrobe for the small hole.

"There you are," she said, slipping her index finger inside it. Now she plucked away the partition, which was only made of plywood, to reveal a secret storage space at the rear. Deborah kept all her private belongings in here: love letters Peter had sent her, back when she thought he actually knew the meaning of the word 'love'; old photographs from when she was at school, kept in cardboard shoeboxes; report slips; certificates; her dreaded wedding video; a clay elephant she'd made at an evening class once, glazed and fired which everyone else thought was hilarious, probably because it didn't even remotely resemble an elephant, but which she secretly had a soft spot for; and some of her old clothes that were sadly out of fashion, yet had tremendous sentimental value. The storage compartment was also a good hiding place for Christmas presents. Isabel, the junior detective, hadn't found it yet, but it wasn't for the want of trying.

Deborah removed the presents one by one. Wendy Harrison had done the actual shopping, and a good thing, too, what with everything that'd been going on at work lately, but she had provided the list, gleaned from intensive interview sessions with Isabel. There was no point buying loads of surprise gifts because Deborah had about as much idea of what was 'hip' nowadays as *her* mother did when she was young. Although that hadn't stopped her from indulging in one or two things that Isabel didn't have an inkling about. One was a gold bracelet with her name on it you couldn't go wrong with jewellery. Another was a pair of trainers Isabel had mentioned once but Deborah had frowned upon because they were too expensive. Well, Christmas comes but once a year…

The rest were assorted computer games (nothing violent Deborah *hoped* just your average scrolling level descendants of *Donkey Kong*), clothes, Blu-rays and books. The Blu-rays fell into two categories: cartoons and soaps. This was the kind of present they could both sit and enjoy together.

Her mother's gift was hidden in here as well, because Wendy Harrison was just as nosy as her granddaughter. *That's probably where she gets it from,* thought Deborah dreamily. *Probably where I get it from, if it comes to that!* For her, Blu-rays of the old musicals she was so fond of. Deborah thought they might pass the time when both her and Isabel were out of the house. She'd also bought her some perfume Wendy's favourite brand because she hated to be unpredictable. These presents she'd managed to somehow acquire herself.

The bedroom door rattled, handle turning once, twice, with no joy. There was a knock, then: "Mummmm! Let me in!"

Quickly, Deborah transported the wrapped parcels to the bed, then bundled everything else back into the wardrobe. She'd tidy up and put the secret panel back in place later when she had more time.

"Muuuummm!" screeched Isabel with excitement.

"Okay, okay. I'm coming." Deborah removed the chair, putting it back in its place, then opened the bedroom door.

"It must've been stuck," said Deborah. "Fancy that."

Isabel pouted, then spied all the presents on the bed. The sudden transformation was remarkable: she beamed from ear to ear.

"What? Oh yeah. Well, it's a funny story. Er…you see, I heard these bells so I went to the window to check it out. And guess what I saw parked outside on the road… A sleigh."

Isabel looked at her doubtfully.

"True as I'm standing here," Deborah said as seriously as she could. "Anyway, I thought I heard someone behind me, so I turned around and saw all this stuff on my bed. It gave me the fright of my life. By the time I looked through the window again, the sleigh was gone. Good job, as well, because I would've had to have gone down and had a word with the driver for parking next to our gate."

"You would've arrested Father Christmas?"

"Depends whether his reindeer licences were in order."

Isabel giggled. "Silly, that can't have happened."

"And why not?"

"Everyone knows he parks his sleigh on the roof, not on the road," said Isabel, cheekily. Now *she* was playing games with her mother. "And he comes down the chimney—"

"Ah, but we have a gas fire."

Isabel pondered this, then said, "Yes, but why'd he leave them in your room and not in the living room, under the tree?"

"Er…" *She makes Mason look like an amateur,* thought Deborah.

Another figure appeared in the doorway, yawning. "Merry Christmas, love," Wendy said to her daughter.

Saved! "Merry Christmas, Mum."

"Haven't missed anything, have I?" asked Wendy, starting to yawn again.

"Just in time to help us carry these prezzies downstairs."

Isabel rushed over to the bed and gathered some of the boxes in her arms.

"I've got one or two tucked away in my room, as well," Wendy whispered.

"Right then," said Deborah, joining her offspring, "let the fun commence!"

By seven a.m. the living room looked like a paper bomb had detonated inside it.

Brightly-coloured wrappings, with pictures of Christmas trees, crackers and snowmen covering the surface, were everywhere. Isabel didn't so much unwrap as savage her presents, ripping off layer after layer with glee and tossing the remnants over her head.

Once she had finished stripping them bare and marvelling at the contents, she kissed Deborah and thanked her, then did the same with her gran who'd spoilt her rotten with a selection of the latest CDs. Then Deborah brought out the cards for Isabel from various relatives and old friends scattered around the country. She made sure Isabel was careful with these because most would contain money, which the seven-year-old would very sensibly divide and put half in her savings account for a rainy day.

Wendy was overjoyed with her movies, as indeed was Deborah with her mother's gift. She'd opened the small velvet-covered box to find a ring inside, a ring her mother usually wore on *her* right hand. The simple beauty of this gold circle, with a minimum of detailing on the sides and a single ruby stone in its centre, never failed to astound her.

"Can't go wrong with jewellery," Wendy Harrison told her, echoing Deborah's own sentiments.

"Mum, I—"

"It used to belong to my mother, your grandmother, as I'm sure I've probably told you before. She gave it to me when I was about your age, just before…" Deborah's grandmother had died of a brain tumour when she was little. She remembered everyone being very sad, but could never recall her grandmother's face without the aid of old photographic prompts. "Well, anyway, I figured it was high time I passed it on to you. You take it. I want you to have it."

Deborah looked concerned. "You're not trying to tell me something are you, Mum?"

Wendy touched her chest with a finger and laughed. "What, me? No, it's nothing like that. I'm as fit as a fiddle!" Relief flooded through Deborah. "I just thought the time was right, that's all."

"I don't know what to say, Mum." Deborah hugged her mother hard, then kissed her cheek. "I'll never take it off."

It was the only ring on her hand, on either hand, the wedding ring Peter gave her having been consigned to the secret place in the wardrobe…though it almost ended up in the nearest river when she first yanked it off. Throughout the day Deborah would keep admiring it, holding out her finger to see how the light glinted off the gold, off the jewel in the middle.

Isabel spent most of her morning flitting from the TV, to the computer, to the CD player. She did all this in her pyjamas, her new surprise trainers setting off the ensemble. Deborah spent her morning preparing lunch and telling Wendy to go and sit down and relax.

"I've got it covered, really," she said in her most

authoritarian tone of voice. "I *can* cook when I put my mind to it, you know."

But the work was so monotonous, she often found herself thinking back about her last case. She'd tried hard to block it out for the sake of her family, especially over Christmas, and by and large she'd succeeded in doing just that. However, every now and again she'd see Anton Craine's face.

His laughing, staring face. *I am The Gemini.*

What a bad end to come to. It was a hell of a way to commit suicide. You could take away belts, laces, stop prisoners from hanging themselves or slitting their wrists with a buckle although there was always the option of biting through the vein… But how could you stop a person doing something like that? You couldn't take away their teeth, prevent them from sticking out their tongue. From going into shock and dying.

The thought almost made her want to retch as she cooked the sausages for dinner.

They'd never really get to the bottom of those killings now. Never know what really motivated Craine to do those horrible things. If indeed that was his real name: they were still no closer to finding out exactly *who* he was. You could speculate, could make assumptions like Dr Grieves had done, but nobody would ever know for sure. They'd probably never find the missing body parts, either, which meant that the victims would never be 'complete' in their final resting places, much to the distress of the families. What a Christmas they must be having, the Redbrooks, the Archers, George Lovesy's wife and children. All the more reason to savour her own and be thankful she could enjoy it with her mum and her daughter.

And what kind of a Christmas will Jack be having?

The stray thought trespassed before she could stop it, sneaking in subconsciously. Deborah concentrated on the tasks at hand, but now couldn't stop thinking about him.

She shook her head. No, she really didn't want to go down that particular road, thank you very much.

Is he still staying at the hotel, or had he moved on by now? Back home, to his real home?

"I couldn't care less," she grumbled quietly to herself. She hadn't spoken to him, much less seen him since he'd shown up at Yardley Street. Deborah had been very lucky to get away with what she'd done. Very lucky. And there was still a bit of an atmosphere at work.

You have your family, he has no one. And it's Christmas.

"That's not my fault. I'm not going to feel guilty about it."

"Guilty about what?" Isabel had wandered into the kitchen to grab a biscuit from the cupboard.

"Nothing you need to concern yourself about. Just your old mum going senile and talking to herself. Hey, don't eat too many of those," said Deborah as Isabel took out the packet of chocolate biscuits.

"But I'm *hungry.*"

"Comes from having your breakfast at the crack of dawn. Just save some space for all this lot, okay."

"Yes, sir," Isabel replied, giving her mother a mock army salute.

Deborah glanced out of the kitchen window. From here she could see past her gates and onto their road. A couple of children rode by on bikes, the paintwork gleaming and new. A handful of others were testing out roller-blades and scooters, their elbows and knees padded, their heads protected by helmets. Here and there were tiny islands of snow, mainly on the grass verges   the only evidence of their recent fall. Anyone who'd bet on a white Christmas this year would be sadly disappointed. So near and yet so far.

Locking all thoughts of Craine, of the murders, and of Jack, away in the secret compartment in her mind, Deborah opened the oven to see how the turkey was doing.

The sound of hymns breezed through from the living room   her mother stealing a quick peek at the morning services while Isabel was otherwise engaged. Deborah hummed along to 'Away in a Manger'. It was Christmas, she was at home with her family. And nothing was going to spoil that. Nothing was going to interfere.

She was planning to eat, drink, and be merry today.

For who knew what tomorrow might bring?

CHAPTER THIRTY-THREE

It was the strange limbo period between Christmas and New Year.

One celebration was over and the next was just on the horizon. The time for children and presents and mince pies was over, leaving a sense of sad longing in its wake. Ahead was a night for adults, for staying up late to welcome in the next twelve months with open arms, hoping against hope that they might be better than the last.

They seldom were, of course.

He'd thought about her often over the holidays, alone in his hotel room. Jack had barely set foot outside these pastel walls since that day, except to put in an appearance at the small staff party held one afternoon at *The Imperial*: attended by Miriam, Albert, Ralph and the other staff. Both Albert and Miriam had invited Jack, probably because they felt sorry for him. He'd turned down the offer several times but they just wouldn't take no for an answer.

The staff drank punch and wore party hats, then attempted to dance to a festive CD which played such favourites as Lennon's 'So This is Christmas', Slade's 'Merry Christmas' and Band Aid's 'Do They Know It's Christmas?'

The manager was present also, an elusive chap by the name of Waterston who had all the features and the charm of your average gutter rodent. Miriam told Jack that the big boss fella himself might even show up, but he never did.

Felicity didn't come, either. According to one of her friends on staff, she was at home with her family on the other side of the city. Jack had seen her only briefly since the first and last, as it turned out morning of Twinkle's incarceration. She'd thanked him for getting her inside again, even though it had caused a minor riot at the station. He'd told her she was welcome, and had asked how her sister was, as if he really needed to. Patricia Bailey had been hot news property there for a while, along with her boyfriend Danny Sirk and passer-by Benjamin Tate, though *they* proved to be less photogenic than Patricia, whose fame lasted a good couple of days more.

"She's okay, thanks," said Felicity. "Just glad it's all over really." Then she'd asked him once again what he'd been doing there at Yardley Street. "It's like you appeared out of nowhere just to help me."

It reminded Jack of all the times he hadn't been able to help. All the people dead because he couldn't reach them in time. And it reminded him of what he'd asked Deborah to do. The look on her face when Mason caught her doing it.

"Like I said before, I went there to see someone."

"Oh right, your friend. Was it that nice Sergeant Harrison? Was she the friend you went to see?"

"Yes. Yes, she was my friend."

"Well, happy Christmas anyway, Mr Foley. And thanks again!" Felicity kissed him on the cheek, smiling her sweet smile. Except it wasn't the false one she gave all the guests at the hotel. This time it was genuine, the smile she reserved only for those she thought deserved it.

"Just glad it's all over really." Felicity had said. Her sister

was glad it was all over. So shouldn't he be glad, too? Was it only the guilt about Deborah preventing him from leaving Norchester? That was causing this terrible feeling inside? Or was it the image of Craine, sitting at that table, grinning and saying to himself, "I am The Gemini!" over and over again? And Jack feeling nothing. A hollow emptiness, but that's all.

Why hadn't James given him a sign? All this time, watching slaughter after slaughter, reliving James's death: the escalation of those visions after he arrived in this city. So why…

He'd tried calling Debbie a few times, but had always got the snotty woman from before, telling him that Sergeant Harrison was off duty or busy, or some such thing. At least she was still working there, he hadn't cost Deborah her job. Unless she was being investigated herself and the process took time… Was she working out her notice before leaving? Or had disciplinary procedures only just started against her? Demotion? Jack didn't know enough about the police force to be sure. And he didn't know enough about Mason. One thing he was positive about, though: Debbie was refusing to speak to him this time. He could hardly blame her.

Another knockback yesterday led straight to the drinks cabinet. Jack had never been a heavy drinker   unlike James, who could drink anyone under the table if he had a mind and a reason to   but decided that now was as good a time as any to start. At first it had been hard, the miniature bottles pouring what felt like molten metal into his throat and guts. But the more he drank, the more he *wanted* to drink, until he couldn't stand upright. Until he could just about make it to the bed. It had only taken a handful of bottles to get him into such a state.

Jack spent a couple of hours just laughing out loud, at what he didn't know. His screwed-up life, maybe? Or was it the way the stars now danced up in the early evening sky? Like tiny fireflies forming patterns for his amusement.

He finally passed out around ten at night.

His dreams were infused with bizarre alcohol-induced hallucinations.

In them he saw the faces of Twinkle's victims as large as billboards in front of him. The people James had shown him, had projected into his mind from the killer's point of view. A direct link which left no time to undertake a rescue. The faces blurred into each other, like melting plastic, all screaming for his help.

"What can I do? I don't understand what you want me to do," he blurted out, his words echoing strangely inside his own head. Static came back in reply.

The faces continued to morph together, becoming a wall of lost souls, surrounding him. Jack was in darkness. He felt hot breath upon his neck; another replay of James's death? Not this time.

Jack ran.

"It's over," he wailed. "Leave me alone…" He raced down a series of dark tunnels, turning this way and that. Confused, frightened and tired, he tripped and rolled into a large room. No: a chamber. A single light chased away the darkness, but created shadows on the filthy stone walls. Except one shadow was alive. It moved towards him, disengaging itself from its surroundings.

It bore the frame of a man, and yet was anything but. Around its waist was a belt, the kind workmen wear. Only attached to it were the most horrific instruments of torture imaginable: knives, spikes, a small cleaver… A blackened hand reached round the back of the belt, and the shape grew taller and taller.

"No, no! You're dead, Craine. Twinkle is dead!" Jack

reminded him.

But still it came, bringing out its preferred weapon. The twin-pronged fork. And Jack realised it wasn't Twinkle who was dead.

It was him.

Twinkle's other hand was closed around something. Now, as *He* came closer, the hand sprang open. In its palm was a human eyeball, tendrils of flesh still attached to the orb. It was the same grey-green colour as Jack's own eyes. It was the same colour James' eyes had been. In fact it *was* James' eye, and Jack could now see through it. See himself as a victim, the fork raised high, ready to plunge into him…

Jack awoke violently, trying to crawl away but aware that his body was still a liquor sponge and he'd soaked up far too much to move. He lay on the bed, breathing heavily, and within moments was asleep again.

Dead to the world.

He opened his eyes, the lids fluttering like butterfly wings as he endeavoured in vain to focus.

The light in the room was dim. Early morning, he concluded. His head was throbbing and he felt queasy. There was a furry taste in his mouth. Slowly, he lifted himself up and looked at the clock. It was a jumble of unidentifiable, blurry numbers.

The first clue as to how long he'd been asleep were actually the missing bottles of alcohol. It was obvious somebody had been in his room and tidied up; Miriam, back from her short vacation over Christmas. She'd probably left him in bed to sleep it off, worried but knowing there was nothing she could do about it. He was a grown man, after all.

Which meant what? That the sun wasn't coming up, it was actually going back down again.

Twilight.

Incomprehensible images from the night before, from his dream, floated back to him. He saw the faces, the passageway, the flickering light. And Twinkle approaching, the twin prongs of a fork. Saw them being sharpened.

No, that couldn't be right. That hadn't been a part of his dream. But nevertheless he saw the action, the stone grinding against each prong until it was razor sharp.

It took Jack a moment to grasp it. That these weren't remembrances from his dream, his terrifying, horrific dream. These pictures were live, happening right now. This minute! He stared at the wall of his hotel room, not seeing it at all.

The fork was ready, holstered on the belt. Then the belt was strapped around him.

Jack climbed off the bed, felt woozy, and sat back down on the edge.

As *He* moved down that selfsame passageway, taking Jack with him…

Then Jack lost the signal.

Not quite sure what he'd seen, he sat there burying his head in his hands. Maybe he was mistaken; he wasn't quite feeling himself today. Perhaps this time they *were* just figments of his imagination.

Jack hoped to God they were.

Because if they weren't, if what he'd seen was real… If what James was trying to tell him was right, then it could only mean one thing. Twinkle was somehow still alive.

And he was preparing to go out and kill again.

CHAPTER THIRTY-FOUR

The sound of his footsteps echoed all around.

Why shouldn't they? This was a place of echoes, was it not? At one time its walls had echoed to the sound of voices giving praise, the sound of singing, the laughter of children. Not any longer. Now it was just an empty husk. A memorial to a once-great creed. Stuck in the past, always in the past.

The Reverend Jeremiah 'Jerry' Young arranged the hymn books on the benches, their covers battered, tattered, and on the whole generally the worse for wear. Their pages yellowed and creased, some even missing in action: torn out by those vandals who'd ransacked the church on numerous occasions. It made his heart bleed to think of them in here, those thugs. The police still hadn't caught anyone and he was positive it was the same gang every time. They'd robbed from the charity boxes, stolen silver candleholders and the like. Daubed obscenities on the walls, the language disgusting. He worried about their immortal souls, he really did.

But that was the way of the world today. And it was why no one would be coming to his service tonight the ones he held every night between Christmas and New Year, and had done for the last five years. The place would be empty, just like last night and the night before. There hadn't even been that many worshippers over Christmas itself; Jesus' birthday, for goodness sake! Now that the celebration was commercialised, people had forgotten the real reason for it in the first place. Just like the yobs who'd broken in here, the population of Norchester had not a religious bone in their bodies. No respect for the House of God, which – they thought – was only for baptisms and weddings anyway, wasn't it? And that just about summed up most folk's attitudes in the modern world. Why, only the other week he'd been watching a discussion programme and someone had said that in the future there would be no such thing as religion. His 'job' his *calling* would no longer be needed. No religion, no churches, no men of the cloth. That was the way it would be if the young people of today carried on along the path they were traversing.

"You have said terrible things about me," says the LORD. "But you ask, 'What have we said about you?'…You have said, 'It is useless to serve God. What is the use of doing what he says or of trying to show the LORD Almighty that we are sorry for what we have done? As we see it, proud people are the ones who are happy. Evil men not only prosper, but they test God's patience with their evil deeds and get away with it.'"

It was from the Book of Malachi, but as apt today as it was back then as most parts of the Bible tended to be. Evil men *were* prospering in this new age of marvels, and seemingly going unpunished. While those who did the Lord's work were struck down with disease or went hungry or… You only had to look at that incident a few years ago where a church roof had collapsed on a congregation, killing them all. It was like a sick practical joke.

An act of God.

What with all the famine, the poverty, homelessness

and killings going on all around the globe…and here in this very city! There was little wonder people were turning their backs on The Lord. Doubting whether He even existed. It made Jerry wonder sometimes what kind of Divine Being would let such things happen, and if he didn't have his own deep-rooted faith the answer might well be very different to the one he often gave himself.

And yet, wasn't that faith simply an extension of his own father's beliefs? A vicar himself, Frederick Young had preached to his boys at every opportunity, using them as guinea pigs for his sermons each and every week   his wife dutifully playing hymns on the organ in the other room. It used to drive Jerry's brother, Luke, up the wall.

But while Luke rebelled against religion *because* of his father's teachings, Jerry embraced the Christian way of life for much the same reason. Immersing himself in the scriptures, always finding something new, something *different* in them. It delighted him when his father developed a relevant interpretation of a parable, made him want to study them himself, come up with fresh takes on them and share this with others. Luke was forced to attend church every Sunday until he was old enough to refuse, but Jerry went willingly to Sunday School, to services. Much of his childhood was spent in preparation for the vocation he was now lucky enough to find himself in. There was never any doubt in his mind that he'd follow his father into the church.

So he'd studied hard and became a vicar. The happiest day of his and his father's life had been when he received his first posting, to a small country village with a friendly community. He'd felt like he could take on the Devil and all his armies that day. Luke, of course, went his own way. Off to art college, then abroad to make a name for himself in the world of modern sculpture. Didn't fare too badly, either, if his letters were to be believed…although some of his work Jerry found most distasteful. The separation had been difficult, after all those years together, but it was what Luke wanted and in the end Jerry knew his brother had to follow his own calling. He'd last spoken to him on Christmas day, when Luke promised to come back for a visit soon.

Jerry had served as vicar in two different parishes since then, before finally returning to the city of his birth, and the church his father used to preach in   actually taking over when the great man started to go downhill. The dementia was so severe now, he couldn't even remember his own name let alone Jerry's. Another sick joke? In that time Jerry had noticed the changes, the dwindling congregations, the lack of funds, the total absence of regard for his profession. Sometimes, God forgive him, he even thought it was better that his father *didn't* know what was happening to his beloved church.

Jerry remembered the services when he was growing up, where you couldn't find a seat in this place, it was so packed. And Christmases? Well, they were magical, magical times. Now all that seemed so very long ago. Not twenty odd years, but twenty thousand, twenty million.

Jerry finished spacing out the hymn books on that particular row, then moved swiftly on to the next. Could you blame people for losing their perspective? Probably not. But it was terrifying nonetheless.

To think that the time of angels was now long gone.

Landmarks. That's what he was looking for, any distinctive buildings…

Or street names. *Come on, come on! Give me something to work with here…*

Jack had tuned back in to the signal. Now it was coming through loud and clear. This was it, he knew it was. His big, possibly his only, chance.

Twinkle had emerged and was on the move again. Jack saw what *He* saw, could feel his movements just as before silently gliding along, sticking to the shadows. This was no replay. *He* was out there tonight, a hunter searching for quarry.

Jack's brain felt like it was about to overload at any minute. What a time to have a hangover. Not so much the morning after, as the evening after the night before.

You idiot!

All along he'd known it in his heart. Twinkle wasn't dead, how could he be? Jack would have been aware of it, would have felt his passing. Maybe even travelled with him into nothingness. The final journey. He should have realised it the second he set eyes on Craine.

Forget about that, pay attention. You have to go with him, now. Maybe he'll look up, maybe…

A fleeting glance, that was all. But Jack saw it, a street name. Was James showing him this? Did it matter? What did the sign say? Cram…Crom…Crompton Road. Splitting his mind in two, Jack continued to run with the beast, but at the same time he snapped on the overhead light Jesus, did that hurt his eyes! and fumbled around in his coat for his *A-Z*. He focused so hard he thought his eyes would jump out of their sockets.

Just like the one in Twinkle's palm, like the one—

The index informed him where to look. Not too far away from his hotel. But not close, by any means.

When he bent to put on his boots, Jack nearly blacked out.

Stay with us. Stay with us, Jack. His own voice or someone else's? The same but different.

Jack pulled on his boots, tying them as best he could. Then he grappled with his coat, thankful that he'd fallen asleep in the rest of his clothes yesterday, and grabbed his keys. Swaying slightly, he made it to the door. Outside, he saw first a street, then a corridor. He tottered down them both, heading for what he hoped was the lift.

Jack's hand hovered over the call button. He extended a finger and poked it hard.

Sure enough, the doors opened and Albert was there as always. He seemed surprised to see Jack.

"Jack. Er…ground floor?" he asked as the guest ambled in. Jack gave a half-hearted tip of his head.

The cage dropped, leaving Jack's stomach behind on the level above. He shook, his head bobbing from side to side, still partly engrossed in the hunt…

"You don't look so good tonight, son." Albert knew all about the drinking session Jack had participated in the day before. But even if he hadn't, the stink of booze gave this man away. Miriam had told Albert she'd found him spark out this morning, the drinks cabinet raided. And he looked like he'd only just got up, in no fit state to be going anywhere. "Jack?"

Jack mumbled something he didn't quite catch.

"Jack, I really don't think you should be going out tonight."

"Going for…a little drive…Albert."

Drive? He'll kill himself. Either that, or the police'll pull him over…

"You're in no condition to—"

"Crompton Road…"

Crompton Road? It wasn't *that* far away. If Jack really needed to get there, he should think about walking. The night air might do him some good. Besides, what the heck was so important in Crompton Road? Nothing as far as Albert knew.

"Have to…get to Crompton Road, now…"

The lift came to a juddering halt and Albert opened the doors. Jack still looked determined to drive there; the key in his hand already. "What about a taxi—"

"No time! Don't you understand?" snapped Jack, frustration and anger was creeping into his voice. He hauled himself out of the lift, his eyes glazed over, and he began walking towards reception and the outer doors.

Albert shook his head, then stepped out of the lift as well. He'd been doing this job for more years than he cared to remember had only kept his job because he was part of the fixtures and fittings…that and the fact he was so cheap but for half an hour the guests here at *The Imperial* could find their own blessed way up to their rooms. If they weren't clever enough to figure out a lift, there was always the option of the stairs. Albert trotted after Jack. He wasn't very fast on his feet these days, but then neither was Jack tonight.

He took the keys from Jack's hand. The man barely seemed to notice.

"Crompton Road, you say?" Albert confirmed. "Don't worry, son. I'll have you there in a flash."

He moves swiftly.

Though his bulk is large, he treads the streets like a ballet dancer, barely touching the concrete at all. The 'tools' on *His* belt make no sound, cushioned as *He* runs almost flying, in fact through the night.

He becomes the darkness.

He's tried to resist as long as possible, but only needed another one…

Then nothing will be able to stop *Him*.

His time is at hand.

His is the way forward.

Albert was rusty, there was no doubt about that. He had no need, no desire to drive and hadn't done so in ages; he virtually lived at *The Imperial*. But he still had his license, a spotlessly clean one to boot, his eyesight was still keen   if he wore his spectacles   and he knew the city like he knew the lines on his face. Both maps were imprinted on his mind. He reckoned he could make it to Crompton Road without causing any major accidents.

Jack led him to the red Mondeo. The crook lock was on, but through trial and error Albert worked out which key fitted in the slot. The night air did seem to rouse Jack considerably, but he still appeared to be somewhere else. Daydreaming for want of a better description.

Albert placed the lock on the back seat and got in, Jack slumping down beside him in the passenger position. The dashboard looked like something out of an old Buck Rogers serial to Albert, but there was a steering wheel, three pedals, a handbrake, and a gear stick. That was good enough for him. He took his glasses out of his pocket, put them on, made sure the car wasn't in gear, then started her up.

"Lights," he muttered to himself, and messed about with the tip of the indicator stick until the headlights came on. "Right then, off we go."

The Mondeo lurched out of its parking space, kangarooing up to the gate.

"I'm sorry. Not used to the car," he explained apologetically. *Not used to* cars, *full stop!* But by the time they got out onto the road, the Mondeo was motoring quite smoothly. Albert drove her to the next junction, then turned left. "Crompton Road here we come."

CHAPTER THIRTY-FIVE

Wait till he told Miriam about this.

Maybe he could even think about a part-time job as a chauffeur? Nah, *The Imperial* was his life, the lift like his personal cocoon, somewhere he went to escape from the outside world. Yet here he was venturing out into it again.

You're only doing this as a favour, Albert reminded himself. *Don't go getting carried away.*

So far the traffic he'd encountered had been minimal, mainly because he was sticking to the backroads. Albert doubted very much whether he could cope out there in the middle of the city, what with all that congestion and road rage. Knowing his luck, he'd get clobbered by some gorilla with a short fuse.

Just get Jack Foley to Crompton Road and—

Then what? Drop him off and hope he could find his way back on his own? Return the Mondeo to the hotel car park, and go back to the lift? On his way out, Albert had asked Ralph to cover for him, but he really should get back as soon as possible. Or would Jack expect him to wait? It all depended on what he was going to do when he got there, didn't it? Albert was afraid to ask.

Perhaps he should just find out how long they were likely to be, to put his mind at rest. Albert looked across at the owner of the vehicle. Jack was in pain, breathing heavily through his nose, eyes on the road ahead.

Ask him when we get there. Yes, I'll do that instead.

He looks at the front.

It's an intricate building, *old* and intricate, with spirals reaching up towards the heavens. And it is illuminated by several streetlamps, the notice board itself possessing a small tubular light above it. The poster pinned to the flat piece of wood reads: JESUS SAVES.

But the words mean nothing to *Him.* The building is simply a building. All that is going through *His* mind is the light, and how *He'd* better go round to the back. Enter through the small car park, the dark, secluded car park: it wouldn't be the first time.

So *He* goes, smartly and silently.

Eager to be finished and yet wanting this to last forever.

Jack clutched at the side of the door.

"Church," he gasped. "Church… Where's the nearest church to Crompton Road?"

Albert frowned. Now Jack wanted to go to church? First booze, then repentance. "What kind of church? Catholic, Methodist, C of E?"

"Doesn't matter. The nearest one…"

"That'd be St Christopher's."

"Take me there." Jack looked across, pleading with Albert.

"All right, whatever you want."

"And hurry, please. For God's sake hurry."

Jerry Young heard a noise. Only faint, but the church amplified it a thousand-fold.

At first he thought it might be someone trying to get in at the front. He'd been too hasty in his condemnation of this city after all. There *were* some people who still wanted to—

But then he realised the church had also distorted the sound when it increased its volume, bent and contorted it until it appeared to be coming from behind him. When in fact it was coming from ahead, past the altar and inside the vestry.

The only way in through there now was via a medium-sized window, the old wooden door having warped and jammed with age. It was how the vandals always got inside, no matter how many times the window was fixed. Jerry paused, hymn book in hand.

They'd returned, no doubt hoping the Christmas 'rush' had bolstered the coffers little realising there was a service supposed to start in half an hour's time.

What should he do?

Tackle them directly, go back there and demand an explanation. Not that talking would do any good. And he was a pacifist. Even if there turned out to be only one or two thugs and not a gangful he'd still probably end up with his face punched in. That would be the ultimate irony, surely. A better joke than his father's illness, than those people who'd died when the roof collapsed.

Maybe it was nothing, old buildings did make strange noises sometimes. St Christopher's had been known to creak and groan on the odd occasion, and the heaters *were* on full blast tonight.

That was no ordinary creak or groan and you know it!

Jerry contemplated calling the police, but the only phone was…was in the vestry. He could always slip out and run back to the vicarage. But by the time he'd rung the police and returned, the damage would probably be done.

No, Jerry made up his mind. He put down the hymn book he was holding, and put his faith in the Lord. One foot in front of the other, he headed in the direction of the vestry.

"We're here," said Albert.

"Can you take me round the back?" Jack was waking up as if from another deep sleep.

"I-I should think so."

"All right, then. But kill the lights."

Albert looked puzzled, but Jack made no effort to explain. The old man did as he was told.

Right, you're here, thought Jack. *Now what?* He realised he had absolutely no idea what to do. He'd been in such a hurry to get to Twinkle, to catch up with him, finally, that he'd given no thought as to how he could possibly stop him. His head was still pounding, which didn't help matters, and his hands were shaking.

Jack reached under the seat for his flashlight. *That* he would need. It was pitch-black at the back of St Christopher's. Twinkle was attempting to gain entry right now, even as the Mondeo pulled up: Jack knew exactly where to find him.

"Pull over here on the road, please," said Jack. "And whatever happens, stay in the car." Jack reached up and flipped off the car door light. Then he opened the door.

He sees the door opening.

The door connecting the vestry to the inside of the church.

Someone is lingering in that doorway and calls out: "W-Who's there? T-The police are on their way, you know."

No they aren't. The police don't have a clue what's going on. *He* pulls back from the window, keeping out of sight. *He* has to time this to perfection.

Closer. Come closer.

He can see the vicar's dog collar shining brightly in the darkness. The man was feeling around for the light switch. *No you don't.*

On his haunches, he gets ready to spring in through the vestry window.

Now, do it NOW!

Jack swung the crook lock like a club.

It connected with the back of Twinkle's head, making a firm, but faintly moist noise   like a tenderiser striking a hunk of meat. There was a grunt. Not the yelp Jack had been expecting to hear, but a definite grunt.

The dark figure spun around.

It towered above Jack; he could barely see where the edges of it stopped and the night began. Jack brought the heavy metal lock up again. It pounded Twinkle across where his shoulder should have been, the blow knocking Jack backwards rather than his opponent.

Another swing, but Jack aimed low this time. It glanced off a rock-solid leg. He felt like a woodsman trying to fell a mighty oak with the tiniest of axes. Then the lock was snatched out of Jack's hands. He heard the clanking sound it made as Twinkle flung it aside.

Jack tried to edge away. But before he could shift, something flat and hard hit him squarely in the chest: the palm of Twinkle's hand. He was knocked off his feet and flew back several metres. Jack landed hard on the concrete floor, air bursting out of his lungs, his body crying out in pain.

The night descended upon him.

He rolled over as Twinkle lunged at him, frantically

trying to get his hand into his coat pocket.

Annoyed at missing Jack, Twinkle rose and tried again.

"Who *are* you?" Jack shouted at the fiend: he got no answer. Twinkle was almost on top of him now, he had to act quickly…

Jack finally tore the torch from his pocket and hit the button. The powerful beam bit deep into Twinkle's face. No, wait…there were four eyes blinking, not two…a pair of noses…

The torch was kicked out of Jack's hand, but it didn't go off. Instead it picked out Twinkle reeling backwards, temporarily blinded. There was the sound of a car engine, Albert driving into the car park.

He accidentally clipped Twinkle, spinning the killer around. The mighty form dropped sideways out of sight. Jack rose, snatched up his torch, and staggered towards the car.

Someone was calling after them from the vestry window; Twinkle's intended victim?

Jack hobbled around the side of his Mondeo, searching for Twinkle, the flashlight passing over barren concrete. He shone it in every direction, but saw nothing. He tried to bring an image to mind, to discover where his enemy might be hiding. It did no good: the link was broken again. His opportunity wasted. Jack slammed the top of the car with his fist.

"Jack?" said Albert, the driver's window descending he hadn't gone against instructions, he *was* still in the car. "I thought I just hit something. Jack? Are you all right?"

Panting, Jack hung his head.

In the vestry, the reverend Jeremiah Young was trying to make sense of what he'd just seen…or thought he'd seen. Something had happened here tonight. He'd felt death's presence, his time almost up. Only to have his execution stayed at the last second.

And to Jerry, the man out there standing next to the car, lit up by the wash of a torch, looked very much like an angel sent down from heaven above.

CHAPTER THIRTY-SIX

Jack had asked Albert to drive him back to the hotel. That was all.

He didn't stop to talk with the vicar at St Christopher's. He didn't say anything else to the lift operator, even though he knew the old man was full of questions. Jack just asked him to drive them 'home'.

Home, sweet home. That's how Rosy Lim had described it after dropping him there. For Albert, and now Jack, that's what it was. What it had become. On the way, Jack had gobbled a couple of aspirin from the glove compartment to fight back his headache.

Albert parked the car again and locked it, then they headed inside. Ralph gave the pair a funny look as they passed through reception, Jack especially with his coat ripped at the back and his hair a mess. Albert gave Jack a ride back up to his floor, then said goodnight as if nothing had even happened   as if Jack had just returned from having a drink down in the bar or something. And Jack appreciated that. He was in no mood for talking.

When he got to his room, he noticed the door was ajar. *That's how you left it, you stupid prat!* Of course. He'd been in such a rush to go out and save the world (pah, that was a joke) he'd wandered off and left his hotel door open. Thank goodness he had his wallet with him. Jack patted his pocket. There was nothing there. Had he dropped it in the fight?

No, he'd taken it out of his pocket the other day, Christmas Day in fact, to look at the photograph the photograph of himself and James and he hadn't put it back. That meant it was still on the bedside table and his door was unlocked…

Jack lumbered into the room, closing the door behind him and praying his wallet was still there.

He'd forgotten to switch off the overhead light as well; with a bit of luck anybody passing would have thought he was still in his room. He went past the bathroom, turned the corner and—

Almost jumped out of his skin.

Sitting in the chair next to the bed was Detective Sergeant Deborah Harrison.

"Jesus!" said Jack. "You almost gave me a heart attack."

"Jack," acknowledged Deborah. She was wearing a long anthracite trench coat, which was pulled around her in spite of the central heating, and her bag was on the floor reared up against a chair leg. Her hands were in her lap, holding Jack's wallet. It was open, exposing the picture of Jack and James. "You know, you're lucky I was the one to come up here and find this."

"What are you doing here?"

"I seem to recall asking you that same question once. Never did get a satisfactory answer." Deborah rested her chin on one hand. "I dropped in on my way from the station. The desk clerk said you were out and when I showed him my ID he told me I could wait up here until you got back. Actually, I kind of insisted. Never imagined the room would already be open, though. What was the big panic?"

"No panic," said Jack, closing the door. "I didn't notice your car outside."

"Didn't you? It's out there somewhere, the man downstairs—"

"Ralph."

"Ralph. He had it parked for me."

"Great. He probably thinks I'm in trouble with the law now. So why *did* you come here tonight?"

"I-I'm not sure. I think I came to talk."

"I've been trying to get in touch with you."

"I got your messages but… I didn't know whether I wanted to speak to you again, after…"

Jack closed his eyes, then slowly opened them again. 'I know, I'm sorry. Did I get you into much trouble?'

"It was touch and go there for a while. And I'm still not sure where I stand with Mason."

And all that for nothing, thought Jack. "I don't know what else to say."

"What happened to you, anyway? You look dreadful."

"Thanks. You're the second person to tell me this evening, and that was *before* I went out."

Deborah stood up, placing the wallet back on the bedside table. "Are you going to fill me in?"

"Are you sure you want to hear about it?" Deborah raised an eyebrow. "You're not going to like it."

"Now you *have* to tell me."

Jack took a deep breath. "I saved someone's life tonight."

"You did what?"

"A vicar at…St Christopher's, I think the name was."

"What were you doing in church?"

"I wasn't exactly *in* church, I was round the back. Trying to stop Twinkle from—"

Deborah cut him off. "Hold it, did you just say what I think you said?"

"It was James, he showed me the—"

"Jack, Twinkle's dead. He committed suicide in the cells at Yardley Street. It was in the papers, you can't have missed it."

"That was…someone else. Not *Him*."

"No, Jack. Anton Craine *was* Twinkle. You saw him in the interview room, remember? I showed him to you, though God knows why."

"*He* was going to kill him," Jack insisted…

Deborah tilted her head.

She'd always known Jack was a little…peculiar, but this was beyond the pale. It had been a mistake to come here, she'd known it even as she was parking the car, as she was entering the hotel – but had done it anyway. And now this? Was he so obsessed with his brother's killer that he'd pretend the man was still alive just so he could go on pursuing him? So he could have a purpose to his life? Or was guilt driving him because they hadn't been speaking when he—

As she walked towards him, drawn again in spite of herself, Deborah detected the faintest whiff of alcohol. "Jack, have you been drinking?"

"It's funny you should mention that."

"Look at me, Jack," she said, gripping his forearms. "It's over. Twinkle's dead."

"No, Craine might be dead, but… *He*'s still out there."

"You have to let it go. This isn't doing you any good."

Jack pushed himself away from her. "I know what I

saw. I know what I *felt*. If you don't believe me, ask Albert out there in the lift. He damn near ran Twinkle over. Or go and ask the vicar at St Christopher's." Jack turned, and it was only now that she saw the state of his coat.

"My God!" Deborah placed a hand on his back and he flinched. "You're hurt."

He laughed. "Look, thanks for stopping by and everything, but I think you ought to just go."

"It's obvious *something's* happened tonight. You were attacked. This needs reporting."

"I'm tired and I ache all over, so if you wouldn't mind…"

"I'm not going anywhere until we get this straightened out," she told him.

"Fine, then *I* will." Jack stormed off towards the bathroom, slamming the door behind him. Deborah sighed and sat down on the edge of the bed. She waited several minutes for Jack to come out, but it began to look less and less likely that he would.

"Right," she said to herself. "I've had enough of this." Deborah went to the bathroom and, without knocking, tried the door.

"Jack, we have to sort this—"

The door was unlocked and flew open in her hand. Jack was standing at the sink. His coat, shirt, and jumper were in a heap on the floor. She could see the red marks dotted here and there on his back, burns bordering on cuts. He had a wet flannel in his hand and was attempting to dab them. When he turned in her direction, she was also graced with a view of his chest. A purplish bruise was flowering there.

"Oh my God," repeated Deborah. "Who did this to you?"

Jack dropped the flannel in the sink and leaned against its edge. "I told you already, but you didn't believe me, *remember?*"

Deborah came further into the bathroom. She reached out a hand, then withdrew it instantly. She bit her lip, eyes rambling over the welts on his back. Deborah undid her coat and shrugged it off, then folded it over the side of the bath. Next she removed her charcoal jacket, before rolling up the sleeves of her white polo-neck jumper.

"Here," she said. "Let me…"

Suddenly, she was at the side of him; so close Jack could smell her perfume. Her hand dipped into the sink, squeezing the flannel to get rid of the excess water. "Don't worry, I've had plenty of practice at this sort of thing with Isabel," she said. But when the rough edge of the flannel touched his skin, Jack went rigid. "Sorry."

"It seems like we're forever apologising to each other," Jack said.

"Yeah."

Deborah dabbed at the sore patches, now and again washing out the flannel. Jack forgot all about the pain; the gentle motion of her patting felt wonderful. He groaned with relief.

"Do you have any antiseptic? Any plasters?' asked Deborah.

Jack wagged a finger towards his overnight bag. "In there."

Deborah dug out the small first aid kit inside containing a bottle of antiseptic, a bag of cotton wool balls, and some decent sized plasters. "Think of everything, don't you?"

"Most things." But not this, he never would have imagined this…

Now Deborah daubed on the antiseptic, blowing each sore to dry it. Then she stuck plasters over the worst of the burns. She told him to turn around so she could examine the bruise on his front. The flesh there was discoloured, but still as smooth and soft as the rest of his chest. As she applied more antiseptic, she looked into his eyes: those same grey-green eyes she'd seen on Fagin's Row, by the canal, outside George Lovesy's home, at the station...

Why *had* she let him see Craine that day? It was a question she'd asked herself a million times since it happened. She couldn't blame Jack entirely, she was a police officer, it was her duty to—

But where Jack was concerned, duty had a way of getting trampled underfoot, didn't it?

And why had she *really* driven here tonight? Not just to make sure he was okay. She'd denied it to Mason, to Rosy, even to herself. But being in this room, so close to him—

Deborah stopped dabbing his chest. She broke eye contact and started pulling away. "Maybe I *had* better go."

Jack barred her exit. "No, please..." His hand was on her shoulder; it was shaking. She felt the tiny vibrations travelling down through her body. "Debbie, I—"

She placed a finger on his lips. The next thing she knew, she'd brought her own mouth up to touch them. The kiss was tender and sweet. There was no urgency to it, only inevitability.

Deborah realised she'd been wondering what this would feel like since the moment she met him, even down that dead end road she'd known he wasn't a killer.

Had he felt the same way, or was this just another dead end?

They stayed like that for some time, not daring to even

hold each other. Then the kiss ended naturally. Jack inched his head back, a little dazed, and more than a little confused.

"Where did that come from?" he whispered.

"I don't know. But I'm not sorry this time. Are you?"

Jack shook his head. They kissed again. It was like they were suddenly under a spell, filling up each other's senses. The only two people on Earth. Now their hands did explore, fingertips meeting foreign objects skin connecting with skin in her case; with the wool of her polo-neck in his. Jack lifted his hands up and held her shoulder-blades, drawing her even closer.

When they parted a second time, Deborah smiled. Saying nothing, she took his hand and walked out into the hotel room. Jack obediently followed. She was only halfway inside the room when she felt him straining at her grasp. "I-I'm not sure this is such a good idea."

"Me either." She tugged on his hand, and he gave in to her.

"It's been… What I mean is, I haven't, you know…for a long time."

Deborah reached round and clutched the back of his neck. "Me either," she repeated into his ear. "But they say it's like riding a bicycle…"

It was Jack who smiled now, albeit nervously. "Not quite," he replied. What was happening to him? Drinking, brawling, women… One woman, he reminded himself, a very special woman. But that was James, not him. This wasn't him. He wasn't the confident one.

Stop trying to analyse everything. Go with the flow…

Easy to say, not so easy to do.

And after everything else that had happened tonight… Pain and pleasure, pleasure and pain indistinguishable, inseparable.

Somehow Deborah had manoeuvred him around to the bed. Now he was sitting down on its edge while she undid his boots, slipping them off with his socks. Then, holding on to his shoulder for support, Deborah removed her own ankle-length boots. The well-heeled footwear gone, she lost a couple of centimetres in height; barely noticeable if Jack hadn't been watching so intently…

Deborah stepped back, untucking the jumper. Then she shoved an elbow into the bottom corner for leverage, and hoisted it up. It was an effort to force the polo-neck back over her head, just as it had been to put it on that morning, but Deborah eventually triumphed.

Next she undid the button on the front of her charcoal trousers, immaculately creased from waist to foot. She brought down the zip with a flourish and the trousers fell to the carpet. As with her other clothes, Deborah neatly folded these and placed them on the chair, more to delay the inevitability of what was to come than anything.

Standing there in her cream-coloured bra and briefs, she waited for him to undress. To meet her in the middle…

As he'd confessed, it had been a long time since Jack had found himself in such a situation, and he'd never felt especially comfortable even then. He was no Romeo or gigolo. Not even close.

But at that moment his body was crying out for Deborah. So much so that to deny it would have led to madness. Jack stood and mirrored her actions, undoing his belt, releasing the clasp on his trousers, revealing navy boxers beneath. He hopped out of the trousers, not bothering to pick them up…

They came together like magnet and metal, unable to resist the attraction.

A third kiss, held for so much longer this time, culminated in a sideways shuffle towards the bed. One eye on what she was doing, the other on Jack, Deborah pulled back the sheets. She climbed in, Jack seconds behind her. Now she kissed his body, his shoulders, his chest, his stomach; eyes swivelling upwards in their sockets – studying his reaction.

Jack offered her the same, carefully easing down one strap of her bra to press his lips against her flesh. The sensation was incredible, and he wanted more. Somewhere along the line, undergarments were discarded.

Jack vaguely remembered Deborah reaching round to unhook her bra, hitching up in the bed to yank off her briefs, but the actual procedure seemed to have been performed as if by magic. And the same was true of his boxers. One minute he was wearing them, the next they were gone. Naked and free, they both continued their investigations. With fingertips, with mouths, with tongues.

Deborah guided Jack's hand downwards. He kissed her throat as she bucked beneath him. They were both charged. Alive with electricity, desperate to release it for fear they might spontaneously combust. With her it was all so easy, like he'd known her for centuries. With each kiss, with each stroke of the hand, his hang-ups, his reluctance faded away. And so did Deborah's.

When they finally embraced again, it was like nothing he'd ever experienced before. No. He *had* experienced this closeness, the feeling of two people melting into one, before. But only once. It was a trace sensation rather than a memory, of being two people in the same body. Sharing a womb.

Deborah felt it too, through Jack. She'd told herself she couldn't really understand because she wasn't a twin. But she understood at least some of that intimacy now…it was something she'd never once shared with Phil. That affinity. She and Jack were bonded, and it felt like nothing in the world could ever tear them apart.

The connection, as they gazed into each other's eyes, was nothing short of a phenomenon. They moved together like a single entity, beyond moans and sighs. Beyond sweat and gasps. Pleasuring, tasting, but above all simply basking in this thing they'd discovered. They never wanted it to end, and for a long time it looked like it never would: both figures trapped in the moment. Pressed together so tight it was hard to differentiate between them.

But end it did, with an explosion of pure joy – and mixed in with it, pure sadness. They both felt the loss afterwards, but cradled each other, trying to get it back. Knowing that lying in each other's arms wasn't enough.

That it would never be enough.

Deborah used her mobile to call home, telling her mother not to wait up.

Isabel was at a friend's house, she explained, and her mum was used to her not arriving back until late…if at all. For a while they talked, about Isabel, about Isabel's father. Deborah told Jack things she'd never told anyone else before. What was the point of secrets when they already knew each other inside out?

Then they talked about Jack's family. About how his parents had both died in a plane crash when he and James were fourteen.

"Dad was an astronomer, an Advanced Research Fellow in Theoretical Cosmology to be precise though it was really more of a hobby for him: a passion that he was paid for. Our family had plenty of money anyway, you see, on Mum's side. Her parents, my grandparents, were something to do with mining abroad. I've never really bothered to find out the details. Isn't that strange? I've spent the whole of my life digging into other people's pasts and yet I know hardly anything about my own." Jack sucked in a tiny breath before continuing. "When they died, it all came to us. It paid for us to be looked after, paid for our education, but neither of us would touch a penny after we left university. When James... Well, let's just say I'm the last remaining Foley and it all came to me. And though I've wished to God many times it hadn't, the money *has* helped finance my little...journeys."

After this, the conversation moved on, to Jack and James, James and Jack, with Deborah commenting about the similarity between them in the photograph.

"You said once that you weren't friends towards the end, that you had a falling out. What came between you?"

Jack stroked her arm. "It seems wrong to talk about it here, somehow. But it was over a woman."

"*Really*? I'm jealous."

"No need. It was a long, long time ago."

"Was she...was she the one you meant before? You know, 'It's been a long time?'"

Jack nodded. "Stephanie. There's been no one since her. She messed us both up pretty bad."

"She was going out with *both* of you at the same time?"

"We didn't have a clue until it was way too late, of course. James was always a bit of a ladies' man: the slick one. I thought she was just another one of his conquests. But she meant more to him than that."

"And she meant more to you than that, too, obviously."

"Yes. I was in love with her." He said this as a statement

of fact, nothing more. "What I didn't realise was that she simply wanted to make it with a pair of identical twins. I don't know, maybe she was scoring us both or something. I wouldn't have rated very highly against James, I'm afraid."

"Oh, I don't know," said Deborah, softly patting his stomach.

"Anyway, it all came out in the wash one day, and ever since then…Well, you can imagine. With James, it seemed to make him even worse. It was as if he was determined to punish every girl he ever met because of what Stephanie had done."

"With you it had the opposite effect?"

"You could say that. I swore I'd never let another woman get to me like that again. What did I know?"

It didn't take Deborah long to steer the discussion back round to Jack's adventures earlier, though, and this time he told her the entire story beginning with the part where he got drunk because she wouldn't answer his calls. "Don't worry, I don't make a habit of it," Jack said, remembering Deborah's horror stories about her husband. "In fact I hardly ever drink at all. Guess I just wanted to erase the last few weeks."

"You know," said Deborah once he'd finished, "I've been thinking. It could have been someone working with Craine who attacked you."

"What, you mean like a partner? Then how would I have known where to find him? And besides, look what he did to me. I hit him three times with a car-lock, he barely felt it."

"Could've been drugs. They say you don't feel pain on some of the harder ones until you come down."

"I suppose. But you saw what happened to the snooker cue at George Lovesy's house."

Whoever did this was strong, Rosy had said. Craine had

the build, but…

"And this guy blinked with four eyes, Debbie. I saw it."

"Jack, that could have been anything. You said yourself it all happened really quickly. And you were in a bit of a state."

"We're not dealing with any ordinary murderer here, I'm certain of that. I've often wondered if he was some sort of… Well, twins sharing the same body?"

"A freak of nature you mean?"

"I don't know… It would explain a few things. Ever heard of vanishing twin syndrome?"

Deborah shook her head; it hadn't cropped up in her research.

"Where one or more embryos appear to be developing, then the 'twin' just disappears. Then there's the parasitic twin, where a baby can be born with genetic material from a twin that didn't develop attached to it."

"Christ, sounds like something out of a bad horror movie…" Deborah was silent for a moment or two, then suddenly lifted her head. "I've just remembered something, another theory. It kind of relates to what I was thinking before when Craine was caught."

"I'm listening," said Jack.

"Well, I wondered if maybe he'd had a twin who'd died and he was trying to offer sacrifices or perhaps killing twins as a revenge thing."

Jack frowned. "All right."

"It was just an idea… But listen, what if Craine *did* have a twin, and what if he were still alive? What if that's who attacked you tonight? He might have been the original killer…or, or maybe both of them working together?"

"That could explain why I didn't get any vibes from Craine…" Jack shook his head. "However you look at it, the killer is still out there. And he's not going to stop until he's finished whatever it is he's doing."

"I don't think Mason will go for it."

"Forget Mason. Are *you* with me?"

Deborah thought for a minute. Jack would know if she were lying, would be able to see it in her eyes. Just like Mason when he'd questioned her loyalty that day in the interview room. "Yes, Jack. I'm with you."

He relaxed, and she rested her head on his chest.

"Then I'm not on my own anymore," said Jack.

"No. You'll…you'll never be on your own again," Deborah replied.

CHAPTER THIRTY-SEVEN

They made love twice more that night, striving to get back the closeness, the oneness.

Then they slept beside each other, exhausted but content.

Jack awoke when his arm instinctively reached out for Deborah and discovered her missing. It was still dark outside, so he turned on the overhead light. The clock at his side informed him it was seven-thirty.

"Debbie," he called out. "Debbie, are you there?"

No answer. And her clothes were gone from the chair.

Jack got up, feeling weak as a kitten. He'd put his body through the wringer in more ways than one over the last forty-eight hours, done more with it in that short space than he had in a lifetime of sitting behind a desk, and now he was feeling the after-effects. Jack took two more aspirin. His back felt better than it had last night, however, thanks to the ministrations of Sergeant Deborah Harrison.

Should have been a nurse, not a policewoman.

Jack pulled on his boxers, which had ended up on the floor near the window, and padded round the corner. He heard the sound of a shower running. So that's where she was. Not a bad idea, really. He could definitely use a wash himself, except he would probably dislodge all those plasters. Jack rubbed his chin and felt the onslaught of bristles. A shave wouldn't go amiss, either, it seemed.

He thought about walking in and surprising her. Wasn't that what lovers were supposed to do? But last night had been almost like a dream. If he hadn't heard the water running, he might well have convinced himself that it *had* been a dream. Just like the dream of the—

Jack paused.

The passages: those long, winding passages, leading… Leading to somewhere. Twinkle's lair. Darkness folding in upon itself and a single light flickering at the other—

The water stopped running. Jack waited for Deborah to come out, which she did a few minutes later, dressed and towelling her hair.

"Good morning, you." She kissed him lightly on the mouth.

"Hmm… A very good morning."

"I thought you were fast asleep."

"I was, but I woke up. Wondered where you'd gone."

"Not far. I'm not the kind of girl to up and leave after… well, after what we did."

"I'm glad to hear it."

Deborah rubbed her damp hair furiously. "Listen, I want you to come to the station with me this morning. Tell someone all about last night."

"What, everything?"

"You know what I mean."

"You think it'll do any good? You're the only person who believes me about…Twinkle – God, that name! – and you took quite a lot of persuading."

"Point taken," Deborah said. "But you *were* attacked. It

doesn't matter who did it."

"Strictly speaking, I was the one doing the attacking."

"With good reason by the sound of it. If the killer is still…" She paused, rephrasing what she was about to say. "The killer *is* still out there, Jack. We need to do something before he comes out to play again, and I don't mean waiting for you to have another one of your…whatever they are, and then go haring off after him."

"I don't see what else we can do."

"I mean it, Jack. Even if I have to place you under arrest, you're not going near him again. Not now. It's too… What's so funny?"

Jack was grinning to himself. "Nothing. I'm just remembering the first time you arrested me."

A self-conscious smile formed on her lips. "Now, I never technically arrested you. I just wanted you to answer some questions."

"You handcuffed me!"

"And I'll cuff you again if you don't do as you're told."

"Is that a promise?"

"Go on and get ready. I'll wait for you." As Jack turned, she flicked the towel playfully at his legs. But what he didn't see was that after he shut the bathroom door, her expression changed to one of concern. All this was an illusion, wasn't it? A brief respite. It was all starting up again and Jack was stuck slap-bang in the middle. They could never be happy until it was over.

One way or the other.

On the way down, Jack introduced Albert to Deborah. She resisted the urge to question him there and then about last night, but said the police might want to talk to him in due course. He looked scared to death.

"I'm not in trouble, am I?"

"Not at all. In fact I'm glad you were there to help," Deborah told him.

Ralph wasn't on duty that morning unlike Albert, he did tend to leave when his shift was over otherwise Jack would've had to clarify things with him, too, assuring him he wasn't a bank robber or a fugitive from justice.

They took Deborah's car, which was parked right at the very back. The conversation was easygoing, just as it had been last night. When Deborah spoke of Isabel again, Jack told her how he'd like to meet the girl sometime.

"Maybe, one day. When she's ready."

"I'm not talking about adopting her, Debbie," said Jack. "It's just…well, she sounds like a great kid."

"She is. Better than I deserve. I've been very fortunate. Look, I'm sorry, it's—"

"There's that word again, 'sorry'."

"Yeah, sorry. See, I've said it again. The fact is she's going through a bit of a funny phase right now, asking about her dad and stuff. I don't want to confuse her."

"I understand."

Deborah nodded. "I know you do. Thanks." Then she turned and asked: "Did you never think about starting a family, Jack?"

The question took him unawares. "What, with Stephanie you mean?"

"Possibly. You know, if things had been different."

"I don't think she was the maternal kind. But yes, I suppose it did cross my mind."

"I think you'd make a wonderful father."

Jack blushed at the compliment. "Well, for what it's worth I'm sure Isabel thinks you're great too."

As they pulled round behind Yardley Street, Jack

fidgeted in his seat. "What about Mason?" he said eventually.

"He'll have to find out sooner or later. This was…*is* his investigation."

Jack got out of the Peugeot. "But won't I get you into more trouble?"

"It's a free country, last time I checked. Mason can't stop you from reporting a crime. Besides, we have two witnesses."

"I-I may have exaggerated a bit about that. I don't think Albert or the vicar saw that much. It was very dark at the back of the church."

Deborah nodded to him over the roof. "*You* did, that's good enough for me."

It was Jack's third time in the station and once again he got that strange agitated feeling as he walked through the doors. The first time he'd put it down to just being in a police station (for many, the sight of a police car driving behind them was enough to trigger a case of the jitters), the second time he'd been on his way to see his brother's killer…or so he'd believed. Plus he'd just been punched in the stomach.

Evil was here, he could sense it…

So what was causing such dread now, the thought of another confrontation with Mason? No, it was more than that.

Deborah said hello to Sergeant Kilbourne as she led Jack through the entranceway. To their left were the cells, where some of the journos had been taken the last time Jack had been here, and where Anton Craine had taken his own life.

The cells.

Jack stopped abruptly when he saw the bars that cut this part of the station off from the rest. Thick, black bars… Rusted? No, these were clean. Virtually new.

So where were—

He saw rusted, crumbling bars. The railings near the canal? More like ancient prison bars. A dungeon even. Where was he?

"Jack, Jack?" It was Deborah's voice but from very far away.

A long, narrow tunnel, a flickering light. A hand opening, and an eye in its palm.

Evil. Evil is *here!*

Startled, Jack fled from the building. Deborah and Kilbourne watched his departure, the latter with a bemused look on his face.

Not again, thought Deborah. *Oh please Lord, not again!* It was just like the scene in the pub.

She sprinted out through the station doors and into the winter sunshine. Jack was leaning up against a wall, catching his breath. When she put a hand on his shoulder, he twitched.

"Deborah?" He behaved as if he didn't know where he was, let alone how he'd got there.

"Jack, do you want me to fetch someone—"

"Deborah, listen to me," his voice was hardening. "I know where *He* is."

"What? Jack, what're you talking about?"

"Twinkle." He almost spewed the word up this time...

"I think I know how to find him."

CHAPTER THIRTY-EIGHT

He wouldn't – couldn't – tell her. Not until they'd visited the library.

Unfortunately it was closed, the opening time half-past nine. Then Deborah spotted the sign stuck to the window. "Jack, look at this. They're still closed for the holidays."

"Damn."

"Are you going to let me in on what you saw back there?"

Jack pressed his face up against the glass, the place was in darkness.

"Come on, it'll have to wait."

"It *can't* wait, Debbie. I have to get in there."

"What's so important? Where's Twinkle, Jack?"

Jack banged on the glass, then on the door. Nothing.

"There's no one inside."

Jack bowed his head. Deborah was right. It was hopeless. Of all the weeks for this to—

A modest light came on at the back of the library. Jack squinted inside; he saw a figure moving about. He banged again, more urgently. The figure drifted into view and Jack recognised him as the man he almost tripped over last time he was in the library.

The slender chap put on his glasses, which were still hanging from his neck on a chain. His eyebrows shot up several inches when he saw the two visitors at the door. Hurrying across, he punched something into a box on the wall the alarm, Jack assumed and then undid a series of locks with keys attached to his belt on another chain.

At last the glass door was open and he greeted Deborah first.

"Inspector Harrison," he said, shaking her hand. Deborah winced at that, Jack noticed, but didn't correct him about her title. "My word, what are you doing here at this time in the morning? If it's about those books, you're free to keep them as long as you want. There won't be any fines." He spoke only in hushed tones, even though the library was empty.

"No, it's not about the books. It's..." Deborah paused, probably realising she didn't have the first idea why they were there. "It's police business," she said.

"Really?" His eyes lit up. "Well, in that case...please, come on in."

Deborah crossed the threshold and held the door open for Jack. "This is Mr Foley, he's...working with me on this matter."

The man scrutinised Jack. "Foley... Foley? Haven't I seen you somewhere before?"

"Ah...yes. I stopped by here about—"

"No, that's not it. But it'll come to me. I never forget a face, you know."

He locked up again behind them and set the alarm. Then he joined Jack and Deborah at the issues desk.

"I hope we're not disturbing you, Mr..." Deborah frowned, obviously trying to remember a name.

"Hole," he said. "Marvin Hole. That's Hole with a 'H' not a 'W'." Jack could imagine the jokes he'd heard in his time, at school and at work. "And no, you weren't disturbing me, Inspector. I was just doing an inventory of the new stock while the library's shut. It's so much more peaceful when there's nobody around."

So this was the famous Marv... "You don't happen to know Albert from *The Imperial* hotel, by any chance?" asked Jack.

"Works the lift? Certainly do, I've known him for years. Haven't seen him for years either come to think of it. Interesting place, *The Imperial*."

"Well, he speaks very highly of you," Jack said. "Anything we need to know, you're the man to see."

Marvin was delighted. "Is that what he said? Really?"

"And you were so helpful the last time I was here," butted in Deborah.

"Yes, I read that you caught that maniac," whispered Marvin, as if he'd had a personal hand in Craine's capture. "Terrible business. But anyway, how can I assist you both today?"

Deborah looked to Jack for the answer to that question.

"Marvin, do you have anything on local history?"

Marvin smiled. "Follow me."

Norchester's central library did indeed have the largest archives section in the area. Marvin took them down into the records department, explaining that a lot of this information was waiting to be scanned and then transferred onto the library computer network so that anyone could access it. The finished results would probably even end up on the internet as well, available through the library's own website. But it was a tremendous task and there were very few people willing to volunteer for it.

"It's not compulsory, you see," commented Marvin. "Not part of the job description. What they don't realise is it'll make their lives a lot easier once it's all been fed into the hard drive. I do what I can, as a matter of fact I was planning to put in a few hours this afternoon. But there's only one of me."

There certainly is, thought Deborah. *One Marvin Hole in the* whole wide *world.*

Once they were down there, Marvin asked Jack what he was specifically after, and if there was a way of narrowing the search parameters. Local history covered a multitude of sins.

"I'm particularly interested in the history of Yardley Street, the buildings on that street, and especially the police station," Jack clarified.

Happy with this, Marvin tottered off to start gathering the appropriate information.

"What's all this about, Jack?" asked Deborah again, once he'd gone. "You think Twinkle's hiding in one of the buildings on Yardley Street, is that it?"

"Not exactly."

"Then what?"

"I'd rather wait until Marvin comes back."

They didn't have to wait long. Marvin prided himself on his speed and efficiency. He returned with a number of books, some old, some quite new: written by local amateur writers who'd already researched the area, thus saving them the trouble of doing so.

"I've got it!" Marvin exclaimed as he placed the books next to Jack.

"Have you?"

Marvin pointed at him. "It's John Foley, isn't it? The historian?"

"John?" Deborah was puzzled.

"I prefer Jack, personally, but John looks better on the cover of a book so I'm told."

Marvin shook Jack's hand. "I've read a number of your publications in the past. Riveting, absolutely riveting."

"Thank you, Marvin."

"I think you have a fan, Jack," said Deborah.

"You know, I dabble myself a little bit… Nothing in your league, but perhaps sometime you could have a look at a few of my ideas."

"I'd be happy to," Jack told him. "But first…"

"Oh, certainly. Of course, of course!"

The new books had indices, Marv explained, so it was relatively easy to find Yardley Street. Jack got stuck in, while Deborah picked up a couple and strummed noncommittally through them.

"It would help if I knew what we were looking *for*," she said.

"This," said Jack, pointing to a column of text.

It read: *Yardley Street police station   or at least the building that is now used for such purposes   was built between the years of 1945 and 1947, along with those buildings standing on either side of it, as part of a major renovation exercise, once funds became available.*

"So what?"

"Keep reading. Look, this bit here."

During the 1939-1945 conflict, more accurately in the bombing raids of the provinces which took place after the sustained attacks on London, Norchester was one of the northern population centres most heavily bombed. This was in no small part due to its metal-working factories being used to produce weapons for the war effort. In one such night-time attack, the entirety of Yardley Street was levelled, destroying, most notably, the police station   which had served the city for nigh on a hundred years. Fifteen members of Her Majesty's Constabulary were known to have perished in the attack.

Next to the text was a picture of King George VI and Queen Elizabeth with the then Lord Mayor and Lady Mayoress of Norchester on a visit in 1941, inspecting the damage done to Yardley Street the previous year.

"Well, you learn something new every day," griped Deborah. "Jack, I never once thought that Yardley Street nick was the city centre's original police station. All right, I *didn't* know that it had been built on the exact same site as the old one, and I *didn't* know that the old one had been bombed during the Blitz. But what does that prove?"

"Maybe nothing. Maybe everything. Marvin, do you have anything else on the station house itself? That's the original station house, not the one built in 1945."

"We should have," responded the librarian. "Give me a minute, Mr Foley, sir."

"It's Jack, Marvin. Just Jack."

In fact it took Marvin ten minutes to locate the necessary information, but it was well worth the wait. One book in particular about the subject, a tall leather-bound affair, even included detailed plans of the building, taken from original drawings done by the artist Luther Simpson. They were incredibly, intricately, neat, and although it was difficult to make out the old-fashioned handwriting, Jack seemed to find what he was looking for straight away, probably used to studying such documents in his line of work.

"Look, here's the station house," he said.

Deborah brought the book nearer. "It's tiny compared to today. Where did they put the prisoners?"

Jack smiled. "That's just it. The prisoners went below, *underneath* the station house itself. Where the old Norchester dungeons used to be. Two separate parts. I suppose they thought there'd be less chance of them escaping from there. Ah, pay dirt. Here's a layout of the cells."

"Okay," said Deborah slowly.

"So, let's assume that the bomb only took out the top portion of the station house. What do you think the builders would have done in 1945?"

"It's only a guess, but wouldn't they just have… Oh my God." She exchanged glances with Jack.

"Each time I've visited that station, I've had the feeling that something wasn't quite right there. This morning I was certain *He* was around. But somewhere dark, hidden away. And that's not all. I saw rusted bars, the kind you might find in a dungeon or a jail."

"I'm sorry to interrupt," said Marvin. "But who're you talking about?"

They'd both forgotten the brittle-looking man was still with them. "Marvin, could you make us some copies of these?"

"Of course, but—"

"Thanks," said Deborah. She watched him take the book upstairs to the photocopier. "Jack, if this means what I think it means…"

"Then the bastard's been right under your noses all this time."

CHAPTER THIRTY-NINE

Now that they knew, the next question was what were they going to do about it?

Jack still had no idea *how* Twinkle entered or exited the underground cells, the only thing he had to go on being his fragmented recollections and dreams. The most obvious choice was the sewers, of course...the tunnels, the darkness he'd seen.

"It's just so..." began Deborah as they sat in the car outside the library. "I mean, come on. The sewers for Heaven's sake!"

Jack grimaced. "It'd be perfect for him. The melodramatic son of a bitch would get off on it."

"I don't know... Perhaps there's something in one of the nearby buildings?" offered Deborah.

Jack was just about to suggest they do a little scouting around when Deborah's mobile phone went off. It was Mason, wanting to know where she'd got to again.

"Sorry, sir. I'm just at the library."

"We don't pay you to help your daughter with her homework," Jack heard the man say loudly. "There are cases pending on your desk."

"I know, sir. Yep, I'll be there right away."

When she was finished, she turned to Jack. "I don't need to tell you what that was all about."

He shook his head. "You'd better get back, I've held you up for long enough as it is."

"What are you going to do?"

"I'm not sure." Jack tapped the photocopies Marvin had made. "Maybe do a little wandering about near the station."

"No way. Not without me."

"We have to do *something*, Debbie."

"I could try talking to Mason, see what he says."

"I know all too well what he'll say. As far as he's concerned the case is over and done with. He's not going to listen to you, and he's certainly not going to listen to me. The man hates my guts." Jack took her hand. "The only way he'll listen is if we give him something concrete, prove how our guy gets in and out of those cells. If anyone can find that out, it's me."

Not only did he have the historical knowledge, he also had that blasted sixth sense when it came to Twinkle. At first Deborah hadn't believed a word of it, but now...

"Okay," she said reluctantly. "But we're in this together now, remember? Just give me a little time to sort things out at the station, then we'll work out where to go from there."

Jack said nothing.

"Jack?"

He nodded.

"Right," said Deborah, then started up the car.

The drive back to the station was a strange one. Deborah felt as though she wanted to get there, but at the same time couldn't care less if they never arrived. Maybe she should just ignore Mason, or fob him off somehow. She could tell him the car broke down or something. No good, he'd keep ringing her on the mobile; would probably send out a whole fleet of breakdown trucks. She could turn off the phone. But then he'd worry about why he couldn't get through. It was no use, she had to go back and placate her boss.

They finally arrived at the station, and Deborah pulled into the side-street, then the car park. "I won't be long, I promise," she told him as she opened the door. "You wait right here and I'll be back soon…"

Jack nodded again.

"I don't want to use the cuffs, but I will if I have to." Deborah smiled weakly.

"I'll be here."

She leaned across and kissed him softly on the mouth. "You'd better be." Then – although it was the last thing in the world she wanted to do – Deborah was rushing off inside the station…

"Glad you could finally make it," said Mason as she finally entered the office.

"Sorry, sir. Like I said I was—"

"At the library, yes I know." Mason was perched on her desk, right knee raised, one buttock on the woodwork. "Care to tell me why?"

Deborah hung up her coat, doing her level best not to look directly at him. "I…had to see a man about some books. The ones I took out about twins."

"Right, of course," said Mason. "Well, you're here now, so let's get started."

It was the waiting that finally did it.

Jack kept looking at his watch, then across at the station. There was no sign of Deborah. Already it had been half an hour. Mason might keep her in there the rest of the day for all he knew. And by night-time… No, Jack didn't even want to think about it. For once, they had the upper hand. He was no longer trailing behind. Now they had an idea where the killer might be, and finally they could do something about it before anything else happened. But the longer Deborah was in there, the longer it would take. Jack's legs felt cramped and he opened his door to stretch them out.

What harm would it do just to have a little walk around? He'd only be a few minutes. Back before Deborah could—

No, he'd promised her he would stay in the car. Actually, she'd told him to wait here. She hadn't said anything about having to remain inside the Peugeot. Jack climbed out, resting his arms on the roof of the vehicle. He stared at the station for a short while, then walked around the side of the car. Taking one look at the side-street, and another back at the station car park, Jack strolled out of the gates as casually as he could.

He began his trek around the building, looking for anything suspicious, anything that might possibly be an entrance or exit. There were buildings on either side of the station, as he'd noted when he first came here, two narrow side-streets separating them from each other. The buildings were in use, but that didn't necessarily rule them out as entrances or exits.

He went round the other side of the station, down the alleyway there. Behind the station house were a couple of empty smaller structures at least they were empty as far as he could tell. They were also locked. Jack scanned the photocopies he had and found that they'd be unlikely suspects anyway, seeing as the back wall of the underground cells faced east. If Twinkle was somehow coming and going through these locked buildings he could get in and out of locked buildings easily enough: even ones with security alarms, which never seemed to work when he was around there'd be twenty, thirty feet of solid earth between him and the cells to plough through.

Jack wandered up and down the alley. The surface had been concreted over after the bombing raid. Concreted. It would take a pneumatic drill to get through, and those things were hardly inconspicuous; besides, who would be stupid enough to use one with a cop shop right next door? This was ludicrous: there were no elaborate Batcave entrances like you saw in the movies, no secret James Bond doorways or hatches… Which only left the explanation he'd thought of first. The simplest, most obvious explanation.

He scanned the road ahead and his eyes were drawn to it straight away. A manhole cover. Not necessarily the one Twinkle used – they were everywhere! – if he even used them at all, but it was a place to start.

At long last Mason left Deborah alone. There'd been no chance of slipping quietly away while he was hovering around and she didn't want to risk telling him any more lies. So she'd ploughed on with her work in the hopes that he'd simply get fed up and wander off eventually, as he was apt to do. Once or twice she'd opened her mouth and almost told him the truth about the situation, about what they'd found out. But then she remembered what Jack had said. Mason hated him, that was true, and probably still thought he had something to do with the murders in the first place. No, it was best this way. Best that she and Jack—

Jack. Deborah looked at the clock. God she'd been in the office ages, leaving him outside to wait for her. She went to the window, looking out on to the car park. At first she couldn't find her car, then she spotted the small Peugeot. From this angle it was difficult to see inside, to see Jack. But she could see the passenger door clearly enough. And it was open.

"Shit," she said under her breath. Where the hell was he? She'd told him to stay right there. Right *there!* And he said he would. *Don't panic*, she told herself. *He can't be far away... Can he?* She'd been stuck in here with Mason for what seemed like centuries. Sure he could. Jack could be anywhere. Although she had a pretty good idea where he might be.

Deborah whirled around, grabbed her coat, and made a dash for the door. By the coffee machine she saw a familiar figure. It was young Peel, and he was chatting with Clark.

"Peel?" she called out. "Peel!"

He held up his free hand, the one without coffee in it, to say hello. "Sarge. Is everything all right? You look a little—"

"You doing anything?"

"Just about to go on shift, if—"

"Consider yourself already on it. You too, Clark. I want you both to get your gear on and come with me."

Peel frowned. "Where are we going, only—"

"I'll tell you when we get there. Come on, look lively."

She waited for them to get ready and then they were marching off down the corridor together. They almost made it to the lift before a booming voice called them back. Deborah swore softly again, then turned to face her inspector. His knack for being in the wrong place at just the right time was impeccable.

"What's all this, Blondie? Where are you lads off to?"

Peel shrugged. He couldn't tell Mason something he didn't know himself.

"Sir, I can explain—"

Mason took her to one side. "Then explain away, but you'd better make this good bearing in mind what happened last time." Deborah stared at him. He stared back.

She had seconds to decide between her future here...

And her future with Jack.

CHAPTER FORTY

Jack gazed at the manhole cover, an inexplicable compulsion washing over him. Why was he so eager to lift off that square lid and descend into the sewer's depths? Why so impatient? Jack should go back and wait for Deborah at the very least. He had promised…

But he'd started this on his own, hadn't he? Maybe it was compulsory that he finish it the same way. The torch was still in his jacket pocket from last night, the one he'd used against Twinkle. He could—

Don't be so ridiculous, Jack chastised himself. *How are you going to find your way around down there?*

But he'd find his way all right, even without a map of the system. He'd…follow his nose.

No, he *had* to wait for Deborah.

Do you really want her involved in this? You know the way you feel about her, it'd be your fault if she got hurt. She'd never forgive him if he went down alone. But on the other hand, he'd never forgive himself if he let anything happen to her. He'd lived for long enough with the death of…of a loved one (was that how he thought of James now? it was how he had thought about him once…) and he wasn't even directly responsible that time. Imagine the grief if Deborah—

Stop it! he told himself. *I'm not going down there, I'm going back to wait for Deborah.*

So why was he now looking around for something to lever the cover off with?

"Help me…"

If he still had the car-lock, that would be perfect. But it was somewhere in St Christopher's car park.

"Help…"

Nearby there was a skip some workmen had been using, forsaken now it was the holiday season. Inside, Jack found a long piece of metal. It wasn't very wide, so it might just slot into the T-shaped cavity on the cover.

Seconds later, and Jack was using it to yank off the hatch. He grunted, the barrier heavy, but his efforts soon bore fruit. Jack prised off the cover and gazed down into the shaft.

Surely it wouldn't hurt to just climb down and have a look around. Before he knew it, that was what he was doing, stuffing the cell plans into his coat and descending into the darkness.

Halfway down the rungs, Jack flipped on his torch. It smelt terrible down here, but it looked even worse. He figured this system had probably been added just thirty or forty years ago, but decades of dealing with the city's filth had soiled its once clean tunnels. His torch beam was eaten alive by the black. From somewhere up ahead of him he heard the squeaking sound of rats, the splashing their paws made in the rancid stream running down the centre of the tunnel. This was the conduit he'd seen, or a passageway very similar.

Jack looked on this as another adventure. He was an explorer again, just like when he was a kid. Only instead of fields, woods and rivers, he was venturing into a more urban 'playing ground'. Water came up above his ankles, but he tried to keep his light focused ahead of him at all times. He had no inclination to see the things floating past his feet.

He traipsed on through the muck and sludge, the watery mire and the slimy overhangings, attempting to figure out his position in relation to the police station above…and the cells below. Once or twice he consulted the photocopied sheets again, but in the end decided to trust in his own judgement. He'd know when he came upon something unusual.

The tunnels began twisting and soon he was disorientated, unsure as to whether he was even going in the right direction anymore, and unable to find his way back. His first instincts were to doubt his own senses, then he quickly dismissed them.

Evil was down here, he felt it more strongly than he ever had above ground. All he had to do was follow its trail.

Which led to an uneven section of tunnel.

The brickwork was shot through with damp and there were jagged gaps in the tunnel wall. Someone had replaced the bricks in an effort to make it look normal, and it probably would have passed a cursory examination. Jack tapped on one of the bricks with the end of his torch; it gave way a little. He brought up his foot and kicked at the wall. It fell inwards with little effort, the loosely piled bricks toppling over. Someone, it wasn't hard to guess who, had caved in this portion of the passageway – quite possibly with a hammer or something similar. Had *He* needed a hammer? Jack touched his chest, remembering Twinkle's strength. He was suddenly conscious of the fact he'd come down here unarmed. Last night he'd had the car-lock—

But look where that had got him: precisely nowhere. Jack still had his torch, though he doubted the same trick would work twice. Twinkle was far from stupid. If he was to be defeated it was going to be by methods other than brute force. He didn't know exactly how yet, perhaps James would tell him when the time came. His brother had brought him this far… He had to trust him one last time.

Jack climbed through the broken bit of tunnel.

And found himself in a no man's land: a dense, black void that swallowed his torch-beam. He pressed forwards and kept walking for about five minutes or so before hitting a dead-end, some kind of stonework. The jailhouse wall? Had to be!

Jack flashed his torch left and right, searching for a way inside. But there was nothing as obvious as the sewer wall, so he switched off his beam. If he was right, Twinkle would guide him the rest of the way. Sure enough, he saw flickering coming from another makeshift doorway, which was this time in the stonework itself. Jack shuffled sideways. It took him only moments to reach the source of the light.

Jack poked his head into the ragged fissure.

Close now, so close.

He had to be careful. The light was still dull compared with his torch, but it afforded Jack enough illumination to see the bars. Rusted, crumbling, these were the bars that had held a thousand prisoners in their cells. That kept thieves and murders, rapists and maniacs away from the good people above.

Jack stepped cautiously through into what appeared to be another cell. Shadows danced around the stone walls, the light source still unknown. He stood there for a good while, trying to work up enough courage to go any further.

Suddenly there was movement to his left. Jack spun around, snapping on his torch.

What he saw made the hair on the back of his neck stand proud.

CHAPTER FORTY-ONE

There, trapped in the shaft of his torch, with dust motes floating all around it, was a body.

A dead body.

The rodent that had alerted Jack to its proximity now scuttled away. Job done, mission accomplished.

But this body was old. There was no more flesh on its bones: it *was* only bones, that and a few scraps of worthless cloth. The skeleton was propped up against the stone wall of the cell, leaning slightly forwards, a bit like Stuart Redbrook's corpse must have been back on that night something like a month ago down Fagin's Row. Its smile was far from perfect, several of the teeth having remained unaccounted for even before its death. Jack thought of the thing as an 'it', because he had no idea what sex it had been, probably male but not necessarily and this also helped him to think about it as an inanimate object, something that hadn't been alive, something that hadn't lived and breathed and—

Its eye sockets were hollow now, hollow and black. It 'looked' at Jack in an accusing way. Not blaming him for its demise, but simply for living when it could no longer do so itself. Jack switched off the torch, mainly so he didn't have to see it staring at him. Though at the back of his mind, he also knew that the light could give him away.

Only when it was safely covered up by a blanket of darkness once more, just an indiscernible shape against the wall, did Jack wonder who it was. Then what he'd read in the local history book a few short hours ago came back to him. Of course, the author had only mentioned the policemen who perished during the Nazi attack, but that didn't mean the cells below had been empty. This was probably one of those prisoners cut off down here with no means of escape. Peacekeepers and criminals both in the same boat, the rubble of an entire building above them, dying from lack of food, water…air. Jack could scarcely imagine what it must have been like for them in their final few days, their final few hours.

There were bound to be more bodies, perhaps huddled together in the other cells, perhaps moved there by Twinkle. Either way, Jack didn't wish to know. This place reeked of death, just as it reeked of evil. A fitting hideaway for his brother's murderer.

The presence of the skeleton prompted Jack to move forwards, to take a hold of the cell door, which was ajar the locking mechanism having long since disintegrated and pull it towards him. It made a grating sound, the metal hinges remonstrating.

Had Twinkle left it shut as some kind of improvised early warning signal? If so, it was better than any of the hi-tech devices protecting George Lovesy's abode.

Jack took it slowly, gritting his teeth. The sound lessened considerably and he felt confident he'd got away with the noise so far.

Get out of here, said his fear given voice. *Get out of here now before it's too late. You know* He's *down here somewhere. He'll kill you, Jack, and then what'll you do?*

It was a stupid thing to think. He wouldn't *do* anything, he'd be dead. But Jack got the point. This was a bad move. Coming down here was probably the worst decision he'd ever made in his life. Just like walking home that night had been for James.

"Help me…"

But Jack was tired of this game, of chasing, of pursuing, and getting nowhere. He'd almost had him last night—

Oh, is that right? Who exactly had whom?

This would end here and now. If he was killed, then so be it. He didn't care anymore.

No, a part of him *did* care. He had Deborah now, and that changed everything.

But he still found himself moving out of the cage, moving into the corridor. He surveyed the other cells and saw more blurry shapes, just like his 'bunkmate' back there propped up against walls, lying on the hard, stone beds. Jack didn't use his torch this time, didn't care to see what time and vermin had done to them. He hurried past the chambers of the dead. Heading towards the light.

Jack pressed his body up against the archway; according to the plans it was the bit that connected the jail section to the entranceway, back when there had been an entrance and stairs leading up into the police station above. Jack risked a quick glance inside. It appeared empty.

He saw a huge wooden desk, part of one side rotted away, and he saw gas lamps and candles: the only means of light in this electricity-free environment. The whole place was like a darker, older version of the entranceway upstairs. And probably the cells too, though he'd never had the privilege of spending a night in one. *Not like Anton Craine.*

The same place but different. A warped mirror image.

A twin.

Holding his breath, Jack walked into the entranceway. As he cleared the arch he saw something that made his experience back in the cell look like a fun day out at a theme park.

The collection was arranged on shelves, some that had probably held reports or documents in the age before computers and some much newer. Or at least most of it was on these shelves. The collection spilled out onto the floor: its number the result of countless attacks. Twinkle's pride and joy.

His mouth open, and feeling sick, Jack approached the grotesque assortment of jars. Resting behind glass was all manner of human organs and limbs. Some Jack had seen *Him* take, others he had not.

In smaller jars he saw fingers and thumbs, from both left and right hands, and the same number of toes as well… there was even a separate quantity of toe and fingernails. Two halves of different noses, the parts containing the nostrils, were inside another couple of jars, and alongside them two lips upper and lower from different mouths. Ears, eyebrows, teeth: these were suspended in a kind of putty mixture instead of liquid, enough to make a whole new set of dentures if gathered together; cheeks, elbows and knees, with bones still underneath the skin; two spherical grey-purple things that Jack didn't recognise at first and then wished that he hadn't, causing his own testicles to withdraw slightly; nipples, from men and women; two unequally-sized breasts whole this time a left half of someone's brain, and a right half of someone else's…

Then he came to the larger objects: legs and arms, buttocks these looked as if they'd been treated somehow, because they wouldn't fit in jars; feet and hands, calves, thighs, forearms, biceps… And now bits from the inside: lungs, kidneys, curled up veins that looked like tapeworms, sections of the heart, muscles with the layering stripped off. Anything the body had two of had a *copy* of it was here.

There were even bones, every conceivable bone, mounted like trophies; which was what they were in fact, trophies of Twinkle's safari. His killings, his eradication of the twin species. A lifetime's work.

Jack almost gagged, would have gagged if he hadn't been so angry at the perversity of all this. At the waste. All those deaths, and for what? To build up a bizarre museum of body parts Ripley would have been proud of, to create an exhibition not even Hurst would have attached his name to?

The demented, depraved…

"You're admiring my collection," came a voice from behind, so deep and tinged with malice it might have been Satan's own.

Jack turned around to see a huge figure filling the archway he'd just stepped through. One of the dead from the cells had awakened.

The huge presence was dressed in black. From the belt around his waist dangled the instruments of his ghastly trade, though the implement he used to kill was in his hand. A twin-pronged fork, the fork Jack had seen so many times, inflicting pain on so many people.

And as he raised his head, cocking it back, he revealed his countenance. A face split in two. No, not split in two but rather there were two faces. Duality in the extreme. Two noses, two mouths, two pairs of eyes. This was no mask. This was real.

The moment had arrived.

And Jack was facing the one, true Gemini again.

CHAPTER FORTY-TWO

Twinkle entered the room, his movements lithe and graceful, which was surprising considering his gargantuan size.

But Jack couldn't take his eyes off that visage, the taut skin, unwillingly accommodating the extra features. Evidence that the parasitic twin theory he'd had was right…

No.

Though it was hard to tell at first, the more he looked the more Jack realised those two faces weren't the same. One had a woman's lips for a start; the other sported a moustache. Twinkle wasn't two twins in a single body then   although it would have accounted for his strength and build. So what in God's name was he?

Like gunslingers in a spaghetti western he and Twinkle stood at opposite ends of the room. The only difference being that the larger man had already drawn, and Jack had nothing *to* draw. No weapon as such, just the torch in his hand. Twinkle flipped the fork around in his huge gloved paw, expertly twirling it.

"I know you," said Twinkle at last in crisp, deep tones. *Twinkle*. That epithet seemed even more absurd now the 'man' was in plain sight, the contrast risible.

Jack tried to speak but the words wouldn't come.

Twinkle smiled using two mouths. The effect was chilling. "Someone has been a very naughty boy…James."

"Jack," said the historian finally, his voice fluctuating like a teenager in puberty. "My name's Jack."

"Oh, I know *that*," Twinkle replied, as if the fact had never been in any doubt. "He shouldn't have brought you here. It wasn't necessary. You didn't have to die."

He was talking as if it was a foregone conclusion, which, given the circumstances, seemed about fair.

"And they did?" asked Jack, pointing to the collection. Twinkle nodded.

"Why?"

"You wouldn't understand."

No, he wouldn't, but he wanted an explanation anyway. "Tell me!"

"It serves no purpose. If you hadn't got in my way last night, this would all be over. I have been patient. I have waited. Just one more piece, that's all I need."

"For what?"

"For *it* to be complete, of course. And with it, myself." Twinkle was moving forward, almost without moving at all.

"Then what happens?"

"No more talk." In the blink of an eye, Twinkle had obliterated the distance between them. Jack dived sideways to avoid him, and only just made it. He scrambled to his feet, tossing the torch at Twinkle. The missile bounced off the side of his head. Jack saw the skin there ripple slightly, then set itself again. Staggering backwards, Jack almost knocked over one of the candles.

"Jack be nimble, Jack be quick," said Twinkle laughing. "Jack jump over the candlestick!" He leaped towards Jack, grabbing him by the shoulders like a wild animal. In a single movement, Twinkle swept Jack off his feet. There was a hand around his neck, right the way around. Fingers wrapped themselves tightly round Jack's throat like baby boa constrictors. He fought for breath that wouldn't come.

Twinkle raised his fork. He obviously didn't relish using the weapon like this, but there were no two ways about it: Jack had to die now.

For a fraction of a second everything was still. Jack looked into Twinkle's eyes, all four of them, and saw the awful truth. He saw beyond the façade, into the man's very soul. And he saw James trapped inside, pleading with him for release.

"Help me…"

Maybe it was the lack of oxygen, Jack wasn't sure, but there were all the victims of Twinkle, writhing within: feeding him, empowering him. A different kind of parasite.

But the moment was soon gone, and then all Jack could see was the flashing glint of fork prongs in the gas and candlelight.

CHAPTER FORTY-THREE

"Police. Put him down, right now!"

The command carried authority, but also overwhelming concern.

Twinkle turned his head to gaze in the direction of the archway. He saw four people there, a woman pushing in front. It had been her voice he'd heard.

"Did you hear what I said? Put him down!"

"Jesus," spluttered one of the men dressed in black and white, his torch clattering to the ground. "Look at his face!"

At Peel's request, the others – P.C. Clark and Inspector Roy Mason scrutinised Twinkle's face, but all Deborah could see was Jack being held several feet above the ground by his neck. 'Spread out!' said Deborah to her team, still taking the lead.

Twinkle started to lower Jack gently, then simply dropped him on the floor, where he crumpled up into a heap.

"Good. Now step away and lose the fork. Slowly… slowly," ordered Deborah.

Twinkle looked her up and down, could see she had no weapon, just like Jack, but did as she asked. The two constables had drawn their batons, clutching them in case of trouble.

"What's wrong with his face?" Peel blurted out, his fear and fascination growing.

"Never mind about his fucking face! Just get up here and help me," snapped Deborah. "Sir…Sir?" She looked round for Mason, but he was rooted to the spot. "Inspector Mason!" Her cry seemed to snap him out of his stupor, yet still he refused to move.

"It's true, Blondie," he mumbled. "All true… I never believed…"

"Call for backup, sir. Preferably armed backup. Now!"

"Right, yes…" Mason reached into his pocket and held his mobile to his ear, shaking his head. He'd get no reception down here, though. If only they'd brought more people with them in the first place, thought Deborah. But then as Mason said: he never believed he'd find this down here; it had taken all her powers of persuasion just to get him to come. And no one would have given permission for armed response units, even if there had been time. Who in their right mind would have thought it possible? Had Deborah believed it, *really* believed it until she'd seen that hole in the sewer wall, until she saw Twinkle for herself?

Then Clark noticed 'the collection', Twinkle's stockpile of gruesome body parts. "Oh my… Sergeant Harrison, look."

Deborah whipped her head round in the direction of the shelves, the sight momentarily throwing her. When she turned back, it had already begun.

"Watch out!" shouted Mason, but his warning came too late.

Twinkle swung a fist, lifting Peel off his feet. The constable was hurled high into the air and landed awkwardly on the old desk at Twinkle's left-hand side. Deborah ran at

Twinkle, not knowing quite what she'd do when she got to him. Near enough now, she twisted herself around and rammed into him with the full force of her body. It knocked him back a millimetre or two, but did more damage to Deborah's shoulder and elbow than it did to his torso.

She screamed, then felt two enormous hands clamping down on either side of her skull. The pressure was incredible, like being in a vice. Twinkle squeezed harder, ignoring Deborah's pounding on his forearms.

Clark swung his baton and hit Twinkle in the 'face'.

Suddenly Deborah was toppling backwards. Twinkle shook his head and Clark gaped in amazement as the features changed. Molecules were manipulated though whether it was an unconscious act or a deliberate one was anybody's guess flesh reforming like clay, and the faces of that young woman and moustached man were soon replaced by those of Stuart Redbrook and George Lovesy, deformed but side by side.

Clark hesitated. What he'd already seen was beyond his experience and comprehension, but this took things to a whole new level. His floundering proved costly. The knife was already detached from Twinkle's belt and arcing around towards him. Clark's blood was unleashed, splattering Twinkle, and Jack Foley's body on the floor. Clark let out a shriek of agony, before dropping to his knees and falling flat on his face, blood from the knife slash still pouring out of him.

Twinkle tossed the knife from hand to hand, bearing down on Deborah.

The world exploded in front of her.

Twinkle was suddenly glowing red and yellow. The knife fell from his hand as he backed off. Deborah wriggled backwards as the man spontaneously combusted, his clothes melting on his body. She moved away from him, a hand up to ward off the heat and flames. Then she saw what was left of the gas lamp at Twinkle's feet, the golden holder, the bits of shattered glass. And she saw Peel next to the desk, holding on to it for support and smiling.

"Got you, you bastard!" he shouted.

Deborah watched as the fire enveloped Twinkle. But he did nothing to stop it. He didn't roll around on the floor, clap himself like a frozen man in the arctic, or panic and run round pleading with people to help him. He merely stood there and let the blaze engulf him, blacken him, char his muscular frame. He reminded Deborah of one of the superheroes in those Saturday morning cartoons from her childhood (*"Flame on!"*) or a stunt man in an incredibly bad action film.

The king of light in a room filled with smaller subjects.

Then the fire went out. Just like that.

Twinkle was now completely black, but this wasn't the colour of his clothes. It was his skin, some of it still bubbling and blistering. Peel hobbled over to Deborah as she got up, and they both looked on, unsure what to do. Any second now he'd fall over. No one could survive such extensive injuries.

Jack and P.C. Clark lay behind Twinkle; Deborah's first thought was to go to them, but Peel held her back.

"Wait," he said. "Look!"

Four eyes opened and two sets of teeth shone, the whiteness vivid against the rest of his body. Twinkle spread his arms wide like he was waiting for a hug.

"Still they do not realise," the giant said gruffly. "Is this how I'll be received when the time comes? Will I have to constantly prove myself?"

"*How* can he still be alive?" Peel asked Deborah. "I cooked the fucker! He should be dead." And then to Twinkle: "*You* should be dead," as if by telling him he would make it so.

"You *can't* kill me," said Twinkle. "I... I am The Gemini!"

With that, his flesh began to heal itself, skin turning from black to red to pink. Naked, he stood before them in all his glory. But now they could see what his clothes had hidden. Faces, dozens of faces covering the entirety of his body, on his chest, his arms, his belly, his legs; in a state of perpetual flux, they writhed beneath the surface, mouths open in anguish.

"Oh no," whispered Deborah.

Twinkle nodded. "Oh *yes*. Now you understand. I am The Gemini.

"I *am* The Gemini!"

CHAPTER FORTY-FOUR

It was perfectly obvious who those faces belonged to.

The aspects straining under Twinkle's hide represented every kill he'd made in the past. Each twin he'd taken a life from over the years. Deborah thought she even spotted Haley Archer at one point, though it was impossible to be sure.

It was such a mesmerising sight, a living work of art in some respects, not meant for their eyes…yet. Twinkle or should that be The Gemini? wasn't quite done. His task remained unfinished. *He* remained unfinished…

And so it was that he began striding towards them again.

Deborah twisted to search for Mason, but he was now staring uselessly at the scene, mouth open in a state of utter shock. "Run," she said to Peel. "Go and fetch help."

It was too late for that. The Gemini grabbed Peel before he could move and the P.C. began to scream. The Gemini lifted this young man up above his head and Deborah could do nothing but watch as the policeman was brought down over his knee. She focused on Peel's face, so innocent, full of hope and dreams all dashed with one almighty splintering of the spine. Blood ran freely from his lips and Deborah saw the life extinguished from his eyes.

Peel was cast aside like some temporary amusement, a puzzle now solved that had lost its appeal.

She was next.

There was a hand around her neck before she could blink. One sharp movement left or right and it would be broken.

"Noooo!" The outcry came from behind them. Deborah recognised the voice as Jack's and realised it was the last thing she would ever hear.

But suddenly The Gemini was stiffening up, shuddering, grimacing with his Redbrook-Lovesy aspect. The tension was gone from around her throat. She staggered to the left slightly, trying to steady herself and see what was going on.

Jack rounded the huge figure, having pulled something out of Twinkle's back. Something that glinted in the candle and gaslight.

The mighty figure sneered. "You shouldn't have done that," he said. But then he reached round, touched his back and his hand came away wet where the fork had dug in. The Gemini's facial muscles seemed to contract, wiping away Stuart Redbrook and George Lovesy like chalk from a blackboard. And in their place: one single countenance. James Foley's.

"Now! Do it now!" barked James, urging his brother to act. "Help *us*!"

Jack looked at his sibling and for a moment Deborah didn't think he was going to do anything at all, the sudden eruption of his brother's persona sending him into shock.

Then anger took over. Gripping the fork with both hands, Jack slammed it into Twinkle's chest. Right where the heart should be, like Van Helsing staking his arch nemesis,

Dracula. And where his own brother had been pierced so long ago... Sparks flew out of the wound like metal on a grinder.

Enraged, Twinkle pushed Jack backwards and he went flying into the side-wall of the entranceway, twenty metres away. The sound of bones crunching echoed around the room.

"*Jack!*" screamed Deborah.

Twinkle whirled in agony as he struggled to remove the fork from his chest. With a tremendous heave, it came out. But blood wasn't the only thing that emerged this time.

A sparkling white light seeped out of the two holes in his chest, the faces disappearing from underneath and heading for the light. As more and more emerged, the spirits spun around him like a tornado. Deborah flinched as she heard jars shattering on shelves, the collection splashing to the floor and creating a gruesome mess of body parts there. An eyeball rolled across the floor: James' grey-green eye, exactly like Jack's...

Electricity crackled in the room.

Round and round the twins' souls went, hoisting The Gemini up into the air, tugging him in all directions. The candles blew themselves out, leaving only the light of the gas lamps and the transcendental glow of the killer's tormentors to see by. Some had been in captivity for years, others were more recent additions, but they all had one thing in common: each and every one had served time in Twinkle's personal, private jail. Now they were all free. Free to wreak havoc with the vessel they had maintained and empowered for too long. Free to have their revenge. And they were going to savour every fleeting moment of it.

They slashed The Gemini's flesh with slivers of light, leaving only his head intact, featureless now that the spirits were free. Blood splattered the walls, catching Deborah full in the face and blinding her.

Now all she heard was a loud whooshing sound, then a high-pitched wailing noise that could only have been The Gemini himself. If he was begging their forgiveness, he was wasting his final few breaths. Then the howling stopped.

Deborah wiped the blood from her eyes, clearing it out in time to see a train of pure brilliance winding up into the ceiling. The busted and reddened body of The Gemini sagged, and fell to the ground, dividing into pieces.

One tiny spark broke off from the pack.

It floated over to where Jack lay, barely conscious, up against the wall. The light tilted itself and looked down on him, then it pressed itself against his forehead before being sucked back into the group.

The glow – the spirits – disappeared.

Then there was silence.

The only light now came from the gas-lamps and abandoned torches, pointing in various directions. The room looked like a warzone. Bodies and body parts scattered all around, blood and guts painting the walls, weapons on the ground including the charred toolbelt that Twinkle used to wear.

Deborah began walking over to Jack.

There was a whimpering from behind her, from Mason. It just went to show you that no matter how strong you appeared to be, a thing like this could—

Something hard connected with her left shoulder.

Deborah went down.

A heavy foot stamped on her left leg, and she felt the bone snap like a brittle twig.

She yelped, the pain incredible. Deborah rolled onto her back to get a look at her attacker. Maybe Twinkle wasn't dead after all.

But no, there he was, what was left of him at any rate.

She could see his diced body through her tears, his decapitated head, a new face now forming in death: the one he'd been born with.

And it was a face she knew. The face of her superior, Inspector Roy Mason.

She was hallucinating. The pain from her leg was tremendous; it was making her see things. That had to be the answer.

Then who had just done this to her?

Deborah saw Mason standing over her, his face red, as wet with tears as her own. In his hand he held a baton. Peel's or Clark's: it didn't matter which.

"Look what you've fucking done," he spat. "Look what you and your fucking interfering boyfriend have done. You've killed him, you bitch!" He kicked her in the side to emphasise his point.

"You've gone and killed my only brother!"

CHAPTER FORTY-FIVE

Deborah found that she couldn't process the information.

It wasn't because of the intense discomfort she was in – *discomfort*: now there was an understatement – and it wasn't because she hadn't worked out the answer; Mason had just told her for Christ's sake! It was more to do with the fact that she didn't couldn't believe what her eyes and ears were telling her.

That Mason was Twinkle's…*The Gemini's* twin brother. It was ludicrous. He'd just spent the better part of a month trying to capture the man. Or had he? They hadn't actually got anywhere with their investigation, had they? The only reason Craine got caught was because three members of the public had brought him down. Craine? Now what about Craine?

No, again: it didn't add up.

All those times…all the cases she'd worked on with the inspector…her respect for him, the way she'd felt guilty about lying to him, sending him off to Bingham's office so Jack could sneak a look at Craine. And all the while he'd been living the biggest lie of all.

No. She couldn't believe it…

So what was he doing above her now, his face twisted with anger, spittle flying from his mouth as he told her he was going to make her pay?

"Sir? What…what are you talking…"

"Je-*sus*, *Blondie*," the nickname was spoken with utter contempt this time. "You'll never make inspector *that* way." He kicked her again, then cast a glance back over at Jack. "I knew something was going on with you two. I just knew it! That's why you took him to see Craine, isn't it? Because he was fucking porking you? Answer me, God damn you!"

"No."

"Liar!" He slapped her this time.

Now Mason became Phil in her confused mind. She was the punching-bag again, taking it over and over again. Well, he'd gone too far! He'd broken her leg, kicked her. No more. No more…

No more.

Mason bent over her, and she lashed out with her fist. Her mother's ring caught him across the cheek, opening up a deep cut. Taken by surprise, the inspector keeled over sideways holding his face.

Deborah levered herself backwards, wincing at the white-hot agony of her broken bones. With her good leg, she managed to kick out, knocking Mason even further off-balance.

He got onto his hands and knees, touching the gash in his face. "We could have had something special, Blondie. Can't you see that?" Were his words designed to hurt her emotionally, as he had done physically, to turn their relationship into a farce? Or were they just the sick ramblings of another maniac? Two brothers alike? The same but different? "Surely you knew…knew how I felt? There was a place for you…*afterwards*. But it's too late now. Too late…"

Mason clutched the baton again and dived at her, shoving it up against her throat, choking her. His legs rested on either side of her stomach, the full force of his upper body pressing down on her windpipe. In terms of weight she was no match for her superior officer.

"Too late…all too late," he repeated.

She saw something out of the corner of her eye, and wondered momentarily if it was the Grim Reaper. To survive The Gemini, only to be killed by his brother: it would be laughable if it weren't so real, so painful. But this person *was* real, and although dressed in black, there was the occasional dash of white to balance it out.

Clark tackled Mason, the momentum of his charge rolling him over Deborah.

"Stop!" said the P.C.

"Get off me!" shouted Mason, somehow believing that his orders would still be followed without question. Clark hung onto him, only relinquishing his grip when Mason elbowed him in the torso, mere inches away from where his knife wounds were, and then brought a fist back into his face.

Mason shrugged off Clark and set his sights on Deborah Harrison once more.

Deborah was continuing to wriggle backwards, feeling around on the floor as she went. Mason came at her with the baton again. "Now, where were we?" he said.

The sergeant's fingers found something round, then a handle. As Mason jumped on her, she brought up the weapon, turning it around in her hand, forcing it upwards with all of her strength.

Twinkle's knife entered Mason under the chin, moving swiftly through and into his mouth, skewering his tongue before emerging out of the bridge of his nose, showering her with cartilage, mucus and blood.

He dropped the baton, his eyes rolling back in their sockets. Mason attempted to say something, but the knife held his tongue fast: all that came out were wet splutters and gasps, like a patient trying to talk in the dentist's chair.

Then he flopped on top of her, twitching in the throes of death.

Disgusted, Deborah rolled him off. There he lay next to his dismembered brother, face against face, hideously identical.

Deborah caught her breath, inhaling the dank air. She manoeuvred herself around and dragged herself over to Clark.

"Are you all right?"

He was holding his nose, but nodded. "I'll live," he said.

Relieved, Deborah patted him on the leg. "Thanks."

Relief turned to dread, as she remembered what she was doing when Mason attacked. She remembered Jack, the wall, the crunching sound.

Without a second thought, she began crawling, arms and hands working as they'd never worked before.

She had to get to him.

She had to get to him now.

CHAPTER FORTY-SIX

Deborah kept telling herself he'd be all right. He had to be, if only for her sake. It was a selfish reason but it was a powerful one.

But even she could tell, as she hauled herself over the debris, that Jack was very badly injured. With each lunge she recalled his bones cracking as he hit the wall, the same sound her own leg had made when Mason brought down his size ten on the bones. She ignored that particular pain for the time being, shut it away in the storage compartment in her head.

At last she reached his crumpled form, and she could see the darkening redness on his lips, a smear of the same running down the wall itself probably from a head injury she couldn't yet see. She reached out quivering hands and laid them on him, willing Jack to heal. Endeavouring to transfer some of *her own* energy to him, to bring this man back to her.

He groaned, and for an instant she thought the process might actually be working. But when he opened his eyes she could see one was almost black with blood. God knew what was going on inside his head, or the rest of his body for that matter.

"So…sorry," he gargled, smiling.

"Shhh. Don't speak, Jack. Save your strength."

"I…had…." His chest heaved each time he spoke. "Had…to come… You…understand?"

Deborah flattened herself against him. "I understand. For James."

Jack tried to nod, but gave up halfway through. "You… you think we might…might have had something….?"

"We *do* have something, we always will. Now stop talking like that—"

Jack took her hand and squeezed as tightly as he could. "Want…you to know…"

"I already do. I feel the same way." As Deborah kissed him lightly on the cheek, he pulled her in closer and whispered something.

Then she felt his grip slacken. Deborah kept her own grip tight to make up for his, but it was over. Jack's mouth drooped open and the spark in his one clear eye went out. He was gone.

Deborah closed her eyes. Tears travelled down her cheeks. She laid her head on his chest, just as she'd done last night: holding him, simply holding him.

In time Clark came over to her. His nose was almost certainly broken and he clutched his torso where his cuts were. But as he'd said before, he'd live. He'd live. Which was more than could be said for the others.

He left her alone for a moment or two, cradling the man on the floor then said, "Come on, it's over. We need to get out of here."

Deborah knew he was right, for one thing they both needed medical attention. She even nodded, but couldn't seem to move. They'd both seen things today no one should ever be expected to see in a lifetime, had gone through things no one should have survived – lost people they cared about and she doubted whether they'd ever sleep straight through the night again. "Come on," he repeated and this time she went with him; *needed* to get away from this place in fact. "It'll be okay, Clark added."

But she knew he was wrong. It wouldn't, not really.

It would never be okay again.

CHAPTER FORTY-SEVEN

The days were so long in here.

Nothing to do but think and stare out of the window. It was a private room, only the best for the 'hero of the hour' face in every paper, on every news broadcast which meant that there was nobody to talk to, no other patients to pass the time with.

To help her forget.

Deborah Harrison glanced at the clock again for the hundredth time in ten minutes. Most people would have wanted to be alone after what she'd been through, after what had happened to Jack, but she would've preferred the distraction of idle chit-chat.

So why was it that when certain visitors came she felt like telling them to get out as soon as they stepped through the door? Certain visitors…not all. She couldn't wait for the frequent visits from her mother and daughter, even though Isabel had been distraught the first couple of times. And there had been that unexpected visit from Albert, along with a woman called Miriam who Deborah had never seen before a cleaning lady at *The Imperial* apparently. Jack had made quite an impression on them both in his short stay there. Just like he had on her. And though she could see both were clearly shocked and saddened, they never once asked about his death: only about her own wellbeing.

Which just left colleagues from work, and it was largely these people she didn't want to see. P.C.s and members of the division she hardly even knew came to wish her a speedy recovery. She felt more than a little guilty about taking their chocolates and flowers then wishing they would just piss off out of her sight. She'd even been ratty with Bingham when he called in to see his 'favourite sergeant'. Deborah knew she'd probably make inspector because of all this – there was an opening after all – and could even make a fortune out of it if she were that kind of person: TV rights, book deals...the dream of living on Partington Lane now hideously within her grasp.

But, of course, she wasn't that kind of person. Right now her future was as frightening and uncertain as Jack's had been. It was a New Year, so maybe it was an opportunity for a new start? She had plenty of time to consider her position: Deborah wasn't going anywhere soon with her leg up in plaster, and even then she had stacks of sick leave owing.

Was it because of Mason that she didn't want to see her workmates? His *betrayal*? Did it remind her each time of the way he'd been manipulating her, manipulating the case? "You know me too well," he'd said to her once. If only. (This was one of the reasons why she'd finally decided to tell Isabel the truth about Phil lies only came back to hurt you eventually.)

That part of it had come out, of course, and would have been an embarrassment to Yardley Street had it not been for her courageous actions deflecting most of the criticism. Mason's secret twin, one that not even he'd known about until a few years ago when Twinkle had found him. They discovered letters in Mason's bachelor flat, with dates and times of meetings. A diary with his thoughts and feelings. As Roy had got to know his brother it seemed to fill a large gap in his life, something he'd been missing all this time.

There was never any mention of the killings, though, nor of his brother's feelings about the same, although they discussed the state of the world and how it might be changed for the 'better'. Deborah wondered what Mason had said when the guy told him he was a cold-blooded murderer for the first time, that he was *different*? It seemed obvious that he was the dominant one in that relationship. Had he won his sibling around that way? Perhaps he was even controlling him somehow? It didn't matter now. In the end Mason had proved just as demented as his twin.

Had he even helped Twinkle set up his little base camp under the station? He knew his local history, having lived in Norchester the whole of his life. Had he arranged for the transportation of those body parts? Or constructed a suitable display wall in the entranceway of the old jail? The least he could do really for the brother who'd been taken away from him at birth, taken far away from the city he called his own: the city that had spawned the twins in the first place? No, Mason's reaction in the cells…that had seemed genuine…

And so her theory about why *he* came to Norchester was wrong, well at least partially. He'd returned not just because the city was rich in victims, but also to be close to his brother again as he finished his work.

The letters and diary entries also solved the mystery of 'Anton Craine', Twinkle's adoptive younger brother. All that was left now of his adoptive family in fact. Christ, what that kid must have gone through…what Twinkle must have done to him mentally; was there even some warped hero worship in there somewhere? she wondered. It would explain how he was talked into doing what he did that night. To take the fall and fool everyone into thinking it was over. It also explained Mason's hatred of him, some of which had slipped out during that interview session. Craine had grown up with *Twinkle*, had lived with him, played with him…

Promises had no doubt been made, of power, of rewards beyond Craine's imagining. But the guilt had proved too much, and in the end he actually believed *he'd* killed those people.

That still left the question of what exactly Twinkle was, and why he'd embarked upon his culling spree. Deborah had a few ideas of her own ideas about it, but saw no way of substantiating them, not since the 'powers that be' had finally stepped in and swept so many things under the carpet. A task force she'd never even heard of called the Serial Crime Initiative, which had some real clout, had taken charge – had taken all the evidence with them too – and that had been that.

Didn't stop her thinking about it, though. She'd read that some twins could deprive their siblings of nutrients in the womb, take the lion's share of blood and food: literally sucking the life out of the other and forcing doctors to deliver early in order to save both children. So what if *He* had been just such a baby, only somehow he'd retained the ability to do this in later life? To suck the very essence out of other twins, to feed himself and keep their spirits locked away inside? A freak of nature as they'd speculated? Or something else?

I am The Gemini!

But what of the parts he took? Were they merely souvenirs or did he need them for some reason? To keep pieces of his victims 'alive'? Maybe they *were* offerings of a sort, retained for a freakish ritual? Or a rite of passage? Before everything had been whisked away, forensics had confirmed that Twinkle had almost completed his collection. Had almost gathered together every single 'twin' body part there was: and by twin, that meant those numbering in their twos. All that was missing was another eye, like the one stolen from Jack's brother. What would have happened when he'd finished, once he'd completed his undertaking? What other powers would he have possessed? What exactly would he have become?

"And still they do not realise. Is this how I'll be received when the time comes? Will I have to constantly prove myself?"

More importantly, what would have become of the rest of them, of their world? How would *He* have changed it? Would it have become the same but different a distorted mirror image of its former self?

*"There was a place for you…*afterwards. *But it's too late now. Too late…"*

Neither Deborah nor P.C. Clark would speak much about what they'd actually seen in the underground jail that day in the weeks to come, even to each other. And especially to the counsellors who would keep pestering them. This was partly because no one would have believed a word of it, and partly because it eventually got a bit clouded in their minds. Or perhaps they were both just scared to relive it? Deborah did recall Jack using the fork to release the spirits, the weapon that had been used to conduct them into Twinkle's body in the first place, but the official line was more mundane so she kept quiet. What good would it do anyway? The case was closed now, the 'Masons' gone. And she still had Jack's funeral to come yet. A twin funeral now that she knew what Twinkle had done with James: a location whispered to her as Jack lay dying in those cells.

The only colleague she didn't really resent dropping by was Rosy. Perhaps it was because Rosy was the only one she could talk to about Jack. She told her the regrets she had. If only she'd spotted what was going on sooner, got in touch with Jack earlier than she had they might have spent longer *together* not left him alone so he could search for Twinkle's underground house of madness, realised that Mason seemed to know his way around down in the sewers much better than he should have done once they'd found the open manhole. All the remorse came out when Rosy called to see her.

"You can't blame yourself," Rosy told her. "Jack wouldn't have wanted that."

"I can't help it. I let him down."

"You were there when he died, how could you have prevented it without getting yourself killed as well?"

"Maybe I should have done. I'd change places with him now if I could."

"You don't mean that. What about Isabel, what about your mother?"

"We didn't have long enough…"

"You had more than some people get, Debbie. People who never take that chance, who go through their lives wondering what it might have been like."

The words were cold comfort, but Deborah thanked her for the support.

Now, as she lay back in bed, another day grinding to a halt, she switched off the soaps on the TV above her unable to concentrate on them since that day a week or more ago.

Deborah looked out through the window in her hospital room instead.

At the night sky, at the stars shining so brightly outside. Deborah watched them, captivated. She wished she knew more about astronomy, so she could locate the constellation they called Gemini. The true Gemini. But she searched for it anyway, remembering the tiny circle of light that had touched Jack's head as he lay dying. Somewhere up in the heavens there would be two such stars glistening side by side now.

Jack wasn't on his own anymore. He was back where he belonged, just like Mason: back where he'd started, with his brother, exploring, all the troubles of life forgotten. And this thought consoled her, allowed her to rest more easily.

He wasn't on his own.

And neither was she…

EPILOGUE

Inside Deborah's body, changes were taking place.

Just over a week ago, seed had encountered egg, energising it with life. It had withstood the traumas she went through down in the cells, and it had begun to grow   only subtly at first, but it grew. At some point during the course of the week, the egg split: a consequence of the conception taking place in this particular city, which had, once, countless centuries ago, been a sacred site for ancient religious sects practising bizarre fertility rituals beneath the light of the stars. If Jack had had time to take Marvin Hole up on his offer, they might have uncovered all this… Likewise, he might also have been interested to learn that his parents had stayed in Norchester almost thirty years ago, his father attending an astronomy conference at the local university and booking into a well-known hotel in the area…

Suddenly there were two identical eggs, genetically indistinguishable. Exact duplicates that would emerge in something like eight or nine months' time. Twin boys. Jack's legacy, and two younger brothers for Isabel. They would be the same in appearance, in looks if not in personality… though they would be more alike than either of them would ever realise. And no matter how 'individual' they grew up to be, the fact remained that they'd started off as one.

Inside the womb the developing foetuses would interact.

They'd nudge and kick each other, communicating in their own distinct and secret code. Perhaps trying to get back that which they had lost. One would be dominant, taking more sustenance from the mother: but they'd share a bond with each other that could never be broken. Not by time nor distance, nor even by the blackness and finality accompanying death itself.

But all that was in the future. For now they were nothing but clusters of cells in the womb. Waiting, patiently waiting.

Because the miracle, the natural marvel that still remains a mystery even in these times of scientific wonder and technological achievement, was only really beginning.

The miracle that remains purely and simply:

The Gemini Factor.

GEMINI RISING

Property of the Serial Crime Initiative
Evidence Log No. 07 – 52 – 1465
Description: Selected extracts from a journal recovered after a fire beneath Yardley Street police station, Norchester.

SATURDAY, MARCH 15 – 1980.

My name is Maxwell Craine Jr, and I'm so alone.

No, that's not true. I feel alone, even though there are people around me. Anton, my little brother, follows me around like a lost puppy. It's quite sad. He's always done that, even though Mother disapproves. 'Hero worship' Father calls it. Intensely annoying, I say… Luckily, he also does what I tell him, so I can send him off on stupid, pointless errands (I'm a patient person, but my brother tests this). Once I sent him off into the garden to count the blades of grass, and he went – he actually went!

Back to the point of this, my diary. Father was the one who suggested it, ages ago, but I was already thinking of doing something similar. Like I needed to get my thoughts down on paper.

I'll start with a little about myself. I'm thirteen years old, I live in a small village called Cambley, just outside Brenton – which is where Father (who I'm named after) works as a doctor at St Augustine's Hospital. Mother doesn't work, she just stays at home all day. She doesn't even do any housework, because we have someone who comes in on a Monday and Friday, a widow called Mrs Thomas. Mother does nothing except play her instruments in her music room: violin, cello, but her favourite is that damned harp. She used to have a career of sorts, playing in an orchestra. I'm not sure what happened, but she doesn't do that anymore.

Oh, and she drinks. A lot.

She thinks she's good at hiding it, but she really isn't. I've lost count of the amount of times Anton and I have returned home from school to find her passed out on the couch. I'm in secondary, but Anton's primary school is on the way home. I have to call there so we can walk home together. I make him trail behind me…several paces.

I quite like school. Well, the learning side, at least. I like finding things out, investigating. I'm good at history and the sciences, but rubbish at maths…and P.E. I *hate* P.E! Mainly because—

[Fire damage]

—enjoy *some* games. Puzzles anyway, jigsaws, that kind of thing, because you can do them on your own. And I'm into comics, which I buy with the pocket money Father gives me. We have a local shop that stocks the popular ones, though they get them ages after America. *Spider-Man*, *Batman*, *The X-Men*, *Hulk*. I love them all. I wish sometimes that… No, it's silly. Just a dream.

I'm a nobody, just like Mr Gregson says.

I'm a nobody and I'm so alone.

I don't feel like writing any more.

WEDNESDAY, MAY 14 – 1980.

Someone new started at school today. Her name is Lucinda. We were in the middle of English – *To Kill A Mockingbird* – when our head of year, Miss Berkley (whose hair is pulled so far back on her head she has a permanently surprised expression) knocked on the door and ushered her in.

Lucinda is almost my height, with auburn hair. She has freckles on her nose and cheeks. Miss Berkley told us who she was, that she'd just moved to the area. She told Lucinda to go and find a seat. The one next to me was free, it always is. Lucinda came and sat down there. I think we're going to be friends. Maybe.

But the strange thing is, as soon as I saw her I *knew*. Even before her sister appeared behind Miss Berkley, so she could introduce her to the class next. Miranda *her* name is, and she's the complete opposite of Lucinda. A negative of her. Where Lucinda's all smiles, Miranda could scowl for England. Miserable cow! She took a seat near the back, glaring at Lucinda as she passed by. Very odd. I've never seen any before. I mean, I've seen them in photos or on TV, just not in person. Not in the flesh.

Twins… Lucinda and Miranda. Fascinating!

But how did I know? How did I know?

PAUL KANE

TUESDAY, MAY 20 – 1980.

I had that weird dream again last night, the one I've been having ever since I can remember.

I'm standing, gazing into a mirror. But the reflection isn't really me, at least not the me I am right now. More like the me I *want* to be. My reflection is…more confident-looking, doesn't wear glasses (I've had them since I was seven); I'm standing prouder, taller, instead of slumping.

Usually it's just staring back. But last night, for the first time, it moved. It pointed, as if it was accusing me of something. Maybe of not being him?

When I woke up, my covers were tangled and drenched in sweat. I've felt restless ever since. Like there's something I should be doing. I *need* to do.

God knows what it is, though.

MONDAY, JUNE 16 – 1980.

Fun biology lesson today, we did 'abnormally formed organisms'. You know, mutations, two-headed animals, things like that. Really interesting. Miranda calls them 'freaks of nature', but then she would, being one herself – ha, ha!

I like biology. I didn't like dissection at first, we did a frog the other week. But as Mr Lines pointed out, the natural world is a strange and wonderful thing. Bodies are machines, and it's exciting to find out how everything ticks. Or doesn't, if you've just cut it up… Oh, you know what I mean.

I was quite squeamish at first, but put on a brave face in front of Lucy. Now I'm getting used to it.

I think we have a mouse coming up soon.

WEDNESDAY, JULY 30 – 1980.

Father took me with him into work today, for the first time. Anton was really annoyed he couldn't come, but Mother told him he isn't old enough. I think she was happy just to get a day alone with him. He's her favourite.

It was Father's idea to take me. I think he wants me to follow in his footsteps. Well, he did name me after himself.

I enjoyed riding in the car, listening to the music on the radio – more cheerful than the classical rubbish Mother plays. I couldn't believe how big the hospital was when we arrived, it's massive! Father's a consultant there, he's told me before. But I got to see how well respected he is by the staff. Maybe even feared a little. That feeling must be nice. The respect, I mean.

He took me on a bit of a tour first of all and—

[Fire damage]

—until later when we got separated. A group of people came past wheeling a stretcher, there must have been an emergency or something, but when I looked up again there was no sign of Father. I admit, I panicked. And I know from talking to him later on that he did the same. Anyway, I went off to look for him in completely the wrong direction.

I wandered down corridors, searching for him in that maze. Saw signs for departments I didn't even know existed. Walked past wards full of the sickest people, lying in beds, writhing, groaning. Some looked like they didn't have long left, kept alive by machines.

Finally, I backed up through a set of double doors. It was a little darker in that room than the corridor, and when I turned I could see sets of drawers down the sides of the walls, like filing cabinets.

Something about that place drew me further inside and when I touched the 'cabinets' they were ice cold. Then I turned a corner and saw them. Three 'beds'. Except the patients on these weren't moving at all. Two were just shapes, covered with sheets.

One was uncovered. A young man, stretched out on the shiny surface, completely naked. He looked…blue. I bit my lip, but found myself moving forwards, glancing left, right and behind, because I knew I shouldn't be doing this. Shouldn't even be here. But I'd been left alone…

So alone…and…

His eyes were open, not closed as you'd expect. He was just staring up at the ceiling. The closer I came, the more I could see of his injuries. He had some kind of wound on his side, not that big but it had obviously done a lot of damage. There was one on his chest as well, but this had been inflicted afterwards – then stitched up again. I reached out a shaking finger, touched the skin. It was colder than the cabinets.

"What are you doing here?" The voice startled me and I jumped, pulling my finger back quickly. I couldn't speak, couldn't get the words out. I'd been caught doing something I shouldn't, and that always terrifies me.

I turned, slowly, to see a bulky man wearing a blue coat over jeans and a T-shirt. His eyes twinkled when he saw me, and they softened. "Hey…hey it's all right," he said. 'There's no need to be scared. How did you get here?'

I managed to find my voice and explained. He got the hospital to page Father, who came to collect me, glaring at the man – Colin, he said his name was – like it was his fault I'd ended up there. On the way back home Father made me promise not to say a word to Mother, as if I would anyway (I'm not sure whether it was for her benefit, or mine). Father said he knew it must have been a traumatic experience for me.

"There's no need to be scared," Colin had said. But, you know what? I wasn't scared at all.

In fact, in a funny sort of way, I kind of liked it.

FRIDAY, AUGUST 15 – 1980.

I've begun studying medicine and anatomy. Father has lots of books on these in his office at home. He's more than happy to let me read them. I'm not sure whether I'll be going into that line of work, but I do find it all very interesting, the way—

[Fire damage]

—has been troubling me more than seeing that dead man, thinking about those people on those machines. Machines keeping machines – bodies – alive.

I wonder what happens when you die? I used to go to Sunday School when I was little, Mother took us for a while. I remember the teacher telling us that the spirit goes on forever, that it lives on in Heaven. I'm not so sure, looking at those people, at the man who *was* dead. What if the spirit gets... wasted? What if it's just there to keep the machine going, instead of the other way around? Like a battery or something? What if there's nothing afterwards?

Anton was a pain again today, but when isn't he?

SATURDAY, AUGUST 30 – 1980.

Been having the dream again…a lot.

I think maybe it's because school starts soon.

THURSDAY, SEPTEMBER 18 – 1980.

My birthday. The worst yet because—

[Fire damage]

—about any of this. I bloody *hate* P.E!!

WEDNESDAY, JANUARY 21 – 1981.

That bitch, Miranda!

She just can't accept I'm friends with Lucy, even after all this time. Miranda's the dominant one of the pair, I know that because I've been doing some research into their… condition. Doesn't make things any easier to swallow. It's like she controls every aspect of her life. Always has done as far as I can see.

This morning at break time, I was chatting with Lucy when Miranda came along, pushed me over, and dragged Lucy away.

Everyone laughed.

THURSDAY, JANUARY 22 – 1981.

Had the dream again last night.

Every time I see my reflection now, it seems a little bigger, as if it's growing. Growing *stronger*. It's still pointing, accusing, but it was also mouthing something. That's new.

Wasn't until I woke up that I realised what it had been trying to say, and that scared me so much I shivered.

It wanted me to do bad things to Miranda.

It wanted me to hurt her.

SATURDAY, MARCH 14 – 1981.

I'm learning so much from my trips to the hospital. Father thinks I'm studying in the library there, when he drops me off – it *is* a teaching hospital, after all – but really I'm sneaking down to see Colin.

He's worked in quite a few morgues and, strictly speaking, doesn't abide by the rules. Colin told me once that at another hospital, one he'd had to leave, he let students 'experiment' on unclaimed bodies.

He lets me experiment on them, too – I think partly because of who Father is, partly because he just likes me. Colin lets me cut into some of them with a scalpel. It's just like in biology really. He lets me see inside.

They're so pretty.

TUESDAY, APRIL 7 – 1981.

Bloody Anton! The snooping little bastard!

He found my diary. I walked in on him reading it in my room. "I-I just wanted to see," was his whiny explanation. Looking back, I don't even think he understood half of what he was reading. I'm not sure I understand it myself and I wrote it.

I just saw red, I suppose. The next thing I knew I'd

grabbed him by the throat with one hand and was squeezing, hard. With the other I'd taken out my pocket-knife and flicked it open.

Then I had a better idea.

I've been wanting to test the limits of how far I could push Anton for some time. So I told him to go and play on the main road.

And he went! I don't know if it was because he felt guilty or just wanted desperately to please me, but he *actually* did it. I watched him through the window as he headed up the hill next to our house, towards the road.

It was as he stood there, watching the cars speed by, that I had second thoughts. This was my brother. I was about to run downstairs when I saw one of the cars stop. Someone got out, and snatched up Anton just as he was about to—

That was one of our neighbours, a lawyer called Mr Mowberry, on his way back from work. He brought Anton home, told Mother what had happened, where he'd found him. I watched from the top of the stairs, as Mother slurred her thanks, then clutched Anton to her.

Father was less forgiving. He spanked Anton, drumming into him that he must not play up there, that it was dangerous. "Why on earth did you do it?" Father kept asking, but Anton just stared across at me when I finally came down, saying nothing. I think Mother caught the glance, though.

I'm going to need a much better hiding place for my journal.

The basement, maybe?

SATURDAY, MAY 16 – 1981.

It happened again today.

I was visiting Colin when one of the orderlies brought a 'package' in. It's what they call the bodies, I guess so they don't sound as creepy. He was a tall, thin man, with greying hair. Louis, Colin called him.

And I *knew*…as soon as I saw him, from my hiding place (I wasn't supposed to be there). I had that same feeling as—

[Fire damage]

—likes to chat, so I asked about Louis while we were eating our sandwiches. *How* I knew, I can't explain – but I was right. And it must mean something.

Louis has a twin. An identical twin brother called Dennis.

SUNDAY, JUNE 7 – 1981.

I'm not sure how to start this…

I overheard them last night. Mother and Father.

Mother spent the day playing her music, tuning and retuning her strings using her fork – not realising that the reason they never sound right is because she's always drunk.

By bedtime, she was blotto again, falling asleep on the couch. Father sent us to our rooms, but around midnight I heard raised voices. I've always found it hard to sleep and even more so since my dream started to *change*. But I was just beginning to drift off when the argument began. Anton, of course, won't have heard a thing. Once he's asleep it would take a nuclear explosion to wake him… (No, not one of those, poor choice of words.)

Mother had obviously woken, because I heard her

slurred bawling quite plainly by the time I reached the top of the stairs, inching down them a step at a time.

Now I could see into the living room, saw Father had a glass in his hand, half-filled with scotch (it took quite a bit to drive him to the bottle, I think because he's seen the damage it can do at work). Mother was on her feet, without a drink for a change, finger raised and pointing in his direction.

"...always been something not right about him," I caught, before Father told her to keep her voice down. Fortunately, I was close enough now that I could hear anyway. I wished afterwards I'd simply gone back to bed. "You can tell just by looking in his eyes," Mother continued, voice lower but still full of hatred. "He's *different*."

I thought at first they were talking about Anton. He's certainly different, and when you look in *his* eyes you can see there's something wrong. I've known it all my life.

But no. Mother meant me, though Father was quick to jump to my defence. "That's nonsense, Angela. And you're never sober enough to notice *anything*." Then he took a sip of his own drink.

"Why do you think I started!" she answered. Now she was jabbing Father's chest. "You're to blame, it was your idea. What you did, how we... If we'd just waited – but *oh, no!* You had to have a son. Had to have one immediately, like everything else. Well, some son he turned out to be. *Some son!*" Then her face was sad suddenly. "Secrets have a way of coming out, of coming back to punish you."

Father drained his glass, storming off to pour himself another. "You're crazy," he said over his shoulder. "Delusional."

"I'm telling you, it was his fault. *He* got Anton to go up there, I know he did. That...that stranger upstairs masquerading as our boy." Father spun round, dropping his drink and grabbing her by the shoulders. She began crying, sucking in breaths. He stared at her, letting go. Then he left the room, left the house. I heard the sound of his car starting up outside. Mother collapsed on the sofa, sobbing.

I was in a state of shock, trying to understand what they'd said. No, not understand – part of me understood well enough – more like trying to take it in. Absorb it.

Stranger? That's what she'd called me. If only they'd waited… Father had wanted a son, hadn't wanted to wait.

I inched back up the stairs, wandered across the landing in a daze. I found myself in the bathroom, pulling the door quietly shut, pulling on the light. I looked at myself in the big mirror hanging on the wall.

"You can tell just by looking in his eyes."

I stared into that mirror for I don't know how long, watching the reflection gazing back.

I was a stranger. To Mother. To myself.

I don't remember leaving the bathroom and going back to bed, but I must have done, because the next thing I knew I was having the dream again. In fact, it felt like I'd somehow slipped sideways *into* the dream.

The reflection – the stronger, more confident me – was mouthing something again and pointing, jabbing its finger just as Mother had done downstairs.

When I woke, it was light outside. I wondered for a second or two whether I'd dreamt the whole thing. The argument, the bathroom. Sadly, no. I'd only dreamed about the reflection, about what it was telling me to do.

Not just hurt someone this time.

It wanted me to kill.

THURSDAY, AUGUST 13 – 1981.

I've been doing some detective work, trying to find out more about my situation.

I know that I'm not Maxwell Craine Jr. Not really. I'm not their son, not like Anton. *He's* theirs. He came along after they'd…what, adopted me? I have no clue. I can't find any information about it. No papers, nothing. I've tried searching the office, my parents' bedroom. I even looked up in the attic, down in the basement.

So many of the pieces don't fit together. And not only—

[Fire damage]

—figure it out. 'Mother' – can I still call her that? – thinks I'm a monster, that much is clear. She can barely bring herself to look at me. She knows what I did that day, and hates me for it. I *should* hate myself. But I don't. Even less so now that I know the truth about Anton. About me. He's not my brother, never was.

I wish he *had* stepped out into that traffic.

I thought about telling Lucy, if I could get her away from Miranda long enough, but decided against it. So I'm doing what I've always done, jotting down my thoughts, to try and order them.

It's not working, though. Not this time.

MONDAY, SEPTEMBER 14 – 1981.

I am *not* a nobody, I'm *not!*

I should listen to my dreams.

THURSDAY, OCTOBER 1 – 1981.

It's the first chance I've had to write about all this… since it happened.

The accident.

It all began with my birthday. Father wanted to take us to the fair camped out near Brenton, to celebrate that weekend. But Mother was in bed not 'feeling well' and I couldn't see any reason to celebrate – apart from everything that'd been happening at school, it wasn't even my birthday really. Father said "Suit yourself" and just took Anton.

It was while they were out that Mother got up. I heard her clambering about, using the toilet. I never intended to get into an argument with her, but there she was, on the landing, staring through the open door into my room. I got up off the bed, where I'd been doing a word search, and asked her what she was looking at. She just kept on staring, as if trying to work that out. And I lost it again, just like I did when Anton found my diary.

"Who am I?" I snapped, approaching her, and she flinched.

"How dare you speak to me like—"

"Who. Am. I?" I said, my voice rising with each word.

"What do you mean?" she asked, shaking her head. For once she actually sounded sober.

"I *know*!" I barked. "Know that I'm not really yours. So who am I?"

She frowned, not understanding how I came by this information.

"*Who am I?*" I repeated, even more loudly. "Where do I come from?"

She waved her hand, turned away. So I grabbed her by the arm, yanked her back. I held her fast and repeated my question. For the first time ever, the woman who called herself my Mother looked afraid. "I-I don't know," she replied.

"Then how did I get here? Am I adopted?"

She bit her lip.

"What? *Tell me!*"

"Y-Your...father handled it all," she whimpered. "The payments and—"

"The *what?*"

Her face creased up, switching from frightened to angry again. "I wish to God he hadn't bothered. You're... there's something wrong with you, *Maxwell*." She said my... the name like she was trying to spit a hair from her tongue. "Your 'father' refuses to see it, because it would make this all his fault, but I've known for a long time. I see it, what's inside you."

I pulled her towards me with strength I didn't even know I had. "You have no idea," I snarled. Then I told her about Anton, about what I'd made him do, that I was glad, that I'd probably do something like it again.

She struggled to free herself from my grip then and—

Suddenly she was at the bottom of the stairs, legs and neck at strange angles. I rushed down, kneeling beside her. She was barely breathing and I knew then she was about to—

"What...what can you see?" I asked, as she stared at me again, this time blankly.

"Noth...nothing," she managed. Then she was gone.

I should have felt sad, should have felt *something*. But I didn't. All I could think was that I'd get the blame for this, if someone came in right now and found us. I'm not sure where the idea came from to fetch the gin bottle, to pour some over her and place it near her hand – wearing my thick winter gloves, so I wouldn't get any fingerprints on anything.

It was only then that I called an ambulance.

Father and Anton returned just as she was being taken away, after they'd officially declared her dead. Father's mouth fell open, then he'd demanded to know what happened. I just gaped at him, until someone in uniform pulled him to one side. Anton couldn't tear his eyes away from the covered-over stretcher (but it was just a dead body, a broken machine).

An accident. That's all it had been. A tragic accident – the police even said so. I couldn't have pushed her back towards the top of the stairs, shoved her down them, because that would mean—

There's something inside me. And there isn't. If anything, I feel empty.

The funeral's this Friday. Lucy's been really great since it happened, we're becoming quite close. Or would be if it weren't for Miranda.

I haven't asked Father yet about the things that woman said. How can I, without giving away that we fought? That I know?

But I can't help thinking about what she said that night I overheard her.

Secrets have a way of coming out.

Of coming back to punish you.

SUNDAY, JANUARY 3 – 1982

'Happy' New Year! Ha! It's—

[Fire damage]

—imagine what kind of Christmas it's been with Fath…Maxwell how he is. He's taken a sabbatical from the hospital, just sits in his office holding his dead wife's tuning fork, listening to morbid classical music.

He's taken up where she left off with the drinking, and the way he looks at me sometimes… I miss how we used to be, even knowing what I do. And Anton is really driving me insane. He's gotten even worse lately, if anything. Thank fuck Mrs Thomas has stepped up. She now does most things round the house, keeps Anton out of my hair…usually.

I'm looking forward to seeing Lucy at school this week, but not school itself.

I forgot to say the last time I wrote, the reflection in the dream shook its head after 'Mother' died. Not sure what that means. I thought it *wanted* me to—

Accident. Just an accident.

WEDNESDAY, MARCH 3 – 1982.

Maxwell Craine Sr might not go to the hospital anymore, but I still do. Colin's promised to show me how they preserve tissue next time I visit.

I'm old enough to go on my own now, pretty much.

FRIDAY, APRIL 2 – 1982.

Looks like we're at war. As if the nuclear stuff wasn't enough, we're fighting the Argentineans now. This world—

[Fire damage]

—someone could just do something. Fix things. Make things better. But you'd need to be…

Someone. Just someone.

TUESDAY, JULY 27 – 1982.

Oh Christ, oh shit!

I did it. This time, this one… I did it. I *actually* did it. I'm scared and excited and… Not sure I can write any more. I just wanted to—

Later.

THURSDAY, AUGUST 5 – 1982.

Things have calmed down a little. Enough for me to try and explain what happened.

If she'd only kept out of things that didn't concern her, she'd still be… She really only has herself to blame. I was supposed to be meeting Lucy, we were going to have a picnic in the meadow. I'd even smuggled a blanket and some food out of the house in a backpack. I could tell, however, even as she walked towards me, that it was Miranda. We've been having…issues for a while now.

But everything came to a head that day.

We had words, she told me to stay away from her sister, that I was a bad influence on her – more like Lucy had been standing up to Miranda recently. Though not enough, obviously, because she'd wheedled our meeting out of her.

The argument grew more heated and Miranda shoved me over again. I fell, hard. When I got up, I had a rock in my fist. It was instinct mainly, a knee-jerk reaction. I swung it and hit her on the side of the head.

Miranda went down, blood pouring from her temple, onto the blanket beneath her. She was mumbling something I couldn't catch, so I leaned in, but it still didn't make any sense. Maybe she was calling me another name? I panicked again a little. Thought about running off and calling 999 from the nearest phone box. But would they even get there in time? And what would happen to me then?

I began to think more clearly, forced myself to. And I thought about what I could do with Miranda out of the way (*To Kill a Mocking...*), about how much easier things would be—

[Fire damage]

—the dream, what it had been wanting me to do to her for a long, long time.

I had my pocket-knife with me, and I took this out. She struggled, so I straddled her, held her down while I pushed the blade into her chest. She began to scream so I put my other hand over her mouth.

I've never felt so alive! There was a charge running through me as Miranda's life ebbed away. I could feel a throbbing in the metal, a pulse that travelled up my arm into my body. At first I thought I was just imagining it, but I could sense the actual moment Miranda was about to die.

Strangely I wanted more than anything to save her, then. Not because I felt any kind of regret: I hated her. And it was too late physically, I understood that. But I wanted to put whatever she'd been, whatever she was *becoming*, to use. To direct it, draw it into me, somehow control that power.

Then the moment passed. Miranda lay still and lifeless beneath me.

I'd been so wrapped up in what I was doing I hadn't

even heard the footsteps behind. Not until they were right on top of me. I whirled, startled, terrified I'd been discovered.

There, watching me with eyes wide open, was Anton. He'd followed me all the way from home. "What are you doing here?" I snapped, a stupid, pointless question. He *was* there, and he'd seen everything.

He didn't answer, so I got up. He started to back away, as frightened as I had been moments before. I had two choices, and one of them involved another killing.

The other one was this: "Hey, it's all right. Don't be scared. Anton, I'm sorry I shouted. But…look, what happened here – it's just pretend. A game! You like games, don't you? We both do." Anton looked unsure. "It can be our little secret." I remembered again what Mother… what *Angela* had said about secrets, but I'd already got him. The chance to be involved in something with his older brother that nobody else knew about? He just couldn't resist.

After I'd given him a moment or two, I set him to work. We had to clear all this up, fast. Not just because someone else might happen along – that was doubtful, I'd chosen this area for its isolation – but because we needed to get back home. Needed to be away from here. Anton helped me gather my things, wrap up the body, and lug it through the woods to the lake. Then we looked for more stones and rocks, tied them up inside the blanket with her, and pushed her into the water. She sank almost straight away and I grinned at Anton. He grinned back. Finally, I tossed in the knife.

We headed the long way home, creeping back inside so I could get out of my blood-stained top. The first chance I got, I took those clothes, that backpack and everything inside it, down to the furnace in the hospital Colin had shown me – where they get rid of 'packages' they can't identify.

I also made sure Maxwell heard us inside the house,

playing. We woke him in fact. He'd fallen asleep in his office, but came rushing out when we started messing about with Angela's old instruments. I've never seen him as angry as he was then, but it was worth the smack I got – not Anton this time, I noted – because I needed him to remember. It was important.

To remember where we'd been that day.

SUNDAY, NOVEMBER 14 – 1982.

God, the last few months…

I've been lying low, haven't dared write anything in here since… Miranda's parents reported her missing, of course. I knew they would. When the police came knocking at our door a few days after she vanished, I also knew that Lucy had given me up. That she'd told about our 'date'.

Maxwell informed them I'd been around all day on the 27th looking after Anton. He was still in a position of respect, a doctor, even if they could smell booze on him. But my whereabouts were also confirmed by my little 'brother'. It was still part of the game we were playing. I told them I hadn't gone because I knew Miranda didn't want me seeing Lucy, that I didn't want to come between two sisters who were so close. That she must have gone missing after heading off into the meadow on her own. One of the policemen looked wary, but the other seemed to buy it.

There was a search, but nobody searched the lake. It's pretty deep anyway, I remember reading that in a local history book. After a while, and a couple of TV appeals that got nowhere, the police went away again. I don't think Miranda's parents will ever give up, though.

Lucy's…different these days. Even if I did want

anything to do with her – and after blabbing, I really don't – she's not nearly as much fun. She *never* smiles. It's like a part of her is missing, the part that used to tell her what to do. Now she just wanders round like she's in a daze. Like Maxwell Sr does most of the time.

I've learned a lot from this experience. Especially from the dreams that followed. My reflection didn't shake its head this time, just mouthed more words – until I was finally able to hear it. Now I understand exactly what a waste Miranda's death was.

Now I know what I must do the next time. How it will bring me closer to the reflection, which is growing bigger each time I see it. I haven't figured it *all* out yet, but—

[Fire damage]

—turned sixteen last month (well, officially, as I still don't know my *real* date of birth). I can leave school soon, whether Maxwell Sr approves or disapproves. Not that I'm being bothered there anymore. People are beginning to look at me differently, as the woman who called herself my Mother once did.

I intend to travel.

A lot.

TUESDAY, AUGUST 30 – 1983.

So much has happened since the last time I wrote in this diary.

Both the dreams and 'Mother' were right. I'm not a nobody, and I am different (though I didn't have anything inside me, not back when she said those words). Pieces of the puzzle are starting to slot together.

I did a test, just like the reflection told me to. I went to a busy place, the market in Brenton. I sat on a bench and cleared my mind. Then I waited and I watched. I saw three that afternoon, a woman and two men. And I could tell, just by looking at them. It's an ability that, as far as I know, only I possess.

I couldn't prove anything that day, but didn't need to. I simply *knew*.

The next step was to attempt what I'd failed to do with Miranda. The key turned out to be that fork, the one Maxwell used to clutch as he increasingly withdrew into himself.

(He's just a shadow, a…reflection of what he used to be; my reflection in reverse. I know I did that to him, but it was necessary. His sabbatical eventually became an early retirement. I don't think he'll ever return to that hospital.)

The knife I'd used hadn't been quite right. I needed something to conduct that energy, that life-force into me. So I 'borrowed' the fork, one night when Maxwell was asleep, prying it out of his hand.

It was a simple matter to sharpen the prongs.

To turn it into a weapon.

Then I—

[Fire damage]

—overcompensated, but I went much further afield to make sure. Mrs Thomas has all but moved in now. She watches over Anton and his father while I disappear for days at a time. Anton doesn't question it, he knows we're still playing the game. Nobody asks where I'm going or where I've been. I think they just assume I've fallen in with a bad crowd. Doesn't matter.

As for money, it's easy enough to forge Maxwell Sr's signature on cheques. He's built up quite a fund in the bank over the years. I know because I saw the accounts while I was still searching for information about who I am.

Anyway, back to the first one I…hunted. Yes, I suppose you could call it that. I tracked him at any rate, got his scent in my nostrils. Followed him, planned it all in advance: what I would wear – all black, including the mask – what I was going to do, where I was going to do it. At his home, where that used car salesman lived out his miserable existence alone. Sad bastard, I was doing him and the world a favour. He was in his forties, so I had youth on my side, but he still put up quite a struggle, even though I came up from behind, grabbing him and choking off his airway with the crook of my arm. We fell forward through the doorway at one point and I remember thinking: *We're making way too much noise!*

Everything changed when I stuck the fork into his back, puncturing his spleen. I felt the jolt, the trembling sensations, same as I did with Miranda, only they were amplified tenfold. And, as I grew stronger, the man I was wrestling with weakened. Not just because he was losing his will to live, but because I was *taking* his will. It was being transferred into me: all his energy, all that he'd ever been…or ever would be. Wasn't long before he was still and I rose, staggering around. It felt a little like that time I'd tried alcohol. I was dizzy, but managed to make it to the front door, closing it.

My whole body felt different and, once things had settled down, I realised that I liked it. A…it's a little hard to describe it, but—

[Fire damage]

—fire this time. It would get rid of everything, just like

the furnace in the hospital. He was a smoker, so it wasn't that hard to fake a gas leak accident. From a distance, I watched the explosion, the flames rising. I felt just like them. Powerful. Dangerous.

I was gone by the time I heard the first sirens.

Sadly, the feeling didn't last. I couldn't hang onto it. The dream told me why, afterwards. I needed to *keep* some physical part, only then would it remain.

You see? Still learning.

The time after that was better. The woman, the whore. I pinned that one on her last client, incapacitating him while he was still on top of her, while he was ejaculating. Then I rammed the fork into her throat before she could get a scream out.

Oh, it felt good.

When I was done, I snipped off her little finger; it was all I needed. A body part that she had a pair of. Then I did things to the rest of her, things that would cover my tracks and ensure her customer would go away for a long time after I placed the knife in his hand.

It was only what was left behind: the machinery. I have the important part inside me – working *for* me.

The finger's in a solution I concocted myself, hidden in our locked basement. I've discovered I like it down there, underground. It's like my...sanctuary. My Batcave. At some point I will need to find somewhere better, though. Somewhere I can keep them all. My trophies. My reminders.

Because there will be *so* many more. I'm only just getting started, but already I have two more parts of my collection, pieces of the jigsaw. And I'm getting...*better* (no glasses now), closer to the reflection with each one I take. No, not take. Store, keep safe, borrow. Like the fork.

Old Maxwell simply sighed when he couldn't find

it, but I said nothing. He's growing frailer by the day. I am growing stronger.

And I'm far from empty now.

TUESDAY, MARCH 13 – 1984.

I had to share this one with you. The latest addition to my collection.

Matt Wilson (names to faces now, faces to names), fitness instructor in a gym. I followed him for four days, the posing twat. I did so enjoy our little 'altercation' out in the car park when he was leaving work late. And he was strong; a real challenge—

[Fire damage]

—warned him that he wouldn't like me when I'm angry. Just my little joke. He had balls, though, I'll say that much.

I took one of them from him as a souvenir.

I. Fucking. Hate. P.E!

FRIDAY, MAY 25 – 1984.

Acid is my new best friend, you just have to be careful when you use it.

I spilt some on myself by accident, and it burned me pretty badly. But my arm healed up in under an hour.

Being a freak of nature has its compensations.

MONDAY, SEPTEMBER 10 – 1984.

I finally showed Maxwell Sr what I am, what I can do. I figured the timing was right, I'd waited long enough. I'm eighteen very soon, it's a coming of age. Time for a little 'Father' and 'Son' chat. Ha!

So I showed him my new trick.

Showed him what happens when I wear one of the faces…or even two. When I *summon* them. It's handy, I don't even need my mask anymore. I also told him it was all thanks to Angela's fork. Just before he had the heart attack (I was wrong, he did wind up back in the hospital; I *put* him there) he asked me what I was.

"That's what *I* want to know!" I grabbed him by his jumper, lifting him off his feet. Even without my new strength, he'd lost so much weight I could have managed it easily. "Where did you *buy* me from?" Buy, like I was some kind of *thing!*

I only found out a few things before the attack came on. He got me from a woman up north sometime in late May, 1966. Where *exactly* I didn't discover. But she'd died in labour, giving birth to—

I dropped him then, leaving him to spasm on the floor, gasping for breath.

I have a brother. A real brother.

An identical *twin* brother.

The irony wasn't lost on me either. That I'm like the people I hunt. (No, I'm so much more than that!) I've wondered a lot of things about my twin since I found out: wondered what his childhood must have been like; wondered if he'd felt alone as well.

Wondered if he kept a diary like mine? If we shared any traits beyond a physical resemblance?

Wondered whether he might be a hunter?

And the reflection in my dream… I'm beginning to question if that *is* me looking into the mirror, or him? My subconscious *lack* of him. Now I'm becoming the mirrored image, does that make him the one I'm addressing? Ordering, as I do with Anton? I have a feeling I am the dominant one. Unless he's even stronger than me – than I *will be* once this is all over?

Not possible. But just in case, I'll wait a while before I track him down. I'll know when the time is right, when we're close to the endgame.

Not much to go on, though, those tiny hints at my origins, I thought. Then it struck me. That's exactly what this is.

My origin story.

I watched him die then, this impostor, this man who'd claimed to be my father, and I felt about as much pity as I did for Angela (now playing a harp of a different kind!). He wasn't worthy, neither of them were. "Secrets have a way of coming out, of coming back to punish you," I whispered. "Some son I turned out to be, eh?" I'm definitely a *stranger*, and proud of it.

I said he ended up back in the hospital, and he did… in the morgue I love so dearly. There's been some mention of Social Services coming in to assess things, but I can handle them. By that time my birthday will have passed (which in itself is a nonsense, my real birthday was months ago!); I'll take over Anton's guardianship, and between us we'll have access to all of Maxwell Craine Sr's wealth. I'll need it to complete my work, complete my collection, honing my skills and abilities as I go. It will take some time, but then I'm quite a patient person – unless I'm tested. Mrs Thompson will continue to look after Anton, until I have use for him, now I know exactly how willing he'll be. How eager he is to play.

But I'll have much more than that. And with great power comes… Well, you know the rest. This world needs to change, needs someone to take command of it. This is a new war, but it's one that's worth fighting.

I'll also have all my 'friends'. They're right here inside me, doing exactly as they're told.

Late May… I just realised what star sign that is, and laughed out loud. A Gemini.

No. *The* Gemini. He has awoken. He is rising.

And I will never be alone again.

THE GEMINI FACTOR

[TV SCRIPT]

By Paul Kane
based on the novel of the same name

Titles: Tight close-up on a cell dividing, this eventually leads to a kaleidoscope of cells splitting, patterns upon patterns... Until finally we see two babies in a womb, curled up side by side like the Yin and Yang symbol, one`s head next to the other`s feet.

EXT. CITY STREETS - NIGHT.

We see feet. A man, JAMES, runs; we hear his breath. He`s alone and there`s not much light on that street, so we can`t see his face clearly. But we hear footsteps behind him, faster and faster.

James rounds a corner, bends, gasps for air. The footsteps following him grow louder. They force him to run again. He stumbles through what appears to be an empty part of the city, up an alley. James pauses and listens - the footsteps have stopped.

Still very much a silhouette, he lets out another breath. Steam flows from his mouth; the relief`s evident.

James hears the footsteps again, backs up against a wall, presses himself tight against it. We see a close-up of his eyes as he watches the gap at the top of the alley. The footsteps grow louder, louder...

Suddenly we see a YOUTH go past, harmless; he`s wearing jeans and a hooded jacket.

James laughs.

>   JAMES
>   (under his breath)
>   Stupid, stupid... Just
>   a kid. Just a bloody

                 kid!

He tilts back his head, but as he does so we
see movement behind him. The wall comes alive.
No, the shadows there are hiding something:
a figure. It rises above him and still he`s
oblivious to it.

Suddenly he realises, turns.

But it`s too late. We see sudden cuts, the
flash of metal - the prongs of a fork?

Then the face of his attacker, TWINKLE, as it
moves slightly out of the shadows, though only
just.

And we see the impossible: a quick glimpse of
two faces where there should be one.

Close up on James` eyes, open wide in terror
- then the camera pulls in tight to focus on
just the one eye: the pupil and a spot of white
against black.

<u>EXT. CITY - NIGHT.</u>

We pull out to see the white spot is now a
pinprick in the sky: a star, soon joined by
more. We pan down to find the city below is
almost a reflection of the sky above. Its
twin. Tiny, sparkling lights from buildings;
car headlights which zoom along roads...

Welcome to NORCHESTER.

We close in on one of these, a large metallic-
green vehicle that looks almost black tonight.
We turn off from the main road into a side-
road.

We hear sirens, see the reflection of the orange and blue lights on walls even before we encounter the scene. They illuminate a sign that reads FAGIN`S ROW. A crowd has gathered at one end and the car noses its way through them gingerly. It guns its engine at a BYSTANDER, who refuses to move.

The car can`t get any closer so it pulls up by the curb. A door opens and out steps MASON, the car rising with relief as he does. He`s early 40s, but looks older. His salt and pepper hair gives him character. He`s a big man - not exactly fat, just bulky - and looks like he`s been crammed into the suit he`s wearing. His collar and tie strains against a bull-neck. He`s wearing an overcoat on top and he pulls this together to keep out the cold.

Another flash of light, white this time, and he shields his eyes. He pushes the PHOTOGRAPHER with the flash-camera out of the way... Only to be confronted with a TV camera almost instantly. A TV WOMAN with a mike steps forward.

> TV WOMAN
> Excuse me... Excuse
> me, Detective
> Inspector Mason. It
> is D.I. Mason, isn`t
> it? Alice Baker,
> Norchester Today. I
> wonder if we could
> have a word?

More cameras and recording devices are thrust in his direction.

MASON grimaces.

> MASON
> I have nothing to say

                    at this time.

                         TV WOMAN
                    Is it true there`s a
                    dead body in there,
                    sir?

                         MASON
                    If you`ll let me get
                    by, I`ll have a look
                    and find out.

                     SECOND REPORTER (O.C.)
                    Do you think this
                    might be a gang-
                    related killing?

                         MASON
                    No comment.

Mason pushes past.

A pair of young POLICEMEN can see he`s having
difficulty and come to help. They hold back
the reporters and crowds.

Mason ducks beneath the blue and white tape
that`s cordoning off the area. He stares up at
the building, a disused factory with spider-
webbed windows. It has probably never seen this
much activity in the whole of its existence.

With a loud sigh, he enters the crime
scene.

<u>INT. FACTORY - NIGHT.</u>

It`s dark in here, except in one corner of the
room. There are spotlights and there`s a frenzy
of activity: men in white suits buzz around,
while another camera blitzes the scene. MASON

walks over to them, he`s definitely in no hurry.

He cranes his neck, then nods when he spots the person he`s looking for. We get his point of view now, on SGT. DEBORAH HARRISON: mid-30s, a little over five feet tall, with chestnut hair in a bob. She`s wearing a trouser-suit and a grey overcoat on top. What little of her blouse is showing shines white in the glare from one spotlight. She acknowledges him as he walks towards her.

>   DEBORAH
>   Sir.

>   MASON
>   So much for the day of
>   rest, Sergeant. What
>   have we got?

>   DEBORAH
>   It`s probably best if
>   you see for yourself.

She leads Mason over to that corner, where bricks have spilled from the wall in several places. There`s the body - slumped against the wall with head bowed, legs splayed. There`s a patch of dried blood staining his shirt at the front and his right hand is missing.

>   MASON
>   Shit, what a mess.

>   ROSY (O.C.)
>   That`s one way of
>   putting it.

Mason spins round to see pathologist ROSY LIM. She`s about thirty, of oriental extraction, her dark hair tied back. She`s also wearing latex

gloves. When she smiles a most inappropriate
smile, dimples form in her cheeks.

                    ROSY (CONT`D)
          ...although I doubt if
          I`ll be putting that
          in any of my reports.

Mason nods a greeting.

                    MASON
          Miss Lim.

                    ROSY
          I won`t keep you in
          suspense, Inspector.
          I`ve given our man
          here the once-over,
          and cause of death
          is probably loss of
          blood, the result of
          puncture wounds on
          the torso. There`s no
          sign of any of that
          blood on the floor or
          walls, though, which
          means he was almost
          certainly killed
          elsewhere and dumped
          here afterwards. At a
          guess I`d hazard he`s
          been dead for several
          days. The hand was

                    ROSY (CONT`D)
          most likely removed
          after his death. A
          clean cut; nothing
          sloppy.

Mason turns to Deborah.

                MASON
Any sign of the hand?

                DEBORAH
    (shaking her head)
Not yet, sir. But the
SOCOs are far from
finished. It`s quite a
large area to cover.

Mason nods, turns back to Rosy.

                MASON

*What can you tell me about the wound itself, Miss
Lim?*

                ROSY
I`ll know more once
I`ve conducted the
autopsy, but if you
pushed me I`d have to
say it was some kind
of spiked instrument.

                MASON
What do you mean, like
a needle?

                ROSY
No, larger. There are
holes in his shirt,
quite large holes.
But no slits. I don`t
believe it was a
knife.

                MASON
Right. Well, thank you
Miss Lim.

He turns away - moves closer to Deborah.

                    MASON
Who found the body?

                    DEBORAH
A group of homeless
people, sir. Broke in
looking for shelter
against the cold, I
expect. Found more
than they bargained
for.

                    MASON
I`m surprised they
called it in. Where
are they now?

                    DEBORAH
Back at the station,
giving their
statements. I thought
it was best not to let
them wander about out
there.

                    MASON
And, of course, they
get to spend the
evening in a nice warm
nick being supplied
with tea and biscuits.
You`re too soft for
your own good, you
know that, Blondie?

                    DEBORAH
Sir.

                    MASON
But you`re right about
one thing, we don`t
want them gabbing

to the press about
all this. Not yet,
anyway. Which reminds
me, someone had
better speak to those
arseholes out there.

                    DEBORAH
And tell them what?

                    MASON
                 (grinning)
You`ll think of
something.

Deborah narrows her eyes at her superior.

                    DEBORAH
And what are you going
to do in the meantime,
sir?

                    MASON
Talk to a higher
authority, Sergeant.

                    ROSY
(nodding at the corpse)
I don`t think
praying`s going to do
much good.

Mason pulls out his mobile phone.

                    MASON
I was thinking of a
much higher authority
than that, doctor...
                 (into the phone)
Hello, could you
put me through to

                    Chief Superintendent
                    Bingham, please.

EXT. OUTSIDE FACTORY - NIGHT.

DEBORAH finishes giving a statement to the
press, who finally disperse now they have a
few crumbs of information. She is about to
turn back when ROSY calls her.

                         DEBORAH
                    All done?

                          ROSY
                         (nodding)
                    Message for you from
                    Mason. I quote: Tell
                    'Blondie` she can
                    get going once she`s
                    sorted the media out.
                    Tell her to go spend
                    some time with that
                    kid of hers.

                         DEBORAH
                         (sarcastic)
                    Gee, thanks Roy. I do
                    all the hard work and
                    he steams in at the
                    last minute.

                          ROSY
                    Isn`t that what
                    inspectors are
                    supposed to do?

                         DEBORAH
                    Maybe it`s just his
                    way of telling me I
                    look like warmed-over

dog crap.

                ROSY
You do look tired...
You okay?

                DEBORAH
            (defensively)
It`s not the first
dead body I`ve ever
seen, Rosy.

                ROSY
I know.

                DEBORAH
            (yawning)
Sorry. Comes from
being awake since six.
I was in the middle
of tying up a robbery
case when this came
in. The joys of

        DEBORAH (CONT`D)
C.I.D.

                ROSY
No such thing as shift
work, Debbie, you
should know that by
now.

                DEBORAH
Yeah, well I`m not
complaining if his
lordship wants to take
command of-

Deborah notices something over Rosy`s shoulder.
Someone in the crowd staring right at her. Part

of the crowd, yet somehow separate from it. JACK: bearded, his eyes penetrating. Briefly everything else disappears around her and she can only see him.

                    ROSY
          Debbie? Debbie?
          Everything all right?

Deborah breaks eye contact to look at Rosy. When she turns back to the crowd the man has gone. Rosy follows her gaze but sees nothing unusual.

                    DEBORAH
          Hmm? Yeah. I just
          thought I saw...
          Nothing. It was
          nothing.

Rosy gives her a worried look, changes the subject.

                    ROSY
          Oh, I know what I
          meant to ask you.
          Something I`ve been
          meaning to talk to you
          about for a while...
          Well, ever since you
          came to our pleasant
          little city, really.

Deborah glances at her sideways.

                    ROSY
          Why does Mason keep
          calling you Blondie?
          Is he colour-blind or
          something? Your hair`s
          brown.

                    DEBORAH
          It`s just a stupid
          nickname that`s
          followed me around.
          Mind you, he`s the
          only one with the
          balls to use it.

                    ROSY
          Let me guess, you used
          to bleach, right?

Deborah lets out an aggrieved snort.

                    ROSY
          Then what? Come on,
          give.

                    DEBORAH
          All right, but don`t
          say I didn`t warn you.
          What`s my name?

Rosy appears puzzled, then a look of
enlightenment dawns on her face.

                    ROSY
          Ah, I get it. Deborah
          Harrison. Debbie
          Harry! Now that is
          lame.

                    DEBORAH
          Told you it was
          stupid.

                    ROSY
          Oh, I don`t know. It
          could have been worse.
          I can think of a few—

Deborah holds up a finger.

                    DEBORAH
          Don`t even go
          there, Miss Lim the
          pathologist.

The pair laugh softly; it`s a release after
what they`ve seen inside the factory.

                    ROSY
          So, I`ll see you
          tomorrow then...
          Blondie.

                    DEBORAH
          You will?

                    ROSY
          The autopsy`s at ten-
          thirty. Mason`s booked
          you both ringside
          seats.

                    DEBORAH
          Great.

The pair say their goodbyes and a POLICEWOMAN
lets Deborah through the cordon. She makes her
way to her silver Peugeot, glances around one
last time, then gets in.

EXT. DEBORAH`S HOUSE - NIGHT.

DEBORAH turns into her street: a quieter part
of the city - the suburbs almost. A haven away
from what she`s had to deal with at work.
She pulls onto her drive to see the curtains
twitch at her living room window. An older
woman - DEBORAH`S MOTHER, WENDY - watches her
approach. Even before Deborah can climb from

the car, the front door is open.

Deborah raises a hand to her mother, who smiles
- a mixture of worry and relief.

                    DEBORAH
               Hi, Mum.

Deborah`s mother kisses her on the cheek.

                    WENDY
               Hello love.

From behind her mum, little ISABEL appears.
At seven and a half, she`s as cute as can be,
but razor sharp with it: something she gets
from her own mother. Deborah bends to kiss the
girl.

                    DEBORAH
               Oh I`ve missed you
               today, Izzy; I really
               have.

                    IZZY
               You said you`d be back
               early.

The little girl looks at her with doleful
eyes.

                    DEBORAH
               I`m sorry sweetheart,
               but something came up.
               I couldn`t get away.

                    IZZY
               I hate it when you
               have to work Sundays.

                    DEBORAH
               So do I, Izzy. So do

                    I.

Deborah gives her a look that says she`s
growing up way too fast.

There won`t always be opportunities to spend
Sundays with her 'little` girl.

                    DEBORAH
          Did you have a good
          time at Claudia`s this
          afternoon?

                    IZZY
          Yep.

                    DEBORAH
          What did you two get
          up to? I hope you
          behaved yourself,
          young lady.

                    IZZY
          Mu-um! I`m not a kid,
          you know.

                    DEBORAH
          Okay, but you do
          realise if you`re
          lying I`m going
          to have to run
          you downtown for
          interrogation.

Deborah tickles Izzy under her arms until the
girl pleads with her to stop.

                    DEBORAH
          All right, on one
          condition. You tell me
          what happened on the
          soaps tonight after

            I`ve grabbed something
            to eat.

Izzy nods and runs off back into the living
room where the sound of an advert jingle can
be heard.

INT. DEBORAH`S HALL - NIGHT.

Inside fully now, DEBORAH starts to shrug off
her coat. WENDY steps forward to help.

                    WENDY
            Here, let me do that.

                    DEBORAH
            I can manage, Mum. I`m
            not a kid, you know.

Deborah pauses, smiles, and shakes her head at
the irony of what she`s just said. She hangs
up her coat.

                    DEBORAH
            Why don`t you go and
            put your feet up.

                    WENDY
            Why don`t you tell me
            what happened today?

Deborah heads into the kitchen, but her mother
follows her through.

INT. DEBORAH`S KITCHEN - NIGHT.

In the kitchen now, DEBORAH walks over to the
kettle. WENDY follows.

                    DEBORAH
          Leave it for now, Mum,
          okay? I just want to
          make myself something
          to eat and drink, then
          sit and watch TV with
          Izzy before she has to
          go to bed.

                    WENDY
          I can`t help it,
          Debbie. I worry about
          you.

                    DEBORAH
          I know, Mum. But
          really, it`s okay.

Deborah fixes herself a cup of coffee, pops
a couple of slices of toast into the toaster.
Her mother waits until Deborah`s put a pan of
baked beans on the hob before she hits her
daughter with a bombshell.

                    WENDY
           (lowering her voice)
          She`s been asking me
          about her father again
          today.

Deborah turns, an anxious expression on her
face.

                    DEBORAH
          And what did you say?

                    WENDY
          It`s not my place to
          say anything, love.
          But she`s curious.
          It`s only natural.

Deborah stirs the beans, head low.

                    DEBORAH
          I don`t want her
          knowing anything about
          him. In fact, I`ve
          been thinking about
          telling her he died
          before she was born.

                    WENDY
               (horrified)
          You`re not, are you?

                    DEBORAH
          He might as well be
          dead. It`s better than
          telling her what he
          was really like.

                    WENDY
          I`m not sure that`s
          such a good idea.
          She`s bound to
          find out the truth
          eventually, and when
          she does she`ll hate
          you for it.

                    DEBORAH
               (sighing)
          I... I just don`t know
          what to do, Mum. She`s
          built up some kind of
          idealised image of
          him in her mind. I`m
          frightened that if I
          tell her, she`ll blame
          me.

                    WENDY
          For what? You have

                    nothing to feel guilty
                    about. You-

There`s a shriek of excitement from the living
room.

                    IZZY (O.S.)
               Mum! Mum! You`re on
               the telly!

Deborah and Wendy exchange looks and rush out.

INT. LIVING ROOM - NIGHT.

DEBORAH trails WENDY into the living room.
She`s shocked to see herself on the TV screen
this soon, but there she is, addressing the
assembled reporters outside the crime scene.

ISABEL is sitting crossed-legged in front of
the television.

Deborah`s image is replaced by the TV WOMAN
from before.

                    TV WOMAN
               Police were refusing
               to either confirm or
               deny the body-

Deborah snaps off the TV before any more can
be said. The picture disappears, the screen
now blank.

                    IZZY
               Mum, what did you do
               that for? I wanted to-

                    DEBORAH
                  (flustered)
               It`s time for bed,

Izzy.

                    IZZY
But you said-

                    DEBORAH
It`s time to start
getting ready for bed.
You`ve got school
tomorrow.

                    IZZY
But-

                    DEBORAH
                  (snaps)
Bed. Right now!

A sulky Isabel rises and marches past her
mother. Deborah closes her eyes and pinches
the skin at the top of her nose. When she
opens them again, Wendy is looking at her,
concerned.

Nothing is said; it doesn`t need to be.

Deborah walks back out of the room.

Wendy just stands there, bites her lip.

EXT. THE IMPERIAL - NIGHT.

We`re outside a large hotel: THE IMPERIAL,
according to the sign. There are a few lights
on in rooms izn the tall, rectangular building
but not many. It gives it the appearance of a
giant hand-held puzzle.

There are columns at the doorway and it is
between these that a bearded JACK from the
crime scene passes. Late 30s and tall, he`s

wearing a green crumpled jacket, black trousers
and boots.

INT. IMPERIAL LOBBY - NIGHT.

JACK enters the lobby. It`s trying its hardest
to be plush, but has seen better days. There
are a few potted plants scattered here and
there, but the maroon carpets are faded. The
oak reception desk he approaches is chipped
in places.

A young girl with auburn hair in her late
teens/early 20s, FELICITY, is behind this. Her
smile looks like it`s plastered on.

She`s wearing a maroon waistcoat with a name-
badge pinned to it. Her voice is sickly sweet
when she says:

                    FELICITY
          Hello, sir. How may I
          help you?

Jack smiles awkwardly. He shifts his weight
from one foot to the other.

                    JACK
          Er... I`d like a room.

                    FELICITY
          Certainly, sir. Can I
          ask if you`ve made a
          reservation?

                    JACK
          No... No, I`m afraid
          not. Will that be a
          problem?

                    FELICITY

You`re in luck, sir.
We`re not fully booked
at the moment.

Her sarcastic smile says they`re never fully
booked.

                    FELICITY
          Will you be wanting a
          single, a double-

                    JACK
          Double please.

                    FELICITY
          All right, well if you
          could just fill this
          in, Mr...

                    JACK
          Foley... Jack Foley.

                    FELICITY
          And do you know how
          long you might be
          staying with us?

                    JACK
          It`s... hard to say.

Felicity looks at him strangely, then smiles
her manufactured smile.

JACK finishes up and puts his credit card in
the reader when instructed.

Then she gives him his key.

                    FELICITY
          Yours is room three-
          oh-seven. That`s on
          the third floor.

                    JACK
          My cases are outside
          in the car, the
          red Mondeo. Do you
          think...

                  FELICITY
          We`ll have someone
          bring them to your
          room and park your
          car.

He hands over his car keys.

                    JACK
          Thanks.

                  FELICITY
          Thank you, Mr. Foley.
          I hope you have a
          pleasant stay with us
          here at The Imperial.

He doesn`t reply, simply gives her a look that
says 'we`ll see` and makes his way over to the
lift. It`s old-fashioned, the cage already at
the bottom.

Even before he gets there the doors have opened
and Jack`s greeted by an old man wearing the
hotel`s uniform. His name-tag tells us he`s
ALBERT.

                   ALBERT
          Pleasant evening, sir.

                    JACK
             (without malice)
          For some.

Albert asks what floor and sits down on a
wooden stool while they wait for the lift to

ascend.

INT. JACK`S ROOM - NIGHT.

JACK closes the door to his room on the porter.
He pockets his keys and stares at two small
cases by the side of the bed. Jack walks over,
rubs his shoulder, and sits on the edge of the
bed. He holds his head in his hands.

We see a quick flash of the metal fork blades.

When he looks up, he sees himself in the mirror
on the dresser opposite. He rubs his beard,
then looks left and right, as if he doesn`t
recognise himself.

Jack scrambles for the TV remote on the bedside
table and switches his set on. Laying back,
he flicks through a few channels; nothing but
dross. Then he catches the end of a local news
broadcast and sits up sharply.

The TV throws out a picture of a woman talking
to the journalists. There is a brief glimpse
of her name: SGT DEBORAH HARRISON in white
letters underneath.

                    TV WOMAN (V.O.)
               ...further when we
               know more...

The NEWS READER goes on to the next story.
Jack jabs at the remote, searches the channels
again, but finds no more news programmes.

Frustrated, he throws the remote across the
room and slams himself back on the bed, arm
across his eyes.

INT. MASON`S CAR - DAY.

Next day: MASON is in the car with DEBORAH, stuck in traffic. A set of temporary lights have been erected; they`ve just turned from red to green. Mason, crammed behind the wheel, beeps the car horn for the driver in front to move.

                    MASON
          Come on, come on!

                    DEBORAH
          I said we should have
          set off sooner.

                    MASON
          Yes, thank you,
          Blondie. We`d be all
          right if those pricks
          in front would just...
          Ah, here we go.

The lights turn back to red again just as Mason`s car pulls up.

                    MASON
          Oh, I don`t believe
          this.

Mason bangs the steering wheel.

                    DEBORAH
          Easy, sir. I`ve
          already had to deal
          with one irritable kid
          this morning.

The Inspector smiles and turns to her.

                    MASON
          Problems?

                    DEBORAH
          Nothing I can`t
          handle. Just the past
          coming back to haunt
          me, that`s all.

                    MASON
          Yeah? It can do that
          sometimes.

                    DEBORAH
          Sir.

                    MASON
          Yes?

Deborah nods ahead.

                    DEBORAH
          The lights.

Mason turns back to see they`re green once
more. He smiles again and puts the car into
gear.

INT. MORGUE - DAY.

DEBORAH and MASON enter a large room with
several tables taking up the floor space. ROSY
stands next to one of them with her assistant,
EUGENE, who looks like he`s walked in off
the set of a Gothic horror movie: short and
stooping, with what little hair he has combed
over the top of his head. Some people suit
their professions and Eugene is a perfect
example.

Both Rosy and Eugene are wearing scrubs and
latex gloves halfway up their arms. On the
table in front of them is the body from last
night. Face up, it stares with dead eyes at

the ceiling.

Eugene is busy taking photographs of it.

                    ROSY
          Ah, Inspector Mason.
          Nice to see you again
          so soon. Don`t worry,
          you haven`t missed a
          thing. I believe you
          know Eugene.

Eugene greets them with a tip of his camera.

               ROSY (CONT`D)
          Hey there, Blondie.

Deborah groans. Mason looks over and raises an
eyebrow; she shrugs.

                    ROSY
          Well, don`t just stand
          around, you two. You
          won`t see anything
          from over there.

                    MASON
          No, I don`t suppose we
          will.

Mason steps forward. He curls his lip at the
sight of the body laid bare like that. He
regains his composure when Deborah stands by
his side.

                    ROSY
          I was just examining
          the puncture wounds,
          the ones I told you
          about last night.

Rosy points a gloved finger at two holes on the

man`s right-hand side: they look like large
craters in his flesh. She taps her finger next
to them.

                    ROSY
          At first glance I
          did wonder if they
          might have been made
          by something like a
          barbecue skewer, or an
          ice-pick.

                    MASON
          What, like in Basic
          Instinct or something?

Rosy`s turn to raise an eyebrow.

                    ROSY
          Never seen it,
          Inspector - not my cup
          of tea - but if you
          like.

                    EUGENE
          Good film.

They all turn to look at her assistant, who
has put down the camera.

He prepares Rosy`s instruments.

                    ROSY
          Right... Anyway, I
          scrapped that theory.
          See how close together
          these holes are?

Deborah skirts around Mason.

                    DEBORAH
          What`re you thinking,

Rosy?

                    ROSY
          In my opinion the
          murder weapon was
          some sort of pronged
          instrument.

                    MASON
          Now we`re back to the
          barbecue motif again.
          What can you tell us
          about the hand, Miss
          Lim?

                    ROSY
          I can confirm it was
          removed after death.

                    MASON
          After he`d been
          stabbed with the fork?

                    ROSY
          That`s correct.
          He`d already lost a
          substantial amount of
          blood before his hand
          was separated from
          his arm. As I said
          before, it was removed
          very cleanly, possibly
          using a sharp hatchet
          or cleaver. One fluid
          motion.

Rosy makes a chopping motion into her palm and
Mason pulls another face.

                    MASON
          All right, Miss Lim,
          we get the picture.

The pathologist lifts the wrist so they can
see it better.

Inside, meat and bone is packed tightly
together.

Mason swallows hard.

                    ROSY
          It wasn`t sawn off,
          because there`d be
          ragged edges here.

She points to the edges of the cut.

                    ROSY (CONT`D)
          But I`ll tell you
          this much, Inspector:
          whoever did it was
          strong.

                    MASON
          What makes you say
          that?

                    ROSY
          What, apart from the
          fact they can chop
          off a hand in one go?
          Have you ever tried to
          detach a hand from an
          arm, Inspector?

                    MASON
          Not lately, no.

Rosy laughs dryly.

                    ROSY
          It would take

                    considerable effort.
                    It`s not like you see
                    in films or on TV.

                         DEBORAH
                    What`s the other
                    reason?

Rosy lets the arm go and skirts up the table to
the head. She takes hold of it, gently lifts.
A breath escapes from the corpse`s mouth,
followed by a moan. Mason jumps back.

                         MASON
                    Jesus!

                         ROSY
                    Oh, don`t worry.
                    They all do that,
                    Inspector. Air leaving
                    the body; his soul`s
                    long gone... If you
                    believe in that kind
                    of thing. Now, take a
                    look at his neck.

Deborah and Mason peer over the table and see
the finger marks there.

                         ROSY
                    This man was held by
                    the throat while he
                    was being stabbed. So
                    tight it broke the
                    bones.

                         DEBORAH
                    That`s why his head
                    was hanging down back
                    at the crime scene.

                         ROSY

Exactly. And I can`t
be one-hundred-percent
certain until I open
him up, but I`d say
our killer rammed the
murder weapon home,
almost to the bridge
of the fork. Probably
popped a lung, too.
I`ll be able to tell
you the length of
it, once I see what
kind of damage it`s
inflicted on the
inside.

Mason folds his arms and takes a step back.

                    MASON
Thank you, Miss Lim.
That would be most
useful, seeing as
we haven`t managed
to locate the murder
weapon yet. Least we`d
have some idea of what
we were looking for.

Rosy acknowledges this with a bat of her eyes.
Deborah stares at the marks on the victim`s
neck.

                    DEBORAH
Could the attack have
been carried out by
more than one person,
Rosy?

                    ROSY
Possibly... But I
would say unlikely in
my opinion. Whoever

> was holding him would
> just have gotten in
> the way of the person
> with the fork.

Rosy waits for any more questions, then begins to prepare for the autopsy proper. She sets up her recorder, picks up her scalpel. The next images are flashes of blood as incisions are made. Mason sticks around for these, but as soon as a saw cranks up he`s gone. Rosy watches him leave with a certain amount of satisfaction. Deborah isn`t long after him.

EXT. OUTSIDE MORGUE - DAY.

DEBORAH finds MASON outside sitting on a wall. He lights up a cigarette, gives her an apologetic look.

> MASON
> Needed some fresh air.

> DEBORAH
> You call that fresh?

> MASON
> Beats what he was
> sucking on in there.

Deborah walks up and down, unable to settle. Mason watches her pace.

> MASON
> Missing your days back
> on the beat, Blondie?

> DEBORAH
> Just thinking, sir.

> MASON

                    Yeah, I know what you
                    mean.

              DEBORAH
          Why the fork, why not
          just a knife or a gun?
          If this is a gang-
          related thing then...
          I don`t know, none of
          this makes any sense.

              MASON
          Who said it had to
          make any sense? Life
          doesn`t make sense,
          Sergeant, in case you
          hadn`t noticed. If it
          did...

Mason shakes his head and takes another puff
of his cigarette. Deborah pauses, then joins
him on the wall. They both sit and stare at
the morgue.

EXT. JACK`S DREAM/FLASHBACK - NIGHT.

Back on the street again, the footfalls: closer
and closer. The streets are a maze and there`s
no escape. JAMES is being chased. He runs for
his life. Still we can`t see who he is, just an
outline against the streetlamps.We`re tight in
on feet pounding the concrete: the hunter and
the hunted. The sounds echo all around and
the scene becomes almost surreal. We`re back
in the alley again, the silhouette of James
pressed up against the wall.

In contrast to the scene at the start, we don`t
even get the relief of the youth interrupting.
This time the footsteps continue to echo up
and along the alley until they`re almost

deafening. Then the whole of the alley comes alive and folds itself around James.

We get a sudden glimpse again of TWINKLE with his two faces.

INT. JACK`S BATHROOM - MORNING.

JACK`s eyes snap open. We`re in tight on his face - his mouth a grimace - and pull out to see that he`s in his bathroom, curled up next to the toilet. He grips a towel in his hand, which covers the lower portion of his body.

One of his legs still hangs over the edge of the bath, where he`d just finished taking a shower. The water from the nozzle is still spraying into the bath.

He shakes his head and gets an arm underneath him. Jack grabs the edge of the sink and hauls himself to his feet. With shaking fingers he reaches over and switches off the shower.

Jack wipes steam from the mirror, getting his breath. Recovering.

Then he rubs his beard. He takes a bag from the top of the toilet and removes an electric razor. In a series a quick shots we see him cleave off the beard. His rubs his clean-shaven face and examines it in the mirror. Jack leans in, eyebrows stooped, lost in the moment.

There`s a noise from outside the door and he snaps his head sideways. He tenses as if expecting an attack. Jack moves slowly towards the door, one hand out for the knob. He opens it a crack and peers out. There`s no one there in the room. Suddenly a figure is on the other

side of the door and he starts. It`s a middle-
aged MAID in overalls the same colour as the
other employees in the hotel.

> MAID
> I`m sorry, I didn`t
> realise anybody...
> There was no 'Do Not
> Disturb`, and I did
> knock...

Jack lets out a visible sigh, relief evident
on his face.

> JACK
> No... that`s okay.
> I was just taking a
> shower. I`ll be out of
> your way in a minute.

He closes the bathroom door again, leans up
against it, bangs his head back on the wood.

Jack closes his eyes.

INT. YARDLEY STREET POLICE STATION, CORRIDOR
- DAY.

DEBORAH waits in the corridor outside the
Gents` toilet; she leans against the wall.

A few seconds later MASON emerges.

He seems slightly surprised to see her there.

> MASON
> Something come up,
> Blondie? Or are the
> Ladies` flooded again?

> DEBORAH

                    Thought you`d want to
                    know about this right
                    away.

                         MASON
                    Please tell me
                    it`s good news.
                    After reading Miss
                    Lim`s report I need
                    something to brighten
                    my day. Have forensics
                    turned anything up?

Deborah shakes her head. Mason sighs and starts
to walk up the corridor.

Deborah falls in step with him.

                         DEBORAH
                    A routine trawl
                    through missing
                    persons turned up
                    trumps. Photograph
                    left by his family
                    matches. Our vic`s
                    name is Stuart
                    Redbrook, 34 years
                    old. He was reported
                    missing on the
                    Thursday of last week.

Mason halts and faces her.

                         MASON
                    How long had he been
                    missing before that?

                         DEBORAH
                    The guy`s a computer
                    programmer at a place
                    called Blue Chip,
                    keeps informal hours.

But when he didn`t
show up to work for a
few days and no one
could reach him at
home, his family was
contacted.

                    MASON
So he has a wife,
then? Kids?

Deborah shakes her head.

                    DEBORAH
His mother registered
the missing person`s
report apparently.
Lives on his own, no
regular girlfriend.

                    MASON
Have the family been
notified?

                    DEBORAH
Not yet. We still need
a positive I.D.

Mason looks at her and she reads his thoughts.

                    DEBORAH
Hey, listen, you know
how I hate giving news
like that.

                    MASON
Someone`s got to do
it. Take one of the
uniforms if you like,
get them to break the
ice. But I want you to
find out

                    MASON (CONT`D)
          if he had any enemies,
          anyone-

                    DEBORAH
          Anyone who might
          want to crush his
          windpipe, stab him
          with a barbecue fork,
          then cut off his right
          hand?

                    MASON
          I wouldn`t put it
          quite like that to
          them, Blondie.

                    DEBORAH
          Do I really have to?

                    MASON
          I think it`s better
          if you handle... that
          side of things.

                    DEBORAH
                (scowling)
          Why, because I`m
          a woman? Tea and
          sympathy, is that it?

Mason walks again and Deborah follows.

                    MASON
                (over his shoulder)
          Is that what you
          really think? All that
          bollocks?

                    DEBORAH
          No. I think you just
          don`t want to do it

                    yourself, so you`re
                    palming it off on me.

They`ve reached a set of double doors and
Mason turns, a grin on his face.

                    MASON
               You know me too
               well. It`s called
               delegation, Sergeant.
               When you`re the
               inspector, you can
               send people off to do
               all the dirty jobs.
               Until then...

He holds his hand out for her to go through
the door.

                    MASON
               Ladies first.

                    DEBORAH
               And what are you going
               to do?

                    MASON
               My job, Blondie. My
               job.

EXT. BLUE CHIP OFFICES - DAY.

MASON stands outside a small building with a
sign on the front that reads: BLUE CHIP. He
enters.

INT. WHEELER`S OFFICE - DAY.

Sat at a desk is a man in his mid-late 20s,
wearing a light blue shirt and tie: the owner,

MR. WHEELER.

A jacket is hung over the back of his leather
recliner. His glasses reflect the laptop screen
in front of him, which he taps at. There`s a
knock at the door but he doesn`t tear his eyes
from his work.

                    WHEELER
                   (snapping)
              Yes, yes! Come in!

The door opens and MASON is there. The two men
regard each other coolly, but Wheeler breaks
eye contact first.

                    MASON
              Mr. Wheeler?

                    WHEELER
              Yes.

                    MASON
              (holding up his I.D.)
              D.I. Mason, I`d like
              to ask you a few
              questions if that`s
              all right.

Wheeler`s whole attitude changes; he breaks
into a false smile.

Mason grins back: the smile of a person who
knows they`ve got the upper hand.

INT. MULTI-STOREY CAR PARK - DAY

As MASON walks around an indoor car park it`s
interspersed with flashes of the conversation
he`s just had with WHEELER.

INT. FLASHBACK, WHEELER`S OFFICE - DAY.

WHEELER wriggles uncomfortably in his seat under MASON`s scrutiny, seated across the desk.

>   WHEELER
>   Dead? God, how could
>   this happen?

>   MASON
>   I`m afraid I can`t
>   tell you that at this
>   time, but we are
>   treating the matter
>   as suspicious. You
>   might have been the
>   last person to see him
>   alive.

>   WHEELER
>   But... But the first
>   to notice he was
>   missing.

>   MASON
>   True.

INT. MULTI-STOREY CAR PARK - DAY

MASON wanders around the car park. He looks from side to side, under cars.

INT. FLASHBACK, WHEELER`S OFFICE - DAY.

MASON leans forward in the chair.

>   MASON
>   So what you`re telling
>   me is that it`s

> standard practise to
> poach employees from
> other companies, Mr.
> Wheeler?

                    WHEELER
> Happens all the time,
> Inspector. It was all
> very amicable.

                    MASON
> Really? I don`t think
> I`d be very 'amicable`
> if someone had just
> lured away a member of
> my staff. Especially
> if he was good at his
> job.

                    WHEELER
> No, I don`t suppose
> so.

                    MASON
> Forgive me for saying
> so, Mr. Wheeler, but
> this operation doesn`t
> exactly strike me as
> topflight.

WHEELER pouts at this comment.

                    WHEELER
> You think I
> blackmailed Redbrook
> into coming to work
> for me, because I
> couldn`t afford to pay
> him?

INT. MULTI-STOREY CAR PARK - DAY

Mason pushes through a set of doors and jogs down some stairs.

INT. FLASHBACK, WHEELER`S OFFICE - DAY.

WHEELER`s eyes are slits now as he fends off MASON`s accusations.

                    WHEELER
          Redbrook`s salary was
          quite a large one,
          Inspector. Feel free
          to check the company
          records if you don`t
          believe me. We may
          not appear 'topflight`
          at a glance, but
          it`s because we
          don`t splash out on
          superficial luxuries
          that we`re able to
          make more money behind
          the scenes. Haven`t
          you heard, it`s the
          way of the future.
          We don`t even have
          our own car park here
          because the space
          in this building is
          rented.

                    MASON
          So... where did Stuart
          Redbrook park?

INT. MULTI-STOREY CAR PARK - DAY

Back in the car park for the final time, MASON walks across to one of the corners. He notices the CCTV camera positioned next to a ticket

PAUL KANE

machine.

Mason looks up at it, then back across the car
park.

INT. DEBORAH`S CAR - DAY

DEBORAH drives, with a very young PC called
PEEL beside her; he barely looks old enough to
vote. To break the silence, he produces a bag
of sweets from his pocket. He puts one in his
mouth and holds the bag out for Deborah.

She gives them a quick glance, shakes her
head.

                    DEBORAH
          And whatever you do,
          don`t offer Redbrook`s
          family any, Peel.

Peel blushes.

                    PEEL
          Sorry, Sergeant.

He takes the bag away, but at that moment they
go over a bump and he spills the sweets on the
floor. Peel searches under the seat for them.

                    DEBORAH
          Leave them, Peel.

                    PEEL
          It`s okay, I`ve nearly
          got them all.

                    DEBORAH
          I said leave them!
          Christ, I don`t have
          this much trouble when

                 my daughter`s in the
                 car.

                          PEEL
                 Sorry.

                        DEBORAH
                      (softening)
                 It`s okay, relax.

                          PEEL
                 It`s just that it`s
                 the first time
                 I`ve... you know.

                        DEBORAH
                 Wish I could say the
                 same. Look, we`re
                 here.

EXT. REDBROOK FAMILY HOME - DAY.

The car pulls up outside a quaint little house,
with hanging baskets of flowers on either side
of the door.

DEBORAH and PEEL climb out of the car and walk
up the path.

                        DEBORAH
                      (whispers)
                 Stay behind. And let
                 me do the talking.

Peel nods. They reach the door and Deborah
raps with the brass-knocker. She fishes her
I.D. wallet out ready, as she hears someone on
the other side. The door opens and we see her
reaction first.

Deborah`s mouth falls open and she drops her

PAUL KANE

I.D.

The camera tracks it to the floor as it falls
in slow motion.

EXT. STREETS OF NORCHESTER - DAY.

JACK walks the streets of this new city he`s
found himself in. He takes everything in; it
looks so different in the daytime.

INT. CAFE - DAY.

JACK has something to eat in a café. A young
girl, PATRICIA, serves one couple at a table.
She looks a lot like FELICITY from the hotel.

Jack squints, but before he can get a good
look she disappears into the back room. Jack
shakes his head, leaves a tip on the table,
and makes for the door.

INT. MORTUARY - DAY.

Inside a white room is a sheet, with the figure
of a body clearly underneath. THEO REDBROOK
and his MOTHER are led into the room by an
ATTENDANT in a white coat. We only see them
from the back. Theo is much taller than the
stooping woman beside him. He has his arm
around her; she leans into him for support.
DEBORAH brings up the rear.

They all draw nearer to the table, and the
sheet. We see the mother`s face now, as the
sheet is pulled back - and STUART REDBROOK`s
dead expression is revealed. Her hand goes to
her mouth, tears flowing down her cheeks.

                    DEBORAH
          Mrs. Redbrook, is this
          your son?

She can`t say a thing, just nods and falls
back into THEO`s arms. It`s now that we pan
up to his face and see... that it`s the same
as Stuart Redbrook`s. Their features are
identical in every way. THEO holds the woman
close as sobs wrack her body.

                 THEO REDBROOK
          It`s okay, Mum. I`m
          here.

As he comforts the woman he`s just as
distraught, but is holding it all in for her
sake. She`s led off, and Stuart Redbrook`s
brother approaches the table on his own. He
leans down and we see the two of them together
for the first time.

A single tear rolls down his cheek as he brings
his face closer. Deborah watches all this from
the side.

                 THEO REDBROOK
                 (whispering)
          Who did this to you,
          Stuart? Who did this?

Theo holds his position there a moment, as if
expecting his brother to suddenly tell him.
Then he falls on the body; he hugs it and
cries.

Deborah stands with arms folded, head bowed.

INT. LIBRARY - EARLY EVENING.

JACK wanders around the city`s enormous

library. He examines shelves of books. This is obviously a place where he feels at home. He walks past the fiction sections and into the HISTORY one, announced by a large sign overhead.

He runs his fingers over the spines. Jack stops to pull a couple out and flips through them. Then he spots something on the bottom shelf of one rack.

Jack stoops to read the title; he cocks his head. Then he pulls this book out and we see the title: THE REAL ROBIN OF SHERWOOD BY JOHN FOLEY. He opens it up, there are hardly any stamps on the issues page. He laughs quietly to himself.

Jack places it carefully back on the shelf and turns a corner. He almost trips over the little librarian, MARVIN, kneeling on the floor.

                    JACK
          Sorry.

MARVIN says nothing, just watches him back away, into the periodicals section. Jacks turns to see discarded newspapers on a table, their headlines catching his eye: FAGIN ROW MYSTERY, POLICE NO FURTHER. He picks one up, then tosses it back down on the table and closes his eyes.

Seconds later Jack leaves the room, and the library.

INT. IMPERIAL FOYER - EARLY EVENING.

JACK walks across the lobby; there`s a MALE RECEPTIONIST on duty behind the desk tonight.

We can see out through the open door that it`s
dark already.

Jack heads for the lift, where ALBERT holds up
a hand in hello.

INT. LIFT - EARLY EVENING.

ALBERT keeps the doors open and JACK nods his
thanks as he enters.

> JACK
> Don`t they ever let
> you go home?

> ALBERT
> Seems that way,
> doesn`t it? So, what
> did you think of our
> fair city, Mr. Foley?

> JACK
> I`ve told you before,
> it`s Jack. Just Jack.

> ALBERT
> So, Jack, what did you
> think of Norchester?

> JACK
> I haven`t seen enough
> of it to judge. But
> what I did see was...
> interesting. You`ve
> certainly got a hell
> of a library here.

> ALBERT
> Biggest in the County.
> Finest records section
> anywhere.

                    JACK
          I only looked at the
          books.

                  ALBERT
          Next time you ask to
          see Marvin. He`ll show
          you around downstairs.

                    JACK
          I`ll do that, Albert.
          Thanks.

The doors open on Jack`s floor and he steps
out.

                  ALBERT
          You have a nice rest
          of the evening.

Jack nods again as the doors close on Albert.

INT. IMPERIAL HOTEL CORRIDOR - EARLY EVENING.

JACK walks down the corridor. He finds his
room number and takes out the key. His hand
shakes as he turns the lock, and he looks down
at it.

INT. JACK`S ROOM - EARLY EVENING.

JACK stumbles in through the door, grips the
jamb. Then he drops to his knees.

He begins to crawl along and suddenly-

EXT. CANAL - EARLY EVENING.

P.O.V. shot of what JACK`s seeing, intercut

with close-ups on his eyes.

It`s dark, but we can see a small path which runs the length of a canal. To the side an embankment leads up to a set of railings, which separates this from the main road.

We hear the tring-tring of a bicycle bell, and look up to see a bike crossing the small bridge ahead.

As it reaches the path and pauses, we see the rider - HAYLEY ARCHER - is wearing a sweatshirt and leggings. Her cap is pulled down low so we can`t see the face - or even make out her sex yet.

Quick cuts show us Jack`s eyes. He`s squinting, which hammers home the fact that this is his vision. He`s seeing this happening right now!

INT. JACK`S ROOM - EARLY EVENING.

We`ve pulled back to show JACK on his knees again. He reaches out but grabs nothing.

EXT. CANAL - EARLY EVENING.

Back to the canal and HAYLEY is on the path, heading towards us, towards the darkness.

The closer she gets, the more we can see it`s a woman bicyclist. She pulls up sharp again, looks ahead - towards us - as if wondering whether or not to continue. Foliage hangs down over the path, creating shadows.

Hayley shrugs; it`s a familiar route.

Then she pushes on.

She`s very close now, still in P.O.V shot.

                    JACK (O.S.)
                     (hissing)
              No! Get out of there,
              turn around and get
              out!

Hayley continues to ride towards us. Closer, closer... She`s so fixated on the path she doesn`t notice as:

Large hands reach out from the bushes. They drag her and the bike into the foliage. Hayley is thrown and lands awkwardly. The cap falls off and blonde hair spills out everywhere.

P.O.V: We look down, as big, heavy feet trample over the fallen bicycle and crush it. The bell gives a tiny tring, then dies.

Over to the fallen woman now, her back is to the viewer as she attempts to crawl away. Her breath comes hard because all the wind has been knocked out of her.

Then hands are on her; they flip her over to face us. Hayley is terrified - but even more so when a hand hoves into view, wielding a twin-pronged fork. She is about to scream, but the other hand grips her throat.

                    TWINKLE
                    (gruffly)
              Ride`s over.

A flash of steel as the fork is plunged into her.

INT. JACK`S ROOM - EARLY EVENING.

We see JACK`s reaction to the fork plunging in, shock and horror etched on his face. But the ordeal is not over yet, for him or the victim.

EXT. CANAL - EARLY EVENING.

Still in P.O.V, we hear voices off to the side. We track up and across as the fork is removed. We head back out of the hedgerow and look up the path. There are figures in the distance.

We return to the prone body and see blood pooling at the stomach, the hip. A knife blade appears, which replaces the fork as a weapon. The hands brush back her hair, exposing an ear.

The knife traces round it, and the camera zooms in. We see the dark outline as blood appears, then the cuts grow more frenzied. TWINKLE is hurrying now, he doesn`t want to be caught in the act by passers-by.

The ear comes away from the woman`s head with a sickening squelch. It`s held up before the camera for a moment.

The P.O.V. rises. One last look at the dead woman, the broken bike and-

INT. JACK`S ROOM - EARLY EVENING.

We`re back in the hotel room with JACK, who lets out a final gasp and falls forward onto the carpet.

Just when we think he`s not going to move again, he gets up and rushes to the bathroom.

We hear the sound of Jack violently throwing up.

INT. CANAL/TENT - MORNING.

Under cover of a tent, the rain pitter-pattering above, we find D.S. HARRISON, D.I. MASON and DR. LIM.

They stand over another victim, and as the camera works its way around them we see it`s the woman from Jack`s vision.

                    ROSY
          I`d say this happened
          last night.

                    MASON
          Time, doctor?

                    ROSY
          Best guess at the
          moment, between 6:30
          and 8. Maybe 8:30.

Deborah steps around the victim, takes in more of the wounds. We flit between her eyes and the blood of the stomach, the gory mess on the side of the woman`s head - in the same way we did with Jack.

                    ROSY
          The murder definitely
          occurred here this
          time. The blood`s
          confined to this one
          area. And her neck`s
          broken, just like
          Stuart Redbrook`s was.

The name makes Deborah flinch, but instead of

staring at the body now, she stares off into
space.

EXT. FLASHBACK, REDBROOK FAMILY HOME - DAY

We pick up after DEBORAH dropped her I.D. on
the floor, gaping at THEO REDBROOK`s face.

INT. FLASHBACK, MORTUARY - DAY

STUART REDBROOK`s bleached face on the slab to
contrast with this. Then back again to:

EXT. FLASHBACK, REDBROOK FAMILY HOME - DAY

THEO REDBROOK, now on the steps of the house
with PEEL and DEBORAH.

                    THEO REDBROOK
            I`m Theo, Stuart`s
            brother. Is there
            something wrong?

INT. CANAL/TENT - MORNING.

Back to the present and DEBORAH`s missed
something; still in a daze, recalling her
encounter with THEO.

                    MASON
            Seems reasonable,
            doesn`t it, Blondie?

Deborah snaps to, faces MASON.

                    DEBORAH
            Sorry, what?

                    MASON
          Are you all right?

He takes a step towards her, and places a hand
on her arm.

                    MASON (CONT`D)
          Look, I know this is
          rough, but-

                    DEBORAH
          I`m fine... Really.
          What was Rosy saying?

                    MASON
          She thinks whoever
          killed this woman
          also murdered Stuart
          Redbrook, and I`m
          inclined to agree with
          her.

                    ROSY
            (points to the body)
          Same M.O. The neck,
          the wound. I can`t be
          sure without removing
          clothing, but I`d
          bet you anything the
          weapon driven in
          there was a dual-
          pronged fork. The only
          difference is the ear.

                    DEBORAH
          With Redbrook the hand
          was missing.

                    ROSY
          Right.

                    MASON

So what, you think
this guy-

                    ROSY
Or girl. We haven`t
established yet that
it`s a man. Okay,
they`re strong, but
I`ve met quite a few
women who were that in
my time.

                    MASON
(looks from Rosy to Deborah)
  So have I. All right,
  you think this person
  is collecting body
  parts?

                    ROSY
Don`t you?

                    MASON
Buggered if I know
what`s going on inside
their mind. And I`m
not sure I want to,
either.

                    DEBORAH
If only there`d been
something on the
security footage from
the multi-storey.

                    MASON
                 (sighing)
Bloody technology, you
can`t trust it.

ROSY looks at them, puzzled.

                    MASON (CONT`D)
          Some kind of radio
          frequency jammer was
          used apparently, or so
          I`m told... Fucked up
          the cameras, and the
          footage.

                    DEBORAH
          Or maybe it was done
          by someone working
          there?

                    MASON
          Inside job, you mean?
          It`s possible. We
          need to look into if
          there`s any connection
          between this new
          victim... what was her
          name again?

                    DEBORAH
          Hayley Archer, 14
          Cavendish Road,
          according the I.D. she
          had on her.

                    MASON
          Right, between...
                    (beat)
          Hayley and Redbrook`s
          firm.

                    ROSY
          There`s one more
          thing. The cuts around
          the ear are quite

                    ROSY (CONT`D)

> ragged. In fact it was
> almost torn off. I`d
> say our killer was
> worried about being
> discovered this time.

The rain patters on the tent again and Mason
looks up.

                    MASON
          Fucking rain. We might
          have been able to
          lift an impression or
          something if it had
          held off long enough.

Deborah sighs and nods, then looks down at
the victim again. She lifts the tent flap and
walks outside-

EXT. CANAL - MORNING.

-into that rain, immediately putting up her
umbrella. DEBORAH steps past the men in white
suits examining the area, and walks back up,
traces HAYLEY`s movements for herself.

Deborah makes her way up along the path running
parallel to the canal.

                    DEBORAH
             (under her breath)
          Come on. Just give us
          a break. Something,
          anything.

She looks up, sees the iron bars separating
the embankment from the road. Behind it are
the assembled media again, though not as many
as before because of the weather.

Deborah takes in the faces - flitting from one to the other in her P.O.V. Someone points a camera at her and snaps off a couple of shots.

She looks away, carries on down the line - then pans back. There`s a face she recognises in the crowd, even without his beard. The same man who was at the crime scene back in Fagin`s Row: JACK.

They lock eyes, and he suddenly looks away. Moves away, pushes aside members of the press and disappears from view.

> DEBORAH
> (to herself)
> Not this time you
> don`t.

Deborah scrambles up the embankment. Two uniformed OFFICERS protecting the gap in the fence notice her approach and move out of the way before she has to shove them aside.

At the top, out onto the road, Deborah scans the crowd. The reporters take this as their cue to move down and chase Deborah. They flock around, shove more cameras in her face, ask for quotes.

She manages to push through them, searches beyond them for Jack.

Then she sees him - crossing the road and getting into a red Mondeo. She drops the umbrella and elbows through the remaining reporters, makes for her own car.

INT. DEBORAH`S CAR - DAY

DEBORAH slides in behind the wheel, pulls on

her seat-belt and starts the engine. Wipers
flick into action as she releases the handbrake
and pulls out into traffic.

EXT. ROAD - DAY.

DEBORAH`s silver Peugeot almost collides with
an oncoming blue vehicle. Horns blare as she
completes her u-turn and sets off in pursuit
of the red car.

INT. DEBORAH`S CAR - DAY

Looking out through the windscreen, from over
DEBORAH`s shoulder, we see the red car not
that far ahead.

Deborah changes gear but is stuck behind a
green vehicle, the road too narrow to overtake.

She gives a blast of her horn, tries to get
the car to move out of the way, but it only
slows up more.

Beyond it, the red Mondeo seems hesitant, as
if the driver doesn`t really know the streets
of Norchester that well.

Deborah grits her teeth, mounts the pavement.

EXT. ROAD - DAY.

DEBORAH`s Peugeot overtakes on the left-hand
side, as the green car`s horn blares.

INT. DEBORAH`S CAR - DAY

DEBORAH shakes her head.

                        DEBORAH
              And you!

More manoeuvring, and now we see her pull out
into a larger bit of road. The steering wheel
slips through her fingers as...

EXT. ROAD - DAY.

...DEBORAH zig-zags in and out of traffic to
try and catch up with the red Mondeo.

There`s a space between the Renault ahead of
her and the Ford Focus ahead of that. DEBORAH
presses her foot down, overtakes again, and
tries to slip into the gap - but a truck is
coming in the opposite direction.

INT. DEBORAH`S CAR - DAY

DEBORAH grips the wheel tightly, hunkers down
over it.

                        DEBORAH
              You can make it... You
              can make-

EXT. ROAD - DAY.

DEBORAH`s car only narrowly misses the truck
as she pulls into the gap.

The DRIVER of the truck mouths something as
it goes by.

The Focus in front indicates and swings off to
the left, which leaves the way clear ahead for
Deborah to follow the Mondeo.

It turns right at the next junction, attempts
to lose her.

INT. DEBORAH`S CAR - DAY.

DEBORAH grins and hits the right-hand indicator.

                    DEBORAH
          Dead end. Got you now,
          mate, haven`t I.

EXT. DEAD END STREET - DAY.

The Mondeo slows and stops just before the
wall ahead.

DEBORAH`s Peugeot isn`t far behind. The car
pulls up, about 20 metres behind, then waits.

Moments pass. Deborah`s door suddenly opens
and she gets out.

She marches down the dead-end street, ignores
the rain still beating down.

It`s only when she`s almost at the Mondeo that
she hesitates, remembers she`s alone.

                    DEBORAH
                  (to herself)
          Christ, what do you
          think you`re doing?

The door of the Mondeo opens.

                    DEBORAH (CONT`D)
          Just hold it right
          there. Police!

She fumbles in her jacket for her I.D., finds

it, and holds it up in lieu of any kind of
weapon.

Deborah edges forward, and sees the man there
behind the wheel. JACK. He looks at her like a
woodland animal in the headlights.

                    DEBORAH
          Get out... slowly.
          Hands where I can see
          them.

The Mondeo`s door opens more fully and he
begins to get out. Deborah backs off a little,
but then Jack`s hands are in the air as he
rises.

The camera pans up and down, taking him in
as Deborah does. He`s wearing a sage-coloured
jacket with jumper beneath, the collar of a
shirt poking out from the top, dark trousers
and boots.

                    JACK
          (squinting against the rain)
            Am I under arrest?

                    DEBORAH
          That all depends.

                    JACK
          On what?

                    DEBORAH
          On why I`ve seen you
          at two murder scenes
          in the last week. And
          why you ran when you
          saw me coming over to
          talk to you.

Jack is silent, drops his gaze.

                    DEBORAH(CONT`D)
          Look, you can either
          tell me here or back
          at the station. It`s
          up to you.

Still nothing.

                    DEBORAH
          Right, hold out your
          hands.

Jack looks up at her, and there`s a defiance
this time. He hesitates, then finally does as
she asks.

Deborah snaps on a pair of handcuffs.

                    JACK
          There`s no need for
          these.

                    DEBORAH
          I`ll be the judge of
          that.

She feels more secure now he`s cuffed, and
doesn`t bat an eye at grabbing him by the arm.

She pulls him off back towards her car.

Deborah yanks open the passenger door and
stands back so he can climb inside.

                    DEBORAH(CONT`D)
          Get in.

Reluctantly, Jack obeys, then appears to
remember something.

                    JACK
          What about my car?

Deborah regards him, then sighs, locks her car up and walks back to his Mondeo. She reaches inside where the keys are still in the ignition and locks that too, all the time keeping an eye on Jack.

Deborah returns to the Peugeot, unlocks it gets into the driver`s side.

>   DEBORAH
>   Okay?

>   JACK
>   (nodding)
>   Thanks.

>   DEBORAH
>   Now then, care to tell
>   me who you are?

Jack is silent again, so she reaches inside his jacket, checks the pockets.

He resists initially, but then she has what she`s looking for.

She looks inside his wallet.

>   DEBORAH(CONT`D)
>   Jack Foley.

Jack says nothing.

>   JACK
>   I haven`t killed
>   anyone, if that`s what
>   you`re thinking.

>   DEBORAH
>   We`ll see.

>   JACK

It`s true.

                    DEBORAH
          Well, right now you`re
          all we`ve got, Mr.
          Foley.

Deborah`s mobile plays a tune and she answers
it.

                    DEBORAH
          Sorry sir, I had to...
          Yes. But listen, I
          think might have
          something, sir. I`m
          bringing in a bloke
          called Foley for
          questioning... Yes, I
          know that, sir. But...
          Yes, I`ll explain when
          I see you... A-huh,
          yep. I`ll meet you
          there in ten minutes.

She hangs up, looks over at the manacled Jack.

                    DEBORAH (CONT`D)
          My boss is quite
          keen to talk to you,
          whoever you are. Why
          don`t you do us all
          a favour and tell me
          what you know.

                    JACK
          (sighs, hangs his head)
          You wouldn`t believe
          me if I did.

                    DEBORAH
          Try me.

Jack looks up, a droplet of rain running down
his cheek. It looks very much like he is crying.

Then he wipes it away with the back of his
hand.

EXT. YARDLEY STREET POLICE STATION - DAY.

Outside a red brick building, sandwiched
between two other buildings that are all glass
and concrete, is YARDLEY STREET POLICE STATION.

The windows have bars across them, and the
building itself is cut off from the road by a
barred set of railings.

A sign hanging from the front of the building
clearly states: POLICE.

The silver Peugeot pulls left into the street
running alongside the station, then manoeuvres
round the back.

It parks up and DEBORAH hops out. She opens
the passenger side and drags JACK from the
car.

Deborah leads Jack in through the back entrance
of the police station.

INT. YARDLEY STREET POLICE STATION - DAY.

DEBORAH keys in her code to take JACK into
the station proper, then walks him past grey
walls, up the stairs, to a room.

INT. INTERVIEW ROOM - DAY.

Inside this sparse room is a table, with four
chairs - two on each side.

On the table itself is a recorder.

DEBORAH motions for JACK to sit.

A CONSTABLE happens by and Deborah stops him,
whispers something inaudible as Jack looks on.

Deborah looks back over at Jack.

                    DEBORAH
          Do you want anything
          to drink?

Jack shakes his head.

Deborah lets the constable go, returns to the
table.

                    DEBORAH
          Is there anything you
          do want?

                    JACK
          (holding up his cuffs)
          These are a bit tight.

Deborah undoes the cuffs.

                    DEBORAH
          Doubt you`re going to
          cause too much trouble
          in here.

                    JACK
          I`m not going to cause
          any trouble at all.
          Look, am I going to

                    be charged, Sergeant
                    Harrison?

                         DEBORAH
                    (taken aback)
                    How do you know my
                    name?

                         JACK
                    (shrugging)
                    You were on the news
                    the night they found
                    Stuart Redbrook. Plus
                    it`s been in the
                    papers.

Deborah concedes his point with a cock of the
head.

                         DEBORAH
                    All right, what about
                    that night. What were
                    you doing on Fagin`s
                    Row?

                         JACK
                    Shouldn`t there be
                    another officer
                    present or something?
                    There always is on
                    television.

                         DEBORAH
                    This isn`t a formal
                    interview. Not yet,
                    anyway.

                         JACK
                    So the handcuffs
                    were just, what,
                    decoration?

                    DEBORAH
                   (irritated)
          I`m giving you one
          last chance to talk to
          me before my inspector
          arrives. I`m not
          stupid, you obviously
          have something to do
          with all this.

                     JACK
          How do you know I`m
          not a reporter?

                    DEBORAH
          Where`s your press
          pass?

                     JACK
          I might`ve left it in
          the car.

She shakes her head.

                    DEBORAH
          Right, proper little
          Clark Kent aren`t you?
          And unless you`ve
          got a camera tucked
          up your sleeve, I`ll
          assume you`re not
          paparazzi, either.

Still standing, she leans on the table, over
him.

                 DEBORAH(CONT`D)
          You`re going to have
          to do better than that

                    when Mason arrives. He
                    won`t stand for people
                    messing him about.

Deborah pulls up a chair, sits opposite Jack.

                    DEBORAH(CONT`D)
               You say you had
               nothing to do with
               those killings.
               Fine. But you know
               something, I can tell.
               Are you covering for
               someone, Mr. Foley?
               Do you have a guilty
               conscience, is that
               why you were there?

                    JACK
               No, I-

The door opens suddenly and the imposing figure
of INSPECTOR ROY MASON fills the gap.

Jack and Mason regard each other, the latter
with the cold, clinical eye of a cop.

                    MASON
               So, what have you
               brought me, Sergeant?

                    DEBORAH
               This is Mr. Jack
               Foley, sir. I saw him
               that night back on
               Fagin`s Row and then
               again this morning.
               The first time I
               didn`t really think
               much of it, but when I
               went over to talk to

him at the canal...
Well, let`s just say
he led me a merry
chase.

                    MASON
          I see.

Mason pulls up a chair and sits beside Deborah,
across the table from Jack.

                    MASON (CONT`D)
          Like hanging around
          crime-scenes, do we,
          Foley?

Jack says nothing.

                    MASON (CONT`D)
          All right. Do the
          honours would you,
          Blon... Sergeant?

Deborah presses the record button on the
recorder next to her.

                    DEBORAH
          Interview with a Mr.
          Jack Foley. Present
          are Sergeant Deborah
          Harrison and Senior
          Investigating Officer,
          Inspector Roy Mason.

                    MASON
          (pointing to the recorder)
          Now this is for your
          benefit as much as
          ours. You haven`t been
          charged with anything,

                you`re just helping us
                with our...enquiries.

Jack nods.

                    MASON (CONT`D)
                What were you doing
                on Fagin`s Row last
                Sunday, Mr. Foley? Do
                you live in that area
                of the city?

                    JACK
                No. I saw the crowds
                and-

                    MASON
                You just happened to
                be passing and you
                were curious. That`s
                understandable.
                There was a lot of
                commotion that night.
                But it`s funny how
                that abandoned factory
                where Stuart Redbrook
                was found is so far
                away from the main
                drag, don`t you think?
                If you`re not from
                around there... I say
                again, what were you
                doing down Fagin`s
                Row?

                    JACK
                Nothing.

                    MASON
                And this morning? You
                were just passing
                again, right?

                    JACK
          Right.

                    MASON
          You get around, Mr.
          Foley, I`ll say that
          much for you.

Mason eases back in the chair and it creaks
under his weight.

                    MASON (CONT`D)
          Perhaps you could tell
          us where you were a
          week ago last Tuesday.

Jack is silent once again.

                    MASON (CONT`D)
          Did you, for instance,
          happen to be in the
          vicinity of Ingle
          Street, near a firm
          called Wheelers`?

                    JACK
          (with complete honesty)
          Never heard of the
          place.

                    MASON
          No? Doesn`t ring any
          bells?

Jack grimaces and his eyes glaze over as he
remembers...

EXT. FLASHBACK, CANAL - EVENING.

A succession of quick cuts, HAYLEY ARCHER
ringing the bell on her bike, then the flash

of metal, the blood, the sound of the bike as it`s trampled on.

Everything JACK saw in his vision.

INT. INTERVIEW ROOM - DAY.

MASON clicks his fingers, tries to attract JACK`s attention.

Jack snaps out of his trance.

> MASON
> Are we boring you, Mr.
> Foley?

Jack, clearly upset, shakes his head. We catch the look DEBORAH gives him, obviously concerned.

> MASON
> What`s the matter,
> bring back bad
> memories for you?

We see Jack clenching his fists under the table.

> MASON (CONT`D)
> (getting louder as he goes on)
>> Were you waiting for
>> Stuart Redbrook when
>> he left his offices
>> that Tuesday night?
>> Waiting in the multi-
>> storey car park across
>> the way perhaps? Did
>> you force him to drive
>> to some isolated spot
>> and then kill him?

                    JACK
          I-I`ve never even met
          Stuart Redbrook.

                    MASON
          You`re lying. You know
          him, don`t you? You`ve
          seen him. Answer me!

                    JACK
               (less certain)
          No...

                    MASON
               (virtually barking)
          You know what I think?
          I think you killed
          Stuart Redbrook that
          night and got a taste
          for it. Then you went
          out last night and
          killed again, is that
          it? Is that what you
          did, you-

                    JACK
          No...

                    MASON
          You`re lying. Tell me
          what you did!

                    JACK
          I...I didn`t...

                    MASON
               (half-rising)
          You sorry piece of-

Mason pauses and looks down, sees Deborah`s
hand on his arm.

PAUL KANE

Her eyes roll up to the camera in the corner of
the room and Mason slowly descends back down
into his seat.

                    JACK
                 (glowering)
          I didn`t do it, Mason.
          You can sit here
          shouting at me all
          day long, but your
          murderer`s still out
          there somewhere. Look,
          I can prove it. Check
          my cards, you`ll see
          I wasn`t even in the
          city last Tuesday.
          I arrived the night
          Stuart Redbrook was
          found.

Mason says nothing.

                  DEBORAH
          I`ll get someone on
          it.

Deborah pulls Jack`s wallet out of her pocket,
opens it up and looks for the credit cards.
What she sees stops her dead in her tracks.

There`s a photo inside. Of Jack, posing with
his arm around someone.

Someone who looks exactly like him.

Deborah gapes from the picture to Jack, open-
mouthed.

FADE TO BLACK - END OF EPISODE ONE

ACKNOWLEDGMENTS

My thanks to Steve Upham, who published the novel originally through Screaming Dreams, and to Peter Atkins for providing the introduction back then. Thank you to Jason Stokes at Gestalt Media for bringing out the first run of the tenth anniversary edition, and to Encyclopocalypse for publishing the current incarnation. As always, hugs and massive thank yous to all my friends in the writing and film/ TV world, for their continual help and their support in the past. A very special thank you, though, to people like Mike Carey, Neil Gaiman, Rio Youers, Jason Arnopp, Tim Lebbon, Michael Marshall Smith, Alison Littlewood, Simon Clark, Joe Hill, Kelley Armstrong, Christopher Fowler, Stephen Volk, Peter James, and so many more. Finally, a massive thank you to my family, especially my amazing wife Marie – love you loads and loads.

ABOUT THE AUTHOR

Paul Kane is an award-winning, bestselling writer and editor based in Derbyshire, UK. His short story collections include *Alone (In the Dark)*, *Touching the Flame*, *FunnyBones*, *Peripheral Visions*, *Shadow Writer*, *The Adventures of Dalton Quayle*, *The Butterfly Man and Other Stories*, *The Spaces Between*, *Ghosts*, the British Fantasy Award-nominated *Monsters*, *Shadow Casting*, *Nailbiters*, *Death*, *Disexistence*, *Scary Tales*, *More Monsters*, *Lost Souls*, *The Controllers* and *The Naked Eye*. His novellas include *The Lazarus Condition*, *RED* and *Pain Cages* (a #1 Amazon bestseller). He is the author of such novels as *Of Darkness and Light*, *The Gemini Factor* and the bestselling *Arrowhead* trilogy (*Arrowhead*, *Broken Arrow* and *Arrowland*, gathered together in the sell-out omnibus edition *Hooded Man*), a post-apocalyptic reworking of the Robin Hood mythology. His latest novels include *Lunar* (which is set to be turned into a feature film), the short Y.A. novel *The Rainbow Man* (as P.B. Kane), the critically-acclaimed and award-winning *Sherlock Holmes and the Servants of Hell* from Solaris, the sequels to *RED* – *Blood RED* and *Deep RED* – *Before* from Grey Matter Press, *Arcana* from WordFire Press, plus *Her Last Secret*, *Her Husband's Grave* and *The Family Lie* from HQ/HarperCollins

PAUL KANE

(as P.L. Kane)

He has also written for comics, most notably for the *Dead Roots* zombie anthology alongside writers such as James Moran (*Torchwood, Cockneys vs. Zombies*) and Jason Arnopp (*Doctor Who, Friday the 13th, The Last Days of Jack Sparks*) and as part of the team turning *Clive Barker's Books of Blood* into motion comics for Seraphim/MadeFire. His stand-alone comic *The Disease*, published by Hellbound Media, was also a 2016 Ghastly Award-nominated title in the 'One Shot' category. Paul is co-editor of the anthology *Hellbound Hearts* (Simon & Schuster) – stories based around the mythology that spawned *Hellraiser* – *The Mammoth Book of Body Horror* (Constable & Robinson/Running Press), featuring the likes of Stephen King and James Herbert, *A Carnivàle of Horror* (PS) featuring Ray Bradbury and Joe Hill, *Beyond Rue Morgue* from Titan (stories based around Poe's detective, Dupin), *Exit Wounds* – a crime anthology featuring the likes of Lee Child, Val McDermid, Dennis Lehane and Jeffery Deaver – *Wonderland* (a finalist in the Shirley Jackson Awards) and *Cursed*, the last three also from Titan.

His non-fiction books include *The Hellraiser Films and Their Legacy, Voices in the Dark* and *Shadow Writer – The Non-Fiction. Vol. 1: Reviews* and *Vol. 2: Articles and Essays*, plus his genre journalism has appeared in the likes of *SFX, Fangoria, Dreamwatch, Gorezone* and *Rue Morgue*. He also co-wrote the afterword to the latest edition of Stephen King's *Night Shift* collection. He has been a Guest at Alt.Fiction five times, was a Guest at the first SFX Weekender, at Thought Bubble in 2011, Derbyshire Literary Festival and Off the Shelf in 2012, Monster Mash and Event Horizon in 2013, Edge-Lit in 2014, HorrorCon, HorrorFest and Grimm Up North in 2015, The Dublin Ghost Story Festival and Sledge-Lit in 2016, IMATS Olympia and Celluloid Screams in 2017, Black Library

Live (Warhammer 40k) and The UK Ghost Story Festival in 2019, plus the WordCrafter virtual event 2021 – where he delivered the keynote speech – as well as being a panellist at FantasyCon and the World Fantasy Convention, and a fiction judge at the Sci-Fi London Film Festival. He is a former Special Publications Editor of the British Fantasy Society and is currently serving as co-chair for the UK arm of the Horror Writers Association.

His work has been optioned for film and television, and his zombie story 'Dead Time' was turned into an episode of the Lionsgate/NBC TV series *Fear Itself*, adapted by Steve Niles (*30 Days of Night*) and directed by Darren Lynn Bousman (*SAW II-IV*). He also scripted *The Opportunity*, which premiered at the Cannes Film Festival, *Wind Chimes* (directed by Brad '*Hallows Eve*' Watson and which sold to TV), *The Weeping Woman* – filmed by award-winning director Mark Steensland, starring Tony-nominated actor Stephen Geoffreys (*Fright Night*) – *Confidence*, directed by award-winning Mike Clarke (*A Hand to Play, Paper and Plastic*) which stars Simon Bamford (*Hellraiser, Nightbreed, Starfish*), and *The Torturer* directed by Joe Manco of Little Spark Films. Loose Canon/ Hydra Films have just turned Paul's novelette *Men of the Cloth* into a feature called *Sacrifice* (aka *The Colour of Madness*), starring *Re-Animator* and *You're Next*'s Barbara Crampton. His work for audio includes the full cast drama adaptation of *The Hellbound Heart* for Bafflegab, starring Tom Meeten (*The Ghoul*), Neve McIntosh (*Doctor Who*) and Alice Lowe (*Prevenge*), and the *Robin of Sherwood* adventure *The Red Lord* for Spiteful Puppet/ITV, narrated by Ian Ogilvy (*Return of the Saint*). You can find out more at his website www.shadow-writer.co.uk which has featured Guest Writers such as Dean Koontz, Robert Kirkman, Charlaine Harris and Guillermo del Toro

ALSO BY PAUL KANE

NOVELS
- Arrowhead
- Broken Arrow
- Arrowland
- Hooded Man (Omnibus)
- The Gemini Factor
- Lunar
- Sleeper(s)
- The Rainbow Man (as P.B. Kane)
- Blood RED
- Sherlock Holmes and the Servants of Hell
- Before
- Deep RED
- Arcana
- The Red Lord
- Her Last Secret (as P.L. Kane)
- The Storm
- Her Husband's Grave (as P.L. Kane)
- The Family Lie (as P.L. Kane)

Novellas & Novelettes
- Signs of Life
- The Lazarus Condition
- Dalton Quayle Rides Out
- RED
- Pain Cages
- Creakers (chapbook)
- Flaming Arrow
- The Bric-a-Brac Man
- The P.I.'s Tale
- Snow
- The Rot
- Beneath the Surface (with Simon Clark)
- Blood Red Sky

- Confessions (as P.L. Kane)
- Corpsing (as P.L. Kane)

Collections
- Alone (In the Dark)
- Touching the Flame
- FunnyBones
- Peripheral Visions
- The Adventures of Dalton Quayle
- Shadow Writer
- The Butterfly Man and Other Stories
- The Spaces Between
- Ghosts
- Monsters
- The Dead Trilogy
- Shadow Casting
- Nailbiters
- Death
- The Life Cycle
- Disexistence
- Kane's Scary Tales Vol. 1
- More Monsters
- Lost Souls
- The Controllers
- White Shadows (as P.B. Kane)
- The Colour of Madness: Official Movie Tie-In
- Traumas
- Darkness & Shadows
- The Naked Eye

Editor & Co-Editor
- Shadow Writers Vol. 1 & 2
- Terror Tales #1-4
- Top International Horror
- Albions Alptraume: Zombies
- The British Fantasy Society: A Celebration
- Hellbound Hearts
- The Mammoth Book of Body Horror
- A Carnivàle of Horror: Dark Tales from the Fairground
- Beyond Rue Morgue
- Dark Mirages

- Exit Wounds
- Wonderland
- Cursed

Non-Fiction
- Contemporary North American Film Directors: A Wallflower Critical Guide (Major Contributor)
- Cinema Macabre (Contributor)
- The Hellraiser Films And Their Legacy
- Voices in the Dark
- Shadow Writer – The Non-Fiction. Vol. 1: Reviews
- Shadow Writer – The Non-Fiction. Vol. 2: Articles & Essays
- Leviathan – The Story of Hellraiser and Hellbound: Hellraiser II (contributor)
- Hellraisers